The
Mother-in-Law

A NOVEL

The Mother-in-Law

A NOVEL

WRITTEN BY

CHLOE KENT

ISBN: 978-1-78324-148-4

Published by Wordzworth
www.wordzworth.com

Acknowledgements

Firstly, I want to thank you, the reader, for picking up my book. It means the world to me that I get to share this story.

I truly hope you enjoy reading it as much as I have enjoyed writing it.

I want to thank my husband for his continued support.

I really want to take a moment to remember my own Mother, who would have been so incredibly excited that I finally turned my story into a book. She fought my corner until the very end.

Lastly, I want to say that I wrote this book during a very difficult time in my life and I want to dedicate this book to anybody who has suffered with their mental health. I want you to know that you are not alone and just like a book, the next chapter is what we make it.

Lots of Love,
Chloe xx

CHAPTER ONE

So here I am, a twenty-something single Mum with absolutely no love life and an unhealthy obsession with romantic comedies. Which may be part of the problem the more I think about it. Maybe my love life suffers so much because I'm still waiting for Channing Tatum to remind me that he is my husband after my near fatal car crash just like in the movie The Vow, or maybe I'm waiting for Patrick Swayze to teach me the Pachanga. Either way, I'm pretty sure my high expectations are at fault here. Love aside, I've achieved some great things this year in my academic life and I'm excited for what the future holds. For now, I'm not looking for love, much to my best friends' annoyance.

"Erm, No!" I say laughing.

"Shakin Stevens is absolutely *not* the best Christmas song, it's the Pogues!"

"Oh Please! Nobody even knows what on earth the lyrics are!" Lana teases as she rolls her eyes.

"Well I think that's a testament in itself really, good old Shane McGowan was half cut, rambling nonsense into a microphone in between a shot of whiskey and yet here we are, thirty years later still trying to sing the bloody thing! Well, us lot with good music taste are anyway." I mock.

Again, Lana smirks and rolls her eyes before taking a big slurp of her Christmassy hot chocolate.

I absolutely adore Lana, we've known each other twenty years now, since we were in primary school and we used to make the boys play kiss chase with us and then we'd fake fall over every ten seconds, so they'd catch us and have to kiss us. It was brilliant until they cottoned on to our cunning yet brilliant plan and labelled us prevents. Perverts, I think they meant. But still, it was worth it.

Although we've been busy in our own lives since those days, we've always made time for a coffee date when we can.

That's the reality of life really isn't it, as we get older our friendships sometimes take a back seat as other life commitments takeover, such as work and families. Before we know it, we are fully functioning boring adults running errands and moaning about council tax and Brexit.

Suddenly, our secondary school fantasies of living a life like Carrie Bradshaw in a glamorous city and sipping on cocktails every evening aren't quite the reality we once dreamed of.

Although these friendships are still the best kind. The ones where you may not see each other for months and months but when you do finally arrange a date you pick up right where you left off. Giggling, chatting, planning, just like we saw each other yesterday.

"So anyway, are we seeing anyone?" Lana asks curiously.

"Not yet. Still nobody since…you know who."

"Connor? I didn't want to bring him up but I'm desperate to know how you're doing. If it doesn't upset, you too much?" Lana asks gently as she places her hand over mine and gives it a little squeeze.

"I haven't heard from him since the judge ruled in my favour and put a restraining order in place. Last I heard he went back to live with his Dad in Liverpool." I inform her quietly, hoping nobody else in the coffee shop hears.

"And how's your head? Are you coming to terms with it all?"

"My head is fine; the MRI scan came back clear. Apart from this lovely Harry Potter style scar, I'm fine. I had some nightmares at first but since the restraining order, all his calls and emails have stopped. It's given me the space I needed to get myself in order again. I genuinely feel much better." I answer truthfully and give her a reassuring smile.

"It makes me feel so bad that these things were happening, and I had no idea." Lana sighs.

Her disappointed look makes me feel guilty. Lana is my best friend; I tell her everything. I wish I had told her all about what was really happening with Connor too, I don't know why I didn't now. I guess he was just very good at getting inside my head and persuading me to keep his secrets.

"I just got so good at hiding it. I thought I was protecting him. I thought it was just the alcohol making him do it. I was naive and confused, nobody would have ever been able to work it out. You have nothing to feel bad about." I say and give her hand a little squeeze back, I'm truly grateful to have such a good friend.

"Mollie, Can I please now set you up with Reuben?"

"I just…I'm…I don't know if he's my type." I respond.

"How can you say that when you haven't met him?" Lana asks.

Even I can't tell my best friend of twenty years that I have basically lost my confidence since Connor, and Rueben sounds too good. I'm used to disaster relationships with idiot men. Give me a dead beat any day, I seem to be able to handle them. But a gentleman who may actually treat me how I deserve? Pure panic.

"Mollie, I have only met Reuben myself a few times, but Mike says he is the genuine article. His last relationship lasted nearly seven years and he was cheated on for most of that. He has been hurt himself, he is probably just as apprehensive as you are about dating. But if you don't try and move on, I worry you'll be a spinster and I'm going to have to start buying you cats." Lana mocks.

"I happen to like cats." I jest.

"Well okay, crazy cat lady, but before you sign up for a life of cat hair, can you just humour me with the whole Reuben thing? He works hard, he has a car, good friends around him…Mike says he is genuinely a good guy."

"How is Mike?" I ask, trying to change the topic.

"He is still wonderful, we're going out to celebrate our ten-year anniversary next Saturday, he sends his love to you as always and he also wants me to tell you that you'll have to do better than that to change the subject." She winks before giggling.

I giggle back a little and roll my eyes.

"Give Rueben my number." I sigh.

3

"Wait, what?" Lana responds as her jaw drops open in shock. Well half shock, the other half is pure smugness that I have already given in.

Even I'm surprised I said it, but she's right. Reuben does sound decent and I deserve to try and meet someone who can actually make me happy. I'm in my late twenties, I can't just give up on the idea of a happy relationship.

"It's okay. You're right. If I don't take a chance on someone new now, then when?" I say.

"Let's do it."

CHAPTER TWO

At the school gates, the crisp January air fills my lungs, I breathe out watching my breath mist up in front of me from the icy weather. I have never enjoyed the school run, it's always chaotic with Mums rushing around in their gym wear, seemingly confident and with their life together. Unlike me, who hasn't seen the inside a gym since I once walked into one by mistake.

It's been a tough year trying to complete my degree and for a little while I started dating somebody who I thought was wonderful, he literally made me laugh so much, I thought he was the funniest person I had ever met. That was until he started drinking heavily and becoming violent if I dared ever question his habits. Connor Campbell.

I wish to God I could turn back the time and never of allowed him into our lives but that's over with now and I learned a lot from that toxic relationship. Mostly I learned to not be so gutless and naïve again. Next time, I'll walk away at the first sign of trouble and not be so foolish.

As I gaze across the playground, I see my beautiful blonde haired blue eyed mini me. My heart aches as I watch her smiling and laughing playfully with her friends as they throw on their coats and scarves, ready to dash across the playground and find their parents. I'm so relieved that those few months with Connor didn't taint her too much. I wouldn't have been able to forgive myself if it did.

Her smile means everything to me right now, so much so that I catch a little lump in my throat forming and my eyes suddenly become glazed with a tear or two. I give a few hard blinks and ensure I hide my emotion. I put on a big smile and bend down with open arms as my little Daisy comes rushing towards me.

"Mummy!" Daisy squeals excitedly.

"Hello, my baby!" I respond holding her tightly for a moment.

As she holds onto my hand and skips alongside me, I can't wait to tell her my good news.

"Mummy finally got the job I've been working towards." I proudly tell her.

"Which job? The one where you'll be helping other kids?' she asks innocently.

"Yes!" I beam. "So that'll mean some after school clubs for you in the week, but your friend Jessica goes to them too, so that's exciting isn't it?"

"Yes Mummy, well done on your job." Daisy smiles.

We walk quietly most of the way home whilst Daisy skips along, and I'm lost in deep thought. I've been working so hard for three years now to complete my studies and finally kick start my career as a social worker. I cannot believe I finally achieved it and now I can settle down. Daisy is settled into school; our new home is beautiful. Things are finally turning around.

It hasn't been an easy ride to get where we are, when I was pregnant with Daisy her Dad died in a motorbike accident. He was only twenty-three. He was so into bikes and racing them, I think he thought he was invincible. He ended up owning multiple motorbike stores which he inherited from his own father and they proved very successful.

Devon would have been a great Dad; I will forever be sad that his chance to have that father-daughter relationship was robbed from him. And Daisy. Devon and I actually separated during my pregnancy, we loved each other but we soon realised the love we had for each other was only as friends. We remained very close and he promised me he would always look after us both and true to his word I found out that a week after he passed away, he had left his entire business to me and Daisy with information of a potential buyer.

We sold the business and used the money to buy our beautiful four-bedroom modern home in Surrey.

We have over an acre of land, a private driveway, two garages, a great big entrance hallway, an open plan kitchen and dining room and beautiful decorated bedrooms. My living room is my favourite. I have a large ash grey corner sofa with a white marble fireplace which has been a life saver this cold winter. Above it is a huge silver chic mirror and underneath a row of my favourite candles dotted along the top of the fireplace. I have a big fluffy silver rug with specs of glitter in it and large patio doors which open up to our garden. Most of the house is decorated with a light grey and white decor. It's quite big but still cosy and it's ours. Thanks to Devon, I was able to buy our forever home. The large cul-de-sac we are on is also very well looked after and well presented.

My favourite thing is those old-fashioned black lamp posts dotted around, I always think they look so smart and remind me of one of those old classic movies. Surrounding the cul-de-sac are fields for as far as you can see, it really is a little slice of luxury in the beautifully picturesque countryside.

Suddenly my phone pings and breaks my thoughts.

"I'm so excited! Don't forget dinner at mine tonight! Rueben will be here! yay! Let me know if you need help choosing an outfit. Did I mention I'm excited?! L xx"

Oh crap. I hadn't forgotten but I hadn't been particularly counting down the hours either. Lana thought it was best to throw a dinner party where me and Rueben could meet on common ground to save it being awkward. Thing is, I'm still rubbish at these social things, always have been. I hate awkward silences, so I tend to just keep talking to fill them, but the problem is I talk such utter nonsense sometimes that I make a right idiot out of myself. It's pure word vomit.

Christ knows what I'm going to wear. It's easy for Lana, the woman has a body like Kim Kardashian. Quite literally, she's always been short, all the way through school and then as we got into year ten her bum filled out and she was ultra-curvy. She hated her big bum for the most part, until Kim Kardashian and Jennifer Lopez took the world by storm with their big booty's and now suddenly, she doesn't mind anymore. I'm curvy too but not quite in the right places like Lana. I'm currently waiting for big bellies to be in fashion and then I can finally have my moment. To be fair, I'm not massive or anything and I still feel quite attractive, but my body has definitely changed since having Daisy. For instance, my boobs used to be on my chest and now, well, let's just say I rely on a good bra.

As the evening draws in, the babysitter arrives for Daisy. She's a lovely girl, one of the neighbour's daughters and very sweet. Thankfully Daisy took a real shine to her, which means occasionally this frumpy Mummy gets to let her hair down. I drag my feet up to my bedroom and look at all my clothing hanging up in my walk-in wardrobe. Nothing jumps out. I don't want to wear anything too over the top and look overly keen and one rejection away from a lonely-hearts ad but yet I don't want to look like I don't take pride in my appearance either.

Eventually I drag out some new Levi skinny jeans and a black roll neck with organza puff sleeves and a Gucci belt. I style my hair quickly into a smart bun and curl some of the remaining bits hanging down at the front. I phish around my make-up drawer for a red lipstick, My Mum always said red is confidence and right now I need just that.

I catch myself in the mirror as I'm popping in my new earrings and actually, I like what I see. I look fresh faced, casual but with a hint of glam.

I throw on my black ankle boots just as my phone pings.

"Rueben's here. Looks hot. Hurry up! L x"

Okay, well off I go. On a weird dinner date type of thing with Lana posing as Cilla Black. A date I was totally not ready for but going anyway to get my best friend off my back. I must remember to check that my red lipstick hasn't smudged periodically throughout the night – Oh and don't say anything dumb.

CHAPTER THREE

I've been to Lana's house many times, but this is the first time I'm arriving with butterflies in my tummy, sweaty palms and my heart racing. Why am I so nervous? I don't even know Rueben. Why would I care if he likes me? I might not even like him.

As soon as Lana opens the door I'm met with her big cheesy grin. Oh god, she's really loving this already.

"Come in, come in!" She squeals.

"I've poured you a Prosecco already, I'm literally about to dish up so you can grab a seat if you like, next to Rueben of course." Lana says with a wink.

I must admit the food smells delicious and I'm not one to turn down a Prosecco.

As soon as I walk into the dining room, Mike, Lana's husband greets me right away with a warm smile and a big hug. I'm very fond of Mike, he just has one of those charming personalities, the type of guy you could never stay mad at and he has made my best friend very happy for the last ten years, so no complaints from me.

I then turn to look at Rueben and sure enough Lana was right; I'm intrigued by him.

He is attractive, very dark hair and green eyes, quite tanned, smartly trimmed beard, well presented, casual jeans but with a fitted white tee which shows off his biceps. He clearly goes to the gym but nothing over the top, just looks like he takes care of himself.

He gives me a smile straight away and stands to pull my chair out.

Very gentlemanly. Damn it, Lana said that about him too. I hate it when she's right. This means she'll gloat even more.

I remind myself not to stare, but I really like his eyes. I never really understood the term puppy dog eyes but right now I think I do; his eyes are so gentle and kind. Almost as if he hasn't got a bad bone in his body.

Lana is an awesome host as always, she constantly keeps the conversation flowing and our drinks topped up, but I don't really feel like I need her to chaperone us too much. Rueben has been openly telling me about his job and his hobbies. He told me he's some kind of contractor and I'm not entirely sure what that entails but I make a mental note to google it later. He has been asking me a lot of questions too and I told him about Daisy almost straight away. Just in case he couldn't handle the thought of a woman with a child and wanted to run for the hills. Least, that's what I've learned from previous experience. Although he doesn't seem phased at all, in fact he tells me how lucky I am when Lana shows him pictures of me and Daisy on her phone.

"She's very beautiful. A lot like her Mum." Rueben smiles flirtatiously and I feel myself blush with embarrassment.

"So, what football team do you support?" I ask to change the subject so my burning cheeks can cool down.

"There's no right or wrong answer but you should know if you say the wrong team, I'll leave now." I joke.

Rueben laughs and I can't help but grow excited about him with every smile he gives me. I love making him laugh.

"I highly doubt that because I support Gillingham, they were my local team growing up. My Grandad used to take me to the home games every other week." He tells me proudly.

"Aah that's OK then, I support Tottenham. No rivalry there then. We're safe! Cute about your Grandad though, how long did you both do that for?" I ask curiously.

"For years really, ever since I can remember. We stopped when I was sixteen because he started to get a bit poorly and he passed away a couple of years later. Left me with the best memories though, I remember how first thing in the morning before it was barely light outside and before we'd leave for the game, he'd be up by five thirty a.m. just to make me a flask of hot chocolate."

"Jesus, how long does it take his kettle to boil?" I blurt sarcastically. Oh god. Word vomit moment.

"HA! HA!" Reuben mocks with fake laughter but then we both fall about laughing.

Thank God he found that funny.

Before I know it, it's half past eleven and we've been lost in conversation for hours. I look up and see Lana and Mike are just staring at us gleefully whilst sipping on Prosecco and whispering amongst themselves.

"Wow, is that the time? I really best get back. I have a babysitter who I'm sure is desperate to get home." I half laugh.

"I'll walk you to your car?" Rueben suggests.

"Sure." I respond trying to avoid Lana's ever-growing smug smile.

I say my goodbyes to Lana and Mike and thank them for the delicious dinner as always before grabbing my jacket and heading for the door with Rueben.

As Rueben holds the front door open for me the frosty cold air hits my face and suddenly, I can feel the Prosecco rushing to my head a little.

"Tonight was way better than I thought it was going to be." Rueben softly says.

"Thanks...I think?" I mumble and nervously laugh.

"I just mean, I really don't do these kinds of things. I don't really date. I've just been so busy with work, I didn't even think I was open to meeting anyone, but then you walked in." he smiles before nervously looking down towards the floor.

I smile at his honesty; I don't want to say too much just yet but inside I'm completely in agreement with him. I almost wish I had taken Lana's advice and met up with Rueben a long time ago. This night has exceeded my expectations hugely. I lean in to give him a kiss on the cheek and I get in the car whilst he watches me drive away.

As I arrive home, I can't help but notice I've been smiling the whole journey back. Rueben was so open and easy to talk too, he found me funny but more importantly he really made me laugh too. I want to text him, but I feel like it could be too soon. Daisy is off for a sleepover tomorrow for her friend's birthday and I'm half tempted to ask Rueben over for a takeaway and a movie. I shouldn't though, right? There are rules with dating, a type of etiquette, I think. I should just wait patiently for him to contact me and I should play it cool.

It feels so good to be in my big double bed and as I turn the light out for some well-deserved sleep my phone pings. Probably Lana making sure I got home OK.

"Tonight, was amazing, can I see you again? Rueben xx"

Instantly a huge smile spreads across my face and before the thoughts of etiquette and dating rules flood my mind again, I find my thumb typing back for me.

"I'd love too. My house tomorrow evening for food and movies? Xx"

I lay there staring at the three dots on my screen whilst Rueben replies. I love how exciting this feels.

"Can't wait, see you then. Sweet dreams xx"

Before I know it, I'm closing my heavy eye lids and allowing myself to drift off to sleep. Noticing how relaxed and happy I'm feeling. This feeling is amazing. Could this really be happening? My career is about to be in full swing and now I could have finally met someone who could be very special? I can't wait to see what this brings.

CHAPTER FOUR

Sitting on my lunch break at work, I can't help but daydream about Rueben.

It's been two weeks now since the dinner date at Lana's and I am ridiculously happy that I gave in to my friend's persistence.

It sounds crazy to actually think about it and even crazier when I try to explain it to people, but Rueben has been over every single night since the dinner date. People must think that's insane, but it's like I've known him forever.

The first few nights we spent most of it drinking wine and talking to each other about our lives, our dreams, some of our past experiences and adventures, pretty much anything and before we knew it, the sun would be coming up.

I have never enjoyed talking to someone so much that the hours just seem to escape from me.

I started my first day at work too last Monday and sure enough as soon I stepped into the building my phone pinged and Rueben had sent me a good luck message. The sentiment is small but means the world to me. By the time I got home that evening Rueben surprised me with flowers, perfume and took me and Daisy out for dinner. Daisy got to choose the restaurant.

That's another thing, Rueben is refreshingly brilliant with Daisy. I introduced the two a lot quicker than I would have ever dreamt of but with Rueben it just seemed ridiculous to wait. I knew he was good for us; I knew Daisy would love him.

By the end of that night Rueben and I were laying across my big double bed, I moved myself up to lay on his chest and as usual he ran his fingers through my hair, stroking my ear like he always does before placing a gentle kiss on my forehead.

"I love you." Rueben whispered gently.

What? Did he just say love? L-o-v-e?

This is crazy, this is too soon. It's been barely two weeks but here I am, turning my head to look up to him and telling him I feel the same. I never want to lose him, he completes my little family, I'm more sure of it than I have been about anything and more importantly I know he needs us, throughout all the late night discussions I've had with Rueben I have always noticed something, he looks a little lost in the world. I can't quite place my finger on why or what has made him to feel this way, but I can just sense it.

"I love you Roo, I am so happy that we met." I smile and he pulls me in closer for a tighter cuddle.

Over the last couple of days Rueben opened up to me more, I learned about his last relationship, he told me how they met when he was seventeen and ended up staying together for seven years. He told me it was tough sometimes because she was at university for three of those years, but they managed to keep the relationship going. He told me how they started putting away money to buy a house, together they had raised nearly twelve thousand pounds but towards the end of their relationship Rueben had found out his girlfriend had been cheating, more than once and whilst she very apologetically confessed to the affairs, she wasn't quite riddled with guilt enough to give Rueben back his share of their savings. In fact, she point blank refused. It was hard hearing Rueben speak about how the relationship ended and much he lost from it. He spoke about it carefully, expressing to me that he has put all behind him now and had learned a hard lesson but you could see the sadness in his eyes as he recalled having to start all over again financially and how this meant he had to stay even longer living at home with his Mum and Step Dad.

I told him about myself although in comparison I don't think I have a lot to tell. I met Devon when we were sixteen, we stayed together until I was nineteen and broke up some months before Daisy was born. I explained how Devon had died and so Daisy didn't get the chance to have a Dad. He expressed the usual kind sympathy that most have shown me over the years if I have ever told them about Devon.

I love how Rueben very sweetly told me he could relate to Daisy in some ways as he lost his own Father when he was just ten years old. Although he said he didn't see his Dad too often before he passed away, his memory of him clearly causes him great grief still because his eyes water slightly when he speaks of him. I get the feeling Rueben doesn't know a whole lot about the man his Father was as his memories are vague but still spoken about with great fondness.

I very briefly told him that I had been single for only several months. I was in a relationship most of last year, if you can call it that. I swerve most of the questions which followed. Not because I am hiding anything but because I find myself finally in a good place and I hate to give time and attention to something which doesn't deserve anymore thought. I do let Rueben know though that he had a serious issue with alcohol and the more I tried to help him the more he would turn on me. I recall how Rueben nodded sympathetically, as if he understood enough from my short description of what went on in that relationship and I needn't say anymore.

Just as I'm completely lost in my daydream, my phone pings making me jump which almost makes me spill my coffee and I look around quickly to see if anyone noticed. It's cold sitting on these benches outside the offices as the end of January approaches but still a welcome relief from the stuffy offices.

"Hey, I have to pop home later to pick up some more clothes, would you and Daisy like to come? My Mum really wants to meet you xx"

Oh God. Meeting his Mum?

After a moment of the offer sinking in, I smile to myself. The fact he wants me to meet his family so soon is actually very sweet and shows me how serious he is about me and Daisy. I feel slightly anxious about the meet, but I reassure myself that I'm worrying over nothing. I'm not some clueless sixteen-year-old. I'm a Mother with my own home, a beautiful daughter and a career. Plus, If Rueben is any kind of example of the type of person his Mum is then I have absolutely no worries. In fact, Rueben must be a credit to her, she's managed to raise a kind, caring loyal gentleman. I'd love to meet the woman responsible.

CHAPTER FIVE

Rueben's car is really stylish, I'm not a car person usually but this feels very smart. It's an Audi but I'm almost too embarrassed to ask which one. The gadgets inside feel very modern, there's a bright colourful screen in front which displays the songs that are playing and little blue LED lights around which makes the inside of the car glow.

Rueben catches me staring so mesmerisingly at all the features his car has that mine definitely doesn't.

"My car is your car now." Rueben says sweetly with a kind smile.

I catch his glance momentarily and smile back. I love how generous he is with me; it makes me feel so important.

"Does this mean I can change the music?"

"Err, What's wrong with Ed Sheeran?" Rueben laughs as he pretends to be offended.

"Nothing…Ed's great, I'm never bored of his music. Even when the radio plays it a thousand times a day and most of his songs sound the same, I just love it…" I tease.

And we both burst out laughing as he gives me a playful glare.

"Ok, ok I'll be nice about Ed Sheeran. I take it you're not into garage or anything like that then?"

"You thought right." Reuben responds.

Despite mocking me and rolling his eyes every time I put on a song that he isn't sure of; the drive is nice. Rueben puts his hand on my thigh and rests it there between gear shifts. It's something so simple and yet it makes me feel totally at ease and loved.

After twenty minutes of driving I realise we are heading into a very familiar area.

"Is this where your Mum and stepdad live?" I ask.

"Yeah, been here forever and my Nan and Grandad, they've been here since they were teenagers too."

"Wow. My family grew up around here too, as did my Nan and Grandad…" I reply surprised.

"Small world, eh!" Rueben laughs.

"Definitely, maybe your Mum might know my parents? They aren't together anymore but they both grew up around here and stayed here for many years, maybe I should ask her?"

"Yeah baby, be a little conversation starter. Can you imagine if she knows them though? We better not be related or something." Rueben jokes with a flirtatious wink.

I playfully swat at him but giggle at the same time. It's nice to drive somewhere familiar and I realise it's actually made me less nervous. As we arrive, I take it all in, looking around and noticing not too much has changed. It's essentially a large estate with many council homes on it, a few pubs and a couple of corner shops. A place I've been many times to visit family when I was a child and my parents always spoke fondly when talking about their time growing up around here.

Rueben pulls up right outside one of the larger looking houses on the street and I soon realise this one is his childhood home.

"Ready?" Rueben smiles as he locks the car behind us.

"Yeah of course." I say a lot more confidently than I think he expected.

As we approach the front door, I follow close behind him. Daisy has suddenly gotten very close to me too; she must be a little nervous.

"Oh yeah, ignore the state of the place, they're in the middle of decorating. Been in the middle of decorating for fifteen years now." Rueben smirks rolling his eyes.

I look around the small entrance hallway noticing immediately the bits of wallpaper hanging off the walls and the ripped carpets on the stairs to the left. You can tell it's been left for some time now but I'm sure it will look very homely when they do finish it.

What I notice most are the tonnes of pictures. Pictures in small frames dotted around the windowsills. As I enter the living room I see even more, lots of family pictures and those professional school photos you always cringe at when you get older. There are so many. Even more on the walls too, collages mounted into frames and canvas prints too. So many of his Mum and his sisters, not as many of Rueben. It comes to my mind that it is slightly odd but maybe it's a boy thing? Maybe Rueben is more camera shy than his sisters.

I stare at a photo proudly taking centre stage on top of their fireplace. It's of Rueben's Mum and his two sisters. They look like they're at a family event, maybe a wedding or something. Rueben told me about his sisters but not very much. I know the eldest, Lily lives in London now, she got into a bad crowd apparently and got quite heavily into drugs. She doesn't come back to visit too often unless she needs money. I know even less about Kelsey, the youngest sister. I didn't want to push it but as far as I'm aware she ran away from home at nineteen and Rueben's Mum was devastated. They pushed and pushed the police to help but apparently because she is over eighteen and not classed as vulnerable there was very little they could do. She's stayed away from home now for nearly two years and although Rueben hasn't said it, I can tell he worries for her. It seems nobody knows why she ran away. I feel sad staring at the picture, a young innocent looking girl with long dark hair, the same colour as Rueben's, green eyes just the same too and a very cheeky grin. She looks sweet. I wonder what might have caused her to feel like she couldn't stay with her family at home anymore. So sad.

"Hello mate, you alright?"

A lady's voice breaks my thoughts. I turn around to see a plump dark-haired lady walk towards Rueben and touch his arm as she smiles and greets him. Her hair is tied up into a scruffy bun. She's dressed very casually in basic jeans and a white tank top. She has big green eyes just like Rueben, although her eyes seem more serious. They go wide as she turns to look at me and she has a sharp stare.

"Mum, this is my girlfriend Mollie and Mollie this is my Mum, Joy." Rueben proudly introduces us.

"Hiya, so lovely to meet you." I smile nervously.

Joy looks me up and down and smiles but doesn't make a whole lot of eye contact.

"Aww It's lovely to meet you too!" She politely responds after a short pause.

"Say hello Daisy…" I say, trying to deflect a bit of attention from myself.

Daisy smiles and gives a little shy wave which makes Joy giggle.

"Would you like a yummy cookie, Daisy?" Joy asks her and Daisy gives another shy little nod and this time changes her wave to a thumbs up.

We all giggle a little and Joy disappears off into the kitchen and rummages around for a cookie.

"Hello, you alright?" I hear a male voice say behind me.

"Yeah, you? This is Mollie, Dave." Rueben responds, introducing me.

"Alright?" Dave asks nonchalantly.

"Yes, thank you." I nod a bit nervously, unsure what to say next.

Dave walks straight past me and into the kitchen holding a pair of muddy boots. He must have just got back from work. Rueben says he works on farms all day fixing milking parlours. He is a short man and has a very stern face. He definitely doesn't seem to be the friendliest but maybe he hasn't had the best day at work.

Joy comes back into the lounge with a plate for Daisy's cookie and a cookie for herself and sits down.

"Daisy is very sweet, Mollie." Joy smiles as she adoringly stares at Daisy munching on her cookie.

"Oh, thank you, it's probably because you have cookies though." I say jokingly.

Joy doesn't seem to cotton on to my joke because she doesn't respond or react much which makes me a little nervous, but I catch Rueben laughing a little which helps.

"Oh Joy, I was just telling Rueben that my parents grew up around here, I just wondered if you knew them? Laraine and Brian?"

Joy stares for a second before giving a small smile.

"Yeah, Yeah I do. Small world!"

I wait to see if she offers anything more about maybe how she knows them or if she recalls any memories of being out with them when they were just kids hanging about the streets, but she doesn't offer much more on the subject.

"So, what have you both been up to today?" Joy asks Rueben, changing the subject.

"Oh, just work really. It's been a bit full on so by the time it hits five o clock I'm pretty much ready just for a bath and bed. I have been pretty tired."

"Oh right, are you eating properly though?"

"Yes Mum" Rueben rolls his eyes at her fussing which makes me giggle. It's sweet that she cares.

"Mollie has started her new job too, so she's been very busy, why don't you tell Mum about it?" Rueben says turning to me.

Awkwardly I begin explaining to Joy that I have just finished my degree and I've just started as a social worker, which can be quite intense but I tell her I'm really enjoying it so far and genuinely feel like I'm finally doing something useful with my time. Joy nods along politely but doesn't seem too interested.

"Have you got my money, Roo?" Joy cuts me off.

Rueben doesn't seem surprised that his Mum just cut me off mid-sentence and instead fidgets awkwardly at the sudden topic of money.

"Well yeah, I do but I haven't been here very much the last two weeks, have I? You're not still expecting more, are you?"

I suddenly feel very awkward listening to Rueben and Joy discuss money in front of me and I turn to concentrate on Daisy instead.

"Well yeah, but whatever you've got on you is fine mate." Joy responds with a smile.

"I've got a hundred on me now if that's OK?"

"Yeah that's alright, just leave it on the side Roo, that'll do." Joy softly says.

It's kind of endearing the way Joy calls Rueben, mate. Almost as if it's her way of expressing her love a little.

I don't usually care for the word but the way it's used between them is almost comforting. I remember how my Mum used to call me angel cake when I was little. I loved that.

"Right, well I'll just grab some things quickly and we best get going. Daisy hasn't had dinner yet." Rueben informs.

I wait downstairs whilst Rueben disappears to his bedroom to grab a few items. Thankfully I don't feel too awkward as Daisy is chatting away to Joy and telling her all about school and starts talking about how they've been learning about different countries. Just recently they learned about Greece and got to try some traditional foods. Joy laughs as Daisy tells her how gross the feta cheeses were and some of the weird dipping oils. Joy looks fascinated listening to Daisy's ramblings, and I can't help but smile watching them. Joy may have come across a little socially awkward but watching her with my daughter is heart-warming. It makes Kelsey cross my mind again and I wonder why she wouldn't want to stay near her Mum. I think of asking Rueben some more questions, but I don't want to make him uncomfortable. As far as possible future mother in law's go, she seems a little reserved but kind at the very least and that's a relief.

As Rueben reappears, we start to say our goodbyes and Joy tells Rueben to take care and look after himself. The usual mumsy stuff. It's cute to watch and funnier to see Rueben rolling his eyes again at his Mum's fussing.

In the car I notice some tension as Rueben sighs and shakes his head a little in deep thought.

"What's wrong?" I question gently.

"Mum sometimes, that's all." he mumbles flatly.

"Did I miss something?"

"Oh, it's just the rent money stuff, she does this all the time. She makes me give her four hundred a month and I still have to pay for my own food, I pay for two of their household bills, I've been lending her money to cover her phone bill and she'll always ask for the money again in front of Dave. She likes to pretend I didn't give her any rent money yet. She knows I won't argue back because Dave just goes mad and I can't be bothered with it. He will always believe her and take her side and keep arguing with me until I just give her the money, so it's easier if I just hand over the cash." Rueben tells me, his voice getting slightly more raised as he becomes more agitated explaining.

"So, you have already given your Mum her rent money? But she acts like you didn't in front of Dave so that you have to hand over even more?" I ask, making sure I fully understand what he is trying to tell me.

"Yep. Sometimes she will just make out I'm a hundred pounds short, but there have been times where she would tell Dave I didn't pay anything at all. So, I've ended up giving her double in the past."

I sit trying to take in what he just told me.

"She has issues with money." he quietly adds.

"Oh?"

"Yeah, just spending habits, I guess. I don't know what she buys but it's just easier to give the money over, otherwise it can be unbearable under that roof."

I watch Rueben stare ahead into the distance as we drive along the country lanes nearing to my home. He seems so fed up and I sense he could do with talking about it a bit more, but I think he is trying not to trouble me with his problem.

"Move in?" I surprise myself by asking.

Wait, was that word vomit? I ask myself. No, I don't think it was. I think I genuinely want to be with Rueben all the time and hearing him stress about rent and his Mum has made me want to fix the issue. I want to make him happy.

"What? Now? So soon? Are you serious?!" Rueben almost shrieks.

"Well yeah, I could do with the rent." I joke.

We both laugh and Rueben reaches over to give my thigh a little squeeze and smiles at me. He doesn't even have to say it, I can see how thankful he is in his eyes and I am so pleased I got to help him. I look over my shoulder to Daisy who smiles at me as if to give me the reassurance that she's happy to have Rueben come and live with us too.

"I'd love too." Rueben responds enthusiastically.

"Well that's settled then, problem solved" I smile.

CHAPTER SIX

Sitting at my desk, I find myself staring at the clock a lot today. Thank god Friday has come around already, I feel absolutely exhausted. It's Daisy's birthday Sunday, she'll be eight years old and I'm trying to quickly get as much work done as possible so that I can last minute internet shop for her.

I'm not usually this unorganised but Rueben has been moving his stuff in the last couple of days and I have been rearranging my own belongings to help accommodate him.

I did smile to myself this morning though as I left the house and clocked Rueben's work boots sat neatly next to mine and Daisy's shoes. It's exciting to see us becoming a little family.

Daisy has an inset day today so no school for her and Rueben decided to take the day off work too so he could spend some time with her and organise the last of his boxes. I'm desperate to call home to see how they're getting on, but I know they'll be fine. I smile to myself again imagining Daisy making Rueben play hairdressers for the eighth time today. I recall how Rueben promised to build Daisy a camp today in the living room that we can all play in when I get home. I love how much he makes an effort with my daughter.

"Mollie, you've got a personal call waiting on the line, shall I patch them through?" The receptionist, Mel asks. I didn't even notice her approach me.

My cheeks feel flushed and hot and I realise I suddenly feel really awkward and embarrassed. Personal work calls can be frowned upon, especially when I have a mobile. Why wouldn't they just call that? Panic starts to rush over me as I wonder if there is some kind of emergency.

"Oh. Yes, please." I mumble awkwardly.

"Hello?" I say nervously into my office telephone.

"Ah Mollie. It's Joy." The familiar voice says.

"Oh, is everything OK? Has something happened?" I question quite abruptly. I don't mean to sound rude or anything, but I suddenly feel anxious. Joy would be the very last person I would expect to call me at work. We've never even spoke on the phone before.

"Yes fine. I just called you a couple of times after getting your number from Rueben, but you didn't answer your mobile and I needed to check something with you." Joy explains sounding rushed.

"Oh, what's up?"

"I was just in the card shop buying Daisy a birthday card and if it's okay with you I have bought her a card which says 'with love from Grandad and Grandma' on the front and I just wanted to check that you didn't have a problem with me giving her that card?"

"I...I...um..." I stumble trying to find the words.

This is so sudden.

Daisy has only met Joy once.

I don't want to confuse Daisy; she already has grandparents in my Mum and Dad, and she knows that Daddy Devon's parents are in the sky with her Daddy too. I'm not sure if suddenly calling Rueben's parents Grandma and Grandad would feel normal for her? And what if me and Rueben end up breaking up, where would Daisy stand? Am I overthinking it? Surely the offer is meant with good intent and I don't want to sound ungrateful.

"Hello?" Joy says loudly into the phone.

"I, erm, Yes. That should be fine." I say unconvincingly.

"Are you sure?"

"Yes. No really that's lovely, I'm sure Daisy would love that." I say, trying to sound a little more confident.

"Wonderful. See you Sunday." Joy responds and the line goes dead.

I rummage through my bag to find my phone and sure enough when I pull it out, I see I've had seven missed calls from a phone number I don't recognise. That must have been Joy. I feel a little frustrated at the persistence of her calls. She knows I work all week and after trying my mobile half a dozen times she thinks it's completely fine to call somebody's work?

I really don't want to start off my relationship with Rueben's Mum negatively though and so there was no way I could express any concerns to her over a birthday card. Even if I do think it's too soon. I wonder if she often puts people on the spot like that. Maybe she's just trying to be involved and more importantly involve Daisy into their family too? If that's the case I guess it's sweet that she's trying to form a bond so soon with my daughter and I can't dislike her for that.

Daisy means the world to me; I have always been extra protective of her throughout her entire life. I have always felt so guilty and so sad for her that she lost her own Dad so soon that I try to prevent her from feeling any further loss or hurt. So, I guess what Joy has done is a positive thing. She's offering my daughter more family.

I suddenly feel guilty that perhaps I didn't come across very grateful to Joy on the phone over her sweet offer, so I decide to send her a quick text.

"Thank you Joy, Daisy will love the card I'm sure. See you Sunday! Mollie xx"

I put my phone away and quickly dive on to the internet and order Daisy the few presents I know she'll love and make sure I get next day delivery.

It's the first day of February on Sunday and I've planned party food and an entertainer to come to the house for Daisy. I've invited a few family members and a group of Daisy's school friends. Nothing huge but I know she will love it. My parents won't be able to come by as my Dad and his wife are currently sunning themselves in the Caribbean and my Mum's working.

Still, Lana and Mike will come by, I haven't even told Lana that Rueben moved in. She'll be unbelievably surprised. Smug. But also surprised.

26

I start to notice it's getting dark outside as I glance up to the clock, quarter to four. Perfect. We finish at four on Fridays and I can't wait to get home to my family. I smile at the word. Family, my little family. I love them so much. I take a large gulp of the last of my tea just as my phone pings.

> *"Our living room camp is ready and waiting! We're just making popcorn. I love you."*

The perfect little Friday afternoon text. Since meeting Rueben I've become excited to get home more than I ever have been. I really feel like Daisy has another person at home to help create fun games and keep her happy. It takes some of the pressure from me when I'm feeling tired. Daisy doesn't tell me a whole lot about how she feels, she's ridiculously laid back and just goes with the flow, she's always been that way. But the way she giggles and lights up when Rueben acts all goofy and they run around playing hide and seek or other silly games it gives me all the evidence that I need to know how happy she is. Then there's me, I go home and feel like I have my best friend waiting. Somebody to sit on the sofa with and talk to about my day. Someone to choose the movie with and actually cuddle up with. He really knows me so well, he always records the programmes he thinks I like so that I don't miss them, especially the Big Bang Theory and Friends. Even though I've watched those episodes a dozen times over, I'm so grateful he saves them for me. When he senses my day has been particularly bad, he runs me a bubble bath and lights a few candles, he knows a bath is my favourite place when I'm feeling extra stressed. It's only early days but I know he is the one. My one.

CHAPTER SEVEN

I wake up Sunday morning with the early sunlight warming my cheeks as it streams through the gaps in the curtains. I roll over to realise Rueben must be up already because he isn't sleeping beside me with his arms draped across my stomach as usual. A quick stretch and I pull myself out of bed to go and find everyone. As I get halfway down the stairs, I already see pink and yellow streamers and balloons hung around the hallway. I walk into the kitchen to find Rueben standing on a dining room chair and reaching up high to hang a happy birthday sign whilst Daisy watches on excitedly.

"Mummy, look! Rueben has put all my party decorations up!" Daisy beams.

I stare at my little girl momentarily, reminding myself she just turned eight. My precious princess a whole year older. She's stood there in her little pink nightie with her long blonde hair a little dishevelled and blue eyes sparkling as she looks around the room with a great big smile, enjoying all the decorations beautifully on display to celebrate her day.

"Happy birthday my beautiful baby girl." I say excitedly.

Immediately she runs towards me, wrapping her little arms tightly around my waist and I kiss the top of her head.

"Sorry, you've already missed birthday pancakes." Rueben smiles.

"That's ok, a coffee will do me just fine." I smile back.

"Thank you so much Roo, this is incredibly sweet." I say, my voice cracking a little. Suddenly I feel quite emotional.

"Hey…" Rueben says softly as he climbs off the dining room chair and walks towards me.

"I love that little girl." he says as he cups my cheek gently and strokes his thumb down towards my lips before giving me a gentle kiss.

"And I'd do anything for either of you."

"I know." I smile.

"We both love you too, I hope you know that."

"Of course, I know that."

"Mummy!" Daisy interrupts.

"Can you save the kissy lovey dovey stuff for later? I really want to open my presents!"

Rueben and I look at each other and then back at Daisy and burst out laughing. She's clearly trying to be serious, but her face is just too cute.

"Of course, baby!" I laugh.

Rueben disappears off out into the hallway and returns with a few presents in hand. I hadn't discussed getting Daisy anything with him, it's still early days and I just assumed I would be the one buying them.

"What?" Rueben smirks

"You didn't actually think I'd forget my Daisy dots, did you?"

Daisy dots is a cute little nickname Reuben started calling her because her favourite puzzle books are the dot-to-dots. One Sunday she proudly showed us about six she had completed and coloured in and Rueben jokingly called her Daisy dots and now the name seems to of just stuck. It's actually pretty adorable that he has a little name for her.

Daisy rips open the light pink sparkly unicorn wrapping paper and reveals some sparkly bracelets, a unicorn diary with a matching pen and a beautiful snow globe that has miniature unicorns flying around as you shake it up. When the sparkles settle, I realise that inside the snow globe is a picture of me, Daisy and Rueben.

Daisy's face lights up as she stares into the globe.

"OK, seriously, how are you so perfect?" I joke.

The present is incredibly sweet and thoughtful.

"Who is helping you? Where did you come from?" I laugh poking Rueben.

"I've not always been like this, least I don't think I have. You just make me want to be a better man. For you and Daisy." He smiles before pulling me in closer for another kiss.

"Seriously guys! Enough with the kissing!" Daisy shouts before giggling and rolling her eyes playfully.

As the afternoon unfolds the party is in full swing. I'm sat around the dining room table with a couple of the school mums and Lana and Mike whilst watching the children run around with the entertainer.

"Wow, they'll definitely sleep well tonight!" Mike chuckles as Daisy and her little friends come running past us mischievously and giggling.

"I still can't believe you're living together though." Lana smiles as she stares at me brightly.

"Oh god, are we going to hear about this for the entire afternoon?" I laugh.

"Seriously, I'm so happy for you both." She confirms softly. She looks at both me and Rueben for a moment before pulling me in for a hug.

I give Lana a big hug back and don't even notice that Rueben has gotten up to answer the door. Was that the doorbell? Did I miss it? It must be Joy and Dave, they did say they would come by. I'm a little nervous now as they have never been to my home before and this will only be the second time meeting them.

I quickly realise I guessed right as Rueben appears back into the dining room with both his Mum and stepdad followed closely behind.

"Alright?" Dave asks in the same flat tone as last time.

I'm starting to wonder if he is just generally a man of a few words. Joy looks a little hesitant as she comes into my home but gives off a little smile. I realise this is my chance to make more of an effort to make her feel welcome in my home and to hopefully grow closer to her.

"Joy! I've saved you a seat, please sit down and I'll grab you a drink of whatever you'd like?" I ask trying to sound as upbeat and friendly as possible.

"Oh, ok. I'll just have a cup of tea then please." Joy responds quietly.

"Same, please." Dave copies.

"Of course! Please make yourself at home and feel free to eat anything from the buffet. The kids haven't bothered with it much." I laugh.

As I make the drinks, I watch Rueben get Daisy's attention so that she can come and greet Joy and Dave. They immediately make a fuss of her and hand over a present and a card. Of course, she rips open the present first, revealing some colouring books and a pencil case. I walk back over placing the drinks down onto the table and watch Daisy intently as she tears open the white envelope. I feel awkward again, I know I told myself earlier that it was very sweet and that I should be fine with it, but I can't help but tense up a little.

Daisy stares down at the card and looks a little puzzled.

"Are you my Grandma and Grandad?" Daisy whispers in Dave and Joy's direction.

Before I have time to interject it seems Joy is already answering for me.

"Well, yes. If you would like us to be?" Joy smiles.

"Mum…" Rueben begins to interrupt his Mum but I cut him off just as quick. The idea of a scene happening right here right now over this quite frankly makes me hope the ground would swallow me up.

"Oh. it's fine Rueben." I blurt out as fast as I can.

I notice everyone in the room has turned to look at me.

"It's lovely, Roo, isn't it, really. Daisy can call them that if they like. I think it's very kind, thank you Joy." I quickly manage to say.

Joy looks thrilled as she lets out a giggle and reaches out to give Daisy a little cuddle. Rueben looks a little uneasy and keeps looking at me to try and read my expressions, but I keep painting on a smile to lessen any awkwardness and not reveal to Rueben how I might feel. The last thing I want is him challenging his Mum on the topic in front of everyone. I can feel Lana staring at me too, but I can't bring myself to make eye contact with her. I know she'll be thinking it's a little rushed.

"Baby, is that really OK?" Rueben whispers as he pulls me to one side.

I pause for a second to gather my thoughts and over Rueben's shoulder I see Daisy laughing with Joy as she shows off her birthday presents, and I'm reminded that Daisy has two people willing to be her grandparents and build a bond with her. This is the most family she's ever had. This could be really good for Daisy. She deserves this.

31

"Actually Roo…I think it's really OK. It's a bit quick yes, but everyone seems happy. So, I'm happy" I say reassuringly.

CHAPTER EIGHT

As Monday morning rolls around I'm back at work diving into my many emails.

This morning was chaotic, I had an extra tired Daisy this morning who really didn't want to get up. I think yesterday's excitement has taken it out of her. Rueben left for work by six this morning, so I barely got a chance to see him either.

He has been a saint this weekend, helping to make Daisy's party as perfect as it could be. He took charge of all the decorating and balloons, picked up her cake and by the time the last guest was leaving he was already halfway through the washing up. I want to thank him in a way he knows we really appreciate him, but I can't think of what I could do. As I get up to fetch another cup of tea it dawns on me as I'm stood in the little staff room. Immediately I pull my phone out of my pocket and send a text to Rueben.

"Late night shopping? I want to buy you something. Meet you at home and we'll go straight away. Also, dinner is on me xx"

I stare down at the coffee machine and know exactly what I'll do. Rueben is surrounded by all mine and Daisy's girly things and although he moved all his belongings in, very little in the home is his. I'll take Rueben shopping and we'll buy some things for the home that I know he'll love. First off, a coffee machine. He absolutely adores his latte's in the morning, maybe this and some new mugs might make a little start in building up his own stamp on the house. After all it's his home too now.

My phone pings as I finish making my cup of tea and I read the message with a smile.

"I'm intrigued? Can't wait for later now, it's a date xx"

By the time work finishes, we head off to Bluewater shopping centre and by the time we arrive it's already gone six. We decide to grab some dinner first as Daisy complains her belly has been grumbling the whole car journey here. A quick burger and a shake in Ed's Diner and we are ready to browse some shops.

I steer Rueben straight for the department store and immediately see all the coffee sets and machines.

"Pick one" I smile.

"What? No? You can't do that!" Rueben responds in shock.

"They're far too much money. You can't spend that on me."

"I can actually. I know how much you love a posh coffee" I tease.

"And it's the least I can do. It's about time you have more of your own things in our home." I smile again.

"Thank you, baby, so much." Rueben says gratefully and carefully studies each coffee machine.

This is definitely the adult version of Toys R Us I think to myself as I watch Rueben enthusiastically choose one.

Between picking up the coffee machine and taking it to the cashier and checking out, Rueben has thanked me another five times. I get the feeling he isn't used to people buying him gifts.

"OK, well let's go to HMV before we go. I want you to pick a new C.D for the car. That way you can't accuse me of only playing Ed Sheeran." Rueben winks.

"Great! Get ready for some heavy death metal then." I say trying to tease but burst out laughing before I can even look at his reaction.

"If you do that, I'm buying Opera." Rueben smirks.

We end up settling on a Disney album for the car, Daisy's choice of course but who doesn't love to sing along to a Disney classic? Just as we are pulling away from the shopping centre and proudly singing along to Aladdin's soundtrack, Rueben's phone starts to ring. The second he answers it I hear so much screaming and shouting down the phone I immediately feel on edge. It's hard to make out who it is exactly but it's definitely a female voice. The mood suddenly changes and so I turn the music right down in the car and wait patiently to hear what is wrong. Rueben's face looks a little confused at times or maybe that's pure disbelief. Either way I see the stress starting to mount. I always know when Rueben gets stressed because he gets a blotchy rash appear around his neck.

"Fine, I'll come over now and sort it out, but this is absolutely ridiculous!" Rueben shouts and hangs up the phone.

Seconds later before I get a chance to ask what has happened Rueben's phone rings again.

"Great, now it's Mum." Rueben sighs.

I stare out the window watching the road signs as we seem to make a slight change in direction and I soon realise we are heading towards Joy and Dave's house.

Rueben continues to argue over the phone but it's really not clear what it's over.

Several seconds later Rueben ends the call and throws the phone down into the cup holder.

"Do you mind if I detour to my Mums? My sisters there and it's just all kicking off." Rueben groans, agitated.

"Of course, what's wrong?"

"Oh, it's pathetic, it really is. It's embarrassing."

"Ok? But what does that mean?"

"When I was packing up my bedroom to move in with you, I left some old pyjama bottoms and joggers in a black bag. I had planned to bin them off really but whilst I was at work today Lily called and said she's staying at Mums for a few days because she's ran out of money again, she said she found my bag of old joggers and asked if she could have them. Of course, I said yes, I mean I have no use for them, so it makes no difference to me." Rueben explains.

"So, what's the issue?" I ask still confused.

"The issue is my Mum gets weird about stuff being given away and has to take control over everything. She's taken my joggers and pyjamas out of my sisters' bag when she wasn't looking and put them in her own bedroom to keep, which is ridiculous because without being rude, they definitely won't fit my Mum. Then Lily went in there to get them off of her and by all accounts they're arguing over it. I could hear Mum telling Lily that she's too fat to wear them and then Lily's getting upset. It's best I just try and go and diffuse it." Rueben says sighing again.

"Your Mum called Lily fat? Over old pyjamas?" I say trying not to sound too judgemental.

"Yep. She just gets weird about stuff like this, I wish I could explain it better, but I don't truly understand it myself. She just has to have everything. Even if it's no use to her." Rueben explains.

"Like hoarding?" I ask curiously.

"What's that?"

"It just means a person can find it difficult to throw items away, they can become aggressive or very upset when somebody might threaten to put something old and broken in the bin. Even though it makes sense to throw it away. A hoarder will want to keep it anyway." I explain.

"I think you might be right. When we get there and I've calmed everything down, I'll take you up to the spare room. It used to be Kelsey's room, but it soon became a place to store more junk. She already used up the loft space. I'll show you and then you can tell me what you think?" Rueben suggests.

"Sure, but it's not unusual for people to store sentimental stuff, even if it just appears like junk to everybody else."

"Wait until you see it" Rueben says with raised eyebrows.

CHAPTER NINE

I can hear shouting and swearing as we approach Joy's house. Rueben looks a little awkward as he fumbles with his keys and I look down at Daisy who looks a little uneasy.

Oddly, as Rueben opens the front door all the arguing suddenly stops.

Lily stomps past us and up the stairs as we enter the hallway and Joy follows her. Nobody really acknowledges that we've arrived, and Rueben just casually tells me and Daisy to take a seat on the sofa whilst he starts heading up the stairs to speak to Lily and Joy.

I haven't met Lily before, but I could tell it was her. She also has the same dark features and with green eyes just like Rueben.

Although I did notice the large bags weighing heavily under her eyes. She looks tired and unfortunately a lot older than her age. You can tell the drug use has worn her down over the years. She's the eldest of the three siblings, thirty-three, but sadly looks very haggard for a woman so young.

Dave smiles at us as we sit on the sofa.

"Hello trouble." He says sweetly to Daisy.

"Hi." Daisy quietly responds but with a smile and a little wave.

"Would either of you like a drink?" He asks looking up at me.

"Um, I think we're okay thank you, we just had dinner and a tonne of milkshake" I smile.

Dave gives a slight nod and turns back towards the television.

Upstairs I can hear the arguing still ongoing, although now it's become hush tones, clearly for my benefit.

"I'm not doing this in front of Mollie!" I hear Joy loudly whisper.

"Then just grow up and let Lily have my clothes! They're my bloody clothes anyway, nothing to do with you!" I hear Rueben say, his voice growing louder as his patience wears thin.

After a few bangs and stomps, Lily appears at the bottom of the stairs with a pile of clothing in her hand which she quickly stuffs into her bag by the door.

"Hiya, you alright?" She smiles as she enters the living room and plonks down next to Dave.

"Yeah, you?" I smile back a little nervously.

"Oh, I'm fine my darling, it's Mother dearest up there driving me mad!" She says pointing towards the ceiling.

She sounds very different to Rueben, he is quite well spoken with an accent typical to our area, but Lily speaks differently, it's very common sounding. You can tell that if she wasn't speaking with a friendly tone, she could easily sound quite aggressive.

Joy appears abruptly at the doorway and shoots Lily a quick unapproving glare before turning her back to her and making a big fuss of Daisy instead.

"Ooh Daisy, I just found some chocolates I saved from Christmas. You can have them!" She offers excitedly.

"Do you want to come with Grandma and go and find them?" She says as she reaches her hand out for Daisy and they both wander off into the kitchen.

"Babe, can you come up and give me a quick hand with something?" I hear Rueben call.

I turn to see him at the bottom of the stairs, gesturing for me to follow him. I do as he asks, and I make my way up to the top of the stairs.

"Are you ready for this?" Rueben whispers.

"Um…sure?"

As Rueben opens the door, I am overwhelmed by what I see. There's barely any floor space to manoeuvre and you have to be careful where you stand because there are piles and piles of books, newspapers, board games, all sorts piled up as high as it can possibly go. Everything is a little dusty and unorganised. So much of it looks ready to be scrapped.

"Check this out." Rueben says as he hands me a box of shortbread. The box is unopened and in good condition, I don't notice too much wrong with it until he points at the sell by date.

'Best before 30/09/2007'

"Woah, it's like nine years out of date" I whisper.

"Yeah and there's five more boxes down there. As well as tins of chocolates, fudge, all sorts of things she's accumulated over the years. Every Christmas she brings them downstairs, but she won't let anyone dare open them. Then every new year she takes them back up here." Rueben explains as he rolls his eyes.

I scan the room and see tatty old puzzle boxes falling apart, they look like something you may have won on Bullseye back in the early eighties.

There's so much clutter I wouldn't know where to start. The mess gives me anxiety. I suddenly feel really bad, I feel as though I really shouldn't be in this room anymore. I'm sure Joy would rather this was private.

"What's that?" I whisper pointing to a yellowish foot shaped mystery in the corner.

"Oh this? Mum broke her foot one year; it was in the late nineties, but I can't remember which year exactly. I was probably around eight or nine years old. She had to wear this cast all through the summer. She moaned that it was so hot, and it made her sweaty. Hence the yellow colour... but oddly, rather than throw it away she's kept it up here all these years." Rueben says, this time with a little embarrassment in his voice.

I didn't want to appear rude but I back away slightly as I catch a whiff from the foot cast. Its musky smell makes me feel a little nauseous and I decide I'm too uncomfortable to stay in here any longer.

"We should leave Roo, this isn't very fair to your Mum." I say gently.

"You're right, I just wanted you to see it. Growing up I thought this was normal but then you said the word hoarding in the car and it got me thinking, that was all."

"Thinking about what, exactly?" I ask.

"I don't know really, just that sometimes Mum does a lot that doesn't make sense."

"Oh…I see." I answer awkwardly.

"Did you manage to diffuse the argument by the way?"

"Yeah, pretty much. I made Mum realise she was being silly and made her give Lily the clothes. Lily can actually get use out of them whereas Mum can't, I just needed her to realise it was ridiculous. But she seems fine now."

"That's good." I say, relieved.

"Plus, she was really embarrassed when she realised you were with me. She wouldn't dare argue anymore." Rueben chuckles.

As we head back downstairs Joy and Daisy are tucking into some Christmas chocolates. Nobody is talking very much, and I feel myself growing awkward with the uncomfortable silence.

"You'll have to come to ours for dinner one evening." I say in an attempt to break the silence up.

"Oh yes please!" Joy perks up.

"We are free Wednesday actually?"

"Oh, sure, yeah that works for us too" I reply.

We briefly iron out a set time for the dinner and get ready to leave. It's getting pretty late now, and Daisy has school in the morning.

"See ya around Mols." Lily calls as I'm heading out the door.

Joy waits by the front door and watches us get into the car. She's still stood there waiting and waving as we put on our seat belts and drive away. Something my Nan used to do. I smile at the memory.

As we head back down the country lanes towards our home, Rueben's phone pings.

"Ah, baby can you read that for me please."

"Sure." I say and grab his phone from the cup holder.

"It's Lily…"

"Thanks for trying Roo but as soon as you left, she took the clothes out of my bag and she's locked them in her bedroom now. Never mind. L xxx"

"Oh, for god's sake." Rueben growls shaking his head.

"Well at least you tried babe, that's all you can do." I shrug lightly.

CHAPTER TEN

I rush around last minute Wednesday evening lighting the candles and putting out my best dinner plates and wine glasses.

I opted for a Mexican theme dinner, my favourite and always seems to go down a treat whenever I make it. The enchiladas are cooking away nicely, and the house is filled with a delicious smell of mixed spices and chicken. The table looks smart, I ended up shopping around yesterday and bought a new silver glittery table runner and matching candle holders.

I pop back into the kitchen to fetch the couple of jugs of Sangria I made and hope nobody mentions the fact that they're more Spanish than Mexican.

"They're here." Rueben calls as he spots their headlights coming into the driveway.

A few touch ups to the centrepieces and I go to the door to greet Joy and Dave. As usual Dave is a man of very few words but polite all the same. Joy asks where Daisy is and looks a little disappointed when I tell her she had dinner earlier and is already in bed.

As they take their seats at the table, Dave and Rueben start discussing work stuff and Joy adds a comment or two occasionally. They don't work together but they often like to compare notes on what they've been up too. I start dishing up the dinner and feel a little proud as everybody tucks into the food without any complaints.

"I must have the recipe Mollie for this Sangria; I've never had any before but it's very nice." Joy says politely.

"Ah of course, I'll write it down for you. It's really simple but I agree, I love it, it's one of my favourite drinks for sure."

I blush a little as Dave virtually licks his plate clean and asks for seconds. I enjoy cooking but I'll be the first to admit I'm not the best at it, so it's a massive compliment when I manage to present something that's gone to plan and is very well received.

"Credit where credit is due, this is handsome." Dave announces whilst tucking into his second round of enchiladas.

"Thank you, Dave! You'll have to save room for dessert though."

"Oh? What did you make?" Joy asks.

"Yes, what was that popular Mexican dessert you made, Mollie?" Rueben mocks playfully.

I swat at him and giggle at his attempt to poke fun at me in front of his Mum and Stepdad.

"OK, OK. It's not quite Mexican, I wasn't sure exactly what a popular Mexican dessert was, so I ended up making a tiramisu." I laugh awkwardly, feeling my cheeks warm with embarrassment.

"So, Italian then?" Rueben smugly points out.

"Ooh well that's my favourite anyway!" Joy interjects.

"OK show off, since you've mocked my poor Italian dessert you can go and fetch it. Grazie!" I wink at Rueben.

Rueben pulls a funny face and disappears to grab the dessert.

"So, Joy, did you ever hang out with my Mum or Dad much when you were growing up?" I ask whilst topping up their drinks.

"Well, not really. She sort of, well it was a long time ago, but she hit me once." Joy declares dramatically whilst looking down at the table.

"What!?" I ask a little abruptly.

I'm shocked, what could she be going on about? I mentioned to my Mum one night on the phone about Joy and she did say she knew who she was, but she definitely didn't say anything like this. She just said she knew of her from living in the same area, but they never really crossed paths and had different friendship circles. My Mum wouldn't lie?

Rueben hands out bowls of tiramisu and I catch him looking a little confused at the sudden change in atmosphere.

I notice Joy is digging into her dessert and not actually responding to my question. Everyone is just carrying on as if I hadn't even spoke.

"I'm sorry Joy, you said my Mum hit you? What happened exactly? I press.

I can tell she doesn't want to have this conversation as she pokes at her dessert with her spoon and avoids my eye contact. But surely, she can't expect to say such a statement without explanation.

"Oh, well, it's just I was babysitting her friend's daughter and she was mad that she wasn't asked to babysit, so she just came up to me and slapped me around the face and walked off." Joy states sheepishly and still without looking up from her dessert.

I realise my jaw is still open in disbelief. What must she think of me then if she believes my Mum is some aggressive nutter who randomly hit her one day over something so ridiculous? It can't be true. Even if it is why is she saying it? Why does it still matter this many years later? If my Mum did that, she'd just tell me. Rueben starts changing the subject by telling me how delicious my tiramisu is, but I can't help but feel a strong urge to speak to my Mum. I excuse myself from the table and casually walk off to the bathroom.

As soon as I'm away from them I pull my phone from my pocket and start finding Mum's number.

"Mum?" I whisper.

"Mollie?" Mum asks.

"Why are you whispering?"

"I'm just having a dinner thing and Joy is here, Mum I have to ask you something…"

"Oh. Okay? What?"

"She's saying that she knows you and that you randomly attacked her for babysitting your friend's daughter? Apparently, you slapped her?" I inform still whispering.

"What?" Mum bursts out laughing

"Christ Mollie that would have been in the late seventies! I can barely remember that far back but she must be thinking of a different Laraine. I barely knew her, let alone hit her. She's either got it muddled up or she's making it up Mollie." Mum says a bit peeved.

"But why would she make it up?"

"Mollie, she was weird when we were all growing up. Honestly, ask anyone who grew up around there at the same time as her. She didn't mix with anyone. She didn't like anyone. She got jealous very quick and just a bit, you know, funny. So, most people avoided her. Sounds like she hasn't changed much."

"But Mum, she's told Rueben that about you. What if she tells other people and it's not even true? They'll judge me...and you." I whine, worried.

"Don't worry about me." Mum laughs.

"You tend to not give a shit about what people may say about you the older you get."

I pause on the phone thinking about Joy's accusations and sigh.

"Mollie...relax. Go and enjoy dinner and forget about me. She can say what she likes, I really don't care." Mum assures me.

As I say my goodbyes to Mum and put my phone away, I can't help but feel a little confused by Joy. I don't want her thinking badly of my Mum or me, she definitely has the wrong person and I need to make that clear.

"There she is!" Rueben greets me with a big smile as I rejoin everyone in the dining room.

"Sorry, I got caught up. I phoned my Mum quick." I say, looking at Joy.

"Oh?" Rueben asks.

"Yeah, she says you must have gotten the wrong Laraine, Joy. She says she didn't really know you and definitely didn't have an altercation with you. So, I guess it must've been somebody else." I suggest assertively.

Joy fiddles with her napkin a little and continues staring down at the table.

"Oh, it was definitely her." Joy says finally.

"Nobody could forget your Mum." she adds with a sarcastic tone.

"Well, it's a mystery!" Rueben quickly interrupts.

"The main thing to remember here is that whatever happened occurred like what? over forty years ago?!"

"Exactly." Dave adds.

Joy doesn't add anything more to the topic and as much as I want to defend my Mum, I admit defeat and let it go. Rueben is right after all; it was such a long time ago anyway. It's almost pointless discussing it. I really wish she hadn't of brought it up at all but maybe eventually she'll remember who the real person was who hit her and stop accusing my Mum.

"So, let's just agree to forget about it?" Rueben says affirmatively.

"Of course!" I smile at Joy making sure I sound as carefree as possible.

I don't want her to know she's offended me, and I definitely don't want to end the night on a bad note, we can forget about this and move on surely.

"Oh Roo, before I forget, can you go and visit your Nan? She's been asking after you a lot. I know you've been busy moving to a new house and whatnot, but you haven't called in for a while now." Joy says as she finishes her sangria.

"That's fine Mum, in fact I was just saying to Mollie that we should call in tomorrow night and see her, isn't that right?" Rueben turns to me.

"Oh yeah, you did. I'm looking forward to it." I reply politely.

CHAPTER ELEVEN

After a busy but good day at work we drop Daisy off to her friend's house for tea before making our way to Rueben's Nans house.

We'll take Daisy to meet her very soon, but she'd been planning this tea party with her friend for over a week now and I didn't want to change her plans.

Rueben tells me during the car journey how he has always been close to his Nan and how he always used to run down to her house if ever he was in trouble with his Mum.

Rueben's Nan, Irene, lives very close to where he grew up, only a few doors down so it's been nice for him to be able to see her all the time. He tells me a story about how one day he was out playing football, he was only about seven or eight years old and the fields were a lot muddier than he anticipated. He had so much fun but his football boots were covered in mud and he was terrified to go home to his Mum because nothing was ever allowed to get dirty, so he'd go to his Nans who would help clean him up as much as possible before he returned home.

"That is so sweet of your Nan! What else does your Mum get worried about?" I query.

"God, loads really. One thing that sticks out is snow! If it ever snowed, we weren't allowed to play in the garden and make snowmen or anything. She'd yell at us if we dare mess up the snow. Like really yell. It just wouldn't be worth it." Rueben tells me.

"Wow, my Mum would throw me outside when it snowed and tell me to make the most of it." I laugh.

I notice Rueben doesn't laugh or smile. In fact, he hasn't really acknowledged much of my reply. He is just staring out into the distance in his own world and doesn't even notice when I place my hand on his thigh.

"Roo?" I ask gently.

"Oh, Sorry." Rueben mumbles.

"Just an old memory came to my mind, that's all. I hadn't thought about it in such a long time and it just made me a little…. I don't know. Sad, I guess."

"Do you want to tell me?"

"Yeah, I think I will. But maybe later? It's just we are nearly at Nans and I don't really want to get into it right before we go and see her."

"No of course not, that makes sense and I totally understand, how about a takeaway when we get home and then we can go into it then? Only if you want too." I reassure.

Rueben nods with a small smile and gives my thigh a squeeze.

As we pull up outside Irene's house, I notice just how close we are to Joy. I can almost see her front door from here. Irene's house looks much smaller but well looked after. Beautiful baskets full of fresh flowers hang down by her front door and the front lawn is extremely well kept with a row of pretty pink flowers lining the pathway.

Inside Irene is sat in an armchair propped up with cushions and a cup of tea in hand. She lives with two of her sons, they're both in their fifties now but have never flew the nest. It sounds like a rather odd arrangement, but Rueben tells me that they both help take care of Irene and they keep her company.

Irene sits up straight as Rueben walks into the living room with me followed closely behind and looks very happy to see him.

There's lots of photos in Irene's home too, mostly of Joy, Kelsey and Lily. Which is odd really because Irene has nine children and five of them have all gone on to have their own children. So, all in all Irene has eight grandchildren in total.

I take a seat on the sofa next to Irene's armchair and smile to myself as Rueben bends down to give his Nan a big hug. As all Nan's do, she makes a great big fuss of him and offers him a drink and food and cake and anything else she can think of. Rueben just laughs and banters with his Nan about her being a feeder and she giggles.

"I will use the toilet quickly though Nan, if that's okay?" Rueben asks politely.

"Of course you can you silly sod." Irene says as she chuckles loudly.

As Rueben leaves the room, I awkwardly realise that he forgot to introduce us.

"I'm Mollie." I announce softly.

Irene turns to me and looks me up and down before shooting me a glare and turning back to drink her tea.

Oh my god. Did that just happen? She was so sweet moments ago, she's absolutely lovely with Rueben. Did I say something wrong?

Maybe she is just a little socially awkward, like Joy.

"How are you?" I ask apprehensively.

"Fine. There's nothing wrong with me thank you very much!" Irene hisses.

I suddenly pick up on the tone and recognise there really is a problem, but I've no idea what it could be. This is the first time we are meeting; how can she be so bothered by me? What could I have done?

This small old lady in her late eighties with her cardigan draped around her shoulders and curls in her hair should be sounding as sweet as she looks. But I honestly feel as though she's about to attack me. Hurry up Rueben. God please hurry up I think to myself.

As Rueben returns, I look up at him in desperation. Desperate to leave mostly.

He takes one look at me and one look at his Nan and immediately senses there's a problem.

"What's going on?" He asks sternly.

"Why did you bring HER down here for?" Irene pipes up suddenly which surprises me and puts a big knot in my stomach.

"What do you mean?" Rueben asks concerned as he crouches down next to Irene.

"Nan?"

"I don't want her in here! I've heard about her Mother! And what she did to my Joy!"

"Nan, has Mum been here?" Rueben questions, frustration thick in his voice.

"Yes. She came by about nine o'clock last night and told me everything. She's very upset and concerned about you courting Laraine's daughter!" She shouts.

"The apple won't fall far from THAT tree!"

As soon as she says it, I realise Joy must have come down here straight after the dinner party last night. Straight after she ate my food and drank my sangria's and promised to let it go, she came down here anyway and made Irene hate me. Even after I assured her, she had the wrong person in mind. Even after I tried so hard to cook her an excellent meal. She told Rueben to come and see his Nan and then she came here and told her stories. Stories that put me and my mum in a bad light and make Irene so upset she's arguing with her own grandson. I can't help but feel as though I've walked into some kind of trap. Irene continues to yell, and Rueben tries hard to diffuse the issue and I feel a lump in my throat and my eyes stinging with tears. How embarrassing. I know I'm sensitive, but this is definitely the wrong time to cry. Don't cry Mollie I think to myself. Do not cry.

I decide I just need fresh air and a moment to compose myself and then perhaps I can explain to Irene too. Perhaps I can make her see she's got it all wrong.

"What you are staring at?!" Irene glares as I stand to walk out the door.

"I...I...I'm not, I'm just going to get some air and I'll be back." I whisper nervously.

"No, wait!" Rueben demands before turning to his Nan in frustration.

"Mum has got this all wrong and blown it way out of proportion! Laraine is not the person Mum has described and Mollie definitely isn't!"

"Is she lying to me then?" Irene asks Rueben seemingly calming down.

"I don't know if she's purposely lied but she's definitely put two and two together and come up with six. Look Nan, you mean the world to me, but I really love Mollie and I would like it if you both got along" Rueben pleads.

Irene huffs with uncertainty but her eyes soften as she stares at Rueben's face.

"Fine, I don't want to argue with anyone." She shrugs.

"I still think I should go." I nervously say to Rueben.

"I'll just go for a walk and let you both spend some time together."

I don't really give Rueben much of a chance to stop me. I give his Nan a quick glance and a small smile to be polite and I get out of there as quickly as possible. As soon as the cold air hits my face I take a deep breath and before I can stop myself a few tears escape my eyes. I'm not sure where to go but I keep walking, being out here is better than being hated in there.

CHAPTER TWELVE

After a long soak in the tub I feel somewhat better but still dejected. I was so looking forward to meeting Irene and I never would have thought in a million years it would have ended with an eighty-eight year old woman yelling at me!

I didn't say much in the car on the way home, Rueben mostly ranted about his Mum causing unnecessary upset and how furious he felt towards her but I just nodded along.

I wrap a robe around me and quickly peep through Daisy's bedroom door to check she's asleep before heading downstairs.

I walk into the kitchen to see Rueben dishing up my jalfrezi, as soon as he sees me walking into the room, he looks a little nervous, I think he needs reassuring that I'm not mad at him. Of course, I'm not mad at him though, I'm hurt and confused by his Mum, but I recognise this isn't Rueben's fault at all.

"Baby! Are you OK? Do you feel better after your bath?" He asks with concern.

"A little…Look, I know I haven't spoken much but that doesn't mean I'm upset with you." I reassure.

"I wouldn't blame you if you were…"

"Rueben, you really don't need to beat yourself up over this. It's not your fault. You also didn't have to come running after me when I left, you know. I told you to spend time with your Nan, I'd have been fine, honestly." I say.

"I couldn't just leave you; I would never do that. You're my priority. I love you. Nan was sorry after you left though."

"Really?" I ask surprised.

"Yeah! Definitely. She said she didn't mean to upset you. Nan gets very easily confused. She isn't as switched on as she used to be. What Mum did wasn't fair."

"Oh. I see, well I really don't want her to be confused. I see how much you love your Nan and if there's anything I can do to help her feel better about us, I will."

"I know baby, thank you. But I think I've sorted it now I really do. Although my Mum is going to get an ear-full from me tomorrow morning!" Rueben angrily declares.

"No, no please don't do that! Let's just let this go. I'm frustrated too and believe me; all I want to do is phone her and ask her what her problem is with my Mum but if I do that then this'll continue to cause problems. We need to be the bigger person and just let it go. As long as your Nan is OK then that's all that matters, right?"

"I really appreciate that but aren't you still mad at her?"

"Of course, but I'll have to get over it. This whole thing is frying my brain and making us both upset. It's just so pathetic. It's a massive misunderstanding and I just want to move on from it, please?" I urge, dropping my head down into my hands.

Rueben brings his hands to mine and pulls them away from my head. I lean into him as he wraps his arms around my waist and hugs me tight. I feel exhausted. It suddenly dawns on me that Rueben was supposed to tell me about the random memory that popped into his head earlier today, I've been so curious about that but after today I'm not sure I have the energy to really listen. Plus, my stomach is doing summersaults, I've been feeling sick on and off all day. I really hope I'm not coming down with a bug, I have only been at my new job for a few weeks and really don't want to take time off so soon. I look down at my jalfrezi and feel even more nauseous.

"I've been feeling quite sick, Roo. Now my head is starting to hurt. I think I might just skip dinner. I'm so sorry, do you mind?"

"Of course, not…shall we just go to bed and watch back to back episodes of The Big Bang Theory?" Rueben smiles.

"You read my mind!" I say as we both laugh.

I feel like I have only been asleep for ten minutes when I'm awoken by Rueben's phone going off. I open my eyes but it's still pretty dark outside.

"Roo...? Your phone." I say as I nudge him gently.

"Mhmm" is all I get as he pulls the duvet up over his head.

I turn back over and try to go back to sleep when his phone starts ringing again. It's barely six forty-five in the morning, who could be calling so early? Our alarm goes off in fifteen minutes now, I may as well just get up. I stretch and groan as I drag myself out of the bed and over to Rueben's phone.

17 missed calls

Jesus. They're all from Joy. God, what if there's an emergency? What if something happened to Irene after we left her yesterday?

1 new voice mail

Pops up on the screen. I look over at Rueben snoring away and contemplate waking him straight away, but curiosity gets the better of me and before I know it, I'm pressing play on the voice message.

"Rueben, answer your phone please! It's important and I'm really beginning to get the fucking hump with you these days!"

The message loudly plays against my ear.

Wow. I have never heard Joy swear before. I mean, I know her and Lily argued the other day, but I didn't actually hear much of it. The Joy I know is usually quite polite and well spoken, especially around Daisy. She makes such a fuss of her and comes off so loving and gentle. But this message is just brutal. I can't explain it really, but her voice sounds just so, so disgusted. It's quite unsettling.

The phone starts vibrating in my hand again. It's Joy. Her eighteenth call. I nudge Rueben harder and tell him his Mum won't stop ringing. He sits up all confused but takes the phone.

"Hello?" Rueben croaks.

"HELLO!" I hear her yell impatiently

"I would like my rent money please. You need to put it in my bank by the end of the day."

"But Mum, I don't live there anymore? I haven't lived there since early January." Rueben calmly says rubbing his eyes.

"So? If you were private renting and had a landlord, you'd have to give him a month's notice, wouldn't you? And pay him a month's rent! You couldn't just disappear! So, I'll have my money, thank you." She demands unreasonably.

"What? But you're not my landlord? Mum this is ridiculous. I live with Mollie and Daisy now, I contribute here. I can't afford to pay you rent as well. I'm sorry but I'm not doing it."

"Right, well we'll just see what Dave has to say then won't we!" Joy snaps in a threatening tone.

"What, Mum, why?" Rueben asks growing frustrated.

"Well, Let's just see what HE thinks about all this!" She screams.

I can feel myself growing angry as the need to defend Rueben becomes greater the more she bellows at him. She sounds so angry. So unbelievably angry and it's barely seven a.m.

She's being so unfair, so unreasonable. My heart aches for Rueben who has barely woken up and is having to deal with this. The colour has drained from his face.

"I'll ring Dave myself then Mum and I'll explain it to him. I'm sure he'll agree with me." Rueben suggests.

"No, you won't!" Joy rages.

Rueben hangs up the phone and throws it down onto the bed. I heard the conversation, so I won't push him for details, but I need to say something. He looks so stressed.

"Rueben, you're nearly thirty years old. Why does she use Dave against you?" I gently ask.

"Because I was terrified of him when I was a kid. She let him hit me and frighten me and as soon as she knew how scared I was she used it to it control me for most of my life. She hates that I'm older and not scared of him anymore, but she still says it anyway, probably hoping it still has some effect." He explains angrily.

"And does it?" I say as I sit on the bed next to him.

"Does it what?" Rueben snaps.

"Nothing don't worry. I don't want to upset you any more than you already are." I softly reply. I'm not even sure if Rueben intended to tell me something so personal. I think being half asleep made him just say it, without thinking.

I half hope Rueben grabs me before I get off the bed for one of his tight cuddles, but he doesn't. We both get ready in silence and as much as I want to make him feel better, I have no idea what to say this time. The only thing that keeps replaying in my head is '*she let him hit me.*'

CHAPTER THIRTEEN

It's a relief to be at work after the last couple of days. Friday's at work are generally more laid back, especially today. It's Mel's birthday and the staff room is full of cupcakes, bags of pretzels and tins of chocolate. Most of the day is spent sneaking off into the staff room alongside my colleagues for more cake and tea.

"Another cupcake?" Mel offers.

"I'd love too but I'm feeling a little sick, I think I've over indulged!" I laugh.

"More for me!" Mel winks as she scoffs another cupcake into her mouth.

I can't help but laugh as her cheeks puff up filled with cake, although thoughts of Rueben keep creeping back into my mind. I want to call him, but I don't want to be pushy either. Instead I decide to go outside for some air and ring Lana for advice.

"Hey you…" I say into the phone after Lana picks up.

"Hey gorgeous! what's up?" she asks cheerfully.

"Can I ask, do you get along with Mike's Mum?"

"Sure!" she responds without hesitation.

"Oh. Does she ever, like, talk down to Mike at all? Like as if he were still a child?"

"No, not really. I mean Mikes a thirty-one-year-old man! I think she realises he isn't a child anymore!" Lana laughs.

"Yeah…" I mumble.

"Is everything OK? Is this about Rueben?" Lana asks in a gentle tone.

"No, not really. I don't know. I was just wondering. Anyway, I'm at work still so I had better go. We'll catch up soon yeah? for a wine or two." I say trying to sound less uptight.

I end the call with Lana quickly and head back inside. I just start walking back to my desk when I notice my head feels all fuzzy and suddenly out of nowhere I can feel vomit rising up from my stomach, with no time to make it to the toilet I end up huddled over an office plant pot as I throw up.

"Mollie!" I hear Mel call as she rushes over and places her hand across my back to comfort me.

"Oh god, I'm so sorry." I whine, wiping my mouth.

"Don't be! I think we can all agree that plant was ugly anyway! I do think you should get yourself home though, you might have a bug. You need to rest." she suggests sympathetically.

I nod in agreement as I grab my bag and car keys and make my way out of there as quickly as possible. I'm too embarrassed to say goodbye to everyone. I just want to get home and climb into my bed.

Before I set off, I send a quick text to Rueben.

"Hey, I'm just letting you know I'm not feeling great so I'm heading home. Hope you're OK. Love you."

Within minutes Rueben is ringing me.

"Hello?" He says sounding panicked.

"Hey, don't worry. I'm OK, I was just sick at work"

"Sick!? Oh no, have you got a bug? I'll head home in a bit, would you like anything? Lucozade? Paracetamol? Anything at all?" He offers sweetly.

I smile at his kind offer. I love how much he cares.

"Thank you, but I think I just need a lay down. Are we OK?" I use the opportunity to ask.

"Of course, we are. I'm really sorry about this morning. I'd only just woken up and to have my Mum shouting down the phone at me straight away was just a bit much. I'm sorry I snapped; it wasn't you." Rueben says sincerely.

"Yeah that's understandable. OK, well we'll talk later then yeah. I'm starting to feel sick, so I best just get myself home."

"OK, drive safe and I'll see you in a little while." Rueben says before ending the call.

By the time I'm home my head is pounding, I barely manage to take my shoes off or my jacket before I plonk down on the sofa. I decide I'll just stay here for a minute and rest my eyes. I don't ever remember feeling this tired all the time.

The next thing I know, I'm opening my eyes to the smell of dinner being cooked and the television on.

"Hi Mummy, you're awake!" Daisy smiles.

I smile a little confused and give Daisy a big hug before going into the kitchen for a glass of water. I see Rueben making a spaghetti Bolognese and as soon as he sees me enter the room, he walks straight over to me for one of his tight cuddles.

"I've done dinner for me and Daisy dots. I didn't make you anything because I didn't think you'd be up for eating yet but you're welcome to have mine if you want. I wanted to let you rest as well, which is why I got Daisy from after school club so you could sleep a little longer." he says whilst still hugging me tight.

"Thank you so much." I say as I lean my head on his shoulder.

I sit sipping my water whilst Rueben and Daisy tuck into their spaghetti's. I offer to wash up, but Rueben doesn't allow me too, instead he ushers me back to the sofa to rest. I must have nodded off again because the next thing I know Daisy is kissing me on my forehead and giving me a goodnight cuddle.

"Goodnight sweetheart, don't let the bed bugs bite." I whisper.

As Daisy goes off up to bed, Rueben comes in and sits next to me on the sofa, pulling my feet up so they're rested across his lap.

"Are you up for talking?" He asks a little reluctantly.

"Of course," I assure, whilst I prop myself up slightly.

"The memory that popped into my head was something my Mum did when I was about six years old." he starts, nervously.

"Ok?" I respond as I rub my eyes and wake myself up properly.

"We were up in Scotland visiting family, as we did every year. You know my Mums sister? And my cousins I told you about?"

"Sure." I confirm.

"Well we were with them and we were all at the park playing games, silly games like stuck in the mud and chasing each other around when I must've tripped on a stick or something because I fell over and ripped my new jeans that Mum had just bought for me. I grazed all my knee really badly too and it bled quite a bit. I burst out crying and my Mum went mad. She started yelling at me for ripping my jeans and told me Dave was going to be so angry. My Aunt came over and got involved a bit, she told my Mum to calm down and said it was just an accident and that we should walk to the shop to get some plasters. On the walk, I kept crying as my knee really stung but my Mum just got angrier. She made me hold her hand and dragged me along, but I started to realise my hand was stinging as well now. I started to see blood dripping down my hand, and I cried louder and begged her to let go. She just kept telling me to shut up because I was showing her up. When she finally let go, I realised she dug her thumb nail into my hand so much that she made it really bleed. God it was so painful. I still have the scar."

Rueben shows me his hand and sure enough in between his thumb and finger is a slightly rounded scar. The perfect shape of a thumb nail.

"Oh my god, Roo!" I gasp.

I lean up and pull him in for a cuddle. I can't believe what I'm hearing.

"Didn't your Auntie do anything?" I ask.

"She was lovely, she took over when we got back to her house and cleaned up my knee and the graze on my hand. I was just a kid, so I don't know if she said much to my Mum about what she did, but she was really great to me. If it wasn't for her that day, I'd have been miserable." Rueben says with a sigh.

"I don't know what to say. Did Dave do anything? Like get mad or hurt you?"

"Not that time. No. Dave did hit me occasionally though, mostly just threatened it more than anything. But you know, I think it's just a generational thing isn't it. Dave is a bit set in his ways and stuck in the past. He probably thinks it's a normal way to discipline." Rueben casually justifies.

"Um, I don't know about that. Punching a kid is a bit more than a generational habit." I say.

"On the occasion Dave did hit me, she'd either keep me off school for a few days until the bruises faded a little or she'd write a note for my teacher and claim I fell out of bed. She told me ever since I was a child that I couldn't tell anyone where any bruises came from. So, I never have. Not until now, anyway.

My Mum would be furious if she knew I told you any of this. She would swear that I was making it all up."

I hug Rueben again and just feel at a loss of what to say. I want to take away all the horrible things his Mum and Stepdad did, but I know I can't.

"I think they've been bettering themselves since then though. They never once hurt my sisters like that. It was just me. Plus, they would never hurt Daisy. I think my Mum knows it was a mistake and it shouldn't have happened. None of it. I don't think she's that person now. Back then people were just stricter." Rueben tries to assure me.

"Well okay, That's good but it's no apology for the past. You didn't deserve that. I hope you know that?" I say with my hand on Rueben's cheek.

"Yeah. I guess" he responds unconvincingly.

CHAPTER FOURTEEN

The weekend goes by with a blur. I've phoned in sick this morning, there's no way I'm well enough for work, I have barely gotten out of bed at all these last two days. I'm still being sick throughout the day and it isn't getting much better.

Joy has been messaging Rueben a lot over the weekend too, mostly apologising and telling him how much she likes me and she's very sorry if we've gotten off on the wrong foot. I'm too ill to spend any more energy on it and so I reassure Rueben that I really appreciate Joy's olive branch and it's all as good as forgotten.

I flick through Netflix and search for a comedy to cheer me up, I decide to settle on a Melissa McCarthy movie and just as it starts to play my phone goes off. I suddenly feel nervous as I look down at the screen. It's Joy.

"Hello?" I answer politely.

"Oh, hello love, I phoned Rueben and he told me you were unwell? Is there anything I can bring over for you love?" She offers in a very soft tone.

I wonder if her calling me love is her way of showing affection, like she does when she calls Rueben 'mate.'

"Oh, thank you so much Joy, but I've got everything. I'll probably just try to sleep again in a minute." I reply gratefully.

"Ok love, well if you need anything at all just give me a call, OK?"

"OK, thank you I appreciate that." I say.

When I hang up the phone, I can't help but look back down at the screen. Was that really Joy? She was lovely and so thoughtful and kind. That's the Joy I really like. I'm really pleased she called now because I feel so much better about our relationship going forward. I'm still sad about the stories Rueben told me last night but I can appreciate it was a different time and maybe they didn't know any better. People do change. I don't want to judge her too harshly. Up until recently Rueben didn't say a bad word about her, so it's not like she's always been this way. The memory of Rueben's scar pops into my head though and my heart immediately aches. If Rueben let that go and forgave his Mum, I must too, I think to myself.

I snuggle back down and allow myself to relax into the movie.

Within minutes though I suddenly feel overwhelmed with nausea again and I'm running to the bathroom.

This is insane. I haven't been this sick since I was pregnant with Daisy.

Oh. My. God. Suddenly my brain is rushing around with thoughts so fast that I can barely focus. When was my last period?

That's the most important question I should be working out first. I leap back into my bedroom and grab my phone. I have been tracking my period on it with some App, I didn't think there was much point to it before but right now I couldn't be more grateful that I downloaded it.

This can't be right. It's telling me my last period was right before the dinner date.

Just before I met Rueben.

I stare down at my phone as realisation kicks in. It is right though; I have had so much on my mind I didn't even notice just how late I was.

By the time the school run comes around I have managed to shove my hair in a messy bun and throw on some clothes. I've decided I'll grab Daisy from school and run into the chemist for a test before coming home.

I don't think I have ever walked home so fast in all my life, but I need to know if this is the reason I am so sick. As soon as we are home, I fix Daisy a snack as she sits and watches some kids show. I pace the kitchen back and forth whilst drinking water and read the instructions on the test, god knows why, it's not like it isn't pretty self-explanatory but I'm anxious and needing to pass the time.

Finally, when I feel the water working it's magic, I grab the stick and rush off to the bathroom.

Two minutes is a long time to wait for the results when the answer changes your life forever.

I aimlessly scroll social media to help pass the time, I decide to wait an extra minute, just to be sure I have given it enough time.

"Negative?" I say out loud to myself.

Just one little line in the window.

Wow, OK then. I wasn't expecting that but it's probably for the best. It's not like this was the best time for a baby, even though I'm not convinced there ever is an exact right time anyway. I feel quite fed up though, I still feel sick and fuzzy, all I can think is that it's a viral thing and I'm just going to have to put up with it.

"Mollie?" I hear Rueben's familiar voice call up the stairs.

"Oh. Yeah I'm in here…just coming." I call as I pick up the stick to throw in the bin.

"Hey!" Rueben smiles as he walks into the bathroom.

"I know you're still not feeling great and you'll only want toast for tea again, so I picked up some nice fresh bread from the bakery. I figured if it's all you can eat right now it may as well be decent."

"Thank you so much, that's thoughtful, I'm looking forward to more toast already." I laugh, but I do feel very grateful.

"What's that?" Rueben stares eagerly down at my hand.

I glance down to see the stick wrapped heavily in toilet paper in my palm and suddenly my cheeks feel flushed as I grow a little awkward.

"Oh! Funny story…I just got myself worked up today because my period was late and I kept feeling sick, my thoughts ran away with me! But don't worry, I was obviously just worrying over nothing because it came back negative, see…?" I say passing Rueben the test.

"But I'm confused?" Rueben says staring down at the test.

"Well I just wanted to rule it out that's all, in case that's why I was so sick."

"No, I get that. But I just thought if it was negative you only get one line. But this quite clearly shows two lines?" Rueben says staring up at me.

"Pfffft" I let out a big laugh.

"Yeah! Of course, it does!" I wink.

"No…really…" Rueben softly says.

"Look…"

I stare down at the stick I held just moments ago showing a negative result but now he is right. It's changed, it quite clearly shows two pink lines. I look at the packaging and realise it says that the results can be read up until five minutes. My god, it's right.

"So, I'm…I'm pregnant." I whisper with my tears filling my eyes.

CHAPTER FIFTEEN

I love May. It's my favourite month of the year. May in England can be quite beautiful, all the flowers come into bloom, the weather starts getting very warm, the country pubs around here have huge gardens with brilliant play areas for the children. Last year me and Daisy had so much fun going for pub lunches whilst she made friends with some of the other local kids and I sat relaxing with a fresh lemonade. I just love knowing we have at least four months of warm sunny weather ahead of us.

Thankfully the sickness passed a few weeks ago and I feel like I can enjoy my days again without having to run to the bathroom every five minutes.

Everyone has been lovely and supportive since we told them I was pregnant, especially Joy which I can appreciate. This is her first grandchild and it must be very exciting for her too. I cried when I found out, mostly hormones but also because I was terrified it would scare Rueben off. But he just laughed and pointed out how we never seem to do anything at a slow pace and It's just becoming our thing.

Daisy was delighted when we told her, she went to school and told her teacher and all her friends and by the time she came home that afternoon she proudly presented us with a 'Congratulations' card. She drew me with a little baby and even the teacher signed it. It was the cutest thing and now takes up pride position on the fridge.

My work has been so understanding. I had to take a whole week off work until I was able to get some tablets from the doctor to settle the sickness and they were very patient with me. Mel says she can't wait to meet the baby just so she can tell him or her that they made their Mummy vomit in a plant pot. I'm not sure she'll let me live it down anytime soon.

Lana practically squealed so loud when I told her I could imagine even the baby needed to put their hands over its ears. She then sent us a beautiful hamper of new-born hats, mittens, baby grows and muslin squares. It's so surreal to have tiny baby clothes back in the home again but also so wonderful.

I'm so excited to start buying things this time around. With Daisy, I had to rely heavily on my family to help me and shop around for second-hand cribs and strollers to purchase. eBay was my saviour throughout my pregnancy, I managed to find so many bargains. Not a lot of it was in great condition but it did the job. This time though I'm going to head straight to one of those big baby stores and choose everything brand new. Brand new pushchair, a beautiful cot set and even one of those fancy bottle prep machines.

"So…last minute guesses?" Rueben asks with a big smile from across the small waiting room.

"A sister!" Daisy cheers.

"I think girl too, sorry Roo but I think you'll be majorly outnumbered!" I laugh.

"I'm still convinced it's a boy, my real Dad had five boys with his wife, so I think that gene is strong." He smugly smiles.

I shake my head at him and let out a little giggle. It's nice being the only ones in the waiting room. We came specifically to this private clinic as they offer 3D scan pictures, I couldn't afford it when I was pregnant with Daisy but now that I'm financially stable I couldn't wait to book it.

"Mum's text again, for the sixth time…" Rueben sighs.

"She's probably just getting excited; you can't blame her." I say.

I know she's a little intense, but I can't tell Rueben I think that way, it'll only add to his irritation.

"Yeah but she keeps asking if we know what we are having yet, she'll have to wait until tomorrow to find out like everybody else." He groans impatiently.

"Oh yeah, about that. It's difficult but I decided not to invite my Mum, instead I'll invite her over for dinner when everyone has gone home and tell her then."

"You can't do that? Not for my Mum anyway?" Rueben says sounding concerned.

"It's not just the thing with your Mum. She really doesn't get along with my Dad or his wife and so I think it'll just be easier this way." I sigh, feeling a little guilty for my Mum.

"Well OK, if that's what you want to do. I'll treat her to a Chinese when she comes over then. I don't want her to feel left out over a gender reveal party."

"Well I was thinking we just won't tell her we had a party?" I whisper.

Rueben nods in agreement. I feel awful about it, I love my Mum, but this is the reality of broken families. Not everybody can get along or stand to be in the same room as each other and unfortunately my Mum is extremely outspoken, she wouldn't be able to help herself. I do love that about her sometimes though, she's very strong and will always stick up for herself without hesitation. More importantly she'll always stick up for me and so I don't think it's best she meets Joy, not just yet anyway.

"Are we ready?" A friendly nurse appears.

"It's time!" I say to Daisy who jumps up and down with excitement.

CHAPTER SIXTEEN

The decorations were a little pricey but it's so worth it. Everything is decorated with a mix of baby blue or baby pink. The two-tier cake is exceptional, two little booties sit on top of a cake half blue and half pink with silver pearls dotted all around it.

My dining table is covered in pink and blue dummy sweets, milk bottle shaped cookies, pink and blue straws, a beautiful cream coloured guest book for everybody to sign for the baby and little individual cupcakes for everyone. I have even scattered pink and blue gems all over the table and in the centre is a large bowl of pick and mix. Huge clear balloons stand around the table filled with a mixture of pink and blue confetti and cute baby photos of me and Rueben are mounted onto the wall. It's a little extra but I couldn't help myself, it's not every day you prepare for a new baby.

I have opted for a white maxi dress today; the weather has really warmed up and I feel like a radiator under this forever expanding bump. So, I made sure to wear something cool but still pretty. My patio doors are both open and I love how the sun brightly floods in despite it being the afternoon now.

My Dad and his wife Sarah arrive promptly and hand me a very pretty card with vouchers inside for one of the big baby stores.

"Thank you so much Dad!" I say, leaning in to give him a kiss on the cheek.

"You're welcome. Can I go now?" He jokes.

"No Dad!" I giggle before rolling my eyes at him.

"Stop being rude!" Sarah jokingly says whilst giving him a playful nudge.

I steer Dad to the dining room and get him to take a seat before he tries to escape, and Rueben comes over to greet my Dad and Sarah.

I start making up some jugs of fresh lemonade whilst watching my Dad and Rueben muttering something under their breaths before laughing loudly, no doubt talking about how over the top my decorations are.

They tend to enjoy poking fun at me when they're together. I don't mind too much though, I'm just happy they all get along so well. My Dad is pretty easy going though so I wouldn't expect any different. I'm really close to my Dad so it's nice when we can all get together and have quality time. Dad has two houses now, one here, around ten minutes away from me and another in Florida. Which means he isn't often around, so I like to make the most of it.

Before long Mike, Lana, Mel and a couple of the other girls from my office arrive. My hallway starts filling up with beautiful cards and gift bags for us and the baby and I can't wait to rip into them later.

Dad is outside in the garden playing with Daisy and everyone else is already getting stuck into nibbles and cupcakes.

Soon the doorbell goes again and this time I let Rueben go and answer it, after all I'm sure it's Joy and Dave.

"Cor, what's wrong with you? Ain't I invited? Could look happier to see me." I hear a familiar voice yell.

I hurry into the hallway to see what's going on and immediately see Lily. Her hair is up in a scruffy bun, she looks worse than she did the other day. Very tired and haggard looking again but this time her manner isn't friendly. She seems on edge and irritable. She's wearing a pink tracksuit and black trainers, totally a different fashion sense from Rueben.

"Alright Mols. Party in there is it? I'm starving!" She says before pushing past me.

Rueben looks a little worried as he stares at his Mum.

"What? She's your sister!" Joy says dismissive and with a big smile on her face.

I didn't realise Lily would be coming, only because Rueben says she usually doesn't come to family events. I would have invited her though to be polite, but I just didn't think. I know Rueben is worried because her temper can be unpredictable, which isn't a big deal when she's just at Joy's house, but I know right now he is worried about how she might behave today.

"Alright. This is for you" Dave says in his usual monotone before handing me a card.

"Thank you, please come through and grab a drink." I insist.

"Before we go in, can you get Lily to tone it down a bit? It's embarrassing. Mollie's Dad is in there!" Rueben pleads with his Mum.

"Oh, I'm not getting involved, mate! She's fine! Leave her alone." Joy huffs.

As we head back into the dining room area, I notice Lily looking around, she starts going through cupboards and looking through my draws quite comfortably as if this is her house.

"Nice house!" She says loudly as she clocks me watching with a kind of what-the-hell-is-she-doing expression on my face.

"Thank you." I smile politely.

"How about now everybody is here, we let Daisy finally do the gender reveal? She's been itching to do it all morning!" Rueben suggests.

Everyone cheers and claps at the suggestion and they all turn to make a huge fuss of Daisy who is now coming back indoors excitedly for the big reveal.

"Oh Dad!" I quickly call.

"This is Rubens Mum and Stepdad, Joy and Dave." I introduce quickly before I forget.

My Dad warmly greets them both and gets the same effort from Dave as I first got, and Joy seems a little shy. Overall though it's a fairly pleasant exchange and I'm sure soon they'll bond over being grandparents.

Rueben brings in the large cardboard box from under the stairs and we place it on the dining table. The lady in the shop put in a large helium balloon after we gave her the nurses envelope with the information of our baby's gender.

"So, if it's blue it's a boy…but if it's a girl, it's my sister!" Daisy proudly shouts as Rueben helps her stand on a chair for the big moment.

"OK, everyone…let's all countdown!" I smile.

…three…

…two…

…one…

Daisy opens the lid of the cardboard box and out comes a big baby BLUE balloon. Everyone in the room erupts, lots of laughter and cheers with offers of congratulations being offered simultaneously.

"I KNEW IT!" Lily bellows over the top of everyone.

"Yeah I knew it too." Joy adds smugly.

"He is going to be EXACTLY like Rueben." Lily claps.

"He is going to be hundred percent his Dad. Lookswise, personality, everything! I'm afraid to say, there won't be much of you in him. We have strong genes." Joy smiles as she turns to me.

"Well…we'll see." I say with a smile and shrug my shoulders. I don't really care for her tone; she can come across a little childish over things like this. It's like everything becomes a competition and as much as it's growing tiresome, I still try my best to put it down to just her excitement.

"Well I hope he doesn't get my big nose!" Rueben interjects carefully to lighten the conversation.

"Well, whatever. I just can't wait to have him at my house every weekend. I'm going out tomorrow to buy a new cot for him." Joy informs us with a big smile.

"Oh? He'll already have a cot here?" I question a little confused.

I look to Rueben to see if he knows what she means but he looks just as puzzled as I do.

"I know but he'll need one in my bedroom for when he comes to stay at the weekends." she confirms.

"Oh Mum…just because I stayed with Nan a lot it doesn't mean I'll be sending our baby to you *every* weekend. That's a little excessive. I want to be a hands-on Dad, but I'm sure we can work something out at some point." Rueben offers diplomatically.

"But she's going to be *his* Grandmother!" Lily weighs in with attitude.

"Yes, I am *his* Grandmother, Roo." Joy adds impatiently.

"Yeah and we are his parents, we'll decide what's best." Rueben says, trying his best to sound authoritative.

"Well it's getting late…" My Dad interrupts a little hesitantly.

"Yeah, actually we best make a move too…" Lana adds.

Great. Together Joy and Lily have made everyone feel uncomfortable. I'm sure they didn't mean to and it's just the excitement but it's really annoying. I head out to the front door and thank everyone profusely for their thoughtful gifts and cards as I wave them off.

"Aren't in-laws' fun?" My Dad jokingly whispers as he hugs me goodbye.

CHAPTER SEVENTEEN

Our Bank holiday Monday has been very successful. We finally decided to go and do a huge baby shop now that we know the gender. Rueben loved picking out some boy clothes and baby grows, particularly the ones with 'I love my Daddy' on the front. Daisy excitedly chose the baby a cute stuffed toy, she chose a blue and green dinosaur and she's promised to look after it until her little brother arrives. Although she's not getting the sister she hoped for she's still pretty happy even if she does occasionally roll her eyes at everything we buy having to be so 'boyish'.

"I think we've bought half the shop!" Rueben laughs shaking his head at me.

"You laugh now but just wait until he is here! We'll be using all of this stuff. Babies are expensive." I say.

"OK, are you sure we've got everything we need? We've got enough bottles. Baby towels? What about one of those grow bags? Do we need one of those?"

"Yes, I've got two grow bags at the bottom of the trolley. We've pretty much got it all. We just need nappies, wipes and milk but we'll get that in my final weeks." I reassure.

I look down into our trolley and feel very proud at how well we've managed to do. I even got the milk bottle prep machine I saw in the catalogue. We just chose a beautiful white and brown wooden cot set.

It comes with a matching wardrobe and chest of drawers and it has little teddy bears imprinted in the wood. It's the cutest.

We also bought a Moses basket with lots of soft blankets, a tonne of baby grows and vests, baby lotion, a baby bath, an adorable cream coloured bouncer with little elephants across the handle and of course Daisy's dinosaur for him.

"Wait, we haven't chosen a travel system? Let's do it now so we can get it on order." Rueben suggests.

"Oh god yes! How could we forget, actually I was browsing online when I couldn't sleep last night, and I found a really smart one I like the look of. I'll see if I can find it." I say with excitement clear in my voice.

I find a sales assistant and describe to her the travel system I found last night online, straight away she knows which one I'm talking about and tells me how popular it is. We head over to the section at the back of the shop where lots of pushchairs and strollers and travel systems are all on display so that we can test drive them and check out all the features.

"Oh, it's lovely!" I smile at Rueben.

"It's got everything we need, the car seat, carry cot and it turns into a stroller!"

"OK, Daisy, throw the dinosaur in the pushchair and we'll take him for a spin around the shop and see what he thinks, yeah?" Rueben offers with a grin.

"Yes please! He'd like that!" Daisy giggles as she places the dinosaur carefully into the car seat part of the travel system.

Rueben whizzes around the shop taking the dinosaur for a brisk walk and Daisy runs after him giggling away.

"We'll take it please!" I say to the sales assistant as we both laugh watching Rueben playfully speed around the isles with a stuffed toy.

As the assistant takes my order and my receipt to the till, Rueben comes whizzing back with a big smirk on his face.

"OK Daisy Dots, what does the dinosaur think?" Rueben playfully asks.

Daisy giggles and grabs the dinosaur and holds him up to her ear as if he's whispering something to her.

"OK, OK Mr Dinosaur…I will tell them…he said he loves it! But he thinks we should buy the blue one so it's a boy one for my little brother! I think he will love that one." Daisy says proudly.

"OK, sounds good to me" I say, and I give her a high five.

"Honestly babe, in all seriousness you've chosen really well. It's so easy to push around. I think it'll be perfect for our little man." Rueben says as he kisses my forehead.

When Tuesday comes around, I find that work has built up quite a lot over the bank holiday and I'm rushed off my feet returning calls and filing reports that I barely stop for lunch. This is the first time in my job where I have felt quite stressed and overwhelmed. I rearrange my desk and prioritise everything as best I can and decide to stop for a quick cup of tea before I get stuck into the rest.

I get my phone out of my bag to check the time and see I have missed three calls from Joy. I really don't have time to stop for a chat but last time I didn't get back to her straight away she called my work and I really don't want that to happen again.

I bite the bullet and decide to call her back now, so I have no distractions for the rest of the afternoon.

"Hello?" Somebody answers.

"Oh? Hello? Is that Joy?"

"No, it's Lily. Mum wanted me to call you. You alright?" Lily loudly asks.

"Yes, thank you. You? What can I do for you?"

"We're just in the baby store and Mums been buying some bits. She's just bought you loads of bottles and wants to know if you need anything else?"

"Oh, that's so sweet." I politely say.

"I can't think of anything else I need at the top of my head but please don't let her waste money on bottles, I literally just bought loads yesterday."

"Oh…" Lily pauses.

"Mum says these are the new Macintosh ones though?" She tells me with a slightly less friendly tone.

"Ah, I bought the Tommee ones, I don't think you can mix different bottles anyway because the baby will get confused by the different teats. I really appreciate the offer though, tell her I said thank you so much for thinking of us. It's just we did a big shop yesterday and we got more than enough, I'm really sorry." I apologise sincerely again.

"OK. No problem then, we'll just get him something else." she responds abruptly.

"Great, that's so kind. Thank you so much." I say.

I let out a relieved sigh as we end the phone call. That didn't go so bad and I appreciate the gesture, I really think our baby is going to help us all bond and grow closer. I start getting back into my work, making sure I complete all the most urgent paperwork so I can still leave on time today. Just when I'm getting into the rhythm of it all my phone vibrates on the desk. Rueben.

"Hello?"

"Babe? What did you say to my Mum?" Rueben asks bluntly, his voice sounding strained and stressed.

"Nothing? I only spoke to Lily and it was about bottles!" I snap defensively.

"Well she's just phoned me, yelling. Saying how you won't let her buy the baby anything and she's asking me what your problem is with her?"

"What? I don't have a problem with her! I literally just said we sorted out our sons' bottles!" I begin to raise my voice.

"Babe…I don't mean to have a go at you, it's just she won't stop ringing me whilst I'm at work and I'm too busy to deal with her stressing."

"Where do you think I'm at Rueben? I'm at work too!" I yell.

"I'm sorry, I know that but she's accusing me of allowing you to push her out of her grandson's life."

"Allowing? ALLOWING?" I shriek.

"I didn't mean it like that." Rueben begins to say before I cut him off.

"You know what Roo, I'm starting to realise that your Mum always has an issue and our son isn't even here yet and she's complaining of being pushed out? I'm tired and hormonal and I'm not putting up with phone calls whilst I'm at work anymore!" I snap before hanging up the phone.

When I throw my phone down on the desk, I look up to see half the office gawking up at me. I feel so embarrassed which just makes me even angrier at Rueben right now. How dare he accuse me of causing his Mum to stress. I shouldn't even really be mad at Rueben, none of this would have happened if Joy didn't phone him at work and stress him out.

All I want to do right now is go home and have a nice bubble bath and soak all this drama away.

CHAPTER EIGHTEEN

"I come in peace!" Rueben says whilst waving a pair of white boxer shorts through the crack of the bathroom door.

"Is that supposed to be a surrender flag?" I giggle.

"Yes…is it working?"

"Sure, come in…" I say softly.

"But I have my best bath salts, my best scented candles and a new face mask on, this is a stress-free zone." I joke with a smile hoping to lighten the mood between us.

"That's good, because I'm really sorry about earlier."

Rueben says as he kneels next to me.

"Roo, can I ask you a question?"

"Sure?"

"Did your Mum like your ex-girlfriend? The girl you were with for so many years?" I ask gently.

"No. It started OK and she'd always be nice to her face but whenever it was just me and Mum again, Mum would constantly tell me she wasn't good enough or find a reason to moan about her. But I'd mostly ignore it because my Mum really doesn't like anyone." Rueben jokes.

"Is there a pattern happening here? I mean do you think she'll continue to find issues in me?" I try to ask casually but my throat is thick as I feel myself growing emotional.

"Mollie, my ex-girlfriend ended up cheating on me for a long time behind my back. Maybe on some level my Mum was right to judge her, I don't know. But you are amazing, you're thoughtful, you're caring, and I love you. My Mum just gets funny sometimes but it's nothing to do with you. She has no reason to dislike you." Rueben reassures me.

"Well, I really hope so. She's been wonderful with Daisy and I have no doubt she's going to be just as wonderful with our son. It would just be nice if things flowed a bit...simpler. I guess."

"They will. She's just a bit of a control freak. She'll soon calm down."

I smile and nod at his efforts to reassure me but in his eyes, I can see hesitation. I'm not entirely sure if he is as convinced as he is making out, but it helps ease my mind a little anyway.

"Oh! Before I forget to tell you, my Mum is coming around tonight for a Chinese takeaway. Do you want some?" I ask.

"Actually, I've had a bit of a migraine since Mum phoned me a million times earlier, if it's alright with you I was just going to have an early night?"

"Of course, it is!" I say sympathetically.

I feel bad for him really, most of the hassle and stress gets put onto him from Joy. I've noticed if she has an issue it's usually Rueben who she phones straight away to take it out on. I know he is trying his best to keep everybody happy and the strain must be a lot to bare. Even I have snapped at him today and I shouldn't have done that. I should know better and take a step back before I react, I know by now that Rueben doesn't mean to stress at me, it's just the pressure he is under.

When I get out the bath, I decide to make Rueben a quick cup of tea and bring some biscuits up to him as a small gesture, so he knows I still love him so much.

Of course, he is so grateful, and we cuddle in bed for a little while before I hear my Mum at the door. I kiss him goodnight and let him rest.

My evening with Mum is just what I needed, I tell her a little about my day and she just makes her usual sarcastic comments and silly jokes which have me in stitches.

"It's just ironic that she's called Joy isn't it?" Mum sneers and I burst out laughing.

I love these evenings. We get comfy on the sofa with a takeaway and just put the world to rights. She's always made this a regular thing since Devon died. Although he wasn't the love of my life and I wasn't some sort of grieving widow, I think she sensed I needed the extra support. Just like many times before, tonight is such a welcome relief. I haven't stopped laughing.

"Rueben is a good person though Mollie." My mum says in a serious tone.

"I know." I agree.

"It can't be easy for him to try and keep the peace with his Mum all the time and also keep you happy. So just be patient with him when his Mum argues on the phone to him, OK? He won't need you stressing at him too." Mum gently advises.

She's right and I appreciate her pointing it out, even though I sort of came to that revelation in the bath it's nice to have someone offering perspective. Mum always sticks up for Rueben, there isn't many boyfriends I have had that my Mum likes but Rueben has definitely won her over.

"I was talking to Sheryl the other day; did I ever tell you that she used to be a dinner lady at the primary school Rueben went too?" Mum begins lowering her voice. I'm assuming so Rueben won't hear.

"No? You never mentioned that." I respond.

"OK, well she told me that when Rueben was only small, he always turned up at school with fresh bruises, some pretty bad ones at that and if anyone ever asked him about it, he'd just tell them he fell out of bed."

"Oh." is all I can say.

I know this story already but I'm not sure I should confirm it. I know Rueben told me in confidence.

"It's rubbish though isn't it? Where the hell was his bed? The top of Mount Kilimanjaro!?" Mum mocks sarcastically.

"It's certainly strange…" I add hesitantly.

"You know what else she told me? She said that he was never given any money for anything. Not for school trips, not for the after-school football club. Not for anything. Apparently, Rueben was obsessed with football at school, it was his favourite thing to do and the school ran a Saturday club which was three pounds a week, but his Mum would refuse to help him. Next thing you know Sheryl saw him selling his belongings at school just so he could make the money to go. Meanwhile Lily, who was a couple of years above him got given everything. Always seen with new school stuff, always had money. She went to every school trip, every club she wanted to go too. For some reason it was just Rueben who was left out. Sad really." Mum whispers.

"He hasn't told me any of that stuff." I mumble.

"People don't often realise they've been mistreated until they're out of the situation. He probably doesn't know any different." Mum says shaking her head.

"Did Sheryl mention anything else?"

"Not a lot. Just that she used to feel really sad for Rueben, so she was pleased when I told her that he turned out to be a really lovely lad." Mum smiles.

"Yeah. Yeah he is lovely" I smile back.

CHAPTER NINETEEN

I'm pleased as I leave work Friday afternoon. This pregnancy is taking it out of me, and I've only made it to June. Three and a half months left though, and it'll all be worth it.

I remember that Daisy is staying around my Mums house tonight, she asked when she came over for a Chinese if she could spend some more time with her and take her to the cinema. Daisy loves cinema trips with her Nana, plus I love having the odd child free night. Although in the past I would use a child free night to drag Lana out to a fancy cocktail bar for happy hour and really let my hair down, whereas tonight I'll probably be asleep and snoring on the sofa by eight.

As I arrive home, Rueben has other plans, on the table is a bottle of grape juice and two new dressing gowns.

"I thought we could have one of those nights that we used to have, where we stay up late talking and drinking wine. Although you can't drink wine now, so I thought we'd both settle for grape juice." Rueben proudly presents to me.

"I love it! But I might fall asleep a lot earlier than I used too." I laugh.

"That's fine by me. I just miss my girlfriend; I know a lot has been going on and I thought it would be nice to have some time just me and you."

I lean into Rueben and smile as I rest my head on his chest. He really is thoughtful.

My evening is beautifully spent with us lounging on the sofa in our new dressing gowns and snacking on pizza. We get onto embarrassing subjects and I start telling Rueben about how one time at school Lana made me laugh so hard I wet myself. He sits laughing away as I cringe at the memory and recall how I tried to hide what had happened by walking backwards out of the classroom so no one could see my skirt but that only drew more attention to me.

Annoyingly, Rueben swears blind that he doesn't have much of an embarrassing story so instead he just tells me about all the random drunk shenanigans he got up to when he was a teenager. Typical lad stuff really, but he laughs at himself through memories.

"Did you see your Dad when you were growing up much?" I ask.

"Not really. I think he was a deadbeat to be honest" Rueben brushes off.

"Oh? What makes you say that?"

"I don't really know much; Mum was pretty vague. From what I understand my dad was married to a woman and they had five sons. He left her and got with my Mum and eventually they had Lily and were really happy. But when I came along, he changed his mind and went back to his wife. Mum said they were together for ten years all in all though." He explains.

"What caused him to change his mind?" I ask curiously.

"I don't know. Lily used to tell me it was because he didn't want any more sons, he already had the five. He just wanted a daughter and he got that with Lily."

"Pffft! That's rubbish though, I hope your mum put Lily straight?" I ask appalled.

"No. Mum would never go against Lily. I just accepted what they told me. Which is that essentially I was the reason my Dad left." He says looking down at his feet.

"No, babe. No. You were just an innocent baby that won't be the reason. But even if it was, what type of man is that? You were clearly better off. Just look at the man you've become...and you did that without him." I proudly point out.

"Maybe. The next thing I knew he had died. But I didn't find out until weeks later, my Mum said nobody told her and I missed the funeral. God, I remember feeling so gutted. I must've cried myself to sleep every night for a week. Still, it's not like he wanted to know me anyway. Is it? It's like Dave used to say to me, my dad didn't care about me, so get over it." Rueben mumbles.

The mood has changed since I mentioned his real Dad and Rueben doesn't seem in the mood to laugh at old memories anymore. Instead he stretches out on the long sofa and lays his head on my lap and rests his eyes as I run my fingers through his hair and down to stroke his cheek. Before I know it, he is softly snoring and so pull the sofa blanket over the both of us and I let him sleep.

My body feels stiff and tight as I start waking up, I realise I had fallen asleep in a very uncomfortable position to accommodate Rueben who is still peacefully sleeping. I rotate my neck trying to relieve some of the pressure and get up for some water. It's just gone ten a.m., We must have needed that lay in, we certainly haven't slept in for that long in a while.

I soon notice Rueben's phone flashing on the kitchen counter and decide I'll bring it in to him and wake him up.

Thirty-seven missed calls

It's Joy. Oh god, I groan to myself. Now what?

I decide this time I'll make some toast and a coffee for Rueben and wake him up properly before he returns her calls. Maybe this way it'll give him a chance to get his head straight first.

By the time I'm done buttering his toast a very dishevelled Rueben appears behind me.

"Oh well, hello! nice to meet you. I'm Mollie and the year is two thousand and seventeen." I banter.

"I've been asleep, not in a coma" Rueben smirks as he rubs his eyes.

I place the toast and tea down for Rueben before handing him his phone.

"Oh no. Not today." Rueben dramatically groans as he stares at the missed calls.

"Well when you speak to her, invite her and Dave over for dinner tonight. I know she said to you she felt pushed out so let's try harder to make her feel included." I offer. Hopefully it'll give her something positive to look forward too and distract her from whatever she is about to create a drama out of.

Within seconds of Rueben returning the call, he tenses up. He leaves the toast and paces around the kitchen looking quite nervous.

"Yes…OK, thank you but we bought one Mum." he responds to her into the phone.

"Well it's, it's a travel system. A really good one Mollie did her research and…"

"…I appreciate that, but it's already been ordered."

"What does it matter which one it is?"

I hear the frustration growing thick in Rueben's voice as he paces faster and starts running his hands through his hair. Something he always does when he gets irritated.

"Stop shouting at me Mum. I don't understand why you're so angry?"

"The lady in the shop said it was the best one on the market Mum, I'm sure it's fine…"

"Oh, for god's sake. It's the Baby Bloomer three hundred. The newest model…"

"Hello…?"

"She's hung up on me." Rueben declares in disbelief.

"What happened?"

"She kept saying she was with Dave and they were in a shop choosing a pushchair for us and the second I told her we already got it, she went mad…" he shrugs anxiously.

Rueben's phone starts vibrating again on the kitchen counter and breaks off our conversation.

This time he doesn't pick it up, instead he leaves it on the counter and puts the phone on loudspeaker.

"Well I've looked at the pushchair you've APPARENTLY ordered. It's a flimsy piece of junk and I am not having MY grandson in it. So, you can phone up whoever the fuck you ordered it from and cancel it, NOW! And me and Dave will order a proper one TODAY!" Joy rages.

"Mum, Mollie has already paid for it…" Rueben tries to interject.

"I don't give a FUCK what your fucking girlfriend has done. I am your Mother and I am telling you now, it is NOT good enough, you really DON'T want to push me here. You'll come unstuck!" Joy threatens.

"What do you mean?" Rueben sighs.

"Well perhaps I'll ring Mollie's Mother and tell her about how we all had a gender reveal party and SHE wasn't invited! Not nice is it!"

"Mum, you're out of line!" Rueben snaps.

"And I didn't want to tell you this, but I know for a fact that your Dad would have been ASHAMED of you for the way you're both treating me!"

Rueben drops his head into his hands at the mention of his Dad and I know he is trying to hide it, but I can tell he is holding back the tears.

"Hello?" Dave's voice bellows into the speaker.

"Dave?" Rueben responds, his voice shaky.

"Now listen here, I've just about had a fucking belly full. I wasn't going to say anything but now you and HER have really upset your Mother and it's not fucking on. You really need to think about your next move here, Rueben, because I am NOT fucking playing!" Dave roars before the phone line cuts dead.

My jaw drops open and I can barely fathom what just happened. I look at Rueben whose trembling with anger and looks as completely bemused as I am.

"What the *hell* was that?" I sigh in utter shock. my jaw may as well be on the floor.

CHAPTER TWENTY

It's been around eleven weeks since Rueben last spoke with his Mum or Stepdad. After her outburst she did call Rueben a few times and leave voice messages apologising and pleading with him to call her back. At one point I felt quite sorry for her as her voice sounded so desperate.

But Rueben won't budge, he refuses to speak to her right now. I know he is deeply hurting over the mention of his Dad. It's a sore subject for Rueben and it always be. It will be because his Dad has gone now, he can't answer Rueben's many questions or fears. He can't give the closure Rueben so desperately needs to be able to move on and stop doubting whether he was enough for his Dad.

Rueben told me this isn't the first time Joy used his Dad against him, she has said similar things when he was just a child. One-time even Dave did too. Apparently, his Mum has a habit of trying to find the worst thing she can think of that might hurt you and when she knows she's got it, she'll use it. No matter how harsh or vile it would be to say, she has no qualms.

After the first couple of days of Joy trying to reach out to Rueben, the phone calls soon stopped. For Rueben's sake it was a relief, I thought maybe Joy had decided to give him space. After all, in situations like this, it's always best to let things settle especially as there was no way Rueben could forgive his Mum so soon.

But after barely a week the calls started again. One morning Rueben woke up to fifty-eight missed called and seven voice messages. The voice messages creeped me out a little, they were so vacillating. One voice message could be Joy apologising as sincerely as she could sound and then a voice message left only moments later would be her screaming down the phone with her saying that Rueben is pure scum and that she hopes he drops down dead. It was constantly from one extreme to the other, which was exhausting for Rueben.

Days after that he came home from work in the worst mood. He went straight to the fridge and cracked open a beer and barely spoke a word for hours. Eventually he told me that Joy had been phoning his work all day, to the point where the Boss got stressed and lectured Rueben about personal calls. I wish they knew how out of his control it was.

"Do you know how embarrassing it is for your Mum to keep calling your work? It's like I'm a child!" Rueben heavily sighs and shakes his head vigorously.

"I don't know why she thinks it's OK to bring personal issues into your work?" I shrug.

"I just wish she'd stop. I feel like I'm suffocating…"

"Oh, not another one…" I sigh as I stare down at my phone.

No caller ID

"Who is it?" Rueben asks.

"I'm not sure, I've had like ten today. I answer and they don't say anything at all. But they just stay on the line until I eventually hang up."

"Let me answer it next time." Rueben insists.

"That's fine but I'm probably going to turn it off now anyway, I've had horrendous backache all day and I just want a bath and bed."

"It's probably all the stresses lately, I'll run you a nice bath and then we'll find a film to watch." Rueben says sweetly as he pulls me in for a cuddle.

Within thirty minutes of me soaking in the bath I feel like the pain is getting worse and spreading around the front of my bump.

"Rueben…" I call from the bathtub.

"I think this could be the start of labour."

"OK, should we go now? To the hospital?"

"Not yet. It might be too soon, let's wait a little longer. But maybe you could drop off Daisy to my Dads now, in case we need to go." I suggest.

"OK! No problem, I'll call your Dad and I'll tell him, and I'll pack Daisy an overnight bag. Call me if you need me, or just call me anyway, yes?" Reuben insists trying to sound calm. But I can see the panic and uncertainty in his eyes.

"Yes, don't worry I'll call if I need anything."

I lay in the bath and practise my soothing breathing whilst I hear Rueben frantically pack a bag and get Daisy's shoes on to go.

Within minutes Rueben has set off and I'm managing well. I got out the bath and threw on some comfy clothes that I kept aside for the hospital. I made sure my hospital bag was packed correctly and ready to go. I phoned my Mum quickly and updated her. She wants me to call her the second I'm ready for her to come to the hospital. I pace around my bedroom and concentrate on breathing through the contractions. The pain is getting intense now though and I find myself pacing by the bedroom window desperately waiting for Rueben to turn into the driveway.

Strangely, a sense of guilt rushes over me. Joy and Dave are the only family who haven't been told that I'm in labour. I know she's been difficult, argumentative and I know how much she's upset Rueben right now with her insults and short temper. But she's about to be a grandmother for the first ever time and it wouldn't seem right to exclude her.

I'm not sure Rueben is ready though to speak to her, perhaps it needs to be me. Without giving it anymore thought I grab my phone and turn it on whilst I continue pacing around my bedroom.

"Hi Joy, It's Mollie. I hope you're OK, I just wanted to let you know that labour has started. I'm just about to head to the hospital so I'll try to keep you updated as best I can. Speak soon x"

CHAPTER TWENTY-ONE

All I can hear are beeps around me. Lots of hospital machines making different noises and I can hear my breath against this oxygen mask.

I'm drowsy and I don't even think I have the energy to open my eyes. So, I don't even try. I can hear everyone talking around me and I know they're mostly talking about me, but I can barely keep up with what's happening.

"Excuse me, Mr. Adams, your Mum keeps ringing the hospital. I told her it wasn't a good time, but she insists it's urgent. She's waiting on the line." I hear a lady's voice say.

"Ok…" I hear Rueben hesitate. Even I can tell he wanted to say no, but he also didn't want to sound rude.

"It'll have to wait now, we're about to put her under." I hear a man reply.

"Roo…" I mumble as I try to reach my hand out to find him but with no luck.

"I'm here baby…" he says softly in my ear and I feel his hands come up against my cheeks.

"Everything is OK. The baby got a little stressed and all the pain relief made you too lethargic to cope any longer. The doctors are here and they're going to put you to sleep now and when you wake up, I'll be here and so will our baby."

It starts sounding like more people are entering the room, I feel scared, but I can't express it. I'm just so drowsy. I whine a little bit and Rueben just keeps his hands on my cheeks, stroking them. It's not a lot but it's very comforting.

"The next time you wake up we'll have our baby, just remember that. I'll be here the whole time." Rueben whispers again into my ear and I try to give a small smile.

"Mollie? Is there anybody else we can call for you for when you wake up?" I hear a different lady ask.

"Please..." I try to nod.

"My Mum."

"I'll make sure we get a message to her sweetheart." The friendly voice assures me, and I feel myself fall asleep.

My first memory of waking up is so vague. I remember feeling so very thirsty and groggy. It was like I was extremely hungover, hit by a bus and then kicked repeatedly for good measure. The pain started to rush through my body the more conscious I became. When I tried to open my eyes, I was panicked as everything was blurry and black dots clouded my vision. Anxiety starting to set in as I grew confused and worried for my baby. Where is my baby?

"There she is...this is your Mummy." I hear the soft voice from the man I love say. Immediately that gives me some reassurance that he is by my side.

I turn and sure enough through squinted eyes I can make out Rueben holding close to his chest a beautiful little baby. My baby.

"His hair..." I manage to whisper. I want to laugh but it's too painful.

I study my beautiful sons' hair, thick black messy hair. Just like me when I was born, I think to myself, as I recall all the many baby photos I've seen over the years. My mum will love that. She'll laugh so much when she sees his hair and tell me proudly how it was just like mine when I was born and how she could put my hair up into a ponytail from the moment I was twelve weeks old.

"He is perfect, and I am so proud of you." I hear him beam.

"He weighs nine pounds and ten ounces, so he certainly is chunky!"

"Like me then." I joke with a little smirk.

"Oh hello! You're awake." A friendly female voice interrupt. I recognise that voice from earlier. I think she was in the room with me, I'm sure she was the lady who promised to call my Mum.

"Hi…" is all I manage to mumble.

I can just about make her out as I strain my eyes to focus on her. It's difficult and the room is quite dark, but I can make out that she's quite young and has a very friendly smile.

"I'm going to be your nurse and look after you through the night. When you're ready and feeling a little stronger, I'll help you sit up and we can try and give baby a little cuddle, does that sound good?"

I nod in agreement but out of nowhere I feel a tear rolling down my cheek. I want to hold my baby now. I feel so sad that I can barely make him out, I can barely move a muscle.

"What's wrong with me?" I manage to croak.

"Absolutely nothing sweetheart, you're going to be fine. The c-section was a success however you lost quite a lot more blood than we would have liked. Because of this you will feel very weak and your eyes will be extra sensitive to light and probably very blurry for a little while, which is why we've turned all your lights down low. We've just started you on your first blood transfusion, but I think the doctor wanted you to have another one. Then after this we'll check your bloods to see if that's enough. Hopefully then you'll start feeling stronger and your eyes will feel much better. I know that's a lot to take in but just know that I will be here whenever you need me tonight. If I'm not in the room, then you just give this buzzer a press and I'll come straight in." She sweetly explains as I feel her place the little buzzer in my hand and I relax a little.

"Freddie." I whisper.

"What's that sweetheart?"

"Freddie." I manage again.

"Can we call him Freddie?"

"That's a beautiful name! Shall I get it written up on his chart?" The nurse smiles as she looks at Rueben.

"Yes please. Freddie it is."

I watch Rueben smile down at Freddie and repeat his name smiling.

"Wait, is this because you fancy Freddie Flintoff?" Rueben asks, his eyes wide and his jaw open as he playfully pretends to be shocked.

I giggle a little and shake my head.

"Mercury." I whisper.

"Freddie Mercury."

Rueben nods with a big smile as he realises where I conjured the name from. Mum and I have a habit of bellowing old songs out whenever we are in the car together. Our favourite is Queen and Mum has always mentioned how much she loves the name Freddie. Plus, Queen was playing in the background at Lana's when we first met. It just fits.

"He has fallen asleep again, so I'll put him down now, shall I wheel the cot right beside your bed?"

"Yes please." I nod.

"I'm going to have to leave for an hour, your Dad text earlier and I'd forgotten to pack the dinosaur that Daisy picked out for Freddie and she's gotten herself all upset. She wanted to bring it up tomorrow with your Dad. I thought I'd take it round and make sure Daisy is OK, I don't want her feeling left out or anything. Then I'll be back." He gently reassures.

"Thank you. Thank you so much for always being there for Daisy too. Please give her the biggest cuddle from me."

"More morphine for you sweetheart." The nurse interrupts as she reappears.

"You're going to feel drowsy and sleepy for a little while, but it'll all help to get you feeling as right as rain."

"I'll go now then if that's OK, I'll let you sleep, and I'll be back." Rueben informs as he gives me a gentle kiss on the cheek before leaving.

"Oh, and good news!" The nurse says.

"When I got to the phone earlier, your Mum was already on the line. She said she wouldn't be long."

Thank god I think to myself. I can't wait for her to comfort me and to meet little Freddie.

CHAPTER TWENTY-TWO

When I start waking up again, I feel a little more comfortable. The morphine must have fully kicked in now because the pain is a lot better. My head still feels fuzzy and heavy though, but still a slight improvement. I start opening my eyes and notice they're still quite blurry and sensitive. It will get better though, I remind myself. A c-section is a major operation, I know it'll just take time.

I thought I had heard voices which had woke me up, but the nurse isn't here. I slowly use my hands to prop myself up slightly. I have been laying in one position for too long and I feel a little restless, so I carefully turn myself over as best I can.

Slowly my eyes start to focus on a figure by the window swaying back and forth.

"There he is." A familiar voice coos over Freddie.

"My little baby boy. Absolutely beautiful and perfect. You look so much like me…Yes you do…But I knew you would."

I rub my eyes in confusion and try to stare at the figure coming towards me.

"Mum?" I whisper huskily as my throat feels strained and dry.

"Well that's what I told them love. But no." I hear Joy smugly say.

"Did you really think I was just going to sit back at home whilst MY grandson was being brought into the world?"

"I…I'm really not well Joy. I'm not supposed to have any visitors yet." I stutter.

"I'm not just a visitor. I am his Grandmother. The most important person in his life." Joy declares whilst shooting me a poisonous glare.

I'm so tired and fuzzy, it's been a long day and now I'm feeling so overwhelmed. I look at her cradling my son and my heart aches with sadness. This wasn't how this was supposed to go, I was supposed to have some time with my son first as soon I was able to and then everyone else could come and visit when we were ready.

"I wanted to be the first to hold my son, after Rueben…" I sob and the tears stream from my eyes and down my cheeks before I can stop them.

"Oh, stop with the water works. You've just given birth for goodness sake. Be grateful." She hisses.

"Joy. I want you to leave. Please."

"I will when I'm ready thank you, but right now my grandson needs me."

I remember the buzzer the nurse gave me and as much as I feel awkward to do it, I'm going to buzz for her and tell her that I want Joy to leave. Only when I look down the buzzer isn't where it was left when I fell asleep, I pull my covers around and look underneath them but there's no sign it.

"Looking for the buzzer?" Joy smiles as she points to it on the table. Completely out of my reach. Her look is boastful, like she's winning a game that I didn't know we were playing.

"Oh, don't look so serious!" She bursts out laughing.

"You can have it back in a minute."

I flop my head back down onto my pillow, feeling defeated. Why does she dislike me so much? Why did she do this? Is it over the bottles and the pushchair? Has she felt that offended that she thought she'd come uninvited and take this moment away from me? Right now, I should be finally holding my son and kissing his little forehead whilst I proudly observe every inch of him that I created with Rueben. But instead I'm stuck here feeling helpless watching Kathy Bates from the movie Misery obsess over my son.

"Thank you for the name. Fred was the name of Dave's great

grandad. He'll be thrilled when I tell him." She smiles.

"Freddie Mercury" I croak.

"We named him after Freddie Mercury."

Joy stares at me confused and displeased.

"He's the lead singer in the band Queen…"

"I know who he is!" She snaps.

"I just cannot believe you would name my only grandson, my beautiful grandson after a flipping homosexual." she huffs, rolling her eyes in disgust.

I watch her in disbelief as she continues to sigh and pace the room. Occasionally looking down at Freddie and then back at me in disappointment. Is Joy homophobic? I wonder to myself. Rueben can't stand narrow minded hateful people; does he know the kind of comments she makes?

"If anybody asks, I shall tell them he was named after Dave's great grandad. He was a wonderful man. It's a good thing Freddie has me to save him from the embarrassment you could have put him through. Honestly Mollie. Freddie Mercury! What on earth were you thinking?" She moans as she finally places Freddie back down into his little hospital cot.

She doesn't say anything more which I'm grateful for and she doesn't even fake a polite goodbye to be friendly. She just turns on her heel and leaves the room. I stare back towards the buzzer still left on the table; she didn't even give that back. The crying and stress has exhausted me but I keep rubbing my eyes and fight to stay awake because I must speak to Rueben. As soon as he gets back, I'm going to tell him everything. How controlling she was, how she belittled me and made me feel. Even how she took my buzzer away like some crazy woman.

I stare down at my baby boy through the plastic sides. His eyes are open, and he stares back at me momentarily. His eyes so bright and curious. Quickly his little eyelids begin to close and sure enough he is settled back to sleep. I reach my hand in and stroke his tiny little fingers and thankfully I feel a lot less stressed and wound up. I just feel happy and content, staring down at my beautiful son.

The next time I'm opening my eyes I realise it's day light and annoyingly I must have fallen back to sleep despite desperately wanting to speak to Rueben.

"Morning baby…" Rueben bends down and kisses me on the cheek.

For the first time since coming out of surgery my eyes feel much better and my head is a lot less foggy. I'm so relieved to see Rueben that I just start sobbing and reaching out to him for a cuddle.

"Hey…what's brought all this on?"

"Rueben, your Mum was here last night, and she was awful to me. She took Freddie and just took over everything, she kept saying she was the most important person to him, then she took my buzzer away when I went to call the nurse back in! And do you know how she got in? She pretended to be my mum!" I say, my words all scrambled and rushed.

Rueben just stares at me bemused.

"Baby…Mum wasn't here last night. I just spoke to her on the phone to tell her about Freddie. She said you had already texted her and she was honestly so grateful Mollie. She kept telling me to thank you and she was really appreciative. She says when you're feeling up for visitors, she'd love to come by, but there's no rush." Rueben reassures whilst tucking my hair behind my ear.

I stare at him completely bewildered by what he is trying to tell me. Is she lying about being here as well?

"Rueben. She *was* here." I say firmly.

"Babe…come on. My Mum is a pain, especially to me but she wouldn't come here without my say so and upset you like that, not when you've just given birth."

"So, you're calling me a liar?" I snap.

"God, no. I know you're not a liar. But I know you were on a lot of different drugs last night and had not long come around from being heavily sedated. You probably got confused…"

"Then why wasn't *my* Mum here?"

"I'm not sure, she phoned me earlier and I told her as well about Freddie. She said nobody phoned her last night from the hospital but that's the nurse's fault and surely my Mum can't be to blame for that?"

"They didn't ring my mum because *your* mum was already on the line! Pretending to be *my* Mum!" I sigh in frustration.

A new nurse strolls in breaking up our conversation. I sit quietly whilst she takes my blood pressure and my temperature. I don't even know what to say at this point, this is not how I saw this conversation going.

"Sorry to interrupt but my girlfriend is saying she had a visitor last night whilst I was gone, does anyone know anything about that?" Rueben queries the nurse.

"I don't think so, we did handover this morning and Mollie's nurse from last night said everything was quiet and there hadn't been visitors.

I don't think you'd have been well enough anyway, poppet." The nurse says turning to me with a smile.

"My girlfriend is absolutely sure though that somebody was here last night, and it's gotten her a little upset..." Rueben surprises me by pressing the matter.

"Well according to Mollie's notes, she had morphine last night, it doesn't happen very often but occasionally it can cause hallucinations. Perhaps that's what has happened. But you shouldn't need any more morphine today so don't worry." She tells me before unstrapping me from the blood pressure machine and leaving the room.

"You see..." Rueben says softly and takes hold of my hand.

"I am so sorry I wasn't here last night when you hallucinated."

"But it seemed so real..."

"I'm sure it did, it must have been very strange. But I know what will make you feel better. Do you want to give your little man a cuddle?" He smiles proudly.

I nod excitedly and pull myself up properly ready to cradle him. Just as I sit up and wait for Rueben to bring me my son from his little cot, I spot something on the table. The buzzer.

I want to tell Rueben about my suspicions again but after what the nurse said I'm doubting myself now. I suppose that buzzer could have been moved by anyone and if the nurse really thinks I have been hallucinating, I don't want to sound crazy.

Maybe it is a bit farfetched to think Joy would just turn up here and be as nasty as she was. Maybe those drugs were messing with my mind, they certainly were strong, but I can't fixate too much on it all right now.

I'm too busy having my first proper cuddle with my son.

"Hi Freddie." I smile proudly.

CHAPTER TWENTY-THREE

So far, I have had a lovely day. I managed to get out of the bed and sit in the chair by the window, the fresh air coming through was a welcome relief. I gave Freddie a bottle and got him freshly changed into a gorgeous soft grey sleep suit with blue stars that reads *"50% Mummy and 50% Daddy"* on the front.

I then took about hundred photos of him or at least so it would seem and Rueben helped me put a brush through my hair so I'm starting to feel somewhat human again. During lunch the doctor came by and told me that my bloods had started to go back to a normal level, so if all continues to go well, I can be discharged tomorrow and get back to my home.

My Mum was here first thing this morning, I desperately wanted to tell her about Joy…or my possible hallucination but Rueben was in the room and I didn't want him to think I was obsessing over it.

As I thought, Mum laughed hysterically at Freddie's hair before telling us the same old stories about how thick my hair was when I was born. I didn't mind listening to it all again though, it was comforting. She gave me a bag of gifts which I didn't expect but it really boosted my mood. I got a big helium balloon for Freddie, a new pair of fluffy slippers and a whole Clarin's face pamper set which I really can't wait to use when I'm home.

By the time Mum left we only had a few moments to ourselves before my Dad arrived with a very excited Daisy in tow.

I laughed as she stood by the door at first looking all excited, curious and nervous all rolled into one. My heart melted as I saw her clutching the dinosaur toy against her chest.

It didn't take long for Daisy's hesitations to fade. She was soon proudly presenting Freddie with her dinosaur that she picked out for him. Rueben and I took even more photos of them together as Daisy happily posed alongside of him with all the sass of a supermodel.

I couldn't stop thanking my Dad for taking care of Daisy and bringing her down to see me. You don't realise how much you miss home and your family until you're stuck in four walls and confined to a bed.

"He really looks like you when you were born Mol." Dad beams as he has his first cuddle with Freddie.

"I've seen the photos! He definitely has your hair baby." Rueben laughs.

"He does. But you're so dark too Roo, it's probably from us both."

"Oddly, I was blonde when I was born! So, this is definitely all you." He proudly smiles at me.

"So, Freddie, are you going to come and play golf with your old grandad when you're older?"

"The next Tiger Woods, maybe." Rueben says.

"Yeah, or the next David Beckham and he'll play for England." Dad continues.

"Or even the next best boxing champion. Like Muhammad Ali."

"Now now, boys. He might be a contestant on Ru Paul's Drag Race and not into sports at all!" I laugh.

"And I really don't care either way. As long as he is truly happy. That's all I want for him."

"Couldn't agree more." My Dad says whilst proudly staring down at Freddie and Rueben nods in agreement.

The afternoon seems to fly by and before I know it, I'm giving Daisy a big tight cuddle and kissing her goodbye. She's sad to leave but I promise her that I'll be allowed to leave the hospital tomorrow and I'm going to treat her to a McDonald's and spend the day cuddled up with her and watching Frozen. Which is still her current favourite.

When we're alone Rueben helps me take a shower. I still struggle to manoeuvre without pain, so Rueben takes off the shower head and moves it around my body whilst I wash. I still can't bend down yet either so after the shower I'm grateful when Rueben helps me get dressed into some fresh pyjamas and the new slippers my Mum bought for me. I decide to sit at the chair by the window again for a little while and eat some of my dinner the nurse brought in.

"So, when does Norma Bates get here?" I ask Rueben sarcastically after a mouthful of pasta.

"Norma Bates?"

"Yeah. You're Mother."

"Oh!" Rueben laughs.

"I assume your hallucination is still making you mad at her."

"*If* it was an hallucination" I scorn.

"Baby…"

"No Rueben. I don't want to hear it again. I still remember it; I don't think it was my mind playing tricks on me. However, I have no evidence and I'm well aware of that. I'm also aware that the drugs I was put on did make me feel very spaced out and confused. I won't mention it again after this, but I want you to know that this is how I feel and those are my thoughts. I'm unsure and I don't like it."

"Ok…I'm sorry you feel very confused and unsure still. But I really believe your mind did play tricks on you, however I trust you and I will always believe you if you a hundred percent know something to be true. So, if you remember anything more, tell me, OK?" Rueben surprises me by softly saying.

"Thank you…I will." I say gratefully as I look up and see a familiar figure hovering at the door.

"Oh Christ. Norma's here." I mutter under my breath.

"Where's my grandson?" Joy asks cheerfully as she helps herself to Freddie and picks him up from his hospital cot.

I then see Dave stroll through the door, followed by Lily.

"Wow, starting to see you a lot." Rueben says to Lily.

"Yeah well, my boyfriend trashed my flat didn't he. I ain't gonna sit in that am I?" She says aggressively with her usual short temper.

"Congratulations Mollie, well done." Dave casually says to me.

"Thank you!" I smile.

"Alright Mol?" Lily looks up at me.

"Yeah, not so bad now." I nod.

"Much better than last night" I say as I look up to Joy to see if she has a reaction to that. But she's too fixated on Freddie.

"Look at my little man!" Joy smiles.

"50% Daddy? More like 100% Daddy!" She giggles as she reads his sleepsuit.

"God yeah, absolutely Roo's double!" Lily adds.

"Definitely. He has hair just like mine!" Joy boasts.

"He looks quite a lot like you actually Mum." Lily continues.

Eurgh. Do they ever see anybody beyond themselves? I think to myself.

I also wonder if Rueben realises that his Mum hasn't acknowledged me yet.

"Who got the helium balloon?" Joy asks Rueben.

"Oh, Mollies Mum, Laraine. She brought it in when she came by this morning." Rueben answers.

Joy responds but it's barely a word. It's like she went to say something but thought better of it. Instead she catches Lily's eye and gives her a childish smirk. Her face says it all. As soon as Rueben told her it was my Mum her face dropped, and she looked disgusted and obviously making stupid faces to Lily is part of an inside joke. I'd love to ask her what her problem is but it's not the time or the place.

"Could you please take a photo of me and my grandson on your phone Mollie? And send it to me later?" She asks.

Oh. Spoke to soon. She has acknowledged me. As a photographer anyway.

"She can't really stand comfortably Mum; I'll take the photo." Rueben cuts in.

I watch as Lily and Joy pass Freddie to each other multiple times as they pose continuously for the camera.

"Do you like his name, Joy? I named him after Freddie Mercury." I say, testing her.

"Yeah! I love it." She smiles. "Although I don't like Freddie Mercury much. It's still a nice name."

"Did you do much last night?" I ask.

"Nope. Not a lot." She quickly responds.

She's vague, but somewhat polite and I can't read her at all. At this point I frustratingly have no clue whether Joy was in my room last night or not. I sit back in my chair and rest my head back. I'm starting to get tired again and my body is slowly beginning to ache. It's been a long day.

"You've had him ages Mum! It's my turn!" Lily snaps impatiently and I look up to watch what looks like is about to be some kind of tug of war with my son.

"Grow up you two or I'll take him off you." Rueben warns.

I'm relieved when a Nurse pops her head around the door and tells them that visiting hours is about to end.

Joy definitely doesn't look pleased and huffs in her usual way as she says her goodbyes.

Lily and Dave are the only ones who give me a decent goodbye. Joy gives a polite nod in my direction but offers nothing more. So even if I was hallucinating last night, it's clear she still has a problem with me.

CHAPTER TWENTY-FOUR

Settling back home as a family of four has been wonderful but tough at times.

The recovery took a lot longer than I hoped and so Rueben had to do a lot of the legwork with the kids. For the first two weeks I couldn't even shower or get dressed without Rueben's help and the broken sleep every night was getting to us all.

It's all been so worth it though; I find myself on Sunday's feeling the most grateful and blessed. It's becoming my favourite day. We tend to take the kids to the park in the morning, Daisy gets to have a run around and get some fresh air, Rueben gets stuck in, chasing her around and playing hide and seek and other silly games. I get to push Freddie around in his pram which always ends with him having a little nap. By the afternoon my Mum usually drops by and we make a little roast dinner. Then finally once we've eaten, we all sit together on the big sofas and put on a movie. It's so simple, but I couldn't be happier.

Freddie is a whole three months old now and Joy hasn't been upset or argumentative once. She's been a little intense at times and there has been quite a lot of phone calls, but I just put it down to her excitement over a new baby in the family. She has been asking to have Freddie stay at her house overnight, but we've not felt ready yet. Thankfully she seems to accept it and hasn't pushed too much.

We make the effort to pop into Joy and Dave's whenever we head over that way, I promised myself I would make an effort so that she feels as involved as possible and hopefully she won't feel so competitive or offended. Anything I can do to prevent her from giving Rueben a hard time on the phone, I will.

Occasionally she calls in at our house too after she's been shopping with Dave and shows us some new clothes that she's bought for Freddie. Oddly though she offers to keep them at her house for when Freddie visits and I think that is her subtle way of telling me she doesn't like how we dress Freddie, but I don't push it. I tend to not question much with Joy, instead I politely smile and nod.

Rueben has taken Freddie and Daisy down to his Nan's house a few times, but I have stayed at home when they go. I haven't felt comfortable enough to see Irene again just yet. I feel really bad about that because I understand how important she is to Rueben. But I still can't shake how disappointed she looked when she first met me and how she kept glaring at me. If there is one thing that I cannot stand, it's an atmosphere. So, for right now it's best I give it time and then approach with caution.

Christmas is only a week away now and we have decided to have a fairly calm and relaxed one and spend it mostly at home. I promised Joy we would drop in on them on Christmas Day evening because I sensed this might cause an issue if we didn't. I did just want it to be us four at home for the day and then make our way around everyone on Boxing Day. But with Joy, I know by now that I have to make extra allowances. After all, it's Rueben who suffers if she isn't happy.

The run up to my first Christmas with Rueben and my first-born son feels very surreal but exciting. Last week Rueben and Daisy put the Christmas tree up in the front room whilst Freddie napped in my arms. I took a photo on my phone of Rueben lifting Daisy in the air to place the gold star on top of the tree, she had the biggest smile on her face. I immediately had that photo printed off and framed it. I even sent a framed copy to my Mum, Dad and Joy too.

Over the last two weeks Daisy started to call Rueben Dad. She started doing it so casually that I didn't even notice. It was Rueben who pointed it out to me. Rueben loves that she's been calling him it, although he did ask if Devon's family would mind. The thing is there is nobody *to* mind. Devon was gone a long time ago now. He didn't have much family and if he has Daisy hasn't met them, nor have I.

I wouldn't even know how to get in contact with them. For as long as I can remember it was only ever me and Daisy, so there *is* no one else to worry about. I assured Rueben that he certainly was not treading on anyone's toes.

I'm stood at the school gates with Freddie asleep in his pram and I'm waiting for Daisy to appear. It's her last day today and then they're all broken up for Christmas, so she's bound to be extremely excited.

Sure, enough she leaps across the playground and proudly presents me with a Christmas ornament she has made for me in class. It's a big silver star with "my family." written on the front and then on the back it says 'Mummy.' 'Daddy.' 'Daisy.' 'Freddie.' In gorgeous Christmassy gold ink.

"It's beautiful!" I tell her whilst she pokes her head into the pram and kisses Freddie on his cheek.

As we start heading home, Daisy chats excitedly about Santa Claus and how she's nearly finished her Christmas letter to him. She asks what a mince pie is and looks confused and equally disgusted when I tell her. Then asks me why it's called mince if it isn't meat. Something I have no clue on, so I make up a reason. She then sings me a Christmas hymn they learned in assembly and then asks me how Santa gets through the front door, plus whatever other question pops into her brain.

"Wow!" I laugh.

"Someone really is getting excited for Christmas."

"Why do you say that?"

"Well for one thing, you've barely stopped talking long enough to take a breath!" I playfully tease.

"I can't help it!" Daisy giggles as she starts skipping ahead.

"Hey Missy, come back I want to ask you something." I call.

"Yeah?"

"Why do you call Rueben, Dad?" I ask casually as if it's an everyday normal question.

"Because he is my Dad, silly!" She smiles innocently.

"Oh! I see. So how do you know that?" I lightly press.

"Um, because he is Freddie's Dad and Freddie is my brother!" She says matter of fact.

I smile at her certainty and her love for everyone. Daisy is so easy going; she always has been. Even from a baby she was so well behaved, so laid back. One thing I adore is how much she literally loves everyone she meets. She's the sweetest kid and I couldn't feel prouder of her grown up little revelation she's having.

"Well then, that's lovely...and Rueben really loves you and is so happy that you think that way." I smile.

"I know that. Silly!" Daisy laughs as she playfully skips off again.

As she skips ahead, I pull out my phone and give Rueben a quick call.

"It's official. She says you're her Dad." I smile into the phone as he picks up after a few rings.

"Yeah I know and she's my daughter. Silly." Rueben says with a laugh and I can't help but roll my eyes at how they use the same words.

"Well OK." I laugh.

"Anyway, I've got to go I'm almost home and I have just seen my Mum pull into the driveway. I'll call you back." I say before hanging up the phone.

Daisy spots my Mums car and runs up to it excitedly.

"Nana!" She screams.

"She's a bit hyper!" I giggle as Mum gets out of her car.

"I thought she would be! I brought you a gingerbread man." Mum says as she passes Daisy a little paper bag from the bakery.

"Thanks Nana!"

"I didn't expect you today?" I breezily ask whilst opening the front door.

"Yeah, I wanted to speak to you about something." Mum says in a quiet but serious tone.

"Oh?"

"Yeah it's nothing that I want you to worry about as such but it's important." She says again firmly.

"OK, let me put Freddie down and I'll put the kettle on."

Daisy disappears off up into her bedroom to finish her list for Santa with her gingerbread man in hand and Freddie barely flinches as I move him from the pram into the bouncer.

"Tired boy." I hear Mum say to Freddie as I switch the kettle on in the kitchen and prepare our drinks.

In the short time it took me to make them Mum already looks a bit pale as she stares at me seriously.

"Do you want any biscuits with it?" I ask.

"No, no that's OK thank you." She says calmly.

I sip my tea awkwardly waiting for Mum to speak but she just sighs a little. It's like she's looking for the words.

"Oh, come on Mum, just tell me. You're not dying, are you?"

CHAPTER TWENTY-FIVE

"That was my JOKE guess!" I bellow sarcastically after Mum doesn't respond.

"No, no it's not quite like that…" Mum calmly begins.

"Do you remember how I said my kidneys weren't working like they were supposed to?"

"Yes. Vaguely." I nod.

"Well, last week the doctor told me that unfortunately I've reached stage five kidney disease, which means I need either a transplant or dialysis. Like now." Mum explains.

I pause for a moment and try to absorb the news.

"OK, well that's not bad, we can surely get you a kidney. Have mine!" I joke nervously.

"No, it's not that simple." Mum sighs.

"I had to have some assessments to see if I could cope with surgery, but apparently I'm too ill. I have that lung condition, diabetes, I'm anaemic…the list goes on. They won't operate on someone in bad health, Mollie."

"Oh." I respond trying to work out what that could mean. I think I know, but I'm scared to assume.

"So!" Mum interrupts my thoughts with a more chipper approach.

"I start dialysis next week and that's what I wanted to tell you. I need to have it three days a week in London, it takes three hours or so they told me and then there's travel time so I just needed you to understand why I might not be around very much."

"And the dialysis is going to keep you alive? And you'll be okay?" I ask with confusion and concern clear in my voice.

"Yes, I'll start the dialysis. There are some side effects I might have but ultimately, I think I'll feel better.

It's not what I would have wanted to be doing at fifty-five years old but I'm not ready to go just yet. I want to see my grandchildren grow up a little more…" Mums voice cracks and her eyes puff slightly.

"Well…let me know if you need anything, OK?" I answer trying to sound comforting.

"Of course! But I'll be fine. The doctors will look after me." Mum assures.

We spend the afternoon trying to find more lighter things to talk about but by the time my Mum leaves the topic is still weighing heavily on my mind. I sit on my phone trying to research kidney failure and educate myself. I read up on prognosis and mortality rates, survival rates, transplants and all sorts of information but nothing much helps me to better understand what is happening to Mum. I come to the conclusion that the outcome of kidney failure depends entirely on the individual and how well dialysis might work and there's no point me trying to guess what may happen in the future.

When Rueben gets home from work, I repeat to him everything my Mum told me, along with everything I researched, and he sits listening intently trying to take it all in. By the time I have finished explaining, Rueben has quite an optimistic approach. He tells me how well dialysis works for many people and that I shouldn't worry myself too much right now. He tells me he'll help where he can, and I really appreciate his support. We decide not to tell Daisy because it's far too much for her to understand and we really don't want to worry her. Mum is still quite young, I remind myself. Her chances of being able to remain on dialysis for the next ten years at least are strong.

"On a lighter note, I've bought home a gingerbread house I thought I could make with Daisy." Rueben suggests.

"Yes! She'll love that. Thank you." I say as I wrap my arms around his neck.

"I really love you."

My evening feels like something out of a Christmas movie. Rueben and Daisy get stuck into creating the gingerbread house and get into a lot of messy fun whilst trying to copy the picture on the box. I notice Daisy giggling as I spot her secretly shoving bits of gingerbread house into her mouth. No wonder they're having a hard time keeping it together, I think as I smile warmly watching on.

I make some festive hot chocolates for us all and even decide to change Freddie into one of his new Christmas sleepsuits. I choose a red one with little reindeers all over it and it's adorable. I take lots of pictures of him in it and as always, I send them on to my Dad, my Mum and Joy.

Before long it's getting late and I notice Daisy starting to yawn. I fix us a quick dinner of jacket potatoes with cheese and salad and when she's done eating Rueben takes Daisy up to bed and reads her a bedtime story.

I give Freddie his last bottle for the evening and settle him into his cot in our bedroom.

Back in the kitchen I clock some amaretto liqueur I was keeping back for Christmas Day and decide that I could really do a couple. I pour Rueben one too and leave it on the kitchen counter whilst I start cleaning up icing and bits of gingerbread off the dining room table.

"This is really shaping up to my favourite Christmas of all time and it's not even here yet." Rueben surprises me by saying as he reappears.

"Oh, really?" I question but I feel the same too.

"God yeah. This is the first time I feel included." He mumbles with sadness in his voice.

I pass him his amaretto and Diet Coke and head to the sofa, taking Rueben by the hand and pulling him along with me.

"Surely you must have had one good Christmas as a kid?" I ask curiously.

"Not really no, I was always forgotten about or Mum and Dave just spent the entire time arguing. I'll never forget this one year...actually don't worry." Rueben hesitates before shutting off completely.

"No come on, tell me. I'm all ears."

"Well this one year." Rueben continues cautiously.

"I was Daisy's age I think, about eight years old and I woke up really early on Christmas morning feeling very sick and hot. I must have had a bug or something I don't really know. As you know our bathroom is downstairs so I got out of bed to get downstairs as quickly as I could but before I managed to reach the stairs the sick just came and I couldn't stop it. I was sick all over the landing. Then I felt so scared about the mess I made, I just stood there sobbing."

"Oh Roo! You poor thing but it's not like being sick can be helped. Hardly something you should have worried about." I add honestly.

"You'd like to think so wouldn't you. But when Mum and Dave came out of their bedroom and saw the mess, they went mad. Started yelling at me and asking me how I could have been so stupid to not of gotten to the bathroom in time. Then they made me clean it. They said I had to fetch a bowl of water and soap and scrub the whole thing before I was allowed downstairs to open my presents with my sisters." He says hanging his head as if he has something to feel shame about.

"Jesus." I manage to mutter.

I have never had to clean up my own sick as a child. My Mum would always comfort me and then put me in the bath and bring me water to sip. She'd always clean up after me. I can't imagine a parent ever reacting differently from that."

"Well, you were lucky then." Rueben replies.

"So, if that's the worst Christmas Day you had, what did you mean about being forgotten about?"

"Oh, they started to stop buying me presents. So, it was boring really."

"What, like, nothing at all?"

"Yeah…it happened on birthdays too. One year on my birthday, again I was around Daisy's age. I got a pair of pyjamas and I was told that's all they could afford. I remember them like it was yesterday, they were Taz Mania pyjamas, I didn't even like Taz. It was like my Mum just picked up any old thing and it didn't matter to her whether I liked it or not. Then a month later it was my sisters' birthdays, their birthdays are three days apart and I remember them getting a huge gift bag each full of stuff. Clothes, C. D's, sweets, books, video games…loads. Lily even got a Walkman; I remember because I had asked Mum for one for months, but she said they were too expensive."

"No way." I add in shock.

"Yep. By the time it was Christmas the exact same thing happened, but I didn't even get pyjamas this time. The older we got it just became the norm. I'd roll out of bed to see that my sisters had a new pandora ring each, a new coat, boots, make up, always a perfume set each in there somewhere, earrings, DVD's and gift vouchers. If I ever asked Mum if anybody managed to buy me anything, she would just say that I was too difficult to buy for and it's not her fault. So, I stopped expecting anything." He shrugs glumly.

"But your Mum was here the other day and she asked you to buy her some Chanel perfume for Christmas?" I say appalled as I recall her asking.

"Oh yeah, she has always expected me to buy her stuff as soon as I started working. Never anything small or cheap either, she's always asked for perfumes which cost like eight or ninety pounds and more! Stupidly, most years I would actually buy it for her too. I think I just wanted her to actually acknowledge me at Christmas or something, I don't know. Sounds stupid when I say it out loud."

"No, it really doesn't Rueben. I can understand that. Sounds like you were just vying for your Mum's attention and love." I say gently.

"Maybe. But look, that's the past now. All I'm saying is that this Christmas is already the best I've ever had, and I have you to thank for that." He smiles adoringly.

"I'm so pleased." I smile back, feeling emotional at the sound of his gratefulness.

"Some of these stories are hard to hear. I know they all seemed normal and natural when you were growing up, but I know different."

"The older I'm getting and the longer I have been away from living under that roof…The more I'm starting to know different too." Rueben declares.

CHAPTER TWENTY-SIX

On Christmas Day morning and I'm awoken by a very hyperactive Daisy jumping on my bed.

"Santa's been! Santa's been!" Daisy squeals excitedly.

"How do you know?" I ask playfully.

"Because I saw his snowy footprints outside my door just now!" She declares and I smile to myself as I recall Reuben and I up late last night creating those footprints together with flour and glitter.

"What time is it?" Rueben groans.

"Five thirty a.m." I say.

"God. Are we really going to do this now?" He mumbles.

"Apparently so!" I laugh and I reluctantly pull myself from the bed and wrap a dressing down around me.

I scoop Freddie into my arms who is still sleeping and follow Daisy down the stairs. To my surprise Rueben got up pretty quick too and soon starts playing along and making a fuss of the snowy footprints and pretending he has no idea how they got there. All of course adding to Daisy's excitement.

We get comfortable on our sofa and watch Daisy's face light up as she discovers all the presents that Santa left for her.

"Thank you so much Mummy and Daddy! And Santa!" She screeches after opening each gift.

I pull Freddie up onto my lap and open his presents for him to see.

We didn't go mad this Christmas for Freddie as it's only his first and he's a bit oblivious to it all. So, we just got him a big teddy bear with *'my first Christmas'* written on it as a little keepsake and a jumperoo with lots of fun sensory things for him to play with.

Rueben proudly hands me a bag of presents and I'm more than grateful when I realise, he has bought all my favourites. Make up, Valentino perfume, a big fluffy scarf, a new purse, some pyjamas and a Jo Malone candle. He has tried so hard with these gifts, I'm so grateful but I'm also excited to surprise him with his hamper. I know he hasn't always felt very included or thought of at Christmas, so I hope my gift goes some way to change that.

"What's this?" Rueben gasps staring down at the huge hamper.

"Well, I know you said you have always wanted to go to America, so until we can all go, I decided to bring a little bit of America to you." I say proudly.

Rueben stares in awe at the hamper as he carefully studies all the items in it. There's a mixture of cereals and imported candy, crisps, root beers, Mountain Dew, Hershey's, Twinkie's, Milk duds, ranch sauce and all sorts for him to try. Also, I added a few pin badges from various teams in the NFL as I know he collects football badges in general anyway. I have also put in an American football to play with, a Patriots football jersey and new Nike trainers.

"Babe...wow. I'm speechless." Rueben stares up at me with a big smile.

"Don't be silly!" I laugh.

"It's not *that* much. But I thought you'd like it."

"Like it? I absolutely love it. I think this is the most anybody has ever done for me."

"Aww don't say that." I say a little sadly.

"It makes me think back to that horrible story you told me, and I don't want us to think about that today. Today is about giving you the best Christmas you've ever had."

"It already is." Rueben softly smiles and pulls me onto his lap for a tight cuddle.

I cuddle him tightly back and for the next half an hour and I don't move, instead I bask in this moment whilst I watch Daisy open her last few presents.

As per my usual traditions, I put the snowman on the television for the kids and start prepping dinner. Rueben sits in the front room putting together the Jumperoo so we can let Freddie try it out. I make Rueben and I a snowball and put on some Christmas music, kicking it off first with a bit of Wham. It's already shaping up to be a great day.

Thankfully, I manage to not have too many kitchen mishaps and my Christmas dinner looks pretty professional when I serve it up.

Daisy giggles as she pulls on her Christmas hat from her cracker and Rueben happily cradles Freddie with one arm whilst eating his dinner with the other.

"I can take him if you like?" I offer.

"No, honestly I'm OK. This is perfect. I'm eating a tasty dinner made by my beautiful girlfriend and I have my son contently in my arms. Then in a minute, me and my Daisy dots are going to make slime. I wouldn't change a thing. I only wish we didn't have to go out and see my Mum later." Rueben half jokes.

"I know but if we don't go, she'll only ring you forty-seven thousand times." I mock.

"OK, well let's just stay an hour or so. I really just want to spend my evening with you on the sofa watching Home Alone with a glass of Bailey's in hand." Rueben sighs.

"We will, I promise. Plus, I think we can only manage an hour or so anyway because Daisy looks shattered already!" I laugh.

"I guess that's what a five thirty a.m. start to the day will do for you!"

After dinner I make a start on the cleaning up and start loading up the dishwasher. Rueben wheels the jumperoo in and places Freddie in it for the first time. He has only just started to smile and adorably his face lights up at all the colours and noises the jumperoo makes. We get so many photos of him smiling, my phone must nearly be at capacity with the amount I take.

It's soon time to head to Joy's house and when we eventually arrive, she greets us all with a warm welcome.

As we walk into the front room, I notice Lily first, she's sat on the floor surrounded by gifts and bags.

"Hi Daisy!" She smiles cheerfully.

"Is that my little Fred's too? Auntie Lil wants a big cuddle off him in a minute!"

Daisy excitedly sits on the floor next to the Christmas tree.

"Have you had a good day then mate?" Joy asks Rueben as she sits back down on the sofa.

"Yeah it's been really nice."

"What have you been doing?" She asks again.

"Not a lot, the usual. We had a nice dinner and opened our presents and watched movies." He replies flatly.

"Whilst you two catch up can I get anyone a drink?" Dave politely interjects.

"Yeah please, just a Diet Coke if that's OK." I smile.

"No problem, I'll get Rueben a beer too and I'll get Daisy some blackcurrant."

"Can I fetch the kids their presents now?" Joy asks eagerly.

"Yeah of course." I smile and I get myself comfortable on the other sofa as Joy disappears off into the hallway. Daisy comes to sit next to me as she excitedly awaits her presents and Rueben sits at the other side of the room and feeds Freddie his bottle.

"I'm skint as always, so I'm afraid I didn't manage to get anyone anything." Lily laughs casually.

"Oh, that's OK, we understand. We got you something though." I say politely and hand Lily her gift.

"They're white gold." I add as Lily rips open the packaging and stares down at the pair of elegant earrings I picked out.

"Oh, thanks!" She smiles politely but sounds a little underwhelmed.

"Here we go!" Joy cheerfully announces as she reappears.

The gift bags she brings in are ridiculously huge. I literally think I could fit into one quite comfortably. The bags are full to the brim with presents too. I don't want to seem ungrateful, so I keep a smile painted on my face but inside I'm a little overwhelmed. This is a lot for a three-month-old baby and Daisy whose bedroom is only small. Daisy's face is quite the picture though as she's presented with her bag.

"Wow! Thank you!" She squeals.

"Do you see this Daddy!?"

"Yeah, I see it baby, lucky girl!" Rueben politely responds.

"Here you go Joy this bag is for you and Dave this one is for you." I say.

"Thank you." Dave mumbles in his usual monotone as he tucks his present down beside the sofa instead of opening it.

Joy tears into hers revealing a small canvas print of Daisy and Freddie that I had taken by a professional photographer, a pair of earrings and a set of bath salts.

"Oh lovely!" Joy smiles as she examines the canvas.

Silence fills the room as we sit, and watch Daisy open the rest of her presents and Joy begins opening Freddie's presents for him. She looks thrilled to be proudly showing him each present. I've been wondering all the way here whether she was going to buy something for Rueben this year, or for me just to be polite but any hope I had is quickly dissolving.

"Have you had a good day, Lily?" I ask.

"It's been alright, ain't done a lot. I got spoilt though thanks to Mother dearest." She gloats as she starts pulling out all her presents to show me.

"I got two boxsets of my favourite t.v shows, I got a new Superdry coat, a pair of Timberland's, some clothes, this Pandora bracelet, some chocolate, oh...my favourite Angel perfume too, a couple of pairs of pyjamas and this new dressing gown...I think that's everything."

I look up at Rueben and worry if this is reminding him of all the Christmas' he wanted to forget about. Sure enough, he is looking down at the floor looking insulted and hurt.

"Fucking joke." Rueben mumbles, as he passes Freddie to his Mum and storms out of the room and out to the back garden.

CHAPTER TWENTY-SEVEN

"I'd ask you if you're OK, but I think I know the answer." I say gently as I step out into the garden.

Rueben turns around abruptly to face to me and shakes his head in disbelief.

"What the fuck have I done?" He angrily asks.

"I don't know, Roo." I shrug.

"You know what, I was used to it to be honest. But then to watch you pass them gifts that you put thought into and for them not to even have the good sense or grace to buy you something…anything at all, it's embarrassing. I am embarrassed." He sighs.

"Maybe they just didn't think. They did spend a lot on the kids though…"

"Yeah and that's a joke as well. My whole life I had virtually nothing and then she completely spoils Freddie and Daisy in front of me. It's like a slap in the face. Don't get me wrong, I'm so pleased that she's made an effort for them but it's not fair. She's sitting there proudly presenting them with all these lovely gifts. Why couldn't she have been like that with me?" Rueben sighs, running his hands through his hair.

"I don't have all the answers Roo, maybe this is something you'll have to bring up with her." I suggest softly.

Rueben laughs and shakes his head.

"Mollie, she'll deny it. She'll deny every bit of it. She won't want anyone to know how she used to treat me. She has an image to obtain. She'd sooner people believed that I was some manic compulsive liar than for her to take any responsibility." He huffs.

"What do you want to do?"

"I want to go home. I mean it. I don't want to sit here anymore with Lily acting so spoiled and watching my Mum act so sweet. It's fake and I hate it." Rueben says.

"OK, let's go then. If that's what you want. But your Mum hasn't had much time with the kids so you might need to figure something out." I suggest, knowing full well how Joy might react if we just leave now without promising her something to keep her happy.

"OK, what about New Year's Eve? She mentioned to me on the phone that she wanted to take them to Crystal Palace Park in London sometime soon and for some lunch. Why don't I offer to drop them off here in the morning and then they can drop them off to us by about four in the afternoon when they're finished. That way when the kids arrive home, we can get them settled, bathed and in bed at a reasonable time and then you and I can see the New Year in together. Just us." Rueben smiles as he walks over to me and wraps his arms around my waist.

"There we go, problem solved. Check us out, all adult and stuff." I say, which makes Rueben laugh and loosen up a little before we begin to head back inside.

As we reappear back inside, we see Joy and Lily fussing over Freddie, bickering as usual over who gets to hold him. Daisy quietly plays in the corner on her own with her new toys Joy just gave her.

"OK Mum, I think we are going to head back now. I'm sorry but I have a huge migraine and I can't shake it." He tells her. We both know it's a lie and I can't help but feel some admiration towards him for still choosing to spare his Mum's feelings by making up an excuse instead of arguing with her.

"Oh." Joy stares up at us displeased.

"They haven't had a mince pie yet or some sweets."

I clock Lily rolling her eyes too with a sarcastic smirk as if she fully expected us to come with an excuse to leave.

"Well why don't you save them? Me and Mollie were thinking that perhaps you could have the kids for the day on New Year's Eve?" Rueben says and Joy's expression instantly changes from displeased to happy.

"Oh yes please. We're not doing anything are we Dave, we can have them can't we?" She says eagerly to Dave.

"Yeah that's fine. We'll take them to the Crystal Palace Park like you wanted too." Dave responds.

"I'll drop them off here early in the morning for you but if it's OK I need you to drop them off back at ours by four-ish if that's OK? As we have some plans."

"Yeah that's fine mate. Not a problem at all." Joy smiles in agreement.

"You sure? And you'll definitely be able to get back for four o'clock? Because I really need to settle them before it gets too late, I have some things to sort out."

"Yes mate. It's fine." Joy reassures again, this time a little restlessly as if she is offended by being told when to bring the kids back.

"OK, I was just making sure."

Once we've packed up all the gifts and said our polite goodbyes, I start to wonder about Irene. We are so close to her house and it is Christmas Day. I know I usually avoid it lately, but something tells me it would just be very impolite to drive past.

"I know you're supposed to have a migraine, but do you think it would be OK if we called into your Nan's?" I suggest as we start to drive away.

Rueben looks across to me a little surprised.

"Yeah baby, I think she'll love that. If you're sure?"

"Yeah definitely, come on let's go and call in." I smile.

I'm a little apprehensive as we turn into Irene's instead of going home but this time seems different. As soon as I walk through her front door I'm greeted with a warm smile from Irene and I feel somewhat relieved. I'm still unsure whether she wants me in her home though so I'm a little quiet and leave Rueben to do most the talking.

"Hiya, Nan." Rueben smiles as he bends down to give her a cuddle and a kiss on the cheek.

"You brought the kids to me! On Christmas!" Irene smiles joyfully as her face lights up.

I sit down in the same place again, on the little sofa next to Irene's armchair and keep a smile on my face at all times. Albeit a nervous smile.

I watch as Daisy gives her a cuddle before coming to sit next to me and Rueben places Freddie on Irene's lap.

"Phwoar!" Irene laughs.

"I think he has filled his nappy!"

"Uh oh!" Rueben laughs.

"Come here stinky and I'll change you."

"Where are you going to take him? upstairs?" Irene asks.

"Yeah, I'll go into the bathroom." Rueben says as he gathers Freddie's nappy bag and heads off upstairs.

We really should have thought this through, I think to myself. Leaving me with an elderly lady who made it quite clear last time how she feels is extremely awkward. You could probably now cut the tension with a knife. Thanks Rueben, no really thanks. By the time he gets back Irene will have my head on a stick. Her walking stick probably.

"Mollie?" Irene says and snaps me out of my kooky thoughts.

Oh god, this is it. She's going to scrutinise me again.

"Yes?" I answer nervously chewing at my bottom lip.

"I'm really sorry about before." She calmly says as she takes my hand and holds it in her palm.

"I get really fed up with Joy. She only ever comes down here to moan or rant about someone or something. It's been really getting to me. I have just had enough."

"Oh…" I say totally surprised.

"The family tell me that you really are lovely. I guess it's just Joy that didn't think so. She can be a bit funny." She continues.

"That's really OK. I'm just so happy you've said something, it's such a relief. Thank you, Irene." I smile gratefully at her.

"I'm too old for these arguments anyway." She laughs a little.

"As long as Rueben is happy then I'm happy."

Her entire demeanour towards me has definitely changed and now I can see the warmth in her Rueben must see. I couldn't be happier now that we chose to call in, it's really made my day.

When Reuben reappears with a much better smelling Freddie, he soon spots that Irene is holding my hand. His eyes light up as he realises the air has been cleared.

"Oh Nan, I'm made up!" He beams.

"Well when I'm wrong, I'm wrong. I don't mind admitting it. Unlike Joy." Irene tells him.

"I told you Mum was just causing trouble. But I'm so happy now that my two favourite people are on the same page." He smiles.

"Aren't I your favourite person?" Daisy queries Rueben with her hands on her hips and with a feisty stare.

"Yes of course you're my favourite person! You're number one!" He replies grinning and we all can't help but chuckle at Daisy's sass.

CHAPTER TWENTY-EIGHT

I can't believe it's nearly five o'clock in the morning and I haven't managed to settle Freddie once. I'm feeling more and more anxious with each time he cries. I haven't been able to get him to keep any milk down now and I have tried all the remedies our family doctor recommended, from gripe water to colic syrups but nothing is working. To top it off he has been developing a rash all over his chest and it's looking so sore. My poor little mite.

"Shall we take him in?" Rueben worries.

"I think so. Let's wake Daisy up and go, I can't wait any longer. I'm worried sick." I sigh.

I pack a quick bag for the accident and emergency room whilst trying to wake a sleepy Daisy. I put on a big coat around her and get them both into the car.

The drive up to the hospital is an anxious one, Freddie screams most of the way from the car seat and nothing I do seems to offer him much comfort. Rueben gets us to the hospital as quickly as he can, and I feel somewhat relieved as soon we arrive and see that the waiting room is fairly quiet. Hopefully Freddie will be seen very soon.

I pace around the waiting room with Freddie in my arms as I try to keep him as content as possible. It's approaching six o'clock in the morning now and usually I'd be giving him his feed, but I still can't get him to keep anything down.

Daisy is being so good; she's brought her Harry Potter book with her to keep her occupied and hasn't once moaned about me dragging her out of bed so early.

"Master Freddie Adams?" A nurse calls.

"Thank god." Rueben and I say in unison.

The nurse carefully checks Freddie over, reading his oxygen levels and temperature. She assures us that all his levels appear quite normal, but she has some concerns over his rash, so she is going to put him as high priority for the doctor to come down urgently and start some blood tests. We get shown to a private room with a bed so that we can try and make Freddie more comfortable.

Rueben sighs and paces a lot as he grows more anxious with the passing time. Thankfully the room is equipped with some sensory items for babies and so we manage to distract Freddie long enough to stop crying.

"Hi love. Are we still OK to have the kids tomorrow?" – Joy

"Your Mum has just text." I tell Rueben.

"She wants to know whether she can still have the kid's tomorrow night. What shall I say?"

"Just leave it for now. We'll have to wait and see what happens." Rueben anxiously replies.

A doctor comes in with a nurse and they start checking over Freddie straight away, carefully studying his rash. The nurse takes a blood test from his foot which causes Freddie to scream in distress and sends mine and Rueben's anxiety through the roof as we try to comfort him.

"So how long has this been happening for?" The doctor asks us.

"I'd say about two weeks on and off and the family doctor just said it was probably bad reflux. But the past few days it's gotten unbear-able." Rueben explains.

"And are there any other symptoms you've noticed?"

"Yes, there's also been…" Rueben pauses as his phone loudly starts ringing over their conversation. He fumbles quickly to silence the phone.

"Sorry, as I was saying, he has also been quite constipated too."

My phone then starts ringing loudly and I quickly search through my bag to turn it off. Noticing first that I see Joy's name flashing up on my screen.

"OK, I'm going to put a rush on the blood tests and have a look at what's going on." The doctor informs as Rueben's phone starts ringing again.

"Thank you." I say whilst Rueben answers his phone.

"Yes?"

"Well am I have the kids or not?" Joy asks forcefully.

"Mum, just because Mollie couldn't text you back straight away doesn't mean you need to stress and badger us. We're busy." Rueben says as he chews anxiously on the skin around his fingernails.

"Doing what?" She asks abruptly.

I really don't care for Joy's tone sometimes. When it comes to the kids, she can very easily change her mood. It always feels like we need to walk on eggshells to avoid conflict.

"Well Freddie isn't well." Rueben sighs.

"He has a rash, he's been sick, he cries all the time and we can't settle him no matter what we do."

"It's probably colic." She declares as if it's obvious.

"Well we are waiting for the results with the doctor now, so we'll see what they think soon. I'll phone you when we know something!" He snaps. His tiredness and anxiety making him much less patient.

The next hour goes by a little easier and Freddie manages to fall asleep. I'm relieved he is out of discomfort for a little while. Joy has phoned Rueben another seven times since they last spoke, but he hasn't answered them. Anxieties are still quite high as Rueben grows more agitated with every call Joy makes.

"Hi Mollie. I've tried calling Rueben but no luck. Could you let me know how my grandson is getting on please x"

"Your Mum text again..." I say.

"She's relentless." Rueben sighs.

"I said I'd call her as soon as I knew anything."

"She's probably just worried." I respond trying to ease some of the stresses.

Thankfully we aren't kept too much longer as the Doctor arrives with some results in hand.

"OK, so I think we are dealing with a slight allergy coupled with some severe reflux. I'm going to write you a prescription for some specific milk which will help the issue. The powder will require a lot less water added to it as it's designed to be thicker, this way when he drinks the milk it should stay down a little better. I'm also prescribing you some medicine for the reflux. There's two sachets that you'll need to put in with each feed to keep him comfortable." He explains.

"Thank you so much, that's such a relief." I say.

"Please remember to follow the instructions exactly with the milk, it's important to make sure it is made correctly. Hopefully this will work, and we won't need to see him back here. If it doesn't work and he continues to be sick we will need to see him again as we really do not want him to lose any weight." The doctor firmly informs.

"Absolutely." I say.

"Thank you again."

"He should start feeling better within a few hours once he has had a feed with the new milk and the medicine. You should see some changes straight away." He smiles once again before shaking Rueben's hand and leaving the room.

"Thank god!" I smile to Rueben.

"I'll go to the pharmacy with Freddie's prescription, you give your Mum a call and let her know everything is fine and then let's get out of here. I'm absolutely shattered."

Sure enough, the doctor was absolutely right, and I am so grateful that it's now eight o'clock in the evening and Freddie is settled and sound asleep in bed.

"The doctor was definitely right about the thickness." Rueben laughs as he washes out Freddie's bottles.

"I know, it looks more like cream! But for the first time in days our son is content so I couldn't be happier." I say.

"What do you want to do about tomorrow then? As you know Mum will only start calling me again soon." He says rolling his eyes.

"I don't know. I'm nervous. Do you think it'll be OK?"

"Well the milk and medicine *have* done the trick. Plus, it's only going to be for a few hours or so tomorrow and the fresh air will definitely do them good."

"Will your Mum be able to keep on top of everything though?"

"I'll explain everything to her on the phone and then I'll even write it all down and give it to her tomorrow just so she doesn't forget." Rueben reassures.

"OK and maybe just politely remind her to be back by four and then we can make sure he gets settled again, like tonight." I say.

CHAPTER TWENTY-NINE

I wake up to the house so quiet you could hear a pin drop. Confused, I reach over to my bedside table to grab my phone and see that I have got two text messages. The first one is Lana.

"In case the phone lines are majorly busy tonight I just wanted to wish you a happy new year!! Give my love to Rueben and the kids! L xx"

I smile as I send a quick text back wishing her the same. The second text is from Rueben.

"Hey baby, I wanted to let you have a lay in this morning, so I got up to take the kids over to Mums now. Love you. Xx"

I smile at his thoughtfulness, I wondered why it was so quiet. I check my phone for the time and sure enough it's nearly eleven a.m., I can't believe how long I have slept for, but I know I must have needed it. I decide today I'm going to make an effort. It's the first full day we've had child free for such a long time. It's a special night tonight what with it being New Year's Eve and I definitely want to look good for Rueben. It's time to ditch the dressing gown and pick out a nice outfit. I start by jumping straight in the shower and washing my hair, followed by shaving my legs and trying out a new face mask. I'm already starting to feel so much better.

I decide to opt for black skinny jeans with my Gucci belt and a cream coloured off the shoulder fluffy jumper. I run the curlers through my hair once it's dried and add a little cream head band to match. I apply my make up using some of the new pieces Rueben got me for Christmas and I finish with a few sprays of my Angel perfume. I smile at the reflection in the mirror for a split second. It's refreshing not to just have my usual ponytail, leggings and baggy cardigan on. I actually feel quite attractive.

I'm excited to hear Rueben pull into the driveway as I come downstairs for a cup of tea.

"Well, Good morning." Rueben smiles.

"Did you explain the milk and medicine situation again to your Mum? Did you write it all down for her too?"

"Good morning to you too Rueben! Oh, and thanks for the lay in." Rueben mocks me.

"Sorry!" I laugh.

"I'm just a little anxious. Was everything OK?"

"Everything was fine." Rueben reassures with a smile.

"I explained everything to Mum, and she said she understood but she'd call us anyway if she has any questions."

"OK, that's good then." I exhale, a little relieved.

"You look amazing by the way." Rueben stares looking me up and down.

"I feel it. Thank you for the lay in, I do really appreciate it." I say as I pull him in close for a kiss.

"Well I thought today we could go for a pub lunch; you know the one down by the lake? I reserved a table there on the outside balcony overlooking the water. They've got those outside heated lamps so shouldn't be too cold."

"Oh my god, Roo…that sounds amazing! Literally my perfect idea of a chilled New Year's Eve." I smile.

"Mine too. I then thought we'd come home, and you could play a game with Daisy whilst I keep Freddie entertained. Then we'll give them a bath and get them to bed. And finally, I plan to give you copious amounts of wine whilst watching trash t.v and watching the New Year come in." He smiles.

"Perfect!" I giggle.

"Shall we go to the pub now?"

"Yeah why not, I booked the table for one o'clock anyway so we could sit at the bar for a drink whilst we wait?"

"You had me at bar!" I joke.

"Let's go!"

I can't get over how beautiful this pub is as we turn into the large driveway. It sits up quite high on a slight mount, so you have to climb a few steps to get up there but once you do it's stunning. There's a huge balcony that wraps around the pub with tables and chairs all around the back overlooking the lake. It's so picturesque that I immediately snap up the opportunity to use this moment to get a new photo of me and Rueben together. A nice waiter takes the photo for us with the beautiful lake as our backdrop.

"What would you like?" Rueben asks as we head into the bar.

"I think I'll have a glass of Rosé please." I smile.

"A Rosé and a pint of Guinness please." Rueben asks the bartender.

The inside of the pub is just so beautiful, so much exposed brick but with candles everywhere and a huge fireplace, it has the cosiest feel.

I start telling Rueben about how Guinness reminds me of my Grandad because he was from Belfast in Ireland and I joke about how the family could barely understand what he was saying half the time because of his thick accent. Rueben tells me a little bit about his Grandad who passed away a few years ago and how his Mum ended up being at the centre point of all the drama from that too. He tells me how his Grandad left a significant amount of cash under his bed for his Nan to have but when they went to retrieve it the whole lot had been stolen.

"Oh my god. Who do you think did it?" I ask.

"My Nan will tell you it was my Mum. In fact, the whole family will you it was Mum who stole it." He rolls his eyes.

"Really? How do they know?"

"Because she's obsessed with money and she always steal if she thinks she can get away with it. Plus, the fact that she had a new three-piece suit and a brand-new fridge freezer delivered a few weeks after it went missing was a bit of a giveaway."

"No way!" I gasp.

"Sometimes these stories sound like a soap opera."

"Tell me about it! Nan was absolutely crushed though."

"I can imagine, did anyone confront your Mum?" I ask.

"Nan did, a lot. She often demanded Mum give it back. But typically, Mum just denies, denies, denies! The thing is, Mum was unemployed when that suite and fridge freezer came, it was so obvious it was ridiculous." He shakes his head bemused.

"Yeah, I notice your Mum goes through a lot of jobs. What's that about?"

"She's probably had about twenty jobs since I was a kid. It always ends the same, she always ends up suspended or fired and if you ask her why she'll always blame a colleague or claim she had a horrible manager and was treated unfairly. Although these days she pretends she's hurt her back or her foot and act like she's too unfit to work. It's always the same." He says laughing with his head in his hands.

"Your table is ready." A waiter interrupts.

"Oh yay! Thank you!" I say and I follow the waiter to our table.

Our table is beautiful, it has red roses as centrepieces and half a dozen tea light candles. We both order the same, a beef dinner with all the vegetables. The food is divine, I can't think how I had never heard of this place before. I keep thanking Rueben for this wonderful day and he just keeps smiling back at me.

"It's so beautiful, Roo." I say staring out onto the lake.

"I'm glad you like it; we should come back again sometime."

"Definitely. I could stare at the view for ages."

"Did you see the baby ducklings over in that corner?" Rueben asks.

"No? Where?"

"Right over there, you might have to turn right round to look… can you see them?" Rueben asks again whilst I turn right round in my seat trying to get a better view.

"No? I can't see them anywhere. I bet they were so cute." I say still trying to find them.

"They must have gone." Rueben responds calmly.

"Mollie…"

"Yeah?" I ask as I turn back around in my seat.

Oh my god. Is he…? Is this actually happening? Rueben is perched down on one knee with a dark blue box in hand and a gorgeous white gold ring on display. It has a stunningly elegant oval shaped diamond. It's beautiful. My jaw drops open and I bring my hands up to my cheeks in shock as Rueben stares up at me nervously.

"Mollie, will you marry me?"

CHAPTER THIRTY

"YES!" I squeal.

"A million times yes!"

Rueben takes the ring out of the box and carefully places it on my ring finger. It's stunningly beautiful. I rotate my hand around slightly to see it catch the light.

Rueben leans up for a kiss and I wrap my arms around his neck. I honestly had no idea. We had never really discussed marriage although after Freddie was born, I knew this was it. This is the man I want to spend my entire life with. This is my family and the four of us together are complete.

"Does it fit?" Rueben asks.

"Yes! It does, very comfortably. Thank you so much. I love it." I reassure with the biggest smile on my face.

"That's not all. I asked the chef to make your favourite. White chocolate covered strawberries. He's preparing them now, I thought we could go home and save them for our New Year's countdown with champagne?" Rueben smiles.

"Wow, you've really thought of everything. I don't think I could have ever of said no. Not to white chocolate covered strawberries anyway." I giggle.

"I thought you hated champagne?"

"I do. But isn't that what you drink on special occasions?" Rueben laughs with me.

When we arrive home it's nearly four o'clock. Rueben and I have been wedding planning the whole car journey home. I'm so excited I can't help but imagine Daisy's flower girl dress and Freddie's little suit. I ponder over whether I'd have a big princess style dress or a fishtail shape. Rueben jokes about whether he can get away with just wearing shorts because he wants to be comfortable and I playfully swat at his attempt to tease.

"Where would you want to get married?" Rueben asks curiously.

"I have no idea really, it's such a big decision. I don't really like huge manor houses or old-fashioned churches. I find them a bit daunting." I reply.

"Thank god you said that because they're really not my cup of tea either." Rueben smiles with relief on his face.

"And also, I've never understood why people spend twenty thousand pounds on one day. You could do something so much more with all that money. Create so much more than one day."

"I agree with that too! I've always thought that a place you choose to get married should mean something to you, it should be your happy place."

"Where's your happy place?" Rueben asks.

"Well…it's not in England unfortunately. It's Florida." I say smiling.

"Really?"

"Yeah. I had the best holidays there when I was a kid. There's so much more there beyond the theme parks. It has some of the best beaches in the world. It's beyond beautiful. Not to mention the fact it's probably cheaper than getting married here!" I tell Rueben, who notices my voice growing with excitement.

"Shall we get the laptop on and actually look into that? I wouldn't mind getting married in Florida to be honest…it will finally mean I get to go to America!" Rueben points out as he smiles enthusiastically.

"Out of interest you should call the country pub we were at and see how much it costs to host a wedding and I'll do some investigating into Florida and see which works out better?" I challenge.

Within twenty minutes Rueben and I are totally engrossed in research. Going between our phones and the laptop we work away quickly trying to find out what type of wedding would best suit us.

135

"OK, well I've phoned the pub and they're more expensive than I thought. Their starting rates are six thousand pounds for just the venue. Then I'm assuming food, music, decor, your dress and everything else could be around twelve thousand pounds in total." Rueben tells me.

"Wow that's so much for one day. Well I've been more successful. I can get a villa and flights for us all for three thousand, a hotel venue on the beach with food on a weekday will take that up to just over four thousand! It's a lot cheaper. Plus, we could even save more money and take the kids to Disney. I would much rather have a two-week holiday than one day. Don't you think?" I smile.

"God yeah! Imagine all the memories we could make. We'll just invite very close friends and family. We'll have a very chilled ceremony down by the beach. We can make it beautiful but still have a holiday! Can you imagine the kids' faces?"

"They would love it! We should probably wait until Freddie is a little bit older though. He won't enjoy it much now." I decide.

"You're right. What about next May? Freddie will be eighteen months old by then. He'll enjoy it a bit more. Plus, if we really love it, we can always go again another time." Rueben winks with a smile.

"I like your thinking. It gives us just over a year to plan and save and give everyone else a chance to save and book their flights and accommodation. We should do it. I'm going to love this planning! I'm half tempted to send out save the dates now!" I laugh excitedly.

I turn back to the laptop to start browsing through different invite styles and colour schemes. I really need to pace myself otherwise I'll have this whole thing booked and planned within a week, but I just can't help myself. The excitement has fully kicked in and so many thoughts of our wedding buzz around my brain.

"Wait, what's the time?" I ask Rueben, suddenly aware that all the excitement has distracted me from the fact the kids should be home by now.

"Oh, It's quarter to five." Rueben responds a bit disgruntled.

"Really? They knew not to be late. Do you think there's been traffic?"

"I'm not sure, I'll call them now." Rueben says as he runs his hands through his hair.

I start putting the laptop away and decide the plans will have to be put on hold for now. I wait anxiously for Rueben to find out where they've got too.

"Both their phones are off." Rueben reports with a sigh.

"What? You're joking? Do they often turn their phones off?" I ask as anxiety kicks in.

"Well not usually. Dave is quite forgetful when it comes to charging up his phone. So, there's a chance his has run out of battery. But Mum is always on her phone and it never leaves her side. I'm not sure why hers isn't ringing…"

"I'll try her phone." I suggest as I fumble to find my phone from my bag, and I start calling Joy.

The line doesn't connect, and I suddenly feel so frustrated.

I look up at Rueben and shake my head to show it's still off. I know he's trying not to panic too much because he doesn't want to worry me more, but I can see the concern building on his face.

"It's probably traffic. It's New Year's Eve after all, people are rushing around. It's probably mayhem out there." Rueben calmly says.

Although I know he is just trying to reassure me. He makes a good point. It *is* New Year's Eve after all. The traffic is probably a lot busier than usual and Joy and Dave may not have realised that when they chose to leave Crystal Palace Park.

"OK, well I'll put the kettle on, and we'll have a tea or something." I suggest and I walk off into the kitchen.

Rueben continues to try his Mums phone every ten minutes but still no luck. Both phones are still switched off. As I get to the bottom of my cup of tea, I start becoming restless. It's half past five. They're an hour and a half later than they promised. I start googling the local traffic news but just grow more concerned when there doesn't seem to be any accidents or traffic or anything that could hold them up for this long.

"I'll ring Lily and ask if she's heard from them." Rueben says as he paces around the room.

I sit in the chair staring at the clock and I jiggle my leg with nerves. I have butterflies in my stomach, I feel clammy and my heart is racing a little bit. I hate this. I really hate this. I tried to stay calm but the more the minutes tick by the more I can feel myself freaking out. Did they have an accident? Are they lost? Did one of them hurt themselves?

"Lily hasn't heard from them at all today." Rueben sighs as he hangs up the phone.

"Great. Just great." I whine.

Much to my dismay, the next time I allow myself to check the clock it's quarter past six.

"Jesus Christ. Where the *hell* are, they?" I say as I begin to sob.

"Baby please won't cry." Rueben comforts me as he kneels down beside me.

"I'm going to go mad at Mum when she finally gets here! She's ruined our perfect day."

"But Roo, what if they're hurt?" I sob.

"I'm getting so scared."

I walk out the room to give my Mum a call. She barely has a chance to speak when I'm already sobbing heavily down the phone. I tell her how scared I am that something bad has happened. I tell her how Rueben asked her a million times to be back by four and how Dave promised us he would be back on time.

I can't even tell her about the engagement. None of that matters right now, I just want my kids' home and safe. Mum manages to calm me down a little bit, but she feels quite strongly that we should call the police. I look back up at the clock and see it's twenty to seven in the evening. They should be getting ready for their bath before bed. Enough is enough. I tell Mum I'll call them now and keep her updated. I'm shaking as a hang up the phone.

"Can we call the police now?" I croak.

"It's been nearly three hours."

"Ok...Ok. I'll call now." Rueben tries to say calmly but I see he is just as worried as I am now.

Where are my babies?

CHAPTER THIRTY-ONE

"Wait!" I shout at Rueben.

I see headlights coming up the driveway. This could be them. Finally.

Rueben ends the call to the police and peers out the window with me.

"It's them!" He says with a mixture of shock and relief in this voice. Although the relief quickly fades and instead is replaced with anger. His face is growing red as he watches Joy casually get out of the car without a care in the world.

"Where the *hell* have you been?" He barks at Joy as I swing open the front door and rush to Daisy. I fall on my knees and wrap my arms around her so tightly.

"Thank god!" I cry as I nestle my face into her hair.

I don't think Daisy has any clue why I'm so upset right now, she smiles and hugs me back sweetly but ultimately, she looks oblivious.

Rueben picks up Freddie out of his car seat who is wailing and looking distressed.

"Go to your room sweetheart and get ready for bed. I'll be up in a minute." I tell Daisy.

The tension is thick in the room and I don't want Daisy to witness any arguing. She does as she's asked and waves goodbye to Joy and Dave. I can barely bring myself to look at Joy. She's tutting at our reactions as if this is one huge over reaction. As a Mother she should understand what we've been put through these past few hours.

"Oh, Roo!" Joy huffs irritability.

"We were having fun and time just got away from us."

"But I said to you FOUR O'CLOCK. It's now SEVEN! How can you think that I wouldn't worry? Why didn't you call?" Rueben sighs.

"My phone died." Joy huffs again, this time looking flustered and staring at Dave for support.

"They were perfectly safe. They're with their Grandma." Dave sternly adds.

"I don't care if they're with Mother Theresa!" I blurt.

"Do you have any idea how much worry goes through a parents mind when you don't know where your children are and how to get a hold of them?"

"Mum can you not see where Mollie is coming from? I was about to call the police!" Rueben snaps. He pauses and waits for his Mum to apologise. But nothing.

Joy barely makes eye contact with me; her eyes are wild though. She looks angry. The more we make our point and tell her how worried we've been, the more she seems to get flustered and irritable. What does she have to be annoyed about? I feel my cheeks burning red and I notice I'm trembling as my adrenaline is rushing through my body. She isn't even trying to understand us or apologise. She's looking at us as if she's done nothing wrong. She keeps catching Dave's eye and then pulling a face as if she's being victimised.

"I wasn't going to say anything." Dave raises his voice.

"But we were late because Freddie hasn't been himself, you should go to a better hospital in future and see a better doctor because that idiot that gave you that thick milk and medicine is clueless. That stuff isn't right for a baby! Your Mum changed the dose, so it was actually drinkable. He actually managed to settle for a little while, so you should be thanking her!"

"You did, *what?*" Rueben hisses furiously.

"I know what *I'm* doing. I have had three children." Joy responds defensively.

I feel so much anger bubbling away from the pit of my stomach as he smugly and so very arrogantly announces that they know better than a doctor. So much so that they felt it was totally appropriate to change my sons' dose, something the doctor warned me I must be careful of. How could they be so ignorant? So careless? So damn right delusional and cavalier.

"And I'm sorry if it's not good enough, but I really don't think a baby should be having so much medicine in their milk. So instead of two sachets we only used one and he was fine all afternoon." He adds continuing his arrogant tone.

"Fine? Look at him now!" Rueben shrieks.

"Don't raise your *fucking* voice at me! You need to go back to a different hospital and get better help, that's not us that's done that!" Dave shouts over Rueben.

"I don't shout in your house, so don't shout in mine in front of my kids!" Rueben says, seemingly trying to take a calmer but firm approach.

Joy continues to not say much but huffs and shifts around restlessly.

How can someone who has so much to say on a phone or in a voicemail lose her tongue now?

"He was settled all last night. The milk is designed to be thick, so it stays down and stops causing him discomfort. You've essentially given my son a tiny bit of milk and hot water. He's probably starving and uncomfortable." I try to explain calmly despite my disbelief of even having to have this conversation.

"Also, the sachets were for pain management."

Neither Dave or Joy seem remotely interested at what I've said or believe I know best. Now I know how Rueben feels with those phone calls and horrible voice messages. There's no respect given, ever. It's just being constantly treated like an incoherent child.

Rueben snaps at Joy about not being able to trust her with his kids which causes Dave to jump to her defence and start swearing and shouting louder than ever. Freddie's wailing and screaming adds to the tension, everyone is having to shout over him if they want to say something and at one point so many voices are raised at once that none of us are being heard. I decide to take a step back with Freddie, take him away from the shouting and calm him down. I try to take his snowsuit off him but before I barely undo the zip, he projectile vomits everywhere. Then vomits again.

"The doctor warned us this could happen." I panic as I stare at my pale baby boy with vomit doused all in his clothing.

"We should take him to the hospital again." Rueben suggests as he grabs Freddie's bag and starts preparing it to leave.

"I think you're right." I croak. What a day this is shaping up to be. It started out being one of the best days of my life and now it's one of the most stressful days I've ever had. I feel sick, shaky, tired and mostly just so worried about Freddie. I wish I could take his pain away.

"We can look after Daisy for you while you go?" Joy offers casually.

"I think you've done enough." Rueben hisses.

CHAPTER THIRTY-TWO

We're back in the same room with Freddie as we were last time. Rueben managed to settle him by getting him into some fresh pyjamas and rocking him gently by the window. Daisy is being as good as gold for us and is sat quietly reading her Harry Potter book. I feel so guilty though that we aren't at home and I'm unable to spend a bit of quality time with her before bed.

The one good silver lining is that we've both managed to calm down. The drive here allowed us a breather and now we are too busy concentrating on Freddie that we've managed to push most of it to the back of our minds. That is until we have to keep repeating to a doctor or a nurse that a family member *accidentally* messed up his dose causing him to vomit violently and that's why we are back.

"Are you OK?" I quietly ask Rueben as I notice Freddie is slowly drifting off to sleep in his arms.

"It's my family that did this, I should be asking you if you're OK...." Rueben answers and drops his head down in guilt.

"Roo, you've nothing to feel guilty about. You're a fantastic Dad. What they did isn't your fault. I just...I just can't believe how arrogant they are. How stubborn..." I sigh.

"And what was all that stuff about going to this hospital?"

"Eurgh." Rueben sighs heavily as if I've just asked the most annoying question.

"One of their friends had a bad experience here ten years ago so now they've decided this is a dodgy hospital and they'll only go to the London hospital, forty-five minutes away! They're just weird like that, they do it with everything. They only see one doctor at their surgery, that's the only one they believe is good and if she goes on holiday for two weeks, they'd rather wait with their problem than see a different doctor!"

"Really?" I question trying to understand if that's more arrogance on their part because they always seem to know best or whether that's paranoia.

"Absolutely. They'd have judged us for taking him here in the first place. Like really judge us as if we are negligent and stupid. As if this is some kind of circus and not a hospital."

"Wow. They really really are set in their ways!" I say.

"That's because they know best!" Rueben sarcastically laughs.

The nurse pops her head round the door with a freshly made bottle using the prescription milk again with the correct dose.

"The doctor wants to see if you could try and feed Freddie this formula and see if he manages to keep it down again?" She smiles.

"Sure, thank you so much." I smile back and take the bottle. It will be a relief if Freddie manages to feed again and settles back down. Maybe we could even get home by midnight. At least, I hope.

I pass Rueben the bottle and he coaxes Freddie with it a little until he wakes up enough to start drinking.

"Come on little man, get some food in you and keep it down please." Rueben soothes.

I decide to take Daisy for a walk to the cafeteria whilst Rueben feeds Freddie. She deserves some kind of treat for sitting here bored again and I haven't eaten anything since the pub at lunch time and my stomach is beginning to growl.

"How about a hot chocolate and a muffin?" I offer Daisy as we reach the cafeteria.

"Yes please! That sounds yummy!" Daisy responds excitedly.

I decide to get myself a hot chocolate too and Rueben a coffee. He's probably hungry by now as well so I choose a cheese and ham panini for us both and order them to take away.

"Mum?" Daisy calls as we collect our food and head back to Freddie's room.

"Yeah?"

"Grandma Joy didn't play with me much today...and she got a bit bossy with me." She grumbles.

"Really? How so?" I ask curiously.

"Well she just doesn't let me play with Freddie. She tells me to get off him and sit down. She *always* holds Freddie too and never puts him down again. She says she's too busy to play with me now." Daisy shrugs a little sad.

My mind immediately goes to anger. I'm starting to know Joy; I know how obsessive she can be towards Freddie and it wouldn't surprise me at all if Daisy is taking a back seat because of that. But I try and look at things diplomatically. It was her first full day with Freddie out on their own, maybe her excitement took over and she was a little... consumed.

"Sometimes Freddie takes up a lot of our time because he is quite new and needs a lot of attention. Babies are hard work. Maybe Grandma didn't mean to sweetheart and I'm sure she wouldn't have wanted to upset you." I reassure.

"But if you keep feeling that way, just let me know again, OK?"

"OK Mummy." Daisy smiles and sips her cup of hot chocolate.

When we return back to the room Freddie has managed to finish a whole bottle and is fast sleep. I'm not too surprised though as it's gone half past ten now. Daisy is yawning her little head off but still managing to read her book and being so well behaved. Rueben gratefully tucks into his panini, clearly as hungry as I was.

"Everything OK?" I ask Rueben, noticing his sombre mood.

"Yeah, I guess so. I'm just not looking forward to Mum's phone calls in two days." He heavily sighs.

"Two days, that's oddly specific?"

"Because that's when Dave will be back at work so that's when she will call me. Trust me. She'll have a lot to say, she just didn't want to say it tonight in front of you and Dave. Especially because she likes to be the victim in front of Dave. I just hate it I know it sounds pathetic."

"It's not pathetic. If you're feeling any type of way about this, I want to hear it. I'm always here for you. Nothing is pathetic to me. It never will be." I assure as best I can.

"It just puts me on edge." Rueben mutters.

"It always has. It's like I can't ever relax because I don't know when she's going to do something, like call my work again, or leave me abusive messages, or call me a hundred times making me feel completely suffocated until I feel like I can't catch my breath. Sometimes I really hate the way she makes me feel."

"I'm so sorry you feel like that, Roo." I whisper with a lump in my throat.

The doctor interrupts our little moment as he comes in with some more medicines and notes for Freddie. But I'm filled with hope that this means we can go home.

"I feel quite happy that Freddie has managed to keep his milk down again, so I do feel like it was just the changes of his milk that caused his upset stomach again." He informs whilst he gently feels around Freddie's stomach.

"That's a relief, thank you." I respond although I feel let down by the confirmation that Joy's fussing and arrogance of supposedly knowing better has led us back here.

"Just be really careful at making sure you stick to the correct measurements for the next four weeks so that Freddie continues to maintain a good weight." The doctor instructs in a warm manner.

He is very polite about the whole thing, but I do feel a little awkward and embarrassed. We are his parents and yet it looks as though we couldn't follow simple instructions for our son. I smile and nod as I take the new prescription but inside, I can't wait to get out of here.

"Thank you again, Happy new year." Rueben says as he starts to gather up our belongings to leave.

By the time we pull into the driveway, Daisy has fallen asleep in the car and Rueben gently carries her up to bed whilst I settle Freddie into his cot for the night.

I catch my reflection in my bedroom mirror and I definitely do not look as good as I did this morning when we were headed off to the pub. My skin looks tired and puffy. I grab a wipe and remove all my make-up, throw my hair up into a ponytail and welcome back my dressing gown.

When I get downstairs Rueben is placing down the white chocolate strawberries onto the coffee table in the front room and pouring me a flute of champagne. The TV is switched on to show Big Ben ticking down to midnight and Rueben quickly passes me my champagne and takes my hand into his.

"Five, four, three, two, one…Happy new year, baby." He smiles and kisses my lips softly.

CHAPTER THIRTY-THREE

Unsurprisingly, Daisy slept until just past ten a.m., but I really don't blame her. It was a really late night for her last night. Freddie settled well through the night and has woken up with a few smiles this morning which makes me feel so happy and relaxed now I know he isn't crying in discomfort anymore. We have all woken up fairly happy this morning and I realise the stresses of yesterday have seemingly evaporated from our home.

So far, our New Year's Day is very relaxed but fun. When we got up this morning we mostly lounged around on the sofa and watched The Labyrinth. I put it on for Daisy and told her it was my favourite movie as a child, and she was glued.

Daisy's now been busy playing with her new glitter pens that she got for Christmas and Rueben has been helping me clean up the house a little and prep the dinner. My Mum's coming over for dinner this afternoon and I'm looking forward to the catch up, although I'm slightly worried, she's going to have a few things to say about Joy.

"How about May 8th next year?" Rueben looks up and asks whilst he peels the potatoes.

"Sorry?" I say confused.

"That's the wedding date. We should design our save the dates today and get them ordered so we can send them out. I think that's how we should start the new year." Rueben smiles.

"I love that idea!" I say squealing with excitement.

"OK, tonight when we've all finished with dinner, we can get comfy and design our save the dates!"

As I begin prepping the ham for the slow cooker my phone starts ringing from the counter.

I glance down and see its Mum calling.

"Hey Mum." I say.

"Mol…" Mum croaks.

"Listen, I can't come for dinner. The nurses at dialysis were worried about my oxygen levels so they've sent me to hospital. The doctors think I've got a nasty chest infection. Sorry darling."

I process what she's saying as I grow concerned listening to her voice. She sounds so out of breath and wheezy.

"Oh no! How are you feeling? Are you staying in?" I ask anxiously.

"I'm OK, just a little tired and chesty. Yeah they said I'll be in for a couple of days." Mum breathlessly informs.

Before hanging up the phone I promise Mum that I'll come to visit her this afternoon at the hospital which perks her up somewhat. Rueben is more than understanding when I get off the phone and offers to take over the cooking.

"Maybe I should go now?" I say hesitantly.

"I should go to her house and get her some pyjamas and her toothbrush and things."

"Go baby. If you want to go now, we'll be fine. I'll make sure I save you some dinner for when you get back too, you have nothing to worry about. Just keep me updated." He says softly.

As much as I want to stay home and eat a lovely dinner and snuggle up for another movie with my family, I know I have to go to Mum. She never met anyone else after her and my Dad divorced, and she hasn't really got anyone she can rely on. I know she puts on a brave face for me, but I know that the truth is she gets quite fed up with feeling unwell so often and being stuck in a dialysis centre or hospital for so long.

I swing by Mum's apartment and gather some essentials. I decide to stop by the shop too and pick her up some face cream, body wash, moisturiser and lip balms to make her feel a little better when I get there.

The walk to her ward is long, she's on the third floor and all the way to the other side of the hospital but it's worth it as her face is a picture when I eventually arrive.

"I didn't expect you so soon!" Mum smiles gratefully.

"Well I couldn't leave you here bored annoying all the nurses, now could I?" I joke.

"I got you some of your things from home and some face creams and shower stuff to make you feel a little better later."

"Oh Mol, you didn't have to do that. Thank you though."

"It's fine. I wanted too. So, have you had lunch or anything yet?"

"Yeah I just had some soup though as I couldn't manage much else." She replies, looking a little pale.

"So, what's going on with the mother in law then?"

I did speak to Mum last night from the hospital and tell her the kids got home safe and sound, but now it's just the two of us I go into a lot more detail about what happened. I find myself talking away non-stop about everything that has been going on and it feels such a relief to get so much of it off my chest. I tell Mum that I worry I'll never manage to have a good relationship with Joy and Dave despite wanting to for Rueben's sake and the kids' sake of course.

Mum makes a few of her typical sarcastic comments as we talk it through, and I find myself laughing so hard my stomach starts to hurt. I feel so much better about yesterday after laughing it off with Mum. She never fails to make me giggle.

I decide not to tell Mum just yet about the engagement though and so I make a conscious effort to hide my ring finger whilst we talk. I really want to tell her, but I don't want to do it whilst she's not feeling very well and stuck in a bed. As soon as she's better I'll invite her over for dinner again and me and Rueben can tell her together and we can all plan the wedding.

"Mol, can you go to the cafeteria and get me a nice hot chocolate? These watery teas are not for me." She croaks.

"Of course, do you want anything else?" I offer.

"No thanks, just the drink." She says as she allows her head to fall back onto the pillow and by the time I leave the room she closes her eyes and rests.

On the walk to the cafeteria I give Rueben a quick text message to let him know everything is OK and that I'll probably head home in an hour. The cafeteria is very busy this time and it means I have to join the long queue. Annoyingly, the long queue gives me more time to stare at all the cakes, brownies and muffins behind the glass, but I try to ignore the temptation and remind myself I have an upcoming wedding to think about. I can't go shoving cakes down my throat no matter how inviting they look.

Eventually I get to the front of the queue and order two cups of hot chocolate to go. I notice the cafeteria has emptied quite a lot whilst I've been waiting and it's now a lot quieter.

As I walk through the long corridors and head back to Mum's room, I notice there seems to be some commotion the closer I get to the ward. Two doctors' barge past me as they run through the ward doors and down to the last corridor.

I suddenly hear random words being shouted up and down the corridors.

Most of the words I'm not sure I understand, but then I hear someone shout, "cardiac arrest" and they are stood by my Mum's door. The doctors who rushed past me are heading in there now too.

As I walk closer, I realise all the commotion is because of my Mum. Something is happening to my Mum. There are alarms going off and nurses wheeling different machinery into her room.

"I'm sorry you can't go in there right now." A nurse interrupts my scrambled thoughts as I get to Mum's door.

I feel tears spilling down my cheeks and I realise I'm still holding the cups which are starting to burn my hands.

"Are you her daughter?" The same nurse asks.

I nod and blink as more tears fall down my cheeks.

"Is she OK?"

CHAPTER THIRTY-FOUR

"Roo?" I mumble into the phone.

"Baby?" Rueben responds sounding concerned.

"It's Mum, she's had a cardiac arrest." I manage to say before I sob heavily down the phone.

I pace outside the hospital trying to calm myself down a little. It's gotten dark now as the late afternoon has drawn in. It's really cold but I welcome the frosty air, it's better than sitting inside the stuffy ward, waiting to see Mum again.

"Oh my god. Do you want me to take the kids to your Dad's or something? And I'll come down right now?"

"No, no it's OK. I really don't want the kids to have an unsettled night again. I'm fine. They said they managed to stabilise her but they're moving her to intensive care, and I can't see her yet." I explain, trying to hold back the tears again. My eyes are sore and puffy and crying always makes me feel so tired and drained.

"OK." He says hesitantly.

"Please keep texting me at least so I know you're ok. If you're going to be late home, I'll stay up for you. I want to wait up and see you."

I feel so safe knowing I always have Rueben. He is always so supportive and effortlessly loving. He'll always offer to help me in any way he can, and he hasn't once let me down. Just the short conversation on the phone is enough to give me the support I needed and I soon feel brave enough to go back inside.

When I head back inside, I decide to go back into the cafeteria for something to eat and drink to keep my strength up. My throat feels scratchy and dry and although my worries for Mum are still making me feel sick, I decide to order some toast at least.

A message from Lana comes through on my phone whilst I wait for my order.

> *"OMG Mol. Rueben text me and told me what happened! Is there anything I can do for you now? I can come and collect the kids tomorrow if you want and take them to the park for a few hours to give you and Rueben some time to see your Mum? Xx"*

I'm so grateful by the text and as much as I wanted to spend some time with the kids tomorrow, I'm not sure what is happening with my Mum yet and this will really help.

> *"Life saver. Thank you so much. Freddie is on some strict prescription milk though. It's a bit tricky and he gets easily unsettled. I don't want to put you out?"*

> *"It's fine I promise. Rueben already explained all that. You can trust me. I'll see you in the morning xxx"*

Thank god for Lana I think to myself. I sit by the window watching people come and go as I pick at my toast. I text Rueben a lot too and ask him how the kids are doing, and I keep the conversation fairly light to help take my mind off my worries. The nurse said she'll call my phone when they're ready for me to head down to see Mum but my anxiety creeps in as I realise my phone battery is nearly dead.

I pass some time by heading up to the hospital shop and looking at some magazines. I start staring at all the bridal ones, I desperately want to buy some and flick through all the amazing pictures and ideas it has to offer but I decide my emotions are too all over the place to be able to focus on that yet. Then again, maybe just one won't hurt. I grab some water and give in to allowing myself one bridal magazine.

Finally, I get the call, I can head down to intensive care and I can finally see my Mum again and let her know I'm here.

When I arrive though my stomach is in knots. The nurse greets me at the door and I make sure to sanitise my hands before I enter. It dawns on me very quickly how sick the patients are in here. As I walk past many rooms, I notice how much machinery is constantly beeping in here. All the patients I pass are wired up to a lot of them too. They all look so poorly. It makes me so nervous to see Mum.

When I reach Mum's room I hesitate by the door. I'm almost scared to go in. I can see there's about six of the big machines in there and a lot of wires. She has a nurse sitting by her side and a large oxygen mask over her face.

"It's okay, you can come in." The nurse gestures as she waves me in with a smile.

I awkwardly shuffle in and stand at the foot of Mum's bed.

"Well I don't know about you, but I thought I was off to meet my maker!" She manages to joke, her voice a little muffled behind the mask.

"Well it's a good thing you didn't go then because I'm not sure you're destined for Heaven." I tease and she manages a laugh.

"Has anyone managed to explain what happened yet?" The nurse asks me.

"Not yet..." I mumble.

"OK, well firstly, your Mum should be ok now, we're going to keep a close eye on her tonight to make sure of it. The chest infection started causing fluid on your Mum's lungs which put some pressure on her heart and caused a minor cardiac arrest. We've been alleviating the pressure and monitoring her. I'm going to be sat here with your Mum all night as well." She explains carefully with a reassuring voice. I look back at Mum who is smiling a little too and I feel my tense body relax a tiny bit, but I still feel so emotional at the sight of her wired up to all these huge machines which make her look so small and frail.

"What you got?" Mum croaks through her mask, pointing at my hands.

"Oh…" I say slightly startled as I look down to my hands and realise I'm still holding the bridal magazine.

"I'm…"

"Are you getting married, darling?" Mum manages to whisper.

I nod at her with a little smile and she lets out a slight excitable giggle.

"Rueben's going to be my son-in-law then, that makes me very happy. Tell me everything you're planning so far…" she says and points to the chair next to her for me to sit down.

Before I know it, we are all deep in wedding conversation, me, Mum and even the nurse joins in too. Mum doesn't speak too often because I know she's tired and it's difficult for her to say what she wants with the mask on her face. But she listens intently as I chat away about dresses and colour schemes and first songs to dance too. Her face lights up the more I tell her and occasionally she'll add a few words to the conversation. I notice though that she's drowsy, probably from all the drugs she's had to take but I know she isn't ready for me to leave just yet. So, I continue talking about further details such as cake flavours and bridesmaids.

Soon enough Mum's eyes look heavier as she starts to drift off to sleep.

"I think you gave her something happy to think about, she could obviously relax and get some sleep." The nurse smiles kindly.

"Either that or I just bored the hell out of her!" I joke, making her laugh.

I decide to stay with Mum for a little longer, just in case she wakes again. I organise her clothes and fold them neatly. I put her phone on charge so I know she can call me easily tomorrow and I leave the magazine on a table beside her bed, just in case she wants to look through.

"You should really go and get some rest, it's nearly two o'clock in the morning, I promise you I'll take care of your Mum and I'll ring you if there are any changes." The nurse whispers as she writes some things down in Mum's notes.

I reluctantly agree and whisper goodbye to Mum, careful not to wake her as I leave. Tiredness really starts to kick in during the car journey home, I can barely keep my eyes open. As I pull into the driveway,

I can see the lights are still on in the front room and I actually feel relieved that Rueben has waited up for me.

"Hey…" Rueben says softly as he jumps up from the sofa when he sees me come through the door.

"Are you OK?"

"Yes." I nod.

"Just so tired. I'm really pleased you're up though." I say, relieved.

"I was going to ask you to tell me all about it, but you look shattered. Shall we just go to bed for now? I don't want you too tired if we are going back to see your Mum in the morning."

"Yes, please. I'm going to set my alarm early though. I want to go back as soon as I can so she's not alone in there. It's a bit daunting."

"That's fine. We'll go bright and early." Rueben assures and pulls me in close for a cuddle.

When we get upstairs, I quickly brush my teeth and take off my make-up. As soon as my head hits the pillow my eyes are heavy. Rueben moves closer to me tonight, wrapping his arms around my waist as I close my eyes. I love the feeling of him holding me so devotedly. It helps me relax just enough to fall asleep.

CHAPTER THIRTY-FIVE

The second my alarm sounds on my phone I'm up straight away. I want to get back to the hospital as quickly as possible to see how Mum managed through the night. I know Rueben is tired and is struggling to wake himself up fully, but he eventually gets up too without much complaining. He knows how worried I have been and how eager I am to get to the hospital.

Lana comes by early just as she promised. Daisy's halfway through her cereal when she arrives. I'm so grateful to see her. She surprises me with a big bouquet of faux flowers for my Mum. Apparently real flowers aren't allowed in intensive care anymore for allergy reasons and I smile at her thoughtfulness.

I thank her over and over again for the flowers and of course for taking the kids out for a few hours. Thankfully the new milk is still keeping Freddie content and settled and so I don't think there will be any problems.

I want to tell her the news that I'm engaged but I don't want to be late for the hospital, so I decide I'll tell her this afternoon when she drops the kids back and we'll have a proper chat and I can tell her everything then.

I carefully pack Freddie's bag with all his medicine and milk and give Daisy a big cuddle as they set off out for the day.

"Ready?" Rueben calls from the hallway as I quickly finish my cup of tea.

"Yeah." I respond. I'm not very talkative this morning, I think a mixture of nerves and tiredness has set in already and I'm feeling a little run down.

The journey to the hospital is quick, we don't live too far from it and it's nice we managed to get here early, just before nine o'clock.

As Rueben manoeuvres the car into a parking space the sound of his phone suddenly ringing startles us both.

Somehow, I immediately know it's Joy. Just like Rueben said it would be.

"Great." Rueben sighs as he looks at his phone screen.

"Wow, Dave literally would have left for work ten minutes ago. She really didn't want to waste much time."

"Answer it." I sigh heavily.

"No. I'll ignore it baby. This morning is about your Mum."

"And have her start ringing your phone and mine continuously whilst I'm trying to check on my Mum? I don't think so!" I respond impatiently.

"Eurgh. For god's sake!" Rueben snaps.

"I really don't want this for you today."

"I know. But we know by now that she doesn't stop."

"I'll try and tell her first that we are here and hopefully she'll respect that enough to call back later." Rueben suggests, as the phone stops ringing, and a missed call notification flashes up instead.

"Good one. Now she'll be sending the flying monkeys." I say sarcastically which makes Rueben laugh.

"Are you going to liken my Mum to every movie villain for the rest of our lives?"

"Probably." I smirk.

"Or at least until she stops giving us a hard time."

We both giggle a little which distracts us but as expected, Rueben's phone starts ringing again.

He takes the phone and sets it in the middle of the dashboard and presses loudspeaker as he reluctantly answers it.

"Hello?" Rueben sighs.

"Right, we need to have a chat about the other day and you need to come to my house now and see me. Just me and you. Not her." She demands angrily.

"Mum...before you go on, I am at the hospital about to see Laraine. She's not been well, and I need to be here for Mollie. It will have to wait." Rueben calmly explains the situation without giving too much of my Mum's health problems away.

"So? She's not family. This is more important and I strongly suggest you make your way over to my house straight away!" She continues to threaten.

"I'm not Mum, not right now. Sorry."

"Then you had better tell me right now why you fucking let *her* speak to me like that the other day?" Joy screams into the phone.

"Like what Mum?" Rueben sighs frustratingly.

"For god's sake! This is going to get pathetic. Mollie is entitled to explain how she feels if she's worried about her kids..."

"I'm quite capable thank you very much!" She interrupts.

"Mum, do you know the doctor confirmed that Freddie was poorly because you decided to go against all the directions?" Rueben calmly points out.

"Yeah well Dave thinks that's a load of rubbish as well and you should have gone to a better hospital. It's not my fault at all. I think you'll find that's the doctor's fault! Thank you very much." She spits, arrogance thick in her voice.

"And how dare you give me a *time* to bring them back? You know, I've told your Nan everything and she's *fucking ashamed* of you!"

"Right Mum, I'm hanging up now. I have more important things to do. I'm sorry you're upset but I have to put my kids needs first and I don't feel like you did that when you looked after them."

"Kids?" Joy venomously hisses in a high-pitched tone, as if she's mocking him.

"Let's be honest Rueben. The only kid you have is Freddie. Daisy is *not* yours. Daisy is *not* our family. Come on now. You only have *one* child."

Her words instantly knock the wind out of my chest. Shock and anger bubble up from deep within and I don't know whether I want to burst out crying for my innocent Daisy or to take the phone and scream at the person saying the worst possible things I have ever heard anybody say about my daughter. How could she suddenly exclude her like that? Is she that angry she's prepared to use Daisy to hurt us? To hurt me.

"Mu…Mum!" Rueben stutters sounding embarrassed and shocked.

"How dare you! They are both my children!"

"Oh, come on Rueben…" Joy keeps repeating as if he is being some petulant child.

"That's not fair Mum. You can't just exclude her like that?" Rueben begins to say before his voice croaks and I realise he has tears in his eyes.

"She is somebody else's daughter Rueben." She spits viciously.

Great. Now he is crying so she knows her vile words have impacted us. She knows how to hurt him again. She wanted to achieve this today and now Rueben has shown her she's gotten her way. I sit and watch Rueben buckle under her words and I feel even angrier. Rule number one, don't let them see they've won, I think to myself as I frustratingly hear Joy's smug voice down the phone continue banishing my daughter from their family as if she were nothing.

Yet she was the one who started all this by giving Daisy a birthday card with Grandma and Grandad written on it. She came to Daisy's birthday and announced herself as Grandma. *She* offered my daughter family and now because she's mad she's going to snatch it away. She'll casually use my daughter as a pawn in childish tantrums without any thought of the innocent child she could upset. She's callous and cowardly and right now, I don't think I have ever been so disgusted by any one more.

"Mum…Mum…" Rueben keeps trying to interrupt Joy who is now saying she only wants to see Freddie going forward.

"I don't care about Daisy. She isn't my granddaughter. I just want to have quality time with my Freddie and you better sort that out with *her* and make it happen." She forcefully demands.

I grab the phone without even thinking as my anger bubbles over and I can't control my emotions anymore.

"Listen here you witch." I bellow down the phone.

"I don't want to talk to you! I'm talking to my son!" She tries to yell over me.

"My Daisy was too good for you! And you'll be lucky if I let you see Freddie again after you made him so ill! How *dare* you say such disgusting things about my daughter? Rueben was right about you! You're crazy!"

"I'm not crazy! Your Mother is! And you are!" She shouts over me.

"God Joy, please get a hobby and stop obsessing over my Mum. Goodbye you nasty old hag. I'm going now." I say before hanging up the phone.

"Oh god." Rueben shakes his head.

"What!?" I snap.

"She's going to get so much worse now." Rueben whines looking pale.

"Well obviously I'm going to stick up for my daughter!" I yell.

"Perhaps you should get a backbone and put her in her place and then maybe she wouldn't try and bully you all the time!"

"I know but...but..." Rueben tries to say.

The next thing I know, before he even manages to finish his sentence, he flies open the car door and vomits all over the pavement.

CHAPTER THIRTY-SIX

I stomp off ahead and don't even wait for Rueben who is still trying to compose himself after throwing up.

I look behind me a couple of times and see what a mess he is in. He is visibly trembling and he looks as white as a sheet, apart from his eyes which are red and puffy. I feel so torn as I continue walking ahead. One half of me wants to stop and comfort Rueben, my heart aches at the state he is in.

The other half is just so mad at the comments made about Daisy that I can't help but feel anger towards Rueben about it. He didn't see red like I did. He was quite calm about it. He should have reacted as angrily as I did. We are Daisy's parents; we need to protect her. It's like he is so used to her saying the most vile, hateful things that he is desensitised to it.

I'm so frustrated but I'm nearly at the intensive care ward now and I can't let Mum see I'm upset.

"Mollie...please." Rueben calls as he catches up to me by the ward.

"Not now. I want to see my Mum and not think about this." I quietly snap.

"When then? Please let me know we are going to be fine and you're not going to leave me, are you?" Rueben pleads.

"For god's sake! Get a grip." I snap before storming off.

Even I'm shocked at my reactions now. I'm just so done with constant drama from Joy and the worry I have been feeling for Mum.

Then on top of it, I just feel absolutely crushed for Daisy right now. I'm not even sure what this means going forward, or how I'm going to handle it in a way that ensures Daisy won't get hurt. I can't believe I've found myself in this situation. Poor Daisy. I try to push those thoughts to the back of my head though as I make my way to Mum.

When I reach Mum's room, I'm pleasantly surprised to see her sitting up in bed with a cup of tea and looking much better. I notice she is wired up to less machines, she doesn't seem to be on any oxygen and there is a lot more colour in her cheeks.

"Mum!" I say relieved.

"You look good, like really really good."

"I had a *really, really* good night's sleep." Mum laughs.

"Hey Laraine!" Rueben says as he follows in behind me, looking more composed.

"Hello darling! Are you OK?" Mum says, looking pleased to see him.

"I'm fine, thank you. I'm more concerned for you." Rueben smiles.

"No need to worry about me, the doctor said the pressure is off my heart now and my antibiotics have really kicked in. I should be going back to the normal ward tomorrow." Mum reassures.

"Oh, that's great news. I'm so pleased you're feeling better. Do you need me to go and get you anything? Whilst I'm here?" Rueben offers.

"Actually, if you don't mind could you go to the shop downstairs and get me some magazines please? It's gotten a bit boring in here."

"Yeah, course I can, they do puzzle books too, I'll grab you a couple." Rueben kindly offers as he leaves the room, but not before giving me a sorrowful look.

I smile back at Mum who stares at me curiously.

"Well? Are you going to tell me why Rueben looks like he's about to burst out crying at any moment?" Mum asks me quizzically.

I roll my eyes and huff as I slump down on the chair next to Mum's bed.

"Joy." I mumble with my arms folded.

"I thought it would be. What did she do this time?"

I carefully explain everything to Mum, trying not to miss out any details. At first, she looks furious when I tell her what she said about

163

Daisy. In fact, she looks like she's about to charge out of her bed and go looking for her. But the more I explain about Rueben's reactions the more her expressions soften a little as she listens and nods along.

"And then I pretty much told him to get a backbone and to get a grip." I say regretfully.

"Hmmm." Mum responds unimpressed.

"What?" I huff defensively. Surely, she can understand why I'm so angry.

"Mollie…we all know that Joy is a bully. It's become evident with the more Rueben tells you about his childhood. All these abusive phone calls she makes when Dave isn't around and when she hopes you can't hear them, it's all a type of control. To the world she wants to come across as innocent, as a kind woman and if anything, the victim.

But Rueben knows a very different version. A version that you don't know the full extent of yet.

When I was in care, after your Nanny died, I saw a lot of kids from bad backgrounds who needed therapy. I think Rueben could benefit from it too." Mum explains quietly.

"Why? What makes you think he needs that?" I ask, surprised.

"Well, he's a thirty-year-old man who crumbles under the pressure from his Mum. You told me he was sick outside? That's a clear sign of anxiety.

On the surface, you might see a grown man who allows his Mum to still get to him and talk down to him. In Rueben's mind, he's probably that eight-year-old kid, stuck under the same roof with no place to go and being told he isn't good enough."

"Oh." Is all I manage to add as guilt takes over me.

"It's really good that he doesn't live there anymore, because chances are the more space he has, the more he'll realise that he isn't that child anymore and the way she treated him wasn't right. But you need to support him. I know you're frustrated but he needs you to love him and understand him. He needs you to be patient. What he *definitely* doesn't need is another woman in his life telling him he is spineless or bringing him down. There's only so much a person can take." Mum gently says.

"But Daisy…" I begin to say.

164

"Daisy doesn't even know what got said today and she doesn't need to know. Chances are, Joy has *only* said that to cause hurt and stress for Rueben. She *knows* that Rueben is in love with you. She knows he doesn't want to lose you. So, guess what? She pisses you off and winds you up, in the hopes that you end up arguing. She probably hopes it will cause a divide and you'll push him away. *Hell!* She probably even hopes it'll break you both up. Then where does that leave Rueben?" Mum presses.

"So, what do I do?" I ask.

"Be strong. Do what you think is best but keep supporting Rueben. This is probably why she doesn't like you Mollie. You help make Rueben stronger and independent, don't let her come between you both." Mum urges and I know she's right. Suddenly I see everything so much clearer. A new perspective.

My anger has faded but I'm left with guilt. I'm not sure which feeling is worse. Rueben has never let me down, he has gone off now to buy things for my Mum. He continually supports me and my family and yet here I am, losing my temper with him when he needs me the most.

CHAPTER THIRTY-SEVEN

"Your Mum seemed in good spirits today, didn't she?" Rueben nervously asks me as we drive away from the hospital.

"Yeah. She did. A lot better than yesterday anyway." I reply.

"I'm so sorry Mollie." Rueben blurts.

"I don't blame you if you hate me, if I could stop my Mum from saying these things I would. I'm just as disgusted as you are, I swear. I just don't handle it very well."

"Roo…" I softly interrupt.

"You have nothing to be sorry for. I do."

"Wh…what? No, you don't!" Rueben says surprised.

"Yes, I do. It was nasty of me to insult you the way I did. I was frustrated and upset because of Daisy but that's really no excuse."

"No, you were right, and I deserved it." Rueben sighs, running his hands anxiously through his hair.

"Stop that. You can't just roll over like that and allow your mum or me to insult you. You don't deserve it Rueben. I can't stress that enough. I lost my temper because of Joy but that has nothing to do with you. I was wrong and it's ok for you to agree. You are *not* to blame." I say firmly.

"I just don't want to lose you. You're the best thing that's ever happened to me and I don't want my Mum to break us." Rueben whispers, putting his hand on my thigh.

"I'm not going anywhere, I promise. It's ok for you to be angry or upset or anxious. I want to be there for you. I can't promise that your Mum won't cause me to lose my temper again, because I'll always defend Daisy. And you. And Freddie. But I promise I won't take it out on you again." I say truthfully.

"Thank you. It means a lot." Rueben smiles as he exhales with relief.

"Shall we swing by the supermarket and buy pizza and beer?" I half joke.

"I feel like we deserve it."

"Sounds good! By the way when we left the hospital, I had forty-nine missed calls from my Mum." Rueben says rolling his eyes.

"Ahh, that's not bad for her." I mock as I shake my head.

I feel better now that I have apologised, and Rueben seems happier, but the guilt still hangs around me. I have already decided I'm going to treat him to a few beers and then offer a full back massage, I'm going to let him catch up with Game of Thrones tonight and I'm not going to complain that I'm bored once or moan that I'm confused by the plot. In fact, I'll grab some things in the supermarket and make a homemade Banoffee Pie too, his favourite. I want him to know I'm genuinely sorry and he is just as important to me as I am to him.

"Hey!" I hear a friendly male voice call as we get out of the car.

"Hi! You OK?" Rueben responds and walks over to the couple standing outside the supermarket.

I recognise the man straight away, he's Rueben's uncle Ray. Not one of the sons who still lives with Irene but the one who got married some years ago. I have only seen him in passing a few times. Rueben speaks very fondly of him though. Apparently, he always helped take care of Rueben and even took him on a skiing holiday once when he was a child, which was really generous and kind of him.

"Hi, I'm Carmel, Ray's wife." She introduces herself with a big smile as I walk over. She's very glamorous looking. She's wearing a black fur jacket with a matching black designer bag and the most gorgeous Swarovski watch. She literally looks like the polar opposite of Joy.

"Hey!" I smile at them both warmly.

"We've just been down to see your Nan." Ray tells us.

"Oh yeah? Was she OK?" Rueben asks.

"Sort of. She said Joy had been down this morning kicking off and complaining about you both." He says dismissively as if it was barely worth mentioning.

"Yeah! Especially about you." Carmel tells me as she smirks.

"Well she phoned me earlier and kicked off too. She said my Nan was ashamed of me." Rueben sighs.

"No that's definitely not true. She told your Nan that Mollie wasn't going to let you visit her anymore. Sounds like your Mum is playing games again." Ray says as he rolls his eyes at Rueben.

"I'll ring Nan later and make sure she's OK and assure her I'll be down to see her again soon. I hate it when Mum does things like this. Why does she have to bring everyone else down? Especially Nan." Rueben huffs.

"It's the first time in years it's taken the heat off me!" Carmel tells me with a laugh.

"Really?" I ask curiously.

"God yeah! When I first met Ray, Joy told everybody that I was a gold digger and then she told Irene that I was a cheat, she said my daughters were on drugs, pretty much anything she could think of that would make Irene dislike me and hate me being with Ray. Since you've come along it's all gone quiet!" Carmel says.

"Glad I could help!" I joke and Carmel laughs more.

"Why don't you all come over next weekend or something? And we can have a proper chat?" Ray suggests.

"Yeah definitely, we'd love that. Wouldn't we?" Rueben replies and I nod in agreement as Carmel gives me a warm smile.

"I'll get Ray to text Rueben my phone number for you too Mollie, if you like? You can always give me a call if Joy ever gets too much." Carmel kindly offers before giving me a hug goodbye.

"That'll be nice, thank you." I respond gratefully.

As we walk away after making some arrangements to go over for a coffee, I can't help but think about what Carmel said. Joy didn't like her either and tried to cause issues in their relationship. She said it had been going on for *years*.

CHAPTER THIRTY-EIGHT

It's been a couple of weeks since Mum had a cardiac arrest. She recovered really well and has been at home for nearly a week now. She still has dialysis and regular checks, but she's been much more herself.

My days at home have been a lot quieter now since Daisy has gone back to school and Rueben has gone back to work. It's nice to be in the routine of everything but I do miss having them around every day. Freddie definitely keeps me occupied though, he's five months old now and just started sitting up and even attempts to crawl.

We haven't made it round to Carmel and Ray's house for a coffee yet, but Carmel has phoned me a couple of times since we met which has been really nice. She's probably only one of the few people in the family who seems to make an effort with me and actually wants to get to know me. I really appreciate her for that.

I managed to design and create the save the date cards which I'm so excited about. We've chosen a gold and pastel pink colour scheme which looks so pretty. But we haven't sent any out yet, Rueben couldn't decide whether he was sending one to his Mum or not so I told him we should wait until he has made up his mind. I personally think we should just send one, I know he is struggling with his Mum again, but I know for sure that things wouldn't get any better if we excluded her from our wedding.

Rueben and I have been spending some evenings on the internet planning our wedding and even found a hotel we both really love right on the beach. It's modern but still full of character, there's a huge out-side patio area where we can get married under a chic arch and upstairs the reception room overlooks the beach with huge windows so we can watch the sunset. I sent the information to my Dad and asked him to check it out for us on his next trip to Florida in a few weeks. If it looks as good as the photos online then we're going to book it.

My Dad is really excited about our choice to get married in Florida but I'm a little worried about how everyone else might take the news. Hopefully they will understand our decision. This really does benefit us all, especially Daisy and Freddie who will have the best time having a holiday too.

As I start mushing up some banana for Freddie's early afternoon snack, my phone starts ringing and I'm relieved to see it's Rueben.

"Hey stranger." I smile.

"Hey…" he says, sounding out of breath.

"Are you OK?" I ask.

"Yeah…Listen, do you mind if I drop Lily at ours? She's phoned me saying her boyfriend has trashed her house again and apparently he hit her."

"Oh my god." I gasp.

"She can't go to my Mum's either because she's fallen out with her too. I said she could probably spend the night here. I can drop her off now but then I need to go back to work for a bit. Will you be alright with that?" He asks sounding rushed.

I have never been alone with Lily and I find her a little difficult to talk too. She doesn't really come across as the friendliest person to be around and she's very closed off. Rueben can't even ask her how her day has been without her getting agitated that he is prying. Every time I have seen her, she always has this attitude, as if the world owes her something. It also might be strange because her Mum doesn't even like me very much. But I know that I could never refuse Lily in these circumstances. I know Rueben can't either.

"Yeah." I say trying to sound certain with my answer.

"That'll be fine. Of course."

"Great. Thank you, baby, I'll see you shortly." Rueben replies before hanging up the phone.

I feed Freddie his banana before quickly doing a little tidy up around the home. I fix my hair again and make myself look a little more presentable. I always panic when people come over, even though the house looks half decent I always find myself frantically trying to make it look better.

Whilst I straighten up the curtains in the front room, I see Rueben coming up the driveway in his work van. Only Lily gets out though with a bag and Rueben quickly drives away. He must really be busy at work if he can't come in and say a quick hello.

I kind of wish he had though, even just to break the ice a little between Lily and me.

"Hey." I say as friendly as I can sound when I open the front door to Lily.

"Hi." Lily responds unusually reserved. She looks up at me shyly and I notice straight away the deep purple ring around her eye.

I have never known Lily to be reserved or shy, she's usually so loud and brazen. Her change in personality has caught me completely off guard. I feel sorry for her though as she looks so withdrawn. I think I'd prefer her to have her usual attitude than to be like this.

"Come and sit down. I was just going to make a nice hot chocolate with whipped cream and marshmallows. Would you like one?" I offer warmly.

"Yeah, that would be nice." She smiles as she heads into the front room to see Freddie.

When I bring the hot chocolates into the front room Lily is playing with Freddie but still not talking very much. I ask her if she wants any painkillers just in case she's in any pain around her eye but she politely declines and assures me she feels fine.

"It's not just him to blame, I push him and stuff too. I say the worse things to him I can think of when I'm angry." She tells me as if it's normal.

"Oh." I say, suddenly feeling a little put on the spot and unsure what to say.

"But I still don't think he should be hitting you. No matter how angry he is."

"And what would you know?" She snaps before apologising regretfully.

"I didn't mean to say that. I'm just sick of everyone blaming him."

"Lily…can I tell you something personal? But I haven't even told Rueben the full extent yet, so I would rather it stayed between us?" I ask carefully.

"Yeah? I won't tell him." She responds curiously.

"Well, a while back I met this guy called Connor…"

"Connor who?" Lily interrupts.

"Oh, he wasn't from around here, he was called Connor Campbell. But he has gone back up north now." I reply.

"Anyway, I met him online and we decided to meet up after getting along so well. At the time he was literally the funniest person I had ever met and we just clicked. But after only a couple of months things drastically changed."

"Really?" Lily asks as she listens intently.

"Yeah, well he certainly wasn't that funny anymore. I realised he had a problem with alcohol. It got to the point where he could sometimes be drunk for three days straight and I was getting to the stage where I couldn't sleep from worrying about him so much. I also knew I couldn't have him around Daisy if he would behave like this. So, one night when he came over here for dinner, I decided to tip the remaining wine down the sink, just to see if he could manage without it and well…he really lost his temper. He smashed all my plates up and spat in my face."

"Oh god…Mols…" Lily gasps sympathetically.

"But I forgave him, and he promised me he would change and get help. But a couple of weeks later when he had been drinking for a couple of nights straight again, he turned up at my house at three o'clock in the morning because his paranoia allowed him to believe that I was seeing somebody else. He barged past me at the front door and checked the whole house. I was so frustrated, I threatened him with the police if he wouldn't leave and he ended up punching me and then blamed me for it because he said that I was purposely trying to wind him up." I explain.

"Did Daisy wake up and see all of this?" Lily asks.

"No, she had no idea but by the next day I had a black eye which I managed to hide from her too with a lot of make-up. That day he came back again though whilst Daisy was at school. He fell to his knees begging for my forgiveness, he cried and assured me he would definitely get help. I really believed him and thought this was the turning point. But a few weeks later trouble started again. He stayed here for the night and we had a nice dinner, but when I woke up in the middle of the night, I heard him downstairs, singing and chanting football songs to himself. When I came downstairs, I realised he had found the vodka in the cupboard and drank most of it. He was so drunk he could barely stand. I begged him to be quiet because otherwise he would wake Daisy, but he wouldn't stop. I started packing his things and taking them to the door and telling him I wanted him to leave but he ignored me. He just kept smirking at me as if I was being ridiculous. Then when I grabbed the bottle out of his hand, he saw red. He threw be back onto the sofa and the next thing I knew punches were raining down on me."

"Jesus." Lily mumbles.

"He stopped punching me because he got tired. In his drunken state he just stopped and poured another drink like nothing had happened. I was so dizzy I could barely stand but I saw the opportunity and I ran to my phone and called the police. I hate telling this story, but he could have killed me Lily. I know it's hard because you feel so invested in your boyfriend right now and you feel like you can fix this relationship. But I promise you people like Connor don't change. No matter what they say…you're worth more than being somebody's punch bag." I say gently, hoping that I don't make her feel defensive.

"It's just hard, because he has nowhere else to go." Lily sighs and I feel as though my experience has had some impact on her thoughts.

"But it's not your responsibility to take care of him. Especially if he can't change and he keeps lashing out. You could do so much better." I say encouragingly.

"Maybe you're right. I just need to think everything through and try to put myself first." Lily smiles and I smile back pleased that this is the first proper conversation we've ever had, and I think I may have helped.

CHAPTER THIRTY-NINE

By the time Rueben gets home from work I'm just finishing making a lasagne for dinner.

Lily helped me earlier by going and picking up Daisy from school and now the two of them are doing some colouring at the dining table.

Rueben looks pleasantly surprised as he arrives home and notices we have gotten along just fine.

"Do you mind sleeping on the sofa tonight?" Rueben asks Lily.

"No that'll be fine for me, thank you." Lily responds.

"Mum has been messaging me loads this afternoon asking me where I am but don't worry, I didn't tell her I was here, she'd only go mad."

"Good thinking, best to keep it quiet." Rueben agrees.

"Your Mum will go mad if you have your sister round your house?" I ask a little confused.

"Well yeah. That's Mum for you. She would feel offended that Lily hasn't gone to her and she'll get jealous knowing she's here."

"It's crazy how you know how so many different situations are going to make her react." I say.

"That's because Mum reacts to everything!" Rueben laughs and Lily nods in agreement.

"So, what are you going to do about that idiot living in your house?" Rueben asks Lily.

"Oh Roo! I really don't want to get into it right now. Can we talk about something else."? Lily snaps.

"Alright! Fine, I was only asking." Rueben says defensively.

I plate up everyone's dinner and we continue the evening with lighter conversation and avoid talking about Lily's love life.

"So, what did you and Mum fall out about yesterday then?" Rueben quizzes Lily.

"Eurgh…she accused me of being the reason why Kelsey ran away from home." She says rolling her eyes.

"Really? How on earth can you be to blame for Kelsey leaving?" Rueben asks annoyed.

"Apparently I must have said something to her and upset her. I really don't know. I think she's clutching at straws." Lily shrugs.

"Yep. Always someone else to blame with Mum." Rueben sighs shaking his head.

I sit quietly and let them discuss Kelsey, I can't really comment anyway as I haven't met her, and I have no idea on the situation that took place. But I do feel very sad for them as they discuss their little sister, not knowing where she is.

After dinner, I crack on with the washing up as Lily offers to give Freddie a bath. Daisy sits in the front room and reads her book to Rueben for a little while before bedtime.

Once the kids are settled and in bed, I pour the three of us a glass of wine and we all relax in front of the television.

"What's this?" Lily asks as she finds the pile of save the date cards sat on the coffee table.

"Oh…" I mumble hesitantly as I look at Rueben.

"We're getting married! What does it look like?" Rueben says with a big grin.

"Oh my god! Congratulations!" Lily says as she monitors the card excitedly.

"I haven't tried to hide it from you or anything, it's just I couldn't send them out yet because things between me and Mum are really strained, and I don't want to speak to her at the moment. So, it's not a secret, it just wasn't the right time." Rueben tries to explain.

"It's fine, I understand." Lily smiles reassuringly.

"But if it's Florida I don't think I can come. I'm broke."

"Well I'm sure we can sort something out?" I offer.

"Yeah, we've got a year yet. Maybe we can help you save?" Rueben suggests.

"Perhaps just worry about flights for now. We were thinking of hiring a six-bedroom villa for us to all chip in for, but if money is that tight then don't worry about paying for the accommodation. I'll cover that. Just concentrate on flights." I say.

"Wow, really?" Lily asks surprised.

"Yeah, it'll be fine. We wouldn't want you to miss out." I assure.

When it starts to get late, I head off up to bed and Rueben helps Lily set up the sofa ready for her to sleep on.

"That was very generous of you." Rueben whispers as he walks into the bedroom behind me.

"Well we can't just leave her out. I know you won't agree but I think it's the right thing to do."

"It's not that I don't agree, it was really kind of you. Just don't be surprised if things change, she has a habit of disappearing and hanging out with bad people and then nobody ever hears from her again." Rueben gently warns.

"Maybe it will do her good then to something to look forward too and something positive to plan for." I whisper.

"'Maybe. I just don't know if I like the idea of you paying for her. She's more than capable of getting a job and paying for herself, she just refuses to work and that shouldn't be your problem." Rueben whispers back firmly.

"I just desperately want everyone to get along and be happy." I sigh as I wrap my arms around Rueben's waist and stare up at his concerned frown.

"I just don't want you to try too hard and end up being disappointed."

"Stop worrying about me." I laugh.

"I'll be fine."

"Well in that case I'll be quiet. On a lighter note, I ordered my new passport." Rueben tells me, changing the subject.

"Oh great. I guess I have to go to Florida and marry you then." I tease.

"I guess so." Rueben smirks as he leans down and kisses me.

When I wake up in the morning, I realise there's shouting coming from somewhere. I turn over in bed and see Rueben has gotten up already. I hear stomping and I'm sure I hear Lily's voice. I jump out of bed and wrap my dressing gown around me and hurriedly make my way downstairs.

"What the *hell* do you think you're doing with this shit in my house?" Rueben roars.

"It's nothing to do with you!" Lily screams.

"Give it back!"

I notice Rueben is holding a small plastic wrapper with a white powder in it.

Cocaine.

"Roo?" I mumble nervously from the bottom of the stairs.

Rueben turns to look at me angrily and with disappointment in his eyes.

"Guess what fell out of her bag?" He snaps.

"I can see that…"

"Get your bags. I'll drop you to Mum's now. You're not staying here. No way." He demands as he shakes his head in disbelief.

"You're lucky I don't punch you in the face! I'm older than you, don't you dare talk down to me." She yells.

"Threaten me all you like; I will not have anybody under this roof with drugs. I will not have my children around anybody who takes it. Family or not. Now get in the car." He roars over her.

I stand watching their argument in disbelief, it's so early that I'm having trouble processing all this. When we went to bed last night everything seemed fine, more than fine and now it's suddenly changed again. I choose to stay quiet and let Rueben deal with it the way he wants too. Lily seems to have changed back to her usual bad attitude and short temper that I don't really want to get involved anyway.

"I'm dropping her off and then I'll phone you before I get into work." Rueben says as he turns and kisses me goodbye.

I nod hesitantly as he grabs his things and rushes out the door.

Lily stomps off out of my front door without any acknowledgement or a goodbye and I'm left standing in the hallway a little speechless.

CHAPTER FORTY

"I'm sorry for shouting this morning." Rueben says down the phone.

"It's fine, I completely understand. Did you really mean what you said? About not wanting her around the kids?" I ask, unsure whether Rueben just said it out of the heat of the moment.

"Yeah I meant it." He sighs.

"She's becomes too unpredictable. She's always angry, having violent outbursts and I for damn sure can't have her thinking it's ok to bring this shit into my house."

"OK, fair enough. It's up to you to decide what you think is best. You know her better than me.

What happened anyway when you dropped her off?"

"Not much, Mum was fussing at the front door when she realised Lily had stayed with us and then when I told her about the drugs, she just dismissed it all. She told me Lily doesn't do them anymore and I have it all wrong." He explains with a sigh.

"Then she said if anybody is on drugs it's your Mum."

"Really?" I ask surprised with a laugh.

"Yeah…I'm sorry, I just thought I'd be honest with you." Rueben explains anxiously.

"It's fine, I guess she's just trying to deflect the negativity from Lily and put it onto someone else, it's annoying but nothing you can do. I shall just have to tell Mum later that she's now a crazy drug addict who randomly slaps women around the face, according to Joy anyway." I joke.

"You're Mum will love that!" Rueben laughs.

"So, what are you doing today?"

"Well I'm going to take Freddie for a little walk and then I'm going to get stuck in with some wedding planning. I might even book the villa today." I say smiling.

"Definitely, please do! I need something to look forward too."

"OK, well I'll let you know if I find something, I'll let you get back to work now and I'll see you later. Love you." I say before hanging up.

I love these fresh morning walks this time of year. It's cold but the sun is starting to appear more often, and I love knowing that it won't be long until spring is in the air. I give Mum a quick phone call to check how she's doing and then send a few texts to Lana. I must remember to ask her to be my maid of honour the first chance I get. The thoughts of telling Lana about the upcoming wedding gets me so excited again that I find myself heading home quicker than I planned so I can get back online and look into more wedding fun.

By the time I get home and get Freddie settled, I realise my phone had been ringing in my bag, I have three missed calls from Joy. I speculate over different scenarios which would make her want to ring me. When she's angry, she only ever calls Rueben. When she's trying to be nice, she calls me. I'm not sure if Rueben is wanting me to talk to her yet though. Before I can call Rueben and get his opinion my phone pings up with a new text from Joy.

"Hi Mollie, Lily has let me know the fabulous wedding news. I am so happy for you both and would love to be a part of it all and help if I can. I am so happy to have you as a daughter in law. Please call me ASAP. Joy xx"

Well, there's a turn out for the books. The woman who despises my Mother and seems to be irritated by me constantly, suddenly wants to tell me how thrilled she is for me to be her daughter-in-law. Also,

Lily really can't keep a secret. The text is kind, but I'm not sure I trust the words. For starters she is seemingly pushing her comments about Daisy to one side as if it was no big deal.

If she thinks I can have a relationship with her and be ok with her saying some of the worst things to me or Rueben she's got another thing coming. I couldn't possibly be this insulted and be expected to let it go each time.

I could handle it if she just attacked me immaturely. Perhaps if she just lost her temper and called me a bitch or something equally petty, I could just let it go. But to bring my daughter into her vile rants to hurt me and Rueben, I'm not sure I can be so quick to forget. I worry about what type of woman can so casually be nasty about a child and then dismiss it happened when it suits her.

I decide to not respond to any messages for now, not until I speak to Rueben anyway.

Instead I get back to what makes me really happy and jump back onto the internet to wedding plan.

It doesn't take me long to find a beautiful big villa with a huge outdoor pool and a games room which has me admiring the pictures and excitedly checking the availability. This is the one. I'm sure of it.

Before I can stop myself, I'm grabbing my card out of my purse and putting down a deposit to hold it. I then decide to print off the pictures so I can show Rueben properly when he gets home.

Tonight, I'll cook Rueben a nice dinner and then proudly present to him my amazing find. This will definitely cheer him up again.

As I start packing away the laptop, I see my phone flash up on the table. Thankfully it isn't Joy but Rueben, who is calling again.

"Hey!" I say cheerily.

"Hey." Rueben sighs.

"I'm sorry but I'm going to be late home. I've got to stop by my Nan's after work.

"Why? What's happened? Is she OK?" I ask snapping out of my little happy bubble.

"Not really. Somebody has stolen money from her money box." He says disappointedly.

"She has a money box?" Is what I seem to blurt first.

"Well yeah, we had to get it for her when people kept stealing from her purse. Now they've managed to get into her money box and taken over two hundred pounds and she's devastated."

"Oh Jesus. That's awful."

"Tell me about it. I'm sorry but she wants to see me. She's just gotten herself really upset about it all and I can't leave her like that."

"No, it's fine, you should go to her. I'll put some dinner aside for you, don't worry about me honestly. Just make sure she's ok...and please send her my love." I say sincerely.

Poor Irene. How can anyone be so nasty to an elderly woman like this. Who in their right mind believes they are more worthy over her money than she is? It truly baffles me sometimes how Rueben is so different from his family. He would never steal a penny and yet his Mum and sister would steal your last pound if they could.

CHAPTER FORTY-ONE

It's been on my mind quite a lot all afternoon about Irene and how someone could just take her money.

Rueben didn't sound very surprised when he told me about it, and I wonder if he knows who might have taken it already. I must admit, I have my own suspicions. Judging from our pervious conversations it's likely to be Joy or Lily.

When I get Daisy home, I get organised and make a start with dinner whilst she tells me all about the trip the school have planned for next month. They have arranged to go to a theme park and Daisy is beyond excited that this is by far the most entertaining trip the teachers have ever arranged.

"I'm so grown up now Mum, I'm going on the biggest rides they have!" Daisy tells me with all her sass as usual.

"That's good then! If I give you spending money, you'll have to get a photo of yourself on one of the huge rides!" I laugh, imaging her horrified face on the biggest rollercoaster.

"Deal!" Daisy giggles.

As soon as Daisy finishes her dinner, I head upstairs to bath Freddie and Daisy reads some of her Harry Potter book in bed. Eventually I get Freddie dry and changed and soon settled for sleep.

"Where's Daddy?" Daisy asks when I go in to kiss her goodnight.

"He has gone to visit his Nanny. He'll be home soon." I tell her.

"Oh. But now I won't see him before I go to sleep." Daisy says with sadness in her eyes.

"Don't worry." I smile.

"I'm sure he'll come up and give you a kiss goodnight, even if you are asleep."

"OK, tell him I said goodnight then." She responds softly.

When I head downstairs, I decide to pour myself a glass of wine whilst I wait for Rueben. I made some homemade pizza tonight which I've wrapped up and left aside for him for when he gets back.

Thankfully when I go to sit on the sofa, I see that one of my favourite films is on and I allow myself to get lost in that.

After about thirty minutes or so I see Rueben's car coming up the driveway and I'm relieved he is finally home. I find nights without Rueben a little boring now. It's been this way since I met him.

"Hey." I smile as a tired looking Rueben comes through the front door.

"Hey." He smiles back before leaning down for a kiss.

"Your dinner is on the side? Is everything OK?"

"Not really. My Nan was crying. She's so fed up." He sighs anxiously.

"I can imagine. Does she know who took it?"

"It's either Mum or Lily. They were there this morning, both asking Nan and my uncles for money and when Nan said no, they got angry. Then Mum was ranting at her about the wedding, saying how you're controlling me and you're not letting me invite her." He explains as he rolls his eyes.

"Really? I got a really friendly text from your Mum earlier today. That doesn't make sense." I say very surprised.

"What time did you get the text?"

"It was mid-afternoon, probably around two o'clock." I say.

"She was at Nan's ranting by ten o'clock this morning, she had obviously calmed down a bit before she sent the text." Rueben shrugs.

"That's just Mum being Mum. She'll rant to other people but be nice to you because she wants to be involved."

"Oh. Well I'm actually kind of disappointed. I wasn't sure if I could trust the text anyway but now that I know I can't it's more of a let-down." I groan disappointedly.

"Don't worry about it babe, just leave it for now. I'll speak to her at some point. She rang me a dozen times today and left me a few voicemails, very much similar to your text actually. She was mostly congratulating me and said that I had picked a good one to marry and how excited she was for the wedding." He says with a smirk as if he can't keep up with her sudden change in personalities either.

"Oh." I nervously giggle.

"Well, don't worry I haven't text back yet, I wanted to check with you anyway. So, how did you leave things with your Nan?" I ask changing the subject a little.

"Well I popped to the shops and got her some food because the money was supposed to go towards a big food shop. I'm so angry at both of them. I think personally they both took it. Nan said they were hovering around her bag where she keeps the key and then both went off into the kitchen together, I wouldn't be surprised if they were splitting the money." He says angrily.

"When Nan asked them if they had been doing anything with her money, they told her to drop down dead."

"Jesus. That's so bad, I honestly don't really know what to say. Does Dave know?"

"No way. Dave has no clue that Mum steals money. He knows she has a problem with money though, he knows she gets herself into money issues and debts, but he wouldn't know about this. He wouldn't believe it either, Mum would deny it and Dave would just believe her over anyone else. So, I don't feel like there's a lot I can do. I can't be down at Nan's constantly guarding her money."

"No…that's so frustrating. At least you have done the right thing for now, I think it's really sweet that you went shopping for her."

"It's just the least I can do really. I shouldn't have to but that's the way it is. Anyway, I can't talk about it anymore because I just get upset for Nan and wound up all over again."

Rueben slumps down on the sofa next to me with his head in his hands. I know how protective he is of his Nan and I really wish I could be of more help, but I have never had to deal with a situation like this.

"Ok…do you want some wine or something and just watch a movie?" I offer trying to make him feel a bit more relaxed.

"Actually, there's one more thing I want to talk to you about." He says with his eyes focused on me.

"Oh…ok?" I reply nervously.

"You have Mum and Lily on your social media, don't you?"

"Yeah? They added me ages ago. Why?"

"You need to take them both off. Block them if you have too."

"Really? Block them? But why? Won't that just make your Mum annoyed?"

"Lily is staying at Nan's tonight. She wasn't there when I got there after work though, apparently, she had gone to meet a friend, but she left her phone on charge in the kitchen. I shouldn't have but I looked through it to see if I could find clues as to whether it was her who took Nan's money and instead, I found some stuff about you." He gently explains.

"Me?" I mumble anxiously.

"Mostly you, yeah. It would appear my Mum and Lily have been sending each other screen shots of things they have seen on your social media and basically being nasty and immature about your pictures and things you might have posted. I just don't want you to be their entertainment and I'd prefer it if they couldn't see anything anymore."

"What kind of things would they say?" I ask taken aback. I know Joy has said things about me but knowing she's saying them behind my back and in such a secretive way, somehow offends and hurts me more.

"It doesn't matter. Please don't keep asking either because I really don't want to tell you. It was just immature and it's clear they are only on your social media for the wrong reasons. Please delete them, now?" Rueben pushes.

"OK, fine. I'll do it after my bath."

"No. Now. Please." Rueben pushes again sternly.

"OK!" I say a little defensively at Rueben's demands and I grab my phone.

I'm not sure why but I want to cry. What could they be saying that's so bad it makes Rueben feel as though he can't even repeat it? Why does Joy confuse me with such friendly text messages if she feels something completely different? I'm not sure why I care so much but I'm starting to feel as though the more Joy hates me, the more I want to try harder for her to like me. Yet I have no idea why I'm being so desperate to be liked.

"Deleted! Happy now?" I sigh as Rueben nods.

CHAPTER FORTY-TWO

"I'm sorry for snapping at you yesterday." Rueben whispers into my ear waking me up.

"What time is it?" I croak, rubbing my eyes.

"About nine thirty now. I turned your alarm off, I called in sick today so that we could spend some time together and maybe even do some wedding planning?" Rueben offers sweetly.

"Daisy?"

"I already took her to school. She seemed very pleased to see me this morning" he laughs.

"Yeah, I'm not surprised, she was asking after you last night. You seem to be in a much better mood?" I say whilst sitting up in bed and waking myself up.

"Well, there's no point getting upset over things I can't control. Plus, I spoke to Nan this morning and she feels much better too. I think Ray is going to see her later and get her a new money box."

"Oh well that's good, hopefully it doesn't happen again."

"Well it probably will, but just to some other poor unsuspecting person." Rueben jokes.

"How can you laugh about it?" I ask a little surprised.

"I'm just so used to it. This is what happens. I remember putting a few hundred pounds in my bed side table from my wages, I was keeping it there until I was ready to convert it into euros because I was going on holiday with my mates. Next thing I knew, Mum had been in my bedroom apparently trying to clean it even though I repeatedly asked her not too and the money just happened to vanish from that day. I just laugh it all off now." He says with a laugh again.

"Oh god, please don't tell me anymore of these stories." I half joke.

"They're all so annoying. I just want to tell her off, but I can't."

"Well you can if you really want too." Rueben jokes and pulls a silly face.

"I can't if I'm still trying to get her to like me, as crazy as that sounds! And anyway, I'm pretty sure the moment to tell her off for something that happened eleven years ago has passed." I laugh.

"Well in that case you'll just have to come downstairs and have pancakes with me then." Rueben says as he starts playfully pulling me from the bed.

"OK! OK! I'm coming. Jeez…have you always been a morning person?" I tease.

"Can I at least have a shower first?"

"OK, fine. But don't be long because I'm making your favourite pancakes, strawberry and banana." Rueben announces with a smile before heading out of the room.

Once I'm in the shower and waking myself up properly, I begin to remember the beautiful villa I printed off for Rueben. I wanted to show him last night, but I knew he would be too distracted with his family worries to concentrate on it. I get out the shower and get dressed as quickly as I can so that I can show him now and tell him the good news that I have reserved it. I quickly run the hairdryer through my hair and style it up into a neat ponytail and head downstairs.

"Just in time!" Rueben smiles cheerfully as he sprinkles the remaining banana and strawberries over my pancakes.

"Looks amazing." I smile back, feeling my stomach rumble with hunger. I can't even remember when the last time was that I had such a decent breakfast. I usually survive on coffee and bites from Freddie's rusk.

"I was thinking we could try and book the hotel for the venue, have you asked your Dad yet if he managed to view it?"

"Not yet." I reply with a mouthful of pancake.

"But he told me he would email me about it and forward on any photos that they took of the place."

"OK. Well let's start other bits. Why don't you find a bridal shop you like today and then arrange a day to go and take your Mum to look at some dresses?"

"I like the sound of that! Oh, and I already managed to book one thing…" I proudly announce whilst pulling the piece of paper from bag and sliding it across the counter.

"Wow!" is all Rueben manages to say as his face lights up.

"This looks unreal!"

"I knew you'd love it! It's so close to everything too! Shops, restaurants, Disney parks! It's going to be perfect!" I shriek excitedly. Even Freddie joins in and loudly makes an excitable squeal.

"OK, how about you fire up the laptop and check your emails. Maybe your Dad has replied by now. Then see if you can find a bridal shop. I'm going to look at some suit ideas for me and Freddie." He says with a beaming smile.

"You mean matching suits?" I ask surprised that Rueben would be open to that idea.

"Well why not? I'd love to match with my son on the best day of my life." Rueben proudly says as he smiles down at his phone. Although within seconds his smile fades as he looks deep in thought. He looks a bit puzzled and his happy expressions start turning more into a frown.

"Everything OK?" I ask.

"I don't know. I think so. I'm just…confused." Rueben stutters.

"A woman has messaged me on my social media, saying she's been trying to look for me for years. She's saying she is my Aunty. My Dad was her brother."

"Aww, wow! That's amazing! And so sweet of her to want to find you." I say enthusiastically.

"She's sent through some pictures too, they're of her and my Dad at some park with Lily as well. Dad's holding me and he looks…he looks really proud." Rueben croaks, his voice tinged with sadness.

"No way! Can I see?" I ask as I lean over the counter and see an adorable photo of a very smiley baby Rueben seemingly on a fun day out with his Dad.

"Rueben, that's a beautiful photo."

"Yeah…it is isn't it. It's just…my Mum always told me that my Dad didn't have any other family. She said they were all dead. My grandparents apparently died years before I was even born, and she told me my Dad didn't have any siblings.

"Oh." I shuffle uncomfortably, unsure of what would be the right thing to say. Rueben keeps staring at the photo as if he is trying to figure everything out.

"She's asked in the message if we can meet up, she has more photos she wants me to have." He quietly says in a way that makes me feel so desperately sorry for him. I know how much Rueben needs this. I know how much he wants to finally understand more about his Dad, more about what happened.

"Invite her for dinner. Saturday night." I suggest without hesitation.

"She can come here, or we can go to our favourite little country pub."

"OK…I think I'll ring her; she's given me her number. I'll call her and invite her." Rueben stutters again with a mixture of nerves and excitement.

As he heads out into the garden to make the call, I stare at him anxiously. I know how much this will mean to him and he really deserves this. He deserves to meet more family and to hear some stories about his Dad, anything that might be able to bring him closure and some relief. I see him smiling whilst talking on the phone. She must be friendly and easy to speak too, because Rueben's tense shoulders have dropped a little. He looks more relaxed. I start cleaning up our plates and wait patiently to hear the outcome. Even I'm a little nervous now and it's not my Aunty.

"She said yes." Rueben's face lights up as he walks back indoors.

"Maggie said yes."

CHAPTER FORTY-THREE

The whole of Saturday, Rueben had been on tenterhooks. It started first thing this morning when he got up extra early and gave the house another good tidy and clean despite the both of us doing it yesterday. I know he just wants everything to go as perfectly as it can and I understand cleaning is probably helping to calm his anxieties, but he is also creating an uneasy atmosphere in the house. I wish he could relax but I guess it isn't that easy. I wish I understood more of what could be going through his mind.

Eventually I decided to take the kids to the park for a couple of hours and give him some space. He barely seemed to notice we were leaving and by the time we came back home again I found him hoovering the stairs for the second time today. I know Joy has rang him a dozen times again today too and that hasn't helped his stress either but at least her texts at the moment are apologetic and kinder towards Rueben. Although he still doesn't seem to be willing to respond just yet.

I decide to leave him to the hoovering and just make a start with dinner as I had planned too. Rueben asked me to make a traditional roast chicken dinner with all the trimmings and his favourite banoffee pie for afters, which is what I have promised.

"What's the time?" Rueben asks out of breath as he comes to find me in the kitchen.

"Nearly three o'clock." I answer gently.

"OK. I best get in the shower then…and get changed." He mutters.

"Fine…but when you get out, I'm pouring you a whiskey and Diet Coke. I'm starting to understand the meaning of Dutch courage." I say with a giggle and Rueben gives me a small grateful smile before heading off upstairs.

I decorate the table as beautifully as I can with a nice grey table cover and a silver table runner. I put out my favourite large wine glasses and light a few candles and place them carefully on top of the runner. I add some flowers and silver napkins too and feel quite proud of my efforts as I take a step back and admire my dining table arrangements.

I put another bottle of wine in the fridge and check on the chicken in the oven. When Rueben reappears, he's wearing his dark blue jeans and my favourite white polo shirt of his. He finishes it off with his black leather bracelets and a little wax run through his hair.

"You look really good." I smile as I look him up and down.

"Are you sure? Is this smart?" He asks as he stares uncertain at himself in the hallway mirror.

"Yes! You look really handsome. So good in fact that I think I'm going to get changed!" I laugh as I run up the stairs.

I quickly get out of my jumper and jeans and change into a nice little black dress and style it with some tights and ankle boots. As I start running the brush through my hair, I see a car that I don't recognise pulling into our driveway. This must be Maggie, she's a little early but I like that. Perhaps once she's come indoors and we've broken the ice, Rueben can finally relax.

When I finish touching up my make-up and make my way downstairs, I see a pretty blonde-haired woman wrapping her arms around Rueben's neck as she pulls him in for a cuddle.

"Oh wow. You really do look just like your Dad did." She beams proudly as she stares at Rueben's face.

"Thank you." Rueben hesitantly says with a smile.

"Please come in, I'm so glad you made it."

"Hey!" I smile warmly.

"You found us OK then?"

"Oh yes. Rueben gave me good directions." She smiles as she greets me with a cuddle and looks back towards Rueben fondly.

Maggie has the biggest smile as Rueben directs her into the front room to meet the kids, her hair is styled up quite neatly and she's wearing black jeans with a black off the shoulder jumper and red lipstick. Casual but classy. She seems thrilled to meet the kids and instantly is sat on the floor with Freddie whilst he plays on his baby mat.

"Would you like some wine?" Rueben politely offers her.

"Ooh yes please! That would be lovely." She responds sweetly.

"I'll make the drinks." I say as I smile at Rueben and disappear off into the kitchen. I decide that I'll finally make Rueben that whiskey too for his nerves.

Pretty soon the chicken has finished cooking and I'm relieved for Rueben as I watch him laughing in conversation with Maggie when I dish up the dinner. So far, she's been telling Rueben all the funny things his Dad got up to when he was younger and laughs as she refers to him as a ladies man. I love how Rueben's face lights up with every new story he learns about him.

"So, how's your Mum these days?" Maggie surprises us by asking over dinner.

"Oh...she's good. I haven't spoken to her much lately; she's not exactly been...easy to get on with right now." Rueben stutters awkwardly.

"Oh! That's just how I remember her then." Maggie laughs.

"She didn't exactly get along with me either!"

"She *knew* you?" Rueben asks confused.

"Well yeah, I used to go to her house with your Dad to pick you and Lily up. Didn't she tell you about that?" Maggie asks inquisitively.

"No...she said Dad didn't have any siblings...or any family." Rueben mumbles as he takes a gulp of his whiskey and Diet Coke.

"Mum, can I get down from the table now that I've finished...and can I play on my iPad?" Daisy interrupts.

"Erm, yes, that's fine. You can have half an hour on it sweetheart." I say as I focus back on Rueben and Maggie a little nervously.

"Well he definitely had family!" Maggie snorts.

"Maybe she just meant they had died. Your Nan and Grandad are no longer with us."

"Did they die before I was born?" Rueben continues suspiciously.

193

"No?" Maggie answers surprised.

"Your Nan died when you were around…let's see, you're thirty now, so she would have died when you were around six years old. Then your grandad passed away after your Dad…so you would have been…"

"Wait, my grandad died *after* my Dad?" Rueben interrupts anxiously.

"Well, yeah. You would have been fourteen when your grandad passed away."

"More wine?" I ask as the room is suddenly filled with an uncomfortable silence.

"I'll grab a bottle…or two."

"What exactly *have* you been told about your Dad?" Maggie eagerly asks Rueben with a sad expression on her face.

"I was told that I'm the reason why he left." Rueben let's out a heavy sigh.

"That he only wanted a daughter which he got with Lily. I was told he didn't want me and so he ended up going back to his wife."

"What? He never left his wife, Rueben." Maggie firmly but softly replies.

"And your Dad…your Dad simply adored you."

"Rueben you should probably start from the beginning." I suggest as I stare at both their faces growing more confused.

"Ok…" Rueben says as he takes in a deep breath.

"My Mum said she was with my Dad for ten years or so. He left his wife for my Mum though, so it wasn't easy. My Dad's parents hated her for it and if they ever saw her in the street, they would call her horrible things like a slag and a bitch…" Rueben explains as Maggie interrupts with a gasp at the nasty insults.

I watch as Maggie shakes her head in disbelief, and she takes a gulp of her wine.

"Then Lily was born, and they were thrilled because my Dad always wanted a daughter and he finally had one. But my Mum had to keep Lily away from my Dad's parents because they didn't want to have a relationship with her because of the fact Dad left his wife. But then when I was born my Dad didn't want me and said it was all too much. So, he left and occasionally he would come by to see Lily but pretty soon he stopped coming over altogether. He went back to his wife and she wouldn't allow him near us anymore. I'm sure there's more that she has told me but that's pretty much the gist of it." Rueben finishes as he takes another sip of his whiskey.

I can't bare the tension that has suddenly filled the room. Rueben is hanging his head down as if he has something to feel guilty about and Maggie just stares down at him with the saddest look on her face.

"Oh Rueben…" Maggie croaks.

"I'm afraid you have been lied to."

CHAPTER FORTY-FOUR

"I'm just not sure if I should say anything, the last thing I would want to do is cause any issues between you and your Mum." Maggie softly says.

"If there are any issues between us it's because my Mum caused them herself. Please Maggie, I'm tired of wondering about how my Dad really felt about me, if you can tell me the truth, I would really be so grateful." Rueben gently pleads with her as I refill our drinks.

"OK...I'll do my best." She nervously replies as she sips at her wine before taking a deep breath.

"I was really close with my brother, we saw each other all the time and as much as I laughed and joked about him being a ladies man, sometimes that could land him in hot water. For instance, he never *had* a relationship with Joy. He stayed married and living with his wife the entire time, but unfortunately, he would occasionally go and visit your Mum and I guess you could say they had an affair. But he never lived with Joy or had an exclusive relationship.

Joy started to convince herself though that your Dad would leave his wife and commit to her. Unfortunately for Joy, as much as your Dad was a bit of a love rat and a charmer, he was never going to commit. Soon, Joy started to get restless and that's when the issues begun. She ended up pregnant with Lily. God, I remember the night your Dad told me." She pauses and laughs a little as she recalls the memory.

"Was he scared?" I ask.

"Scared!? He was petrified!" She laughs.

"I remember him panicking because he knew he had to come clean to his wife. I just kept mocking him and telling him it was his own stupid fault! I knew his promiscuous ways would catch up with him eventually!"

Even Rueben lets out a little laugh over the thought of his Dad running to Maggie like a naughty teenager who desperately needed his sister to fix everything.

"Anyway, Joy was the one who was obsessed with having a girl. She wanted to be different and give your Dad something he didn't already have. She started to convince herself that having a daughter might persuade your Dad to finally move in with her and be a family. Which is ridiculous because for your Dad it didn't matter what they had together, he already had sons who he adored already. It all got a bit sticky when he told his wife about the affairs." Maggie smirks.

"Oh, is that why you started coming with my Dad to the house?" Rueben asks.

"Yes, exactly. Your Dad was thrilled when Lily was born and as angry as his wife was with him about the affair, she never once tried to stop him from seeing Lily or you. She just preferred if I chaperoned." She says with a giggle and Rueben laughs along too.

"I'm not sure you chaperoned very well though Maggie because wasn't Rueben born shortly after?" I say teasingly.

"Yes!" Maggie laughs.

"I told you my brother was a nightmare! Even then he still snuck off a few times."

"If it's any consolation to you Mollie, I definitely haven't followed in my Dad's footsteps in those ways." Rueben interrupts jokingly and I laugh as he gives me a playful wink.

"When you were born Rueben, your Dad simply adored you. You looked so much like him...you still do! But your Mum got really fed up. Your Dad stopped going into Joy's house and instead would only come and pick you up and take you to the park or to his house instead for the day. He knew he needed to stay away from your Mum once and for all if he wanted to save his marriage. That *really* irritated your Mum.

As soon as he stayed away, she got nasty. She refused to let my parents see you, which is why she obviously chose to tell you they were dead. Also, my Mum and Dad would *never* in a million years shout insults at somebody in a street! They never even swore, they were always strict about things like that. I'm truly saddened and baffled as to why your Mum would want to paint them in such a bad light."

I give Rueben's thigh a little squeeze under the table to let him know I'm here for him. I know we are laughing and joking along but I also know this must be difficult to hear.

"It got to a point where your Dad would go the house to collect you and your Mum would refuse him at the door. She gave him an ultimatum. It was his wife or her…and when he chose his wife, she slammed the door in his face and vowed he would never see you or Lily again. He still came to the house every weekend for months in the hopes she would change her mind, but she stood her ground. I remember a time when your Dad told me he saw you at the living room window, you were about four years old and you were waving so excitedly when you saw him come to the door. Your Dad was crushed when he had to walk away. Apparently, you were banging on the window for him, but Joy just refused to let him have you again." She croaks as she pauses to compose herself from crying.

"Oh Roo…" I mumble as I see Rueben's eyes filling with tears.

"Your Dad had to give up. It broke his heart to see you like that but not be able to cuddle you and take you off to the park like the good old days. A couple of years later though, your Nan was in hospital, she had been battling cancer and the doctors were preparing her end of life care. We were told she could go at any time. One night, she asked your Dad if she could see you and Lily, just once at least before she died.

Well, your Dad came to your house again, one final attempt. He literally begged Joy to allow him just to have you and Lily for a few hours, just so he could take you both to his Mum so that she could meet you both properly before she died. But again, she said no and slammed the door in his face.

Rueben, I sat with my brother that night whilst he sobbed which really broke me because your Dad never cried. I really don't know why your Mum wanted to paint him in that light, it's not like he is here anymore. But I want to assure you, your Dad desperately tried. He loved you, he really did love you." Maggie assures as she reaches out to comfort Rueben.

"What about Dad's death? How did that happen?" Rueben asks.

"He had a few things wrong with him and was becoming unwell quite fast. Then unexpectedly he had a massive stroke and that was the end. We wanted you and Lily to come to the funeral, but it needed to be me who would have had to come and ask Joy and I wasn't prepared to give her an opportunity to say no and slam the door in my face like she did to my brother for all those years." She answers guilt-fully.

"I can understand that." Rueben whispers as he stares at Maggie reassuringly.

"I sincerely hope I have helped somewhat." Maggie says as she reaches out again to comfort Rueben by holding his hand.

"I always wished that I could have been at the funeral, but in a way, I'm pleased I didn't go. I have never been ready to say goodbye. Not until now anyway, now that I know the truth, I can stop being mad at him. I can stop wondering all the time if it was me who was the issue just like Lily and my Mum had me believe. I feel like I can forgive him now that I understand him. I'll miss him. But I can learn to let him go now..." Rueben whispers softly with a single tear rolling down his cheek.

CHAPTER FORTY-FIVE

"Happy Birthday!" I cheer loudly as Rueben comes downstairs for breakfast.

"Wow…I did not expect this on a Monday morning." Rueben smiles as he stares at the balloons that I blew up last minute this morning and the presents on the kitchen counter.

"I'm full of surprises." I say with a smug grin.

"I can see that. I wondered what you were doing down here so early."

"Daisy drew you a nice picture…see? There is your walking stick." I playfully tease as I point to the picture.

"Oh, and Freddie couldn't quite manage a picture yet, but he can offer you a piece of paper with some dribble, if you'd like?"

"Hmm…sounds wonderful but I think that's a pass." Rueben laughs and he walks over to me for a cuddle.

"Happy thirty-first Birthday." I whisper as I give Rueben a quick kiss before sliding across his carefully wrapped gift.

"Open it!"

"No! Open my present first!" Daisy excitedly interjects.

"OK, OK! I'll open yours first." Rueben laughs as he takes the box from Daisy and starts tearing into the paper.

"Do you like it?" Daisy asks proudly.

"I do! How did you know that these were my favourite chocolates in the whole world?" He asks playfully as he picks Daisy up for a big cuddle.

"Mummy told me! They're from Freddie too but *I* did all the wrapping." She boastfully tells Rueben as she gives him a cuddle back.

"OK Missy, go upstairs and finish getting ready for school." I say to Daisy.

"You know, it's your big one soon isn't it? The big thirty?" Rueben winks.

"When you're this fabulous God rewards you by keeping you in your twenties." I smirk as I put some of the wrapping paper in the bin.

"Ah I see! I didn't realise. My bad." Rueben mocks me as he picks up my gift again and carefully peels back the paper.

"Do you like it?" I ask anxiously as Rueben stares down at the canvas print of his Dad cuddling a cute mini Rueben whilst enjoying a picnic. Both of them with big smiles on their faces.

"It's...it's...how?" Rueben stutters surprised.

"I got Maggie's phone number from your phone the other day and I just kindly asked her if she could send me a few of the pictures she said she had. She sent that one straight away and I loved it, but the photo itself was a little damaged so I took it to a shop in town and they managed to fix it up for me and make it look as good as new." I explain joyfully as I notice how impressed Rueben looks as he traces the picture with his fingers.

"I love it. Really love it. Thank you so much." He gratefully says as he stares at me affectionally.

"I thought we could hang it in the hallway. That way it can be seen all the time." I offer.

"I'd love that. I'll hang it up after work tonight."

"Perfect." I smile.

"Oh, I have a half day on Friday. I have decided I'll finally go and see my Mum after work and hear her out. Do you want to come?"

"Hmmm. That's a hard pass." I smirk.

"Seriously though, I think you two should hash this out between you both for now and then if she wants to apologise for the comments that she made about Daisy then I'll happily speak to her after."

"OK, that's fair enough."

"If you like though we can take my car and I'll drop you off there? I was going to head into the shops quickly on Friday anyway because I could do with stocking up on Freddie's nappies, wipes and other essentials. Then I could come by and pick you up when you're finished?" I suggest.

"Yeah, that'll be nice. I'll text Mum at some point today and let her know."

"Has she not sent you a Happy birthday message yet then?"

"No!" Rueben laughs.

"I doubt she will either. My birthdays are hardly high on her agenda. Come on Mollie, you should know this by now. Try and keep up."

"OK…jeez…a simple no would have done." I joke as I push him playfully.

As soon as I have dropped Daisy off at school, I'm thrilled to see that my Dad has sent me an email. He says he has been to see the hotel that Rueben and I found. He tells me we picked a really good one and he confirms that it really is beautiful inside and the grounds are very picturesque. He forwards me on some photos that he took for me and I can't wait to show Rueben later. It's glamorous but still low key, which is just what we were after.

That afternoon, I stick some stamps on the save the date cards and take them to the post-box. Now that Rueben is planning on patching things up with his Mum, I can finally send them out.

I can't wait for everyone to start planning their trip along with us.

When I'm finished with those, I make myself a cup of coffee and settle down on the sofa to give my Mum a call. She's in dialysis when I get through to her so she's a bit distracted but still sounds thrilled that I've called. We have a little catch up and I tell her a little bit about Maggie and some of the things she told Rueben about his Dad. My Mum doesn't seem very shocked at the revelations, but she does sound sad for Reuben. We then chat about the wedding a little more and Mum tells me that she's seen the most beautiful flower girl dress in a little boutique near her house and I promise to go across there over the weekend and check it out with her.

After I speak with Mum, I give Lana a quick call too. She's busy at work though so it's only a brief chat but I still feel so much better for having had a quick catch up with both Lana and my Mum. Sometimes I get so distracted with things going on at home with Rueben and Joy that I forget how nice it is to talk about other things.

CHAPTER FORTY-SIX

Friday comes around quickly and I'm soon packing Freddie's nappy bag and getting us ready to hit the shops.

"Shall I put him in the car?" Rueben asks.

"Sure, I'm ready now anyway." I say as I grab the car keys from the kitchen counter.

After Rueben gets Freddie into his car seat, I start to notice he looks a little nervous as we set off for Joy's house.

"What's the matter?" I ask.

"Nothing. I'm sure it'll be fine; I just don't want any more grief." He mumbles.

"I'm sure you don't have anything to worry about, she's the one who will be apologising for her comments she made. She's been wanting to patch things up with you, not argue."

"Yeah I know but I still get stressed out. She shouldn't make those comments in the first place and then we wouldn't have to do stuff like this to move forward again." Rueben groans restlessly.

"Well maybe she'll try and control her temper from now on and hopefully everyone can get along a little easier moving forward."

"What should I tell her if she asks about you?"

"Um...I don't know." I sigh.

"I haven't exactly forgiven her for those comments about Daisy. I'm not sure I ever will. But I know that we need to somehow try and move past this."

"Shall I just tell her you need more time?"

"No, maybe just say that I would appreciate an apology but I'm also happy to just move on for the sake of the kids. As long as she can promise she will never say anything like that again."

"Oh, don't worry, I'll be making sure of that myself." Rueben says firmly.

"I can't have her thinking she can just say that in an argument, I can't risk Daisy hearing her say stuff like that either. My Mum needs to accept that I am her Dad, just like she wanted to be her Grandma. And that's final."

"Yeah, just try not to come across *too* pushy. I know it's hard and believe me I want to have my rant at her too but just try and remind yourself that we are all human, we make mistakes. She said what she said in anger and we have to try and be the bigger people and let it go." I say calmly.

"I know, don't worry. I'll sort it all out." He assures me.

As we approach Joy's house, Freddie is already fast asleep.

"Oh great." I laugh.

"That'll be fun getting him out."

"I'm sure he'll be good as gold for his Mummy. Have fun, I'll call you as soon as I'm finished then? I'll stay about an hour or something yeah?" Rueben says.

"Yeah that's fine, just let me know when you're ready to leave and I'll come back." I answer as Rueben leans over and gives me a kiss goodbye.

I watch as he makes his way up the steps to Joy's house and knocks on the door before setting off to the shops.

Thankfully, it's pretty quiet in town and I find a parking space and get Freddie out of his car seat and into his pushchair without waking him. As I go up to the parking machine to get a ticket for the car, my phone starts ringing from my pocket. I stare at my phone a little concerned. It's Rueben, already.

"Hello?" I answer a little surprised.

"Hello? Babe can you please come and get me." Rueben says his voice trembly and anxious.

"Roo? What's happened?"

"Please just come and get me Mollie. I want to go, right now." He pleads impatiently sounding very stressed.

"OK...I'm coming right now. Where are you?" I ask as I start running back to the car.

"I'm walking down towards my Nan's. I'll just wait for you down there, by the road." He says breathlessly.

"OK...I'm coming, I'll be five minutes, absolute tops." I assure as I carefully get Freddie back into his car seat and collapse the pushchair down before haphazardly throwing it back into the boot.

I weave through any traffic as quickly as I can and make my way out of the town and back down towards Joy's road. As I start approaching Joy's front door, I'm half tempted to stop here and go banging on her door and ask why Rueben is so upset. But instead I stay focused on finding Rueben and I reluctantly drive past and follow the road down the hill towards Irene's house.

As I get to the bottom of the hill, I find Rueben anxiously stood by the side of road with his hands in his pockets, head hanging down and looking defeated.

When I stop the car Rueben jumps in straight away and looks at me impatiently as if I should be pulling away instantly. But I can't.

"Rueben, what the *hell* happened to you?" I gasp as anxiety fills my body and I stare in disbelief at all the marks on his body.

"Let's just go home and I'll explain." He sighs as if he is exhausted.

"No, how about I go and ask her." I angrily suggest as I turn my car around and drive to Joy's front door.

"Don't babe! She won't answer the door to you. You're just wasting your breath." Rueben pleads as he takes me by the arm to stop me from getting out of the car.

"Rueben look at the state of you!" I scream.

"So? It doesn't matter. Let's just go and I'll explain. Please. I'm embarrassed enough as it is. Please, just drive away." Rueben begs and I snap myself out of my rage just enough to realise that I should be listening to what Rueben wants. No matter how angry I am.

"Fine." I snap as I take a deep breath and drive away. I quickly take us to a quiet pub car park for some privacy and look to Rueben for answers.

I stare at his injuries. He has red marks all over his arms, neck and face as if he has been hit with something repeatedly. But the most concerning injury is the deep cut and graze across his forehead. It's been bleeding this whole time despite Rueben trying to stop it with tissues from the glove box.

"She started kicking off the second she opened the front door." Rueben begins to explain as he tries to slow down his breathing.

"She wasn't happy because I didn't have Freddie with me, and she got angrier when I said that you had taken him to the shops because I thought I was there to talk alone with her."

"She attacked you for that?" I gently ask.

"No. Without thinking, this morning I took a picture of my canvas you got me, and I posted it to my social media. She told me saw it and asked me where I had gotten the photo from. I told her that Maggie had been in contact and she came for dinner...and she just lost it. She started screaming questions at me, asking me why I would go against the family and see Maggie. Saying that she's a liar and I should stay away. She said I was disrespectful to Dave for meeting up with my Dad's family. Then she asked why I would care about them when my Dad didn't care about me. She said my Dad hated me and I just look desperate. Then, when I told her Maggie said my Dad loved me, she grabbed the nearest thing to her and started hitting me with it as hard as she could. It all happened so quick, but I think it was a hairbrush or the t.v remote. But then that obviously wasn't enough, and she ended up grabbing the fire poker next to the fireplace and just hit me straight across the head with it. Then she hit me across my back and all down my side. She hit me across my head again and it felt all fuzzy and that's when I realised, I was bleeding..."

"Oh my god, Rueben. This *isn't* normal. This is abuse." I say absolutely disgusted.

"I saw my new passport had arrived on the table so as I turned to leave I reached out to take it and she hit me across the hand with the fire poker again and said I couldn't have it...I just walked out and she screamed after me calling me every name under the sun. That's when I called you." He explains as he hides his head in embarrassment.

"Rueben...I think we should take you to the hospital. Your head is going to need stitches and your hand is already swollen..."

"No way!" Rueben interrupts.

"And say what? My Mum attacked me? Do you have any idea how pathetic I would look?"

"It's not pathetic. It's the truth."

"No, I can't do that. Let's just please go home." He sighs anxiously.

"What about if we went to the hospital and said you were attacked by some random man? We don't have to say it's your Mum." I softly suggest in the hopes Rueben will agree.

"That's the thing Mollie...if it was a man that attacked me, I would fight back. Without any hesitation. But what am I supposed to do when my Mum attacks me? I can't go punching a woman. I have no choice but to take it."

"I understand what you mean but the answer is still *not* that you just sit there and take it. Absolutely not. We will figure something out but for now you need to go to the hospital." I plead again.

"No. I don't want anyone to see me like this. Please Mollie. Can we just go home?"

CHAPTER FORTY-SEVEN

I gave up persuading Rueben to go to the hospital in the end. As much as I am worried sick about the wound on his head, he won't allow anyone to see him like this. He is too embarrassed and ashamed, and it doesn't seem to matter what I say, he can't see it any other way.

Instead, when we get home, I make him lay on the sofa and try to relax. I bring down the duvet and make him some lunch. In just under an hour I have to go and collect Daisy and I have no idea how I'm going to explain Rueben's cuts and bruises to her yet. Obviously, it can't be the truth. I will probably have to say he had a fall at work and hopefully she won't ask too many questions.

After lunch, Rueben puts Freddie on the sofa with him and they both snuggle up together and watch Toy Story. I start noticing though that Rueben can't move around very easily without being in a lot of pain, I'll need to go to the chemist after I collect Daisy and see what the strongest painkillers are that I can get for him. I think Joy may have bruised or possibly even cracked one of his ribs. He even says it hurts to take a deep breath in, but he still refuses a quick trip to the hospital to check it out.

"Are you going to be okay for a little while on your own whilst I go and collect Daisy?" I ask Rueben gently.

"Yeah I think so baby. Don't worry about me." He whispers through the pain.

"I really think you need to get your ribs looked at now…"

"No, I'll be fine. Just some painkillers please." He mumbles through a deep breath.

"OK…you stubborn little sod." I say trying to joke a little.

As I put my boots back on and open the front door, I'm startled to see a police car pulling up into my driveway and two male officers getting out of the car.

"Roo…the police are here." I whisper confused and panicked.

"What? Really?" Rueben responds, concerned.

"Yeah. Oh my god I hope they aren't here to tell me something bad has happened to my Mum or something…"

"No, calm down, don't be silly. It might not even be for us." Rueben says as he limps into the hallway behind me.

"Mollie?" The police officer asks as he approaches my front door.

"Is there a Rueben Adams living here?"

"Erm, yes?" I nervously answer.

"We would like to speak to you both please." The other police officer says as he stares at Rueben's injuries.

"What is this about?" I ask as I fidget uncomfortably.

"You'll know in a minute. First, I would like to talk to Rueben on his own in the kitchen please. You need to stay in the front room Mollie. I am P.C Kingswood and this is my colleague P.C Barnes." He informs sternly.

"Let's go in here please, Rueben." P.C Barnes asks politely as Rueben follows him into the kitchen looking as baffled as I am.

I stand awkwardly in the front room with the other police officer, P.C Kingswood. I pick Freddie up from his baby gym and give him a cuddle as I wait anxiously for Rueben to come back.

"Have you been in trouble with the police in the past?" The officer quizzes me.

"No." I reply impatiently and very confused.

"Have you had social services in your children's lives at all?" He continues.

"No." I sigh.

"Never."

To my relief Rueben is already returning back into the front room as he clutches at his ribs before lowering himself onto the sofa.

"OK…" P.C Barnes announces as he reappears into the front room.

"So, Mollie, we had a very anxious call come through earlier today from Rueben's Mother, Joy. She told us that she saw her son today when he popped over for a visit and she was very concerned to see that he was covered in grazes and bruises. She is very worried that you are hurting her son and that he is lying to protect you which is why we needed to speak to Rueben on his own and understand his version of events."

"Wha…what?" I manage to say as my jaw drops open.

I stare at Rueben briefly who looks ashamed before I turn back to the police officer. I feel sick.

"She's also concerned that these violent attacks are happening in front of your two children who also live inside the home. Daisy and Freddie." The police officer continues.

"But, I would never…" I begin to say as my voice cracks and tears start to fill my eyes.

"Baby, it's okay. I told them it was Mum." Rueben assures me as he places his hand on my thigh.

"We will have to take a statement with your version of events in that case. It will need to go down on file that you are confirming the allegations to be false and claiming the bruises were caused by your Mother after she attacked you earlier today." The officer explains.

"That's fine. But then what are my options?"

"Well we can go and arrest her, or if you feel like it's just been a domestic that has gotten out of control, we can just file it for now without any further action." He explains calmly as I just stare between him and Rueben in complete shock and try to process what is happening.

"I'm happy to do the statement. But I want it filed and no further action, please." Rueben shocks me by saying. How can he let her off so easily? When she's lied to the police with allegations that could have potentially had me arrested.

"That's fine. Because it's a domestic issue though there is a chance that social services may need to do their own investigations. They may want to do some checks with the headteacher and just make sure your child's school have no concerns." The police officer tells me.

"Tell…tell…the school?" I stutter as I panic at the thought of them being dragged into this. What will they think of me?

"Yes. But if there are no issues then you have nothing to worry about."

"Nothing to worry about. Do you know how embarrassed I'm going to feel when I go to those school gates now?" I cry as I stare at Rueben in disbelief.

"I'll talk to the school." Rueben tries to assure me.

"I'll tell them everything. I'll tell them it's all my fault and that it's my Mum just trying to hurt us. Baby, please…" Rueben offers as he tries to comfort me. He tries to wrap his arm around my waist, but I move away.

"My job? Could they be informed? I work with children. I allocate foster families to children in need. That's my job…" I say.

"There is a chance your work would be notified then, yes." P.C Barnes informs.

"I love my job." My voice cracks again.

"Can you imagine what they will think of me?"

"I'm so sorry baby. This is all my fault." Rueben whispers as he reaches out for me again.

"Don't touch me!" I yell as the tears fall from my cheeks. I have never in my life been accused of hurting anybody. This allegation is too much to bare.

"Shall we make a start with your statement?" The officer suggests to Rueben.

"Do I need to stay?" I ask through gentle sobs.

"No, we just need Rueben for this part." He replies.

"In that case, I'm going to collect my daughter now." I mutter as I walk towards the front door.

My legs are trembling beneath me as I hurry to my car. I feel as though I could just collapse. As soon as I make it to my car, I shut the door behind me and before I head off to the school, I take a moment for myself. I drop my head into my hands and cry. I cry through anger, through the stress, the hurt, everything. Right now, I am so distraught. I feel as though I don't even want to go back home. I can't.

CHAPTER FORTY-EIGHT

Without thinking about it, I ended up collecting Daisy from school and going straight to my Mum's house. I can't take Daisy back into the house, not whilst the police are still there. I don't want to scare Daisy, I don't want her to know or have to worry about any of this.

I also really don't think I can speak to Rueben right now. He should be telling the police the truth and sending them straight to her house to arrest her. She should be held accountable for wasting police time with her lies and deceit, but mostly she should be made to take responsibility for the awful bruises over Rueben's body.

I tell my Mum about how frustrated and confused I am. I want to go home and look after Rueben; I want to help him and care for him because I know he is in pain right now and needs me. But I just feel so let down. How much more can he take? I'm not sure how much more I can take, that's for sure.

"Right. What's her number?" Mum demands as I sit wallowing on her sofa.

"You can't ring her!" I say anxiously.

"Why not? How are you supposed to know what you have done to deserve this, if I don't ask her? How is anything going to be solved if nobody speaks?" She says in frustration. I'm anxious, but I know she has a point.

"Fine. This is her number. Just please don't get into an argument

213

because it'll just make matters worse." I say passing her my phone with Joy's contact information on display.

"I'm not going too; I'm going to be polite but direct." Mum says as she starts dialling the phone number and presses the phone against her ear.

"Hello is that Joy?" Mum asks in a friendly tone.

"Yes?" I hear Joy faintly confirm from the handset.

"Hi Joy, it's Laraine, Mollie's Mum. I know what happened today and I'm just curious as to what on Earth is going on and why this is happening?

Both Rueben and Mollie are stressed to bits...

Hello?

Hello...?

Joy?

She's hung up the phone already." Mum shrugs unphased as if she knew this might be the case.

I sigh stressfully as I drop my head into my hands.

"I knew it. She's a bully and a coward, Mollie. She won't speak to me because she knows she can't just lie her way out of it. She's bullied Rueben all his life and now when it suits her, she'll bully you too." Mum warns.

"What am I supposed to do?" I whine.

"That's for you and your future husband to decide, I can't tell you what you should do. But you need to stay strong and rise above it. You're not a silly girl Mollie, you can come out on top against some narcissistic oddball like Joy."

"Oh Mum, you do have a way with words." I giggle.

"I know." She smirks sarcastically and playfully gives me a nudge.

"But now you need to go home and talk to Rueben. He must be worried sick about where you have got too."

"Yeah, I think he is worried. He has called me quite a lot and left loads of messages." I sigh as I stare at my phone.

I give Mum a hug goodbye and head back home. I'm nervous though. This is probably the most upset I have ever been with Rueben in our relationship so far and in reality, it's not even him who started it. I know he is just trying to find the best ways to fix everything. But

I don't think he ever thinks about himself. He gets too consumed with trying to protect everybody else to avoid any further damage.

As I walk through the front door Rueben is waiting in the hallway for me. He looks at me sheepishly and my stomach turns to knots as I see the sadness and desperation in his face. I hate it. He looks so lost.

"I have done Daisy a pizza, it's already cooling down on the dining table." Rueben says timidly.

"Yay, pizza!" Daisy smiles as she skips off to the dining room.

"Mollie...can I talk to you please?"

"Yes." I nod awkwardly.

"OK...erm, please come upstairs with me first." He gently pleads as he heads up the stairs and I curiously follow behind.

When I get to the top of the stairs, I see the glow coming from the bathroom. The bath is filled with bubbles and I can see he has used some bath salts too, it smells divine. Scattered around the bathroom must be twenty or more tea light candles. Next to the bath is a small bowl of strawberries and a glass of wine.

"Oh Roo..." I gasp, taking it all in.

"Please just get in the bath for a bit and unwind and then I'll come back for a chat in a minute." He says nervously and I agree.

As soon as my bare skin touches the warm soapy water, I immediately feel less stressed. I sip my wine and lay my head back, indulging in the moment.

I almost want to cry again at all the effort he has put in for me, but I remind myself that I still have every right to be upset.

"Baby..." Rueben says as he reappears and takes a seat next to the bath.

"Can I talk first and say what I need to say and then you can talk?"

I nod in agreement and let him speak first.

"In the last few years of my life I have realised over time that there were certain things that my Mum and Dave would do, that weren't right. When I met you and moved away from their house, I realised that more than ever. When I came to that realisation, I started having all these random memories pop back into my mind. Like flashbacks. Some of them were pretty upsetting and it's been really difficult trying to make sense of why that happened to me and how I managed to suppress it all this time. I have a lot in my mind that I need to sort out and I need help understanding. So, if you can spare me some evenings, I have found a therapist who deals specifically with childhood issues and tonight I have made contact with them and decided to start therapy every Monday night going forward.

I know I should have told the police to go and arrest her, but I need things to settle down so that I can concentrate on this therapy. If I did that to her, she would definitely react even worse and we would both be under even more stress. Whereas if I let her cool down, she'll probably be sorry again and we can graciously accept, but also keep her at arm's length." He calmly explains.

"So, like a keep your friends close but your enemies closer kind of thing?" I ask.

"Yes. Just for now. Just whilst I figure some things out. I need some time. When I'm ready I'll be happy to share with you all the flashbacks and memories that I'm having but for now, I really want to try and work on this on my own. So that I can be the husband you deserve. I want to be the best Dad that I can be to our children without worrying that I am going to repeat my Mum's mistakes. Does any of this make sense?"

"It does." I sigh.

"It's just hard because I don't want to let her hurt us or walk all over us and you're essentially asking me to stop sticking up for myself and to stop sticking up for you!"

"I'm sorry if that's how you feel. I want to be the one who sticks up for you and protects you anyway. It's embarrassing you even have to feel this way because of my family. You have been dealing with my Mum now for just over a year, believe me I know it's hard. But I have been dealing with her my whole life and I just need a bit of time to get my head straight on a few things and then I promise, if anything else bad happens, my next approach won't be so diplomatic." Rueben says whilst looking at me square in the eyes.

"Okay." I say.

"You have my full support."

CHAPTER FORTY-NINE

Things have been a little better over the past four months. Rueben ended up having two weeks off work though with badly bruised ribs but is finally back to his usual self. We managed to book the hotel in for the wedding once I showed Rueben the pictures my Dad had sent. I also booked flights and the caterers, so we are making great progress and I'm feeling quite organised. We still haven't got Rueben's passport though, on the day when Joy attacked Rueben, she threatened to keep it from him for good and if he wanted it back, he would have to go there on his own again. But there is no way Rueben could risk that again, not when she gets herself into such tempers and acts out the way that she does.

I spoke to Mel regularly via email for the first few weeks after Joy had made those false allegations, but she hasn't heard anything about it at work. Thankfully it seems as though my work are blissfully unaware of the lies my soon to be mother-in-law spouted about me.

True to his word, Rueben went straight to the school the following day and explained the situation in great detail to the headteacher. She seemed pretty sympathetic and understanding. She also assured us that if social services got in contact, she would inform them that the school have no concerns over Daisy's wellbeing, but so far it doesn't seem as though they have.

Since Joy called the police, we haven't heard a peep out of her. It's been extremely quiet. A couple of months ago Daisy had her ninth birthday and I half expected to hear something from her then, but we didn't hear a thing. Nothing arrived in the post for Daisy either, not even a birthday card.

Although it's pretty unusual to be given so much space from Joy, it has really helped. Rueben has been making progress with his therapist and even started to keep a journal which he notes down some of the flashbacks and he adds some helpful coping mechanisms next to it. I haven't seen it yet though, this is just what he has told me so far.

The therapist is really helping Rueben to understand that he is a good person who has done nothing to warrant the treatment he has been getting. She made him understand that he was an innocent child and however his parents chose to treat him was actually their own mistakes and toxic traits and absolutely no fault of Rueben's. It's still going to be a long process, but he comes home a lot more relaxed and self-assured.

My Mum bought Daisy the flower girl dress she had her eye on. It's pastel pink up top and then goes down into a beautiful ivory skirt, finished with a diamanté belt. It's got me so excited for going bridal dress shopping with my Mum tonight. Rueben has his therapy, so I'm taking Daisy and Freddie too and going late night shopping.

So far, my Dad and step mum have confirmed that they will be joining us on our wedding day in Florida as well as Rueben's cousin Leah, Lana and Mike and hopefully my Mum too but she's having difficulty arranging her dialysis out there. Obviously, we haven't heard from Joy and Dave, but Rueben did get a message from Lily and she asked if she could still come along. Rueben hasn't talked to her much about what he found in her bag that day, but he did say that as long as she could stay clean on the run up to the day then we would still help her come to the wedding, even if we have to cover some of her costs. We both agreed we would feel guilty if we didn't try to include her.

By the time I pick up Mum, we're both singing loudly along to some Queen songs on the drive to the shopping centre. I'm so excited to try on some dresses but nervous in case I don't get that amazing feeling brides supposedly get when they have found the one.

"So, what are we thinking Mollie?" My Mum asks whilst I find us a parking space.

"I really have no idea, but I guess it'll need to be light and airy because I don't want to be too hot on the day. It's probably going to be pretty humid, so I need to dress for that."

"Good idea, very true. Well we'll make sure you try on a fair few and get a feel for what you like best." Mum says enthusiastically.

My eyes are wide as we enter the bridal shop and I quietly gasp at the view in front of me. The room is filled with the most beautiful dresses, I'm not even sure where to start looking. A lovely shop assistant comes over and offers us a drink whilst we browse before showing me to my private dressing room. It's huge inside, the carpets are black with sparkles and the walls are silver, there's huge mirrors on every wall and there's two shabby chic chairs for Mum and Daisy to sit on next to a platform where I come out and present them with each dress I try on. Freddie as always misses the excitement and has fallen asleep in his pushchair; it never takes long for him to doze off once he has been in the car.

The friendly shop assistant brings me a few different dresses to try on as we really have no idea where to start. Mum and Daisy excitedly take a seat and eagerly wait to me to get started. My first one is ivory and satin, it's elegant but very plain.

"Hmm…" Mum stares at me underwhelmed as I stand on the platform for the very first time.

"I feel like it's a wedding dress you'd wear if you were in your sixties."

"Yeah Mum, Nana is right. It's a bit boring. I rate this a two out of ten!" Daisy loudly says which makes the assistant giggle.

"Nothing like the honesty of children, eh!" She smirks as she begins unbuttoning me from the gown.

The next few dresses I try on are strapless, but I think I'm almost certain this style doesn't suit me, and Daisy confirms my fears by rating me a three out of ten.

"How about a tulle dress?" The assistant suggests.

"They're usually a princess style with a large skirt but the fabric is very light so shouldn't be too hot under the Florida sun."

"I found a nice tulle looking one when I first came in, can I get it and see what my daughter thinks?" Mum asks as she makes her way to the shop floor and I head back into the dressing room to undress again.

"Here we go." The assistant appears behind me in the dressing room.

"This is the one your Mother chose."

On first glance at the dress I am just as underwhelmed as I have been with the previous five dresses but as I step into it and the dress begins to take shape around my body, I find myself staring at it with an entirely different opinion.

"Oh, Mollie!" Mum gasps as I step out and onto the little platform.

I stare at the dress in the mirror. It's a full skirt but as the assistant promised it is quite light, so I don't feel too bulky or hot. The skirt nips in at the waist and on top I have a lot of lace detailing and off the shoulder straps.

"Have you got a diamanté belt at all?" Mum asks the assistant eagerly.

"Yes, we have a few different styles. I'll grab some." The assistant responds as she disappears to the back room.

I stare at the dress quietly, taking it all in. I can definitely imagine myself getting married to Rueben in this.

"Ahh, they're perfect." Mum beams as she stares at the belts the assistant has brought back.

"This is the one!"

Mum carefully places the belt around me where the skirt pulls in at my waist and I can't believe how something so simple has beautifully completed the dress.

"Oh my god...I love it!" I say excitedly as I admire my reflection.

"I love it! Nine out of ten, Mum!" Daisy calls as she stares at me in amazement.

"Ahh yes, good thinking Daisy, we need the veil to make it up to ten!" Mum reminds us.

"I think you need a full-length floor one. Just like Princess Diana did!"

"Go big or go home." The assistant agrees with a big smile.

"But not a plain one, maybe something with a few little sparkles or crystals in it?" Mum suggests brightly.

I pull my hair out of my ponytail and let it fall down over my shoulders as Mum takes the veil from the assistant and places it on top of my head.

"Oh wow…" Mum whispers.

"Ten out of ten!" Daisy cheers excitedly.

"It's better than anything I could have imagined." I say, as I take in the finished look.

"Are we happy ladies? Is this the one?" The assistant asks.

"Yes." I smile elatedly.

"This is my dress."

CHAPTER FIFTY

"I wish I could show you the pictures of me in it! I can't stop thinking about it Roo!" I say gleefully as I tell him what a success the shopping trip was.

"Sounds great! But as much as I want to see it, I'd rather be surprised on the day, otherwise it's bad luck."

"At which point in this relationship have we had good luck?" I joke.

"Exactly! We really don't need to tempt fate, especially not on a day my Mum will be present on." Rueben laughs.

"God...yeah. I forgot Medusa was coming. Okay, fair point."

"Medusa?" Rueben smirks as he stares at me.

"I thought your favourite one was Norma Bates for her?"

"Yeah it still is, but sometimes I like to mix it up a little." I smirk back.

"Well, since we are talking about Medusa. I want to talk to you about an idea my therapist had, if that's okay?" Rueben asks a little hesitantly.

"Sure." I reply confidently.

"You can tell me anything."

"Well I have been discussing with my therapist about whether I wanted to cut my Mum out of my life completely or whether I wanted to try and give her another chance. It's taken me a while to get to the answer, but I think for the sake of the kids I should give her another chance."

"Okay?" I respond, unconvinced.

"Well the thing is, I grew up really close to my Nan and I just think I would feel guilty if I took the opportunity away. Before anything can happen though my therapist suggested that I invite Mum and Dave over one day for a calm conversation about it all. She thinks I need to tell them openly and honestly about the impact their actions have caused me and how moving forward I'll be setting boundaries and I need them to honour that to move forward." Rueben explains.

"So, what kind of boundaries?" I question curiously.

"Well there's a fair few. But for starters I'll be asking her to stop inundating me with abusive phone calls, she obviously can't ever react the way she has done by lashing out at Daisy and definitely *not* the police again. She has to stop taking over with the kids, like she did with Freddie's medicine. There's a few more things that will probably come up and I want you to feel comfortable enough to talk about your feelings too." Rueben offers as I nod along.

"It's weird because when the police turned up at my house that day, I honestly never thought I could ever stand to be in the same room as Joy ever again. Not for a million years at least. I'm still not sure how comfortable I'll feel around her now if I'm honest…but, if you think this could help you to move forward and there's a chance peace can be resumed then I'm willing to try." I offer supportively.

"I appreciate that. I feel like if we do this then at least whatever happens going forward, we can always say that we tried." Rueben says as he gives me a confident smile before pulling me in for a cuddle.

"Does this mean I'll have to stop calling her Norma Bates and other crazy movie villains?" I mutter into Rueben's shoulder.

"Probably best, least just for now." Rueben laughs.

"How boring." I groan sarcastically and roll my eyes.

"OK, so when is this meeting supposedly happening?"

"Friday night, I think. I'll text her in a minute if you're happy to go ahead?"

"Yeah, okay. I'm following your lead." I assure.

"Am I supposed to be cooking a dinner?"

"No, I think we should keep the meeting as casual as possible. Just a cup of tea or whatever, that'll be fine."

"Yeah that's probably a good idea. Okay, invite her then and we'll go from there. Also, will I need full padding and a helmet for this meeting? And should I hide the fire pokers?" I mock as Rueben shakes his head at me as we both laugh.

As Friday comes around, I give the house the usual quick tidy and I make sure everything is presentable and ready for the arrival of Joy and Dave. I'm a little anxious at the thought of seeing Joy though. As the clock ticks my brain runs wild with all the thoughts and memories of the police standing on my doorstep, accusing me of hurting my fiancé, accusing me of having violent outbursts in front of my children. How vindictive was she that day, she physically attacked her son and then tried to blame me for it? I have never known anyone so calculating. I have to actively keep myself from allowing these intrusive thoughts into my mind otherwise I won't be able to sit in the same room as her, let alone be polite.

I distract myself by setting Daisy up in her bedroom with a new movie to watch and some popcorn. I figured it would be best if we had a chat privately first without the kids, just in case it doesn't go very well.

Rueben surprisingly seems quite calm about the whole thing; He seems willing and able to cope with both scenarios that could occur here. Either we all get along and find some common ground, or we walk away from each other once and for all. Both options do not seem to worry him, not like I thought they would.

The sound of the doorbell breaks my thoughts and I hear Rueben answer the door. They're here. I take a moment to take a deep breath and prepare myself to see Joy before I confidently stride down the stairs.

When I walk into the living room Dave looks like his usual self, he maintains his regular nonchalant manner which is the complete opposite from Joy.

Joy is sat in the corner of the sofa, barely making any eye contact and fidgeting nervously.

"Alright?" Dave mumbles with little effort.

"Hi." I smile as Joy quickly looks up and gives me a nervous smile before looking away again.

I take a seat on the opposite armchair just as Rueben comes in with two cups of tea.

"Did you want a hot drink, baby?" Rueben asks with a surprisingly relaxed tone.

"No thanks, I'll just grab a Diet Coke in a minute." I say as I sit back and wait a little anxiously for the conversation to start.

"Can I just start by saying that I'm really sorry about losing my temper and saying those things about Daisy not being family. I shouldn't have said that. Of course, Daisy is family and I'd still very much love to be her Grandma." Joy surprises me by blurting out.

I nod as I listen to her apology, but I don't rush myself to accept it.

"I am her Dad. That's a decision I made long ago; you have no right to tell me any different in future. You can't just change your mind on being Grandma when it suits." Rueben says calmly but firmly.

"I know. Does Daisy know that I said those things?" Joy asks timidly.

"No. We haven't told her anything, we wouldn't." I respond.

"Mum, what made you go and get the police involved?" Rueben sighs as Joy shifts around her seat awkwardly.

"Well I don't know. I was angry…I thought you was going to go to the police first." Joy huffs anxiously as she tries to give an explanation.

"I had no intentions to go to the police, but you were wrong to attack me like that." Rueben says.

"You have no right to ever hit him, or anyone." I add forcefully.

"If your Mum hit you then you must have done something to deserve it." Dave interjects stubbornly as he stares at Rueben with his arms folded.

I stare at Dave in shock. I can feel myself getting agitated, but I try hard to stay calm for Rueben's sake. Once again, Dave just talks to Rueben like he is a naughty child and plays down Joy's abuse as if it was a little smack on the hand. I glance back at Joy who nervously stares down at the floor and avoids my eye contact and it becomes apparent to me that Dave has no idea about the extent of Rueben's injuries. I want to tell Dave exactly how bad the attack was, but I decide it's not my place.

"I don't feel as though meeting up with Maggie to learn about my real Dad warrants being attacked." Rueben confidently makes his point.

"If you want answers about your Dad you go to your Mother. Not some ditzy old woman like this Maggie who has conveniently popped into your life." Dave says impatiently.

"How can you say she's ditzy when you have never met her? In fact, I am sure Joy said she didn't even know Maggie existed." I say as I stare at Joy for answers.

"I knew she existed. I just forgot." Joy speaks up hesitantly.

"And I wouldn't trust a word that woman says."

I hate that Joy is trying to put a seed of doubt in Rueben's mind. Maggie was kind and considerate to Rueben's feelings, she explained so much more than Joy has ever bothered to do and here she is trying to ruin it for him already.

"I am going to continue seeing Maggie when I want to because I really liked her. I would prefer it if we kept Maggie out of this, in future I just won't mention her around you." Rueben offers as Dave nods in agreement, but Joy still huffs childishly as if Rueben is being unfair.

"Fine. It's up to you if that's what you choose, and it has nothing to do with us. I think your Mum can agree that the police shouldn't ever be involved, that was just a mistake and I'm sure we can all get over it." Dave insists as he looks at Joy for her opinion and she hesitantly nods.

"I understand as well that you have Freddie's best interests at heart and I appreciate you only wanted to help, but please in future if you have concerns and want to change something like his medication, can you run it by us first, please?" I say, changing the conversation from Maggie.

"Yeah…just ring us and talk to us. It's not a problem." Rueben backs me up.

"Right…okay." Joy mumbles.

"In my day you didn't question your grandparents like this. But if that's what you want that's what we will do. But it's not fair that we haven't seen the kids in months." Dave sighs.

"It's difficult to see Mum though when she's swearing at me down the phone, making threats and hitting me. How can I bring my kids around that?" Rueben answers.

"You know your Mum would never lose her temper like that in front of the kids. She loves them." Dave adds.

226

"Right, well I'll try and bring the kids around for more consistent visits as long as Mum stops all the abusive phone calls."

"Yes, Roo. That's fine. I don't want to argue anymore. I *am* sorry. To you and Mollie." Joy apologises sympathetically.

"Ok, well I appreciate that." Rueben replies.

"I think if we try, we can probably all start a fresh." Joy says as she looks at me desperately.

"I guess I'm willing to try and wipe the slate clean. Yes." I say which seemingly brings her relief and she smiles.

"Thank you." She whispers and a for a moment everybody is just quiet and unsure of what to say or do next. "Would it be okay to see the kids?"

"Yeah. I'll get Freddie up from his nap and call Daisy." I say.

Within minutes Daisy comes bounding down the stairs behind me as I carry Freddie down.

"Grandma!" Daisy yells excitedly and gives her a hug.

"Hello, love." Grandma giggles as I pass her Freddie to cuddle.

Joy studies Freddie adoringly as she takes in any changes that have occurred over the last few months.

"Guess what Grandma? Mummy chose her wedding dress; she looks like a princess!" Daisy beams.

"Oh, have you, Mollie?" Joy questions, intrigued.

"I'll look forward to seeing it."

"So how are the wedding plans going?" Dave asks to continue the lighter conversation.

"Yeah really well. We are practically done now. I'll have to show you some pictures of it all soon." Rueben suggests.

"That'll be really nice mate." Joy smiles at Rueben as she continues to cradle Freddie.

"And Grandma, I'm going to be a flower girl! I have a dress!" Daisy says as she jumps up and down in excitement.

"Oh wow. I'd love to see it." Joy says.

"I'll go grab it for you, I offer." As I head up to Daisy's bedroom to fetch the dress.

"It's pink Grandma…and it's has a belt just like my Mummy's dress!" I hear Daisy say.

"Here we are!" I smile as I proudly show off Daisy's dress.

"Oh, wow Daisy! That's beautiful, you're going to look like such a big girl in it, aren't you?" Joy thoughtfully says to a very excited Daisy.

"Smashing." Dave adds with a smile.

"Erm, Mollie. Would it be okay if Lily was bridesmaid?" Joy softly asks.

"We aren't doing bridesmaids, Mum. Just Daisy who will be a flower girl." Rueben answers.

"Oh." Joy responds looking disappointed.

"It's not everyday somebody in the family gets married though. Do you think you could think about it?"

"We'll think about it." I say as I make an effort to keep the evening running smoothly.

CHAPTER FIFTY-ONE

A month later and I had pretty much given in to the bridesmaid idea. But I mostly blame Lana for that.

A couple weeks ago we went out one evening to some new Mexican themed bar in town for cocktails and I was telling her all about meeting up with Joy and Dave and how Joy asked if I would consider making Lily a bridesmaid. Of course, if Lily is a bridesmaid that means Lana, my maid of honour will be one too. The next thing I knew, after a few more cocktails we were looking up bridesmaid dresses online and I ended up sending an email off to the bridal store and asking them if they could squeeze us in for a bridesmaid fitting.

The day went quite well though, Lily was mostly polite, and we did find the most elegant bridesmaid dresses. I didn't expect to find anything I would love *that* much, but Lana spotted a pastel pink chiffon dress with ivory lace detailing on the top and I was just amazed with how beautifully they fit in with my colour scheme and immediately knew they were the ones. I cringed a little as the sales assistant told me the price though. Including alterations, they came to nearly three hundred pounds each, I definitely didn't have anything spare from the wedding fund to spend on dresses, so I've had to cover the costs myself, which hasn't been easy. Especially as Freddie's first birthday is tomorrow and I need to budget carefully for his special little day out.

Daisy is at school tomorrow so me and Rueben are going to head off early and take Freddie to Pirate's Cove down by the seaside. It's a lovely little place that my Dad used to take me to when I was little. It's basically a big outdoor pool with a huge picnic area and in the centre of the pool is a big pirate's ship with lots of fun sensory things to keep Freddie occupied. The water is only really ankle deep too so it's perfect for paddling in and for little kids.

I decided to invite Joy over for when we get back because she's already started sending Rueben lots of messages about wanting to see Freddie on his birthday and I want to do my part to keep the peace, so I have made sure to include her.

By the time the first morning sunlight flows through the cracks in the bedroom curtains, Freddie is wide awake and standing upright in his cot with the biggest smile. My smiley little boy is officially a one year old.

Daisy was a little reluctant to head off into school, but I promised her we wouldn't cut the birthday cake until she got home, I don't want her thinking she's going to miss out.

I help Freddie open his presents and as much as he seems thrilled, he ends up mostly playing with the boxes and the wrapping paper. We bought him a few Peppa Pig toys and a mini ball pit to play in. The George Pig soft toy seems to be his favourite so far.

As expected, it's barely nine o'clock in the morning but it's extremely hot. I make sure to put a big sun hat over Freddie's fair head. The older he gets the lighter his hair is becoming; he really is looking more like Daisy these days with his blonde hair.

On the journey down we make a pit stop and stock up on sunblock and lots of bottled water. When we arrive, Pirate's Cove is nice and quiet and we have most of the place to ourselves, I can imagine this is quite different over the weekend.

Just as we put all our bags down and get settled, I walk an excitable Freddie over to the pool just as Rueben's phone rings and distracts us.

"It's Mum…" Rueben says displeased as he checks his phone.

"You should probably just answer it." I say as I stand and wait.

"Hello, Mum?" Rueben answers.

"Where *are* you?" Joy asks abruptly.

"I'm at the beach, like I told you. Why, what's up?" He says trying to sound light and casual.

"You should have brought Freddie round to see *me* before you went off." She continues impatiently.

"Mum, you're coming over later. This is our day to celebrate with Freddie."

"But I'm his Grandma. I should have seen him first!" She snaps irritably.

"Mum...you promised you wouldn't do this anymore." Rueben reminds her calmly as Joy huffs childishly.

"Fine. What time can I come over then?" She asks as she attempts a friendlier tone.

"Five o'clock will be fine. I'll see you later, bye." Rueben replies before hanging up the phone.

"Well...that's still an improvement." I smirk.

"I suppose so." Rueben says as he rolls his eyes and laughs.

Rueben strides over to take Freddie's other hand and we both steer him towards the pool. Just as I thought, he absolutely loves splashing his feet in the pool and playing with all the baby puzzles in the pirate ship. I take lots of photo's as Rueben splashes around with Freddie and spins him around in the air which makes him giggle so loudly.

After a couple of hours of playing, we decide to treat Freddie to an ice cream and take a little stroll along the seaside. Before we know it, a tired little Freddie has fallen asleep with his ice cream still in hand. I giggle as a I take more photos of him in his sleepy but messy ice cream state and Rueben starts to clean him up before putting him back into the car. He sleeps the whole way home and I can't help but keep turning around and watching him sleep so contently. My beautiful birthday boy.

Daisy is very hyper as she bounds out of school and jumps into the car.

"Hello birthday boy!" She squeals loudly which jolts Freddie awake but he excitedly smiles at his big sister.

"We'll cut the cake as soon as Grandma gets here, okay Daisy Dots?" Rueben smiles cheerfully.

"OK!" Daisy responds as she tickles and plays with Freddie.

When we get home, Daisy sweetly sits in the front room and plays with Freddie and all his new toys. She's such a proud big sister. I carefully take the cake out of its packaging and place it on the dining table ready for later. It's so hot I open both patio doors and make a big jug of apple juice and ice for the kids.

"Mum's here…" Rueben calls as he pops his head around the kitchen door.

"Oh…she's early. But okay…" I say as I quickly straighten myself up a little.

As soon as Rueben opens the front door, Joy strides straight towards Freddie and scoops him up into her arms for a cuddle.

"Happy birthday, Freddie!" She shrieks.

"Hi. Alright?" Dave asks Rueben as he follows behind.

"I'm sorry we haven't got Freddie's presents with us." Joy says as she turns to me.

"But they have to be kept at our house."

"How come? What did you buy?" Rueben asks curiously.

"Well, we got him a swing, a slide, a little red coupe car and a trampoline!" Joy says with a boastful grin.

"Wow…Mum, that's quite a lot of stuff to get him. That's more than me and Mollie even got him." Rueben responds a little offended.

"So? I'm his Grandma." She simply responds sharply.

"I know, but I just feel like as his parents his main presents should come from us." Rueben continues.

"It's a very kind gesture though." I interrupt as I feel the tension rising.

"It'll give both Daisy *and* Freddie lots to play with when we take them for a visit."

Joy gives me a friendly smile and nods in agreement whilst Rueben looks a bit peeved that I interrupted him like that, but we both know it's for the best. Today is Freddie's first birthday and the last thing we want are arguments. We know Joy can be a little eccentric by now, at least her gifts will keep the kids very happy.

"Shall we get the candles ready and cut the cake?" Rueben suggests as he makes an effort to change the subject.

"Ooh yes! That will be lovely won't it, Freddie?" Joy says as she sits down at the dining table with Freddie on her lap.

Just as I start lighting the candles, I hear the doorbell ring.

"Here Rueben, you finish lighting those and I'll just quickly go and see who that could be." I say flustered as I hurriedly make my way to the front door.

"Hurry up! The wax is already melting down onto the cake." Rueben calls behind me.

Just as a I swing open the front door, I'm surprised as I take in a smiley face with a happy birthday balloon and a gift bag. I suddenly feel a wash of dread and nerves come over me. Uh oh.

"Hi Mum…"

CHAPTER FIFTY-TWO

"Well aren't you going to let me in then?" Mum questions jokingly.

"Mum…" I whisper nervously.

"Joy and Dave are here."

"Oooh…So?" Mum sarcastically replies as she shrugs her shoulders.

"So, Joy will freak out when she sees you. She'll kick off I know it!" I whisper as my voice grows more panicky.

"Mollie…" Mum sighs impatiently.

"I really don't feel well today. I just want to come and see my grandson on his birthday. What's wrong with that?"

I stare at Mum for a few seconds and I realise she is breathless again and not looking as well as she did last week. I feel guilty and suddenly silly. This is my Mum. What does it matter what Joy thinks? I take a step back from the door and allow my Mum to come through.

"Hello darling!" Mum calls out as she spots Rueben first, who suddenly looks as panicked and as awkward as I did thirty seconds ago.

Joy immediately fidgets uncomfortably in her chair as she stares at Dave for help or a decision on what they should do next.

I follow behind my Mum and pick Freddie up off of Joy's lap so that my Mum can greet him too and give him a little cuddle. I pretend I don't notice how irritated Joy's expression become when I took Freddie from her.

"Hiya." My Mum casually says towards Joy and Dave who both choose to blank her.

The tension is thick in the room and the atmosphere is extremely awkward. At least Mum tried to make an effort to be friendly and I'm disappointed Joy and Dave are both too childish to do the same.

"Quick, let's sing happy birthday to Freddie before the candles burn out." I say, noticing the wax dripping onto the cake just like Rueben said.

I hold Freddie next to his cake as he stares mesmerised at all the candles. The singing is the most awkward thing ever. Daisy is singing loudly without a care in the world, Mum and Rueben are singing along too as they adoringly stare at Freddie, but Dave and Joy aren't singing at all. To be fair, I can't imagine Dave ever singing anyway, he is far too straight laced to enjoy things like this. But Joy seems to be just refusing to sing along because my Mum is.

She isn't making any eye contact with anyone apart from Dave and she hasn't cracked a single smile since the doorbell went.

When Freddie attempts to blows out his candles everyone claps and cheers, everyone that is apart from Joy and Dave still. I let out a big sigh in frustration as I stare at Rueben, trying to read his expressions. He catches my eye and gives me a hesitant shrug. Neither of us knowing what to do.

"Look Fred's! Look what Nana got you." Mum proudly says as she takes some parcels out of the gift bag.

Freddie's face lights up as he stares at the colourful wrapping paper and excitedly tries to grasp the present. Mum begins helping him to open it by ripping at the paper and cheering on Freddie as he does the same.

Joy suddenly tuts loudly and then huffs as she grabs her handbag, before standing up and roughly barging past Mum as she heads briskly for the front door.

"Careful!" Rueben shouts as he realises my Mum lost her balance and nearly fell into Freddie.

"Oh god, here we go." I mutter to myself anxiously.

Dave nonchalantly gets up and without a word he follows Joy towards the front door.

"Hang on a second!" Mum yells as she storms towards Joy. "What's *your* problem?"

Joy turns to face my Mum but doesn't say anything. Dave continues to the front door and opens it whilst he impatiently waits for Joy to follow.

"Well? What's your problem with my daughter? Tell me." Mum demands and she stares at Joy angrily.

Joy just huffs awkwardly as she shakes her head and pulls up her handbag strap up onto her shoulder.

"You might think it's okay to bully your son, but you have got another thing coming if you think you can bully my daughter!" Mum bellows in her face.

"Come on Joy! Let's go, *now.*" Dave loudly demands.

As Joy turns to leave my Mum pulls her back by the arm and steps even closer to her.

"Why don't you try and bully me instead?" Mum challenges, whilst Joy tries to avoid her eye contact and remains silent.

"Right come on, enough." Rueben intervenes.

"Not today, not on Freddie's birthday."

Mum takes a step back reluctantly. I know she wants answers, but I also know she wouldn't want to be disrespectful and completely lose her temper on her grandsons' birthday.

Joy turns on her heel and stomps off out of the front door and towards their car as Dave follows behind.

"I'm sorry Mollie. I wasn't going to say anything but then she barged past me and I couldn't bite my tongue any longer." Mum apologetically explains as I close the front door.

"It's fine Mum, don't worry about it." I assure.

"I'm sorry Rueben." Mum apologises again.

"It's fine Laraine, honestly. I can't expect you not to stick up for Mollie." Rueben calmly says.

"Has Grandma gone?" Daisy asks confused as she peers into the hallway.

"Erm…yeah. She wasn't feeling very well. Come on, let's tuck into Freddie's cake." I smile as I take her hand and head back into the kitchen.

I have barely managed to cut one slice when Rueben's phone starts ringing.

"This'll be Joy." I sigh to Mum as I worry about the earful Rueben is about to get. Joy never seems to say much face to face. It's always on the phone and it's always to Rueben.

Despite the phone not being on loudspeaker, Joy is shouting so loudly I can hear it all perfectly. I step outside with Rueben so the kids can't hear the call whilst my Mum gives them their cake.

"Who the *fuck* does that slag think she is?" Joy roars.

"Was this some *fucking* set up? To get me and Laraine in the same room?"

"Not at all Mum, we had no idea she was coming…" Rueben tries to explain before Joy interrupts again.

"How fucking dare she speaks to me like that!" Joy spits venomously.

"If I find out you or Mollie planned this, I swear to god I will come down on you like a tonne of bricks!"

"Mum you need to calm down." Rueben interjects.

"Calm down!? CALM DOWN? She's lucky I don't come back over there and smash her face in. As for you Rueben, if you dare defend her then you can drop down dead, you little bastard!" She screams down the phone.

"Mum!" Rueben interrupts impatiently.

"I tell you what you and Mollie are shall I…you both are a pair of…" is all I hear before Rueben hangs up the phone.

"Jesus." I mumble.

"I'm not answering anymore phone calls today. She needs to cool off and remember the conversation we had. If she can't calm down, then we just don't speak to her. Simple." Rueben says.

"OK." I nod.

"Now, I'm going back inside to enjoy the rest of my son's first birthday and not allow her to ruin another second of it. Coming?" He gently asks and I nod as I follow behind him and close the patio doors behind me.

Mum gives me a concerned look, but I decide not to stress her out with any of the things Joy was saying on the phone. Instead I watch my happy little birthday boy squeal in excitement as my Mum spoon feeds him his birthday cake.

CHAPTER FIFTY-THREE

It's been a week since Joy had another outburst after my Mum arrived at the house and we haven't heard anything from her since. Rueben hasn't said very much about it, only that he is growing tired of the same arguments happening again and again. He seems to have very little patience and energy to deal with his Mum's tantrums these days and I don't blame him.

I haven't had the time to think too much about it either as my Mum ended up back in hospital a couple of days ago with another suspected chest infection. Although it ended up being worse than they first thought and they've diagnosed her with pneumonia.

This morning I'm going to get Freddie ready and we are going to visit my Mum again at the hospital for a few hours whilst Daisy is at school and Rueben's at work. I pack Mum a few essentials that I think she'll need, such as more shower wash, toothpaste and my comfiest pyjamas that Rueben got for me on our first Christmas. Just as I get ready to leave, I pick up the post off of the mat and throw it on the kitchen counter, but one of the envelopes catches my eye. It doesn't look like a typical chain mail or a usual bill. I noticed it's handwritten and addressed to me.

I take a seat at the dining table and tear it open carefully to find a small handwritten letter inside.

To Mollie,
I'm just writing to apologise for the arguments that
occurred on Freddie's birthday. I don't want this to
cause issues between us all and I would very much
like to continue to work on our relationship moving
forward. I'm not sure what more I can say, I sometimes
act out of anger and I shouldn't do.
Joy x

It's short but to the point and I guess I appreciate it. It's not very often someone writes me a handwritten letter. I'm confused though as to why she hasn't written Rueben a letter or addressed it to both of us. Surely Rueben's understanding and forgiveness is the most important but either way, I am grateful for her efforts.

I take a picture of the letter on my phone and text it to Rueben. I think he'll be pleasantly surprised that Joy has sent out an apology off her own back.

Maybe Joy is trying to learn from her own mistakes and change into a better person. It seems a long shot, but I don't see why it couldn't be possible. People change all the time.

I leave the letter on the table and put Freddie in the car before setting off to the hospital to see Mum.

When I arrive, I'm pleased to see Mum appear in good spirits as she's sitting up in bed and telling me how the doctor should be discharging her tomorrow.

"I think I'm going to treat myself to a new car tomorrow. Maybe a little upgrade. Will you help me?" Mum asks.

"Yeah of course!" I smile.

"As long as you're up for it."

"I should be, I feel a lot better anyway." Mum assures.

"That's good then, I brought you over some of my pyjamas to borrow if you like, I thought you might want some fresh ones to wear." I offer as I pull out the neatly folded pyjamas from my bag.

"Oh, you're a star!" Mum smiles relieved.

"I could actually do with a shower and getting changed, can you give me a hand?"

"Sure." I say as I help Mum up into the bathroom and start running the shower.

After about ten minutes Mum is settled back in bed with my fresh pyjamas on as I help style her hair a little bit.

"I feel even better now." She smiles gratefully.

"How much longer is it until your wedding?"

"Not long at all now, about six and a half months." I say with a big smile my face.

"Oh good." Mum smiles.

"I can't wait to see how you look."

"I hope I look good…I'm suddenly panicking about it all. I think I need to drop another stone at least before the big day." I say anxiously.

"Don't be silly." Mum laughs.

"Rueben loves you just as you are."

"You have to tell me that, you're my Mum." I mock as I give her a sarcastic smirk which makes her laugh more.

"Oh Mol, before I forget, that new Elton John movie is out next month, Rocketman. Can we go together?" Mum asks enthusiastically.

"Yeah of course. I hope it's as good as the Queen movie was."

"Oh my god that was brilliant, we had the best night!" Mum smiles as she recalls the memory.

"You mean when you kept singing along loudly as if we were in some concert and nearly got us thrown out?"

"Yep! At least we were having fun though, who cares what anyone else thinks." She says with a laugh.

"*You* were having fun! I was embarrassed. It wouldn't have been so bad if you actually knew the right words." I tease.

"Cheeky bitch!" Mum says as we both burst out laughing. I giggle at the memory of Mum badly singing along to Radio Ga-Ga and we both laugh the more we remember from that night.

"Anyway, haven't you got to get back for Daisy?"

"Yeah, I should probably head off. Let me know tomorrow what time the doctors will be discharging you and I'll come and pick you up if you like?" I offer.

"Yeah that'll be nice, I'll call you." Mum says as she leans over and gives Freddie a kiss goodbye.

"See you tomorrow." I smile as I head off with Freddie.

"Bye, babe." Mum calls after me.

CHAPTER FIFTY-FOUR

My phone startles me awake as it rings loudly in my ear. I snatch it off my bedside table quickly to silence it in the hopes it doesn't wake everybody up. I stare at my phone confused. It's two minutes past two in the morning. I don't recognise the number at all. I decide to ignore it and let it ring out.

"Who is it?" Rueben croaks with his eyes still shut.

"Not sure. Maybe a prank caller? Maybe someone drunk with the wrong number? I don't know but I'll leave it." I whisper.

Within seconds the same number rings again as my phone vibrates in my hand.

"Answer it babe, maybe it's important." Rueben says as he starts to wake fully.

"Hello?" I hesitantly whisper.

"Hello? Am I speaking with Mollie, the daughter of Laraine Harris?"

"Yes…?" I confirm as I sit up.

"We need you to come down to the hospital as soon as possible, there's been some changes." The gentle voice explains.

"OK, that's fine. I'll come down now. Has she had another cardiac arrest?" I whisper nervously as Rueben sits straight up with concern.

"Yes…yes I believe so. The doctor would like to speak to you." He calmly responds.

"OK. I'm on my way now." I say.

I jump out of my bed and start throwing clothes on and shoving my hair up as quickly as I can. Waking up so suddenly has made me feel a bit sick but I try to ignore it.

"I'll get the kids up, we'll come with you?" Rueben offers sounding panicked.

"No…no. I think it'll be fine. I can't get them up now, it's the middle of the night." I say.

"But what if you need me? What if she's in a bad way?" Rueben questions uneasily.

"He didn't say but I assume she's back in intensive care again. It should be fine, if I need you, I'll call."

"If you need me where shall I take the kids?"

"It'll have to be your Mum's; my Dad is back in Florida. But I'm sure she won't mind. Even at this time."

"OK…but babe, I'm not sure I should let you go on your own in the middle of the night. I don't think I'd go back to sleep now anyway." Rueben continues with a worried expression.

"Shall I phone him back and ask exactly what condition Mum is in then? And then we'll decide from there?"

"Yeah, do that. Check she's OK and stable first before you go off on your own."

I start dialling back the number as I walk over to the bedroom window and stare out of it whilst I wait patiently for the nurse to answer the phone again.

"Hello?" The same male voice answers.

"Hi, I think I just spoke to you a moment ago. I'm Mollie, Laraine's daughter…"

"Yes, that was me." He softly confirms.

"Hi, I was just calling back to check Mum's current situation now? I mean is she in the same ward or has she been moved up to intensive care already?" I ask.

"Oh…I erm, I think there's been a misunderstanding." He quietly says.

"Your Mum has already gone. I'm so sorry."

It takes me a second, just a split second to realise what he has told me.

I feel my knees buckle from under me and I just scream out in pain as if somebody has just shattered my heart into a thousand pieces. I can hear Rueben rushing across the room to hold me with panic clear in his voice.

"No…no…no she hasn't gone!" He shouts.

I hang up the phone and fall to the floor. I'm crying so heavily I can barely catch my breath. I just keep screaming no, please no. The tears stream down my face, the lump in my throat is so thick it hurts. My stomach is in the biggest knot and it makes me feel sick, my whole body is trembling.

"She's gone!" I wail.

"Oh god, no, please, no."

Everything feels like it's going in slow motion around me. Rueben is trying to hold me up and comfort me, but I can barely comprehend anything else but the feeling of my heart breaking.

"Oh god…My poor Mum." I scream as I look at Rueben.

"I have to get to the hospital, right now."

"OK, OK. I'll get a bag; I'll get the kids up. I'll ring my mum, just sit there. Keep breathing." Rueben cries as he rushes around in a panic.

"Mum…" I hear Rueben sob down the phone within seconds.

"Laraine has died. Can I bring the kids to you?"

Just hearing Rueben say the words out loud make me nearly sick.

The next thing I know I'm already in the car and Rueben speeds to Joy's house. Normally I would hate that, but I think I'm too numb to care.

I notice Daisy is watching me with concern on her face as I quietly sob but I can't bring myself to look at her. I can't tell her yet. I try my best to hold it all in. I'm in such a daze as we drive through the night. I just keep staring out the window in disbelief. My whole body is shaking, my throat is dry and sore and all I want to do is be with my Mum. She shouldn't be on her own.

"Oh god." I sob.

"She's on her own."

"Shhh baby, it's OK, I'll get you there in fifteen minutes. Just hold on." Rueben assures me through his own sobs.

When we get to Joy's, I quickly help take the kids in. She's already at the door waiting in her dressing gown when we pull up. Rueben puts a sleeping Freddie on the sofa and Daisy rushes past me to sit next to Freddie.

"I'm so sorry love." Joy says anxiously as I stand in the hallway staring at the floor.

When I look up, she holds her arms out to me and without thinking I collapse into them. The first real hug I think she's ever given me. She wraps her arms around me as she tries to comfort me and I breakdown again. I sob as she cradles me gently.

"I have to go to my Mum now." I whisper as I pull away and wipe my tears.

"Just don't worry about a thing here, OK. Take your time." She assures softly, the kindest I think I have ever heard Joy speak.

I can't seem to manage a word on the drive to the hospital. I sob quietly to myself and I know Rueben is doing the same, although he is making an effort to hide it from me.

When we arrive to the hospital, Rueben keeps his arms firmly round my waist as we walk to the ward. When we arrive the man, I spoke to on the phone is waiting for me.

"The doctor will be down to see you shortly. You can go and see your Mum now if you are ready." He says calmly.

I nod hesitantly and walk side by side with Rueben towards Mum's room.

I feel like someone has kicked me in the stomach when I see her clothes are already all packed away in a bag and placed neatly on a chair outside her room. Along with her coat, handbag and car keys. All her essentials just left.

Her door is closed and I'm hesitant. I know what I'm about to see but I'm not sure yet if I can accept it. I'm scared.

I stare at her name written in marker outside her door. Laraine Harris. Fifty-six years old. My Mum. My poor Mum. She was here with me only hours ago. She was supposed to be coming home tomorrow.

"Can I go in alone first? Just for a moment." I whisper to Rueben.

"Of course. I'll be right here." He assures.

I pull open the door and timidly step inside. My hands tremble slightly as I close the door behind me and stare down at the floor. When I look up, I glance at her feet first. I notice she's laying on her back with the sheet pulled right up. I'm scared to look at her face. So, I just concentrate on her feet.

The room has been emptied too. All of her medications and drinks she had in here earlier are all gone now. I take a few steps forwards and see she's still wearing my pyjama's.

"Well Mum, you really will go above and beyond to ensure you don't have to give me back my pyjamas." I manage to whisper, knowing if she could hear me, she'd appreciate my sarcasm.

My eyes travel up very slowly to her face and I'm so overwhelmed that I want to look away but now I can't. I study her peaceful face. I keep getting distracted by her mouth, hoping that at any minute she might take a breath. At one point my eyes are watering so much it almost makes it look as though her lips moved. But I know they didn't. I know she's gone. I can feel it.

I quietly call Rueben and he immediately walks to Mum's side. He studies her face just like I did and wraps his arm around my waist to comfort me.

"Is she…is she still warm?" I stutter through the catch in my throat.

Rueben reaches out and gently places his hand on hers. Something I haven't been brave enough to do yet.

"No baby…she's not." Rueben softly whispers.

"Oh." I sob.

"That happened quick."

All the pain I was feeling has now been added with guilt. Guilt that I wasn't here to hold her hand, before she took her last breath.

"She didn't like being cold." I add.

"She'll be okay now, baby. She won't be cold. She won't be suffering." Rueben tries to reassure.

"She wasn't ready to go though Roo. She was desperate for more time. Just enough to see her grandkids grow up a little. She was so scared of going too soon." I whimper.

I feel a little braver, so I reach out and gently place my hand over her leg, but I suddenly feel too overwhelmed and quickly pull my hand away.

An hour ago, I was asleep and as far as I knew my Mum was alive and looking forward to coming home. Now, I am stood here next to her lifeless body. It's all too much for one night.

"God I'm going to miss you." I mumble through sobs. "Bye Mum."

CHAPTER FIFTY-FIVE

The last few weeks have been a blur. I've been trying to keep myself busy as much as possible to avoid wallowing in bed and it worked for a little while. I had a lot to get on with such as clearing Mum's apartment, to arranging her funeral. Ironically as much as I mocked Rueben for liking Ed Sheeran so much, I opted for his beautiful song, Supermarket Flowers to play at her funeral. I felt we gave her a good send off, but it was the hardest day I have ever had to get through in my life.

I now have a newfound respect for anybody who has experienced heartbreak and grief over a loved one. It is the most heart shattering, soul destroying feeling and I know it's going to take some time to heal fully.

Yesterday, I saw my Mum's solicitor and he told me that I am to put Mum's apartment up for sale, whatever it sells for is my inheritance. I have decided however much it'll be I will just put it into our savings account. I have no idea what to do with that kind of money yet, but I want to make sure it's of good use. Something which I'm not mentally prepared to think about right now.

Thankfully, Rueben has been incredibly supportive and encouraged me to concentrate on the wedding and planning fun things for the kids to do in Florida and that has been a great distraction.

Joy and Dave have been taking the kids out regularly to keep them entertained whilst I have been sorting everything out and trying to bounce back. I definitely appreciate the help, although Joy hasn't personally mentioned my Mum to me since the night I brought the kids to her house. I received a tonne of sympathy cards and flowers from Lana and Mike, friends at work, family, Mum's work friends, even the neighbours but nothing at all from Joy, Dave or Lily. I know she didn't ever like my Mum, but a gesture to let me know she cares would have meant a lot. Either way, she has been supportive towards the kids and that means something.

Today has been the first quiet day at home where I haven't had to run around sorting anything or making arrangements. It's been difficult. I started my morning with watching the Queen movie again just because it reminded me of the cinema trip with Mum. Lately, I keep seeing adverts for the Rocketman movie appearing on the t.v and I desperately try to keep the tears back when I see it.

Maybe I'll go and watch it with Rueben one day. Mum would have liked that.

"I've got to go." Rueben says out of breath and panicked as he snaps me out of my thoughts.

"What, where?" I ask puzzled.

"It's eight o'clock in the evening?"

"Nan has been on the phone crying, Lily is down there kicking off because nobody will give her money. I think she's on a drug come down or something because she's aggressive and threatening to smash the place up if they refuse her money." Rueben explains with panic thick in his voice.

"Jesus. Ok…you best go straight away. Let me know if everything is okay." I ask worriedly as Rueben turns to leave.

I would never begrudge Rueben rushing to comfort his Nan but my god, I really miss him when he is gone at the moment. As soon as he leaves and I'm alone with my thoughts I find myself thinking about Mum and quite often before I know it, I'm sobbing whilst looking through photos of her. Rueben has been my absolute rock lately and all I wanted was to spend the evening watching a few films and snuggling into his chest. Why does Lily have to behave like this? It's selfish. Everybody has to run to her every single time and it's not fair. I need my fiancé more than ever.

The house is so quiet too, Daisy is off at a sleepover with her friend from school and Freddie is already settled and asleep for the night. I decide to distract myself from my thoughts and put on some light comedy to enjoy instead. I opt for Trains, planes and automobiles. An absolute classic and one that never fails to make me laugh.

Before long, I start noticing that the movie is nearly halfway through and I haven't heard from Rueben like I thought I would by now, without hesitation I grab my phone from my bedside table and start calling. After a few rings I hear an anxious Rueben answer.

"*Babe, the police are here I can't talk right now.*" Rueben breathes into the phone.

"What? The police? What's happened?" I ask as I bolt upright from my bed in panic.

"Lily…she hit me and then ended up calling the police and telling them that I was the one trying to attack her."

"Wha…what? Surely not! Is your Mum there? Shall I call her and see if she can come down and sit with you? She would surely vouch that you wouldn't do such a thing and that it's Lily on some stupid come down…"

"Mum is here. She's sat with Lily in the other room. She's not helping me…look babe, I really have to go as I'm talking to the police. I'll be back as soon as possible. Love you."

As the line goes dead, I sit for a minute trying to make sense of everything Rueben has said. Lily attacked Rueben. But then called the police and lied. Just like Joy has done before. Is this something that is just acceptable to them? To just hurt people and then lie? My heart aches that Rueben is sat with the police and nobody is there for him, nobody is on his side as usual and they really should be.

After an hour of waiting for Rueben to come home I decide to go downstairs and make a cup of tea as I can't settle in bed anymore. I'm relieved to hear the key in the lock just as the kettle boils.

"Roo?" I call anxiously from the kitchen.

"Hey baby." Rueben sighs and I see exactly where Lily hit him straight away. On the left side of his cheek is a red mark in almost a perfect handprint shape. Adrenaline rushes through my body as I stare in anger at it.

"What the *fuck?*" I blurt out in disgust as I gently touch Rueben's cheek.

"Tell me about it. I only went there to help Nan." Rueben says as he grabs a bottle of Budweiser from the fridge.

"What happened? I can't believe what you told me on the phone." I say as I tip my tea away and opt for a beer with Rueben.

"As soon as I approached Nan's I could hear her screaming from outside. I let myself in and Lily just stared at me with so much hate and anger in her face. She started ranting, telling me I should go home because it has nothing to do with me. Nan was crying, saying she'd had enough of Lily always going to her house and shouting and throwing her weight around, so there was no way I was going to just leave. Next thing I knew she was getting really nasty and saying that she isn't coming to the wedding, apparently, I have changed since I met you. Then, she was in my face, literally an inch from my face, threatening to hit me if I didn't leave. Before I had a chance to even respond she just slapped me as hard as she could across my cheek. Then tried to punch me but I managed to stop her."

"For god's sake. That's insane, what's got into her?" I sigh.

I feel so angry and I am not usually a violent person but right now I wouldn't mind slapping Lily back just as hard as she hurt Rueben.

"It gets worse. She then called the police and started telling them that I was intimidating her and threatening to hurt her." He continues as he rolls his eyes in disappointment.

"Thankfully when the police arrived, they cottoned on quite quickly that it wasn't me causing an issue. They saw the handprint that she left on my face and took me into another room to take photos of it. That's when Mum arrived…"

"And…? What happened?" I ask curiously as I notice how dejected Rueben suddenly looks.

"She walked through the front door. Demanded to know what was going on, the police told her that Lily had hit me and would you believe it…Lily is in the living room and I am in the kitchen with a bag of ice on my face, guess who she went to?"

"God…she went straight to Lily?"

"Yep! And she stayed with her the whole time. She only came out once to tell me off for calling the police. Even when I told her it wasn't me that phoned them, she still looked at me angrily, as if I was the problem and Lily was the victim."

"Oh, Roo…" I mumble sympathetically.

"You're not going to like this next part…" Rueben begins to say as he takes my hand.

"Oh no, what more could there be?"

"They arrested Lily for assaulting me because she was still kicking off and swearing at everyone. After they put her in the police car, I heard Mum whispering in the front room. I stood by the door to hear what was going on and she was threatening my Nan and my Uncle Jon. She told them that when the police ask them for a statement, they have to tell them that I came into the house in an intimidating and aggressive manner and that Lily purely acted out of self-defence."

"What the fuck Rueben? That could land you in so much trouble! What about your ESTA? If you end up being arrested for something like this, you may not pass the ESTA and we won't be able to go to Florida to get married! You don't think they would do it?" I ask in disbelief.

"They probably will. I'm not the only person my Mum has ever bullied babe…they'll say it to avoid the grief. The police are going to phone me to let me know the outcome, I just have to wait." Rueben groans before taking a swig of beer.

My anxiety is so high I doubt I'll be able to relax tonight now. I'm so tired of Joy being so damn disappointing. Why is it always Rueben who continually gets disregarded?

CHAPTER FIFTY-SIX

The next morning, I get up extra early. Today is the day that Rueben and I are going to tidy up my Nan's grave and prepare it for my Mum's ashes. Just like she wanted.

I have bought four pink helium balloons too and some marker pens, I want each of us to write a message on the balloon and we can let them go today after we have buried Mum's ashes. Both the kids are coming with us today too, I didn't let them go to the funeral because I thought it would be too upsetting, so today can be their little goodbye.

We stop on the way to a garden centre and get some white stones to pour on, some flowers and some gloves to pull up any old weeds.

I watch gratefully as Rueben does most of the work when we get to the grave.

Within half an hour, Rueben has already got the grave looking so much better. Before it was overgrown with a fair few weeds and looking a little neglected but now it has white stones down, new edging, a row of pink flowers by the headstone and a plaque for Mum in the centre.

Whilst Rueben starts making a small hole for us to bury the ashes, I make a start with writing messages on the helium balloons.

"Okay Fred, what shall I write on yours for you?"

"Nana!" Freddie proudly babbles.

"Pink…lips…lip…tick."

"You want me to write 'Nana, I love your pink lipstick?'"

"Yes!" Freddie says as he claps his hands with a big smile.

"I love it."

"I've done mine, Mummy." Daisy says as she proudly shows me her balloon.

To my beautiful Nana,
I miss you so much and I promise I will never forget you.
I hope heaven is fun. You were the best nana in the world.
From Daisy x x x

"That's beautiful Daisy! She is going to love that so much!" I say as I give her a tight cuddle.

I finish my message just as Rueben starts to pour the ashes into the grave and I kneel down in between the kids and wrap my arms around them both tightly whilst we watch Mum be laid to rest.

For the first time since Mum has passed, Daisy let's out a few tears as her bottom lip quivers.

"Bye Nana." Daisy whimpers.

"Bye Nana!" Freddie cheerfully shouts as he copies Daisy. I can't help but giggle at his innocence.

"Can we let the balloons go now, Mummy?" Daisy asks as she rubs the wetness from her eyes.

"Yes, we can." I say gently.

"Okay, ready? Three…two…one…let them go!"

All four of us stand watching the pink balloons get smaller and smaller as they drift off up high in the sky. Both Daisy and Freddie wave at them as they float away. The same painful lump is back in my throat, but I try to stay composed for the kids.

Rueben carefully covers up the hole, covering my Mum's ashes and we quickly clean up the weeds as we get ready to leave.

We decide it would be best to do something fun for the kids after an emotional morning and end up choosing to head to the park.

"Oh god." Rueben sighs as he stares down at his phone just as we pull into the car park.

"What?" I ask nervously.

"Lily must be home now because she's managed to do this and send me a picture. Look…"

I glance down at the picture on Rueben's phone, it's a picture of something torn up but I can't quite make out what it is. As I take a closer look, I start to realise.

"She's ripped up the bridesmaid dress!?" I gasp.

"Yep. I'm sorry baby…" Rueben says as he puts an arm around my waist.

"Well, that's three hundred pounds down the drain." I sigh as I help the kids get out of the car and they run towards the park gates.

"I knew she wasn't going to come. I bloody knew it. I should have never of let you buy those dresses…"

"Don't be silly! I'm stubborn! I would have bought them anyway." I laugh reassuringly.

"My family are such a joke." Rueben groans as he runs his fingers through his hair in frustration.

"Roo…you are the one who told me to concentrate on our wedding day and I am. Nothing is going to ruin this. It's only a dress. Let's not allow it to ruin our day. We have so much more to look forward too." I say trying to calm him down.

"You're right. Thank you…" Rueben begins as he gets distracted by his phone ringing.

"Great. Now the police are ringing me. You go ahead with the kids and I'll catch up."

I do as he asks and reluctantly leave him behind to deal with the police phone call. The kids run towards the big slide and I feel a lot of enjoyment as I watch them play and laugh together as they chase each other around and take it in turns on the slide.

Daisy as always starts chatting to other kids in the park and makes friends with them. They all start running towards the roundabout and playing nicely together, so I walk over to the closest bench and let them have their fun.

"What a joke." I hear Rueben say as he marches over to me and slumps down onto the bench with his head in his hands.

"The call went really well then?" I ask sarcastically.

"Lily said it was self-defence. She claimed I came in aggressive and I got in her face and scared her…and of course they have statements from everyone in the house confirming Lily's story." He sighs heavily and throws his phone down on the bench.

"Oh…so your Mum managed to get them to lie for her then?"

"Yep. I told you they would. Do you want to know what else the police said?"

"What?" I reluctantly ask, knowing full well I'm not going to like the answer.

"They said it was in my best interests to not pursue it any further because I could get into trouble for intimidation and threatening behaviour thanks to their lies." Rueben huffs anxiously.

"I…I don't know what to say. You only went there to help, how the hell did it get to this?"

"I'll tell you how…" Rueben says as he turns to look at me intently.

"Apart from a few, my family are toxic. That's how it always gets like this. Whenever I'm near them there's nothing but trouble. I'm not sure I want it in my life anymore. There has to be more to life then dealing with this bullshit. I mean it Mollie, if I could get in the car and move us away from here I would do it right now. I would take us a million miles from here if I could, if it meant we didn't have to deal with this anymore."

CHAPTER FIFTY-SEVEN

As I stare out of the window and watch us take off, I hold on tightly to Rueben's hand.

Yes, I'm a nervous flyer but I'm also holding on tight because I'm so happy we made it. After a long countdown we are finally heading to Florida for a beautiful two-week holiday and our wedding.

We decided to fly out a couple of days earlier than everybody else, Rueben suggested it might be a nice idea to take some time out and just relax, just us. I couldn't have agreed more, it's been a tough year and I'm looking forward to relaxing around a pool.

My Dad and Sarah are already out there in their villa which is around two hours away from us. They live closer to Jacksonville but we have arranged a pre wedding dinner so we can all meet up. In two days', time Lana and Mike fly out along with Leah and her boyfriend James. They will all be joining us in our Orlando villa we've rented. Lastly Joy and Dave fly out, but they're headed to a hotel closer to Disney.

This is their second time in Disney according to Rueben who tells me on the plane. Apparently, they once went for their honeymoon for a few weeks on their own without Rueben or his sisters.

Things have been awkward again since the whole police thing with Lily. Rueben has been fairly amicable with Joy and Dave and arranged to meet them at parks local to their house so that they could still spend time with Daisy and Freddie but that is as much as he is willing to do.

He even keeps to basic small talk with them and hasn't once told his Mum that he knows that she made everybody lie for Lily.

We haven't seen Lily at all since, Rueben told Joy that Lily should repay me for the dress she ruined but Joy disagreed and said it wouldn't be fair on Lily as she has a lot on her plate. It's not been easy to ignore the unjust manner in which they treat us, but we have had to just treat it as another lesson learned and keep moving forward without allowing incidences like this to affect us.

Joy and Dave are also joining us for the pre wedding meal in five days' time. I worry it'll be a little awkward but hopefully the excitement of the upcoming wedding will have everybody in fairly good spirits.

A few movies later and with very numb legs after having Freddie sprawled across me for a long nap, we finally touch down on the tarmac at Orlando airport. Immediately the kids spot Mickey Mouse everywhere around the airport as we grab our luggage and head for the car rental. The excitement is clear on their faces even though they are very tired after such a long day.

The feeling that I get when I step outside of the airport for the first time is like no other. The way the humidity and warmth hits my skin fills me with happiness. The skies are blue, barely a cloud in sight. I immediately realise that we definitely aren't dressed appropriately for this weather as we still have on our jumpers from our early morning start back in London. As soon as we are in the car, I crank up the air conditioning as I excitedly direct us to the villa. The car is so comfortable, it's a nine-seater and so spacious. So comfortable in fact, Freddie can barely keep his eyes open. It is nearly nine o'clock back home after all.

As we get close to the villa we decide to stop off at a Walmart, I grab the essentials to tie us over for the evening. Lots of water, bread, milk, cereal and a couple of pizzas for dinner. We'll come back tomorrow for a proper shop but for now this will do. We are all hungry and tired and want nothing more than to collapse in the villa and relax.

"Here we go kids!" I announce as Rueben pulls our car into the driveway of a huge modern looking villa.

"Wow!" Daisy gasps.

"Are we here mummy?" Freddie croaks excitedly as he wakes up from his sleep.

"Yep! This is it!" I excitedly say as they both hurriedly climb out of the car.

When I open the villa door it's more than I could have hoped for. The air conditioning hits us straight away which is a welcome relief. The floor is tiled white and the whole place has been given a modern but tasteful look. I love that everything is so open plan. I drag the suitcases to the bottom of the stairs whilst the kids run off to find their bedroom.

"This is amazing." Rueben whispers as he looks around the villa.

"Mum! Quick! Come up here!" Daisy squeals from upstairs.

I head up and Rueben follows behind me with the suitcases in hand. As I get to the top of the stairs, I gasp again at how big it is. There's five bedrooms up here, beautiful cream carpets throughout, a large seating area with another television and it's just as beautifully decorated as downstairs.

I head down one hallway and see the kids have found the bedroom opposite to ours.

"Look! Mickey!" Freddie says as he jumps up and down excitedly.

The beautiful room has two beds in it with a Mickey shaped headboard and Mickey Mouse clubhouse duvet covers. Even the television in their room has Mickey ears on it.

"Wow guys! This is amazing!" Rueben says as he playfully tickles Freddie on the bed.

"Show us your room, Mum!" Daisy asks as she jumps from her bed and into the hallway.

As we step into our bedroom, I immediately decide it's my favourite spot in the whole villa. It is so spacious with a walk-in wardrobe, a huge king size bed and a balcony overlooking the swimming pool. In our en suite the bathtub is three times the size of our one back home. Rueben catches me staring at it excitedly and jokes that I'll never get out of the bath again.

"Wait, is that the pool?" Daisy asks as she peers over the balcony.

"Yep! Fancy a swim?" Rueben offers as both Daisy and Freddie squeal and nod enthusiastically.

Once I help the kids get changed in their swimsuits, they're both in the pool without hesitation. Freddie has a little vest on full of small floats and he loves it as it allows him the freedom to paddle in the pool without me or Rueben constantly holding him. He giggles as he splashes his feet and proudly shows us how well he can move in the water by himself.

Daisy opts for cannon balls and makes a huge splash each time. Rueben and I sit on the edge of the pool with our feet dangled in and enjoy the moment as we watch them play.

"Thank you." Rueben whispers as he grabs hold of my hand affectionately.

"For what?" I ask surprised.

"For doing all this. For arranging everything, for choosing Florida. Just look at the kids' faces…you did that." Rueben says as he gazes at me lovingly.

I smile as I snuggle into his shoulder and he reaches down to kiss the top of my forehead.

"Five days until we are Mr and Mrs Adams." I say.

"Can't wait." Rueben softly replies as he wraps his arm around my waist.

CHAPTER FIFTY-EIGHT

The next morning Freddie wakes me up early by running into our bedroom and climbing into the bed for a cuddle. It's only five o'clock but I know the time difference is still causing confusion with our body clocks.

Not long after, Daisy wakes up followed by Rueben who wakes up by six. We decide to make the most of the early start and get up and out the door. That morning we take a drive up to Daytona Beach to view the hotel we will be getting married in and plan to pick up our marriage license.

I had a few nervous butterflies in my stomach the closer we got to the hotel. This is the first time we will be seeing it for ourselves and it's been an eager wait to see if the venue lived up to the beautiful photos we had seen.

My nerves soon drifted away as we approached the beautiful beach-front hotel.

My smile was from ear to ear when I stepped inside and was greeted by the wonderful hotel manager who has been helping us plan the entire wedding. The entrance itself felt very grand and exceptionally looked after. As we were led outside to the patio on the beach front the decor becomes more laid back but still pretty, just like we hoped. After a few last-minute decisions over our own wedding decor, we left happy and excited and made our way to collect our marriage license.

It's crazy to think that when we come back in a few days' time, it'll be to get married.

On the journey back to the villa we stop off for another food shop to grab some more pizzas for everyone when they arrive and more wine. Then drive back to spend the afternoon around the swimming pool and catch some sun.

I decide to open a group chat when we get back to the villa and send a message to everyone, Joy and Dave included.

Hey guys!
Just to let you know, we saw the venue today and it's beautiful!
The villa is lovely, and the kids are already enjoying the pool.
It's been sunny and blue skies since we arrived, the weather is supposed to be glorious all week too.
Can't wait to see you all. Hope you have a safe flight over! Not long now!
Love Mollie, Roo, Daisy and Freds xx

I smile as I send the message, excited to get the wedding celebrations well and truly started.

That evening we decide to head to Disney world and watch the fireworks. It's been so relaxed and enjoyable so far; I'm so pleased we decided to have a couple of days on our own.

We manage to get on a few rides too before the fireworks start and Freddie's face lights up as I take him on the Frozen ride. It's only a little boat ride but it's all in the dark and everything lights up blue as the famous frozen song is played. Freddie stares in awe at all the lights and the pretend snow that surrounds our boat. Elsa has been his favourite character ever since he first watched the movie, probably because Elsa was Daisy's favourite too and he loves to copy his sister.

Afterwards, Daisy spots Minnie Mouse and excitedly poses next to her for a photo and gives her a big hug. We treat the kids to a light up wand for the fireworks and a cone of pink popcorn too.

By the time we get home the kids are absolutely worn out and don't take long to settle in bed. My evening is perfectly finished off with sitting by the pool, drinking a couple of beers and playing card games with Rueben. It's simple, but it's the quality time that I enjoy so much with the man I adore.

The following day, I wake up feeling much more refreshed as our body clocks become more in sync with the time difference. I'm so excited as I wait eagerly for everybody's flight to get in. Rueben's picking up Lana, Mike, Leah and James from the airport but not until five o'clock this evening.

As the afternoon nears, I keep myself busy by unpacking the last of our clothes and making sure everybody's room is tidy and ready for their arrival. The kids have had a habit of running about and jumping on all the different beds in their excitement, so a quick straighten up was definitely needed.

I'm anxious and excited when Rueben heads off to the airport though, I can't wait to see everyone. I find myself clock watching as I impatiently wait to see all my favourite people. The kids have been relaxing upstairs in their bedroom watching a movie together. Our busy couple of days have definitely caught up to them.

"No way!" I hear a loud voice squeal from the hallway as I start putting the pizza's in the oven.

"Lana?" I call.

"Hey!" She screams as she runs up to me for a hug.

"This villa is so beautiful! I love it! Where's my room?" She excitedly asks as she takes in her new surroundings.

"Hey Mol!" Mike smiles as he follows behind dragging all the suitcases.

"Hey!" I say and give Mike a quick hug.

"Don't worry Lana, I've got all the bags." Mike sarcastically says and she playfully sticks her tongue out at him.

"Oh my god, this is going to be the best holiday!" Leah says as she appears in the hallway with her new boyfriend James.

"And wedding...don't forget wedding." James jokingly interrupts.

"Of course! That's what I meant!" Leah laughs as she gives me a cuddle.

"Hi James. Nice to meet you." I smile as he leans over and gives me a polite hug and a kiss on the cheek.

"It's lovely to finally meet you, thank you for having me! This place is beautiful. I can't wait for the big day." James politely responds.

James is very sweet, just like Leah told me on the phone when she invited him. Now that everyone is here, I feel completely overwhelmed with emotion. I couldn't be happier that they are finally here and the realisation that I am soon to be married truly kicks in.

"I'm so grateful to have you all here, I really, really am. Get yourselves sorted and relaxed, I've made you all pizza and picked up some more wine and beers if you fancy a drink." I offer.

"That's so sweet. Thank you." James says.

"I heard wine!" Lana jokes as she gives me a playful wink before heading outside to take a look at the pool.

Rueben appears last, carrying a few more bags and places them by the stairs.

"Did I miss much?" He asks as he wipes sweat from his brow which reminds me to turn the air conditioning up.

"Not a lot, I was just telling everyone how grateful I am to them for flying out to be with us." I answer.

"Let's toast to it then." Rueben smiles as he grabs the wine from the fridge and starts pouring it into some glasses.

"Grab a glass everyone!"

I take a glass as everyone joins us by the kitchen counter.

"I can't believe all the people we love so much have taken time out of their lives to travel all this way just to help us celebrate our day. Mollie and I are truly so grateful to you all. We hope you have the best time on Thursday as you watch us get married and also the best holiday. Thank you, guys, we love you. Cheers!" Rueben smiles as he raises his glass and everyone else copies.

"To the future Mr and Mrs Adams!" Lana adds and we all clink our glasses together before taking another sip.

"Don't forget to give your Mum a courtesy call at least to make sure she landed okay." I suggest to Rueben as the others head off by the pool.

"I will, don't worry." Rueben assures me.

I know it's been difficult but it's important to keep things as amicable as possible. The wedding is nearly here, and I just want everybody to have a good day and more importantly, I want everybody to get along.

CHAPTER FIFTY-NINE

"What's this place called again?" Lana asks as she puts on her seat belt.

"Bahama Breeze, it's Caribbean themed and apparently has the best cocktails too!" I reply with an excitable smile and Lana squeals enthusiastically which makes me laugh.

"Are you feeling nervous yet Mollie?" Leah asks.

"Yeah…I'm anxious to get there quickly, I don't want my Dad and Sarah to just have to sit with Joy and Dave awkwardly until we arrive."

"Yeah that's understandable. I'm going to be friendly and greet them and everything else I need to do but I'm not exactly thrilled to see my Aunty Joy either. I just don't like the way she treats Nan; I mean she's nearly ninety years old for god's sake." Leah sighs.

"I don't like the way she treats Mollie and Roo." Lana adds.

"Exactly. It's difficult isn't it. But it's good to take the high road, I think it's amazing that you guys even invited them in the first place." Leah says with a laugh.

"I know, a lot of people have said the same thing to us. But it wouldn't be right to purposely exclude anyone. As a Mum myself I would be mortified to be left out of my children's wedding. As much as she makes me anxious and frustrated, I just don't think we could be so mean." I shrug.

"You're a better person than I am then." Leah jokes. "I would have just left her at home!"

As Mike gets in the car last, we pull away and head to the restaurant an hour's drive away. After dinner tonight, I go back with my Dad and Sarah to their villa with Daisy and Lana. I decided I wanted to be somewhat traditional and spend the night before our wedding day apart. Plus, it builds up all the excitement and I'm much closer to the venue from my Dad's house, it makes it easier to carry all the make-up, dresses, shoes and whatever else I have packed away in my suitcases. My step mum, Sarah has all the favours, flowers, table decorations and everything else we need to set up in the morning too.

"So, don't we all scrub up well." James says as we start approaching the restaurant car park.

"Most of us. Apart from Rueben." I laugh as I stare at his casual shorts and t-shirt attire.

"Excuse me but this is an expensive t-shirt. Therefore, it counts as formal." Rueben smirks as he gives me a playful glare.

As soon as we head into the restaurant my Dad and Sarah are already seated at a large round table with their drinks.

"Hey baby!" My Dad says as he gets up to greet me with a cuddle.

"Hey Dad!" I say with a smile. I feel relieved to see his face and I stay cuddling him for an extra few seconds as I enjoy the moment of being reunited with my Dad again. I'm instantly less nervous about seeing Joy and Dave now.

"Ready for tomorrow then?" He continues as I take a seat next to him.

"I think so." I smile cheerfully.

Everyone else greets Dad and Sarah before taking a seat. Rueben and my Dad share a few sarcastic comments as usual about having to dress up for dinner. My Dad has never enjoyed being in much more than a t-shirt and shorts either.

The biggest glasses of Pina Colada's I have ever seen arrive for me, Lana and Leah. Even a virgin one for Daisy too. They taste amazing. The guys play it safe with beer and we all get into conversation about our holiday so far as we wait for Joy and Dave to join us.

Around fifteen minutes and half a Pina Colada later, I spot Joy and Dave as they appear at the restaurant door. My Dad and Rueben both wave until they find us, and they head on over.

"Hi Aunty Joy." Leah says with a friendly smile as she stands up to greet her. But awkwardly Joy shoots her a quick disgruntled glare as she looks Leah up and down before turning her back to her completely.

My jaw drops slightly as I notice Joy's hostile and rude approach, but I close it quickly and compose myself before anyone else notices. Leah catches my stare as she sits back down at the table and shrugs.

"That's me told." She whispers as she laughs it off.

"I won't be trying with her again then, not if she's going to act like that…"

My Dad takes over the niceties and shakes Dave's hand before greeting Joy with a kiss on the cheek and they both sit themselves down at the table.

Aside from Joy and Dave acknowledging my Dad and Sarah very briefly, there is very little communication offered to anybody else. They both sit inwardly to each other too and slightly turn their backs from everybody else at the table.

"So, how was your flight over?" My Dad asks breezily.

"Yep. Good, thank you." Dave responds in his typical monotone whilst staring at a menu in front of him.

"I'll get you a drink." My Dad offers.

"It's on me, what would you like?"

"Just a water please." Dave mutters.

"Just a water for me too." Joy adds as she stares at her own menu.

"Are you sure? Me and Sarah are sharing some wine, I could get you a bottle? Or a beer, if you prefer?" My Dad offers again gesturing at the wine menu.

"Water's fine." Dave mutters as Joy nods in agreement.

"Okay…" my Dad awkwardly sighs.

"Two waters coming right up."

Everyone sips at their drinks silently. The serious expression across Joy and Dave's faces make us all feel uncomfortable. They definitely do not look like they are here to celebrate their son's upcoming nuptials. Joy looks distracted and awkward and Dave just looks bored out of his brains.

"So, how are you enjoying Florida?" Sarah asks kindly, I assume to fill the silences.

"Yeah. Good." Joy mutters without taking her eyes away from the menu.

"We've been here before." Dave adds.

"Oh, lovely! Was that when the kids were little?" Sarah smiles at Rueben before looking back towards Dave.

"No. Just us. For our honeymoon. If kids want holidays, then they have to go out and earn it when they're older." Dave responds bitterly.

"Oh…" Sarah replies unsure whether he is joking or not. But I think everybody at the table knows that answer.

I cringe a little at how hard everyone is trying to strike up conversation with them both and how closed off Joy and Dave seem to be. Occasionally Joy glances up at Leah and Lana but with a displeased look across her face. If I know Joy by now, the unpleasant glances are probably because of how dressed up they both are. For as long as I can recall, Joy has always voiced her negative opinion on make-up and anybody who wears it. She'll always come up with a negative reason as to why a girl wearing a pretty dress and make up can't possibly look good. Either she's a show-off, or she's promiscuous, or she's ruining her skin and making herself age. Always something unkind and judgemental. I used to wonder if it was jealousy. I used to worry over what Joy must think about my appearance, since make up is one of my favourite passions. But even if she had a bad opinion of it, she probably wouldn't tell me to my face, so I'll never know.

"What takes your fancy on the menu then Mum?" Rueben asks in an attempt to break the ice.

"Oh…probably just a chicken salad. I'm not very hungry." Joy replies as she screws her face up at the menu as if it has nothing worthy to offer her.

"Here we are." My Dad says as he returns to the table.

"Two waters."

"Thanks." Dave mumbles, straight-faced and without breaking into a smile.

"So, are you both looking forward to tomorrow?" My Dad asks with a proud smile.

"Not really…I didn't realise it was an hour's drive away. I'm not even sure where it is." Dave huffs as he glares at Rueben.

"Well, the whole address is on the back of the invite?" Rueben responds calmly.

"Yeah and I also sent it to you in a text message like you asked me too." I add, surprised that there is an issue over this when they have never said anything about it before.

"If you want me to, I'll put it into your Satnav before we go and then you won't have to worry about setting it up in the morning." Rueben offers.

"I don't really trust all this technology. What's wrong with a map?" Dave responds as he rolls his eyes and the rest of us take another awkward sip from our drinks.

"Well I'll set it up anyway, just in case." Rueben replies softly.

By the time we have all ordered and gotten our meals, most of us are all laughing and in deep discussion about our plans for the next few days in Florida. Apart from Joy and Dave, who still haven't offered much to the conversation and instead just occasionally whisper amongst themselves.

"Are we getting ice cream?" Daisy asks as she finishes her chicken burger.

"Actually, it's getting late, we should probably get home and get ready for the wedding tomorrow." My Dad answers and I can't help but smirk at his response which tells me quite clearly that he just wants to get out of this awkward hell as much as I do.

"Grandads got ice cream back at his house." I smile.

"I'll get you some when we get there."

"Well, we'll settle up our side of the bill and get going. We need an early night since we have that long drive in the morning." Dave slyly digs and I can't help but feel agitated over his exaggeration.

"Okay, thank you for coming. I'll see you in the morning." I smile.

"What time do you want us there?" Joy asks.

"Well the wedding doesn't start until four in the afternoon, but there is lots to do and I'll need help with Freddie if you want to give me a hand? So, I'm getting there for eleven o'clock in the morning." Rueben answers.

"Right, okay then. We will get there for lunch time and I'll come find you." Joy replies as she takes her handbag and walks away without much of a goodbye or acknowledgement to anybody else.

"Oh, shall I come and do the Satnav, Dave?" Rueben offers again as he gets up from his seat.

"No thank you. I'm sure I can find it." He responds arrogantly before following behind Joy.

"Thank god that's over!" Leah giggles as she takes another slurp from her cocktail.

"I can't be bothered to try again with them, that was hard work. In future please don't expect me to be that polite. If it wasn't for you two getting married tomorrow, I would have just got up and left." My Dad says he lets out a heavy sigh.

"Don't worry." I assure.

"I think that this was our first and last dinner date."

"Thank you for trying though. I know it's not easy." Rueben says with a nervous laugh.

"No worries mate." My Dad says as he looks at Rueben sympathetically.

"Come on then, let's go." I say.

"I've got your favourite at home." My Dad says as we all leave the table.

"Sangria!"

I smile gratefully and can't help but giggle at Lana when she wombles a little as gets to her feet she walks out of the restaurant. I can tell she is tipsy. To be fair, I think we all are a little. There wasn't much else to do apart from drink alcohol in the hopes it took the awkwardness away.

"Yay! Sangria!" Lana laughs and we head for the car park excitedly.

I say my goodbyes to Freddie as I get him into the car, he looks so tired now, I wouldn't be surprised if he is asleep before they make it home.

After Leah, Mike and James climb into the back of the car. I wait patiently to have a moment with Rueben alone before he gets in the car too and drives away.

"I love you." He whispers as he cups my cheek with his warm hand.

"I love you too. I'm not sure I'll be able to sleep tonight though." I say with a nervous laugh.

"You will baby. Just enjoy the night with your Dad and Lana and I'll be there waiting for you at four o'clock on the patio." Rueben smiles as he leans down and presses his lips against mine.

"It's a date." I say with a smile as I turn on my heel and head to my Dad's car.

CHAPTER SIXTY

"Oh god…" I say as I sit up and hold my head.

My head feels thick and heavy and I feel as though I have barely slept.

"Yep…I think we may have had too much sangria." Lana says as she squints at the sunlight beaming through the windows.

"I didn't mean to drink that much. I think it was just all the excitement."

"Please…you needed it! You're about to have Joy as a mother-in-law. Hell! I'd be drinking too!" Lana mocks and I burst out laughing.

"Morning!" My Dad says cheerfully as he peeps his head around the bedroom door.

"Get up and get ready and I'll take you all for breakfast."

"Your last breakfast as a singleton…" Lana winks and she heads for the bathroom.

My Dad chooses to take us to a small breakfast cafe right by the beach and I opt for strawberries and banana on waffles. I'm not that hungry but I make an effort to eat as much of it as possible to help get me through the day.

"I sorted most of your favours this morning Mollie, I put the mints and the candies into the little paper bags just like you wanted." Sarah informs me with a smile.

"Life saver! Thank you so much." I say with relief. I'm so pleased to have her help me today.

"What time is your make-up and hair being done?" Dad asks.

"In like an hour! But the room for us to get ready in is already available so we can head over there whenever." I tell him excitedly.

"OK, well finish your waffles and we'll get the car loaded up with all your flowers and everything you need and head over." Dad says with a supportive smile.

The next couple of hours go so quickly. My step Mum and Lana went straight to the reception room upstairs upon arrival and put out the favours, guest book and flowers.

Me and Daisy got settled into the room straight away and started getting ready. Daisy had her hair done first, she has it half pinned up and the rest all down and curly, just like I'm about to have. She was adamant she wanted her hair just like her Mummy today.

For now, I am in my bridal dressing down and having my make-up done. So far, the morning has been so enjoyable. Everyone has been so helpful, and the make-up artist is one of the most down to earth and funniest girls I have met in a long time. We have all just been sat around, sipping coffee and enjoying the moment. Through all the excitement I haven't even thought much about Rueben, until now.

"Wow Sarah, you look amazing!" I say as the hair stylist finishes up with her hair and sprays the final bit of hairspray in to help hold it in place. She's dressed in a royal blue midi dress with nude heels and loose curls to complete her look.

"Thank you!" Sarah blushes gratefully.

"Do you need me to help you with anything else?"

"I don't think so, do you know if Roo is here yet?" I ask eagerly.

"Yeah, he's downstairs with Freddie in their room. Shall I bring Freddie up to see you in a little while?"

"Yes please!" I smile.

"What time is it?"

"It's nearly two o'clock." Sarah says as she glances down to her watch.

"Oh. So are Joy and Dave downstairs with Rueben too?"

"No. Not yet." Sarah replies.

"I'm sure they will be here soon."

"Yeah. They probably got lost looking at their maps." Lana says sarcastically and I can't help but giggle.

Next, Lana gets her hair styled and I help Daisy get into her beautiful flower girl dress that my Mum chose for her. As her memory pops into my mind so does the lump back in my throat. I take a deep breath and compose myself a little. I know for sure my Mum wouldn't want me to ruin my make up on my wedding day.

Everything starts becoming so real as Lana twirls around the room in her bridesmaid dress and her hair beautifully styled into a low bun. Everyone is pretty much ready now and it's just me to have my hair done and get into my wedding dress.

"Look! There's Mummy!" I hear Sarah say as she walks back into the room holding Freddie's hand.

"Hey baby!" I gasp excitedly as I stare at how handsome he looks in his little suit.

He is wearing a white short sleeved shirt with a pair of linen sandy coloured shorts and a matching waistcoat. His face lights up as he looks up at me and runs over for a cuddle.

"Mollie, Joy and Dave still haven't arrived and it's nearly three o'clock." Sarah tells me with concern clear on her face.

"What, really? Where is Rueben now?" I ask anxiously.

"He's been downstairs walking around by himself for the past hour, your Dad was going to come up and see you but instead he is going to keep Rueben company and buy him a drink at the bar."

"Oh…okay. I'm pleased Dad is there but I assumed Joy would be here by now. Shouldn't she be enjoying this moment with her son, straightening up his tie, calming his nerves…doing whatever it is Mother of the grooms do." I sigh.

"I agree. But I guess not." Sarah responds as she awkwardly shrugs her shoulders.

"Is Rueben okay?" I worry.

"Seems to be. I think he is just looking forward to seeing you." Sarah assures.

"I'll take Freddie back down there if you want and he can help keep Rueben company."

"Yes please." I nod as I give Freddie a quick cuddle and a kiss before he heads back downstairs.

"Mollie…do you think there's a chance she's decided to boycott the whole thing?" Lana questions gently.

"It's crossed my mind." I sigh.

"She wasn't exactly enthusiastic about anything last night."

"She sat with a face like an angry bulldog Mol! Something has pissed her off. Maybe she's not going to turn up today…and prove some kind of point." Lana shrugs.

"I don't know…I hope not. It does seem like she uses these kinds of opportunities to throw a tantrum and hurt Rueben though. But surely she wouldn't want to miss this day." I try to reassure myself.

"I'll go downstairs and hang about by the entrance if you want? See if I can spot them?" Lana offers and I nod gratefully.

After another twenty minutes I'm pretty much ready and Sarah comes back up to the room again to help me get into my dress and put my veil on.

"Any news?" I ask anxiously.

"No, nothing I'm afraid. They're still not here."

Sarah tells me disappointedly.

"Can I quickly get some photos of you in the other room? Before we go downstairs?" The photographer asks.

I nod and quickly walk into the other room and stand by the window, the photographer snaps away from different angles, I should be enjoying this moment. But I can't.

I peer out the window and see the beautiful white chairs with pastel pink ribbons all neatly arranged in rows ready for our guests. The white wooden archway is decorated with light pink drapes and tied back with ribbon and white roses. It looks beautiful.

I suddenly see Rueben appear, hands in his pockets, head down, walking along by himself.

My heart aches for him. I don't want any more photos; I don't want to stay up here a minute longer. I want to be with Rueben.

"She was supposed to be here four hours ago!" I whine as I watch Rueben sympathetically.

"Hey…" My Dad says as he surprises me by walking into the room.

"Dave has called Rueben just now and asked if you can hold back on the wedding for twenty minutes because they're going to be late."

275

"What? Just delay the wedding for them. They were supposed to be here hours ago!" I repeat agitatedly.

"I'm going downstairs to get ready for the wedding."

I anxiously get in the elevator and make my way down, I have to speak to Rueben, find out what on Earth is going on and see if he is okay.

When the elevator doors open, I see Leah and James.

"Hey!" Leah Smiles.

"You look absolutely beautiful."

"Thanks…" I smile but I'm too concerned about my fiancé to enjoy any compliments.

"Have you seen Rueben?"

"Yeah, he's on the phone still, Dave's been shouting at him down the phone for the last ten minutes." Leah says as she shakes her head.

"Dave is shouting at him. On our wedding day?" I snap irritably.

"Yep, apparently they're lost and the directions you all gave them were no good."

"If they were lost why weren't they phoning hours ago for help? It's quarter past four. I was supposed to be walking down the aisle fifteen minutes ago!" I sigh restlessly.

"I have a feeling they left their hotel very last minute because perhaps Joy wasn't sure if she wanted to come. It's not like she seemed thrilled last night." Leah replies.

"That's what Lana said too." I say, looking desperately around for Rueben.

In that moment I see Joy and Dave come through the entrance doors of the hotel, both looking a bit dishevelled and definitely not ready to take a seat outside.

"Can we have half an hour to get ready?" Joy asks in a fluster as she runs her fingers through her messy hair.

"They're already fifteen minutes late. You can have ten minutes tops." Leah answers for me and I feel relieved that I didn't have to reply to that.

"Right…" Joy huffs defensively as she heads off to find her hotel room with Dave.

"Come on…" Leah says as she gently tugs my arm.

"Let's get you ready, Rueben is waiting."

Within ten minutes I'm standing by the patio doors. Daisy is waiting patiently in front of me with her basket of petals. Lana is standing behind me looking beautiful in her soft pink and ivory gown and my Dad stands by my side, making a few jokes to ease my nerves.

I pull my veil down over my face and stare out onto the patio to see Rueben, who is patiently waiting for me under the arch. Mike, James and Leah disappear to take their seats along with Sarah and Freddie.

"We're here, where would you like us to sit?" Joy says as she reappears.

"Anywhere is fine." I politely answer.

Quietly in the background I hear the gentle sound of the string quartet version of chasing cars by Snow Patrol start up and I know that's my cue to start walking.

I take a deep breath and step outside as Rueben looks up in my direction, a smile spreads across his face.

I'm relieved when I get to the alter with him, I take his hand in mine straight away and give it a little comforting squeeze. Rueben also looks a lot less anxious to be reunited with me.

I lock my eyes onto his and enjoy this moment, staring at him proudly as I tell him my vows.

Before I know it, Rueben leans down to kiss me whilst everybody cheers and throws petals in the air.

"I'm so pleased you're back, Mrs Adams." Rueben smiles.

"I was a bit lost without you."

"Are you okay though? I heard about Dave's calls."

I whisper softly.

"God it was ridiculous. He really lost his temper. He started swearing and shouting in such a threatening way…but anyway let's not let it ruin our day." He reassures me as he takes me by the hand.

As we head off hand in hand upstairs to our reception room, I watch Rueben's face as he stares around in amazement.

"Wow everything looks incredible." He gasps, taking it all in.

"I know! Lana and Sarah were busy up here this morning…and look at how fabulous the cake is." I say gesturing towards the three-tiered ivory and blush cake.

Mostly everyone has found their seats and is already laughing and chatting away over champagne.

Apart from Joy who has gotten up and heading straight for our direction, surely this will be an explanation and an apology for being so late.

"Just to let you know, we will be leaving in an hour as we have to get back." Joy calmly informs us.

"OK." Rueben responds casually.

"Wait, what?" I ask clearly sounding shocked and disappointed.

"Well, it's just Dave booked us in to a park tomorrow to see some dolphins. Tomorrow was the only free day they had, and we have to get there very early…"

I stare at the audacity as she tries to come up with a reasonable explanation. My mouth drops open and my eyes are fixated on her with disgust. Sometimes, I can't hide what it is I am feeling, my facial expressions take over and make it too obvious.

"You have flown all the way here for the sole purpose of seeing your only son get married and you have managed to make other arrangements, which mean you can only stay at your son's wedding for a total of an hour and twenty minutes?" I ask irritably.

"Do you think we should stay a bit longer then?" Joy asks quietly as she picks up on my temper.

How could a grown woman be asking me how long is acceptable to stay at her only son's wedding. I am honestly bewildered at this point.

"I think you should do what you like Joy…" I sigh and walk away quickly to sit at our table. I don't have the energy to discuss this any further with Joy. I will never understand how or why she wasn't here hours ago to support her son and help him prepare for the biggest day of his life and so I have even less chance in understanding why she is in such a rush to leave. I had started getting used to the idea that Lily came before Rueben, but dolphins? I can't even comprehend her thought process anymore. It's too exhausting.

The drinks start flowing and the evening celebrations really start to begin. Rueben and I spent half an hour back down on the beach with our photographer taking some photos and when we got back Dad made a brilliant speech, along with Lana and lastly Rueben, who's speech brought me to tears. It was beautifully read out and it meant the world considering I know how much Rueben hates public speaking.

The music gets louder and most of us head onto the white tiled dance floor. Daisy and Freddie are the first ones up and running around excitedly and showing off their dance moves.

I'm surprised but pleased that Joy seemingly got the message and is still here, celebrating her son's wedding, even though they decided not to participate in speeches or much else.

Pretty soon the dance floor parts a little and allows room for me and Rueben to share our first dance. For me this is the best part of the day, all the stresses of getting ready and rushing around have passed and now it's just time to enjoy ourselves. Rueben holds me close as we sway gently to the music and he reminds me again of how beautiful I look.

As the night unfolds, the majority of us have gotten a little tipsy. Rueben dances with Daisy as he spins her around and she laps up every moment of it and I have a cheeky Freddie trying to hide under my big skirt and which makes me laugh.

"I think we are going to go now." Joy says as she anxiously paces after me on the dance floor.

"OK, that's fine." I smile.

"I hope you enjoyed yourself."

"It was wonderful, thank you." She replies politely and heads over to Rueben to say her goodbyes.

"Right, thanks then. See you back in England next week." Dave mutters in my direction.

"Oh, come here you!" I squeal before drunkenly throwing my arms around Dave and practically forcing him to hug me.

"You're not so bad you know! I mean your taste in women is a little…frightening. But hey ho, other than that you're a nice little bald man. I mean sometimes you're a bit angry…and then you're a moody little bald man, but we all have our flaws…"

"OK, Mol…why don't we get you some water." Lana interrupts as she pulls me away.

"Did you just call Dave a little bald man?" Rueben smirks as he strides over.

279

"Maybe. Maybe that was the champagne talking." I say through hiccups.

"Come on Mrs Adams…why don't we head down to our suite and have a bottle of water or two on the balcony." Rueben laughs as he puts his arm around my waist.

"OK! OK!" I smirk.

"Champagne drunk is like, really drunk…"

"I noticed!" Rueben laughs as we head out of the room, leaving our last few guests to enjoy dancing the night away.

CHAPTER SIXTY-ONE

"I can't believe it's over." Rueben sighs at he slumps down onto our sofa.

"Back to work Monday too."

"I know, I hate not waking up to a swimming pool every morning, why don't we have one of those!?" I childishly groan.

"Because we're not millionaires…" Rueben smirks.

"Oh yeah, right. That little technicality again." I laugh.

"Overall it was pretty amazing though wasn't it?"

"Best two weeks of my life!" I say with a big smile.

"Even your Mum and Dave seemed to enjoy themselves in the end."

"Yep. Although Dave probably could have done without the drunk infused head lock you put him in at the wedding!"

"It was a cuddle! I still maintain it was a cuddle!" I laugh embarrassed.

"Did you notice Mum and Dave were the only ones who didn't get us so much as a congratulations on your wedding day card…not even a gravy boat. Nothing at all." Rueben says half joking.

"Yeah I did notice. But hey, at least they were there and watched you get married. That's the main thing."

"I know, but you should hear the amount of stuff she bought Lily back."

"Really?" I ask surprised.

"Yep. She even asked me at the wedding if I had room in my suitcase to take some of the bits back. She's got her a tonne of stuff from Disney world, then bottles of alcohol, perfume, t-shirts and then she said she had to get more for her at duty free. Meanwhile, it was my wedding day and she doesn't even think to get me so much as a card." Rueben says with a little more irritability in his voice.

"Come on, let's not dwell. You may not always be your Mum's first thought, but you'll always be mine." I say with a smile and start tackling open the suitcases. I need to make a start in separating them and getting them ready to wash otherwise I know I'll let it sit here for days.

"Thank you, baby…that means the world." Rueben smiles as he stretches out onto the sofa and gets comfortable.

"Shall I go and wake the kids up in a minute?"

"No, let them nap for another hour or so, they didn't manage much sleep on the plane, they will be shattered." I casually answer whilst dividing up the clothes into colours.

"Babe…" Rueben says as he sits up straight on the sofa and peers down at his phone. His face has dropped into a confused frown. He stares at his screen carefully, as if he is trying to make sense of what is in front of him.

"What?" I ask a little confused.

"My…my ex-girlfriend, Jenna. She's messaged me on social media. She wants to meet with both of us…this is so confusing, here, read it." Rueben offers as he passes me his phone.

Hi Rueben,
I'm sorry to have to message you out of the blue but there's some things that have been going on now for over a year and I really think it has gotten to the point where I need speak to you about it, face to face. I think you should bring your partner too as I think she whole thing involves her, or at the very least she should be made aware. I'm not sure if you have much free time, but tomorrow I can meet for a coffee in the morning, if you are both free?
Let me know,
Jenna.

"Right?" is all I manage to say.

"What do you think that's about?" Rueben asks curiously as he studies his phone again.

"I have no idea, you're her ex-boyfriend. Shouldn't you know?"

"No. None. We literally never spoke again after we broke up. It wasn't exactly amicable. I mean there's no hard feelings now, I've moved on and I'm sure she has, but this is just so…random."

"The messaged seemed polite though. So random or not you should take her up on it." I suggest calmly.

"You're coming too!" Rueben insists.

"Really? Are you sure?" I say anxiously as I think how awkward that would be to have a coffee date with my husband my husband's ex-girlfriend.

"Yes. She said you should come. So, we both are. I'll message her back now." Rueben says as he begins writing back a message and arranging a time to meet. My heart quickens a little at the thought of being in the same room as a woman who was with Rueben for such a long period of his life. I'm not sure if I have anything to be worried about or not, but something tells me deep inside that this can't be good news.

"Are you okay?" Rueben asks as he stares at me intently.

"I…yes. I'm just…a little, I don't know. Worried." I manage to mumble.

"I'm worried too. Which is why we have to go. I know Jenna and I know she would never go out of her way to message me unless she felt she *really* had too." Rueben sighs.

"Yeah. But I'm also worried about my husband meeting up with his ex-girlfriend of over six years just weeks after we got married." I blurt. I know I could possibly sound childish right now, even jealous maybe. But it's the truth. I should be in my euphoric newlywed bubble. Not preparing to meet Jenna.

"Come here." Rueben says and I do as he asks and sit on the sofa next to him. He talks to me affectionately but with a serious expression on his face.

"I'm with you. I made vows to you. For better or for worse, from now until forever. I'm sorry we have to go and meet up with an ex. I know how uncomfortable that must be for you. But believe me, I feel just as uncomfortable. I never wanted to see this woman again in my life. But if she has something important to tell us then we should at least hear her out. Together, me and you. As a team."

I nod apprehensively and get up to leave the room.

"You're still upset?" Rueben asks surprised as I get up.

"No, but I'm going to get my phone and see if Lana wouldn't mind watching the kids for a couple of hours tomorrow. I don't think it's best we take them." I say a little sternly.

That night I can barely sleep. Rueben fell asleep pretty quickly tonight, but I've been tossing and turning for hours now. I'm not sure if it's the jet lag or I'm nervous about tomorrow. It's quite probable that it's both.

The kids have been sound asleep since eight o'clock and I really wish that I was too so that I didn't have to lay here with these thoughts racing around my head.

The more I seem to worry about getting some sleep the more it seems I can't. I feel so unsettled and anxious and it's now nearly four o'clock in the morning. What could Jenna possibly have to say? It's not like Rueben has seen her recently. What could be so important that we need to meet face to face?

I pull my phone from my drawer and browse YouTube for some relaxing sounds that I can try and concentrate on, instead of my anxious thoughts.

Eventually I decide on rain and thunder noises and place it next to my pillow whilst I rest my eyes and concentrate on those sounds and nothing else.

It seems to be working as I feel my body relaxing, my breathing slowing, and I feel myself slowly drifting off to sleep.

"Mummy!" Freddie calls from his cot bed and my eyes ping open.

"Oh, no." I groan to myself as I reluctantly drag myself out of the bed and into Freddie's room.

"Hello!" Freddie says with a big grin as I find him standing up on his bed holding onto the sides and clearly wide awake.

"Damn jet lag." I mumble to myself as I pick Freddie up from his bed.

"I guess we are up for the day then, cheeky monkey."

I fix Freddie some breakfast and make myself a coffee. I catch my reflection in the kitchen window and grumble to myself. In a few hours we are off to see Rueben's ex and I look like a pale and tired mess, who has been dragged through a hedge and then fell out of a tree. Fantastic.

As the hours pass, I anxiously get into the shower and desperately try to breathe some life into my exhausted body. I have the shower hotter than usual hoping it gives my face some colour.

"You've just been to Florida for two weeks, you look amazing." Rueben tries to reassure me as I wrap a towel around my body.

"Well I don't feel it." I snap.

"Sorry...I'm just tired."

As I finish drying my hair in my bedroom, I hear Rueben greet Lana at the door. It must mean its nearly time to go and with that thought, the butterflies are back in my stomach.

"What do you think it's about?" Lana whispers as I walk down the stairs.

"I have no idea." I nervously shrug.

"Maybe she wants a kidney?" Lana jokes, which somehow eases my nerves a little as I giggle at her sarcasm.

"I'll tell you everything as soon as we're back." I promise and she gives me a reassuring hug before we leave.

Rueben and I are both pretty quiet in the car. I think we are both just anxious to get there now and find out what the reasons are behind her message.

On the approach to the coffee shop I can feel my heart beating faster, my legs feel like jelly and suddenly I feel much hotter than I did in the car.

"They're over there." Rueben gestures to a table in the far corner of the busy coffee shop.

"They're?" I ask anxiously.

"She's brought her Mum with her." Rueben casually replies as he leads me over to the table.

She's brought her Mum. Jesus what is this? Some kind of weird family reunion I think to myself, as I awkwardly follow behind.

"Hi Rueben." Jenna's Mum says with a friendly smile as she stands up to greet us.

"Hi Kathy." Rueben politely responds.

"Hi...."

"Mollie." I say, politely finishing Kathy's sentence.

"Mollie...of course." She says with a warm smile.

"I know this is a bit strange, but hopefully you'll appreciate us telling you everything."

"Yeah..." Is all I manage to say with a nervous smile.

Jenna hasn't introduced herself to me and hasn't got the same warm approach as her Mum. Instead she keeps more of a straight face and stares awkwardly down at the plastic wallet in front of her. I'm wondering whether this meeting was more Kathy's idea than it was Jenna's.

"Let's just get to it." Jenna sighs as she pulls some paper out of the wallet.

"I have things to do so I can't stay long."

"Ok..." Rueben hesitantly responds.

"I think you need to see these." Jenna says as she places the papers out onto the table.

I glance down to see they're of screenshots and taken from a lengthy social media conversation.

"What's going on?" I blurt out as I anxiously stare at the paper and then back at Rueben who has suddenly lost all colour in his face.

CHAPTER SIXTY-TWO

I stare down at the pages in disbelief. It's just pages and pages full of messages from Joy to Jenna. I keep checking the dates and they started just after I gave birth to Freddie and they've been going on and on.

I never once truly believed I could have a real close relationship with Joy, not when she doesn't even have one with her own son but something about this really, really hurts. I feel betrayed. I can't imagine how Rueben must be feeling.

"They started over a year ago. At first, I thought Joy must be trying to get me and Rueben reconnected but then I clicked on to Rueben's profile and saw that he was in a new relationship and saw that he had just become a Dad. So, it didn't make sense as to why she wanted to speak to me so bad. I thought it would be disrespectful to you both to answer them, so I just kept ignoring them." Jenna explains calmly.

"Yeah…I've been having some issues with my Mum." Rueben mumbles embarrassed.

"She even started messaging me on my birthday and here's one from Christmas morning, here, look…" Jenna says as she shows me a circled message on the page.

Hi Jenna,
Hope you have a wonderful Christmas and a fantastic new year. Me and Dave send our best.

*Hope to see you one day soon, you're always welcome round for
a coffee love.
From Joy and Dave xx*

"What the *fuck?*" I whisper quietly to myself. As I read the word
love I feel like another knife has been pushed into my back. She calls
me love when she wants me to believe she's my friend, when she wants
me to believe she cares about me, when she's sorry for my Mum dying,
she calls me, love.

"I knew something wasn't right, your Mum never liked me Rueben,
she hated it when you were with me for so long. When we broke up
and I had to come into the house to collect my things, she glared at
me the entire time. If looks could kill I wouldn't be here now…and yet
she was sending me messages as if we were the best of friends." Jenna
continues as she fidgets a little nervously with the papers.

"We had a feeling there was some kind of motive and that definitely became clear when Lily started sending messages too." Kathy
adds.

"What, Lily too?" Rueben sighs in shock.

"She sent me a few messages, trying to persuade me to go to your
Mum's house for a coffee. Then she sent me this…" Jenna says anxiously as she hands over another piece of paper with a clear message
from Lily's account.

*Hey Hun,
I know I shouldn't be saying this but as you might be aware
my brother has met some other girl called Mollie. Anyway, she's
ended up pregnant and my brother is in pieces. He said Mollie
has trapped him and that if she wasn't pregnant, he would
come back to you. He really misses you. Shall I give you his
phone number. Maybe you could reach out to him?
Miss you girl,
Lily xxxxxxx*

"I would never say that babe…never." Rueben looks at me panicked. His eyes desperately looking for my reassurance.

"I know. It's okay." I mumble awkwardly. I manage to look calm but inside my anger is bubbling away and if I'm not careful, I could lose all control of my emotions and burst out crying at this very table. I feel humiliated.

"I didn't reply to Lily's messages either. I figured they were trying to stir up some kind of trouble and I didn't want any involvement. My Mum will tell you the next part…" Jenna sighs as she turns to her Mum to fill the awkward silences.

"I was in the supermarket one evening and when I walked outside, I bumped into Joy and Dave. Dave gave me a polite nod before disappearing into the store, but Joy stopped and started talking to me. She told me how much she missed Jenna and kept asking me if I could persuade Jenna to get in contact. I explained to her that Jenna didn't want any involvement with whatever was going on, but she was quite pushy. The more I said no, the more irritable she got. The next thing I knew, she said she would even pay Jenna money to message Rueben a text message. She seemed so desperate; it was uncomfortable." Kathy says considerately as she glances at us sympathetically.

"I didn't engage in that ridiculous talk though. I just kind of laughed it off and walked away."

"I blocked Joy and Lily on all my social media and hoped that would be the end of it. But they then started to message my stepdad, my brothers and even my uncle. Basically, anyone who they thought knew me." Jenna tells us irritably.

"It's been a nightmare. I just want your Mum to leave our family alone."

"I'll talk to her about all of this but I'm not sure she'll listen." Rueben anxiously offers as he drops his head into his hands.

"Well if it doesn't stop, I'll end up phoning the police." Jenna snaps impatiently.

"I think Rueben will be trying his best Jen, but I don't think there's any point stressing at him about this. He can't control his Mum." Kathy gently interjects.

"He really can't." I add.

"I've seen it. She's unpredictable, angry, unreasonable, she lies so much, the list goes on. I wish Rueben knew how to resolve everything, but he can't. He can't keep cleaning up her messes either. We have had a really difficult time with her. I'm so sorry you have somehow been dragged into this."

"I'm so embarrassed. I don't really know what to say." Rueben mutters shamefully.

"It's not your fault. We always liked you a lot Rueben. We just thought you needed to know, maybe we could work out together what's going on." Kathy says kindly.

"I guess she's been trying to split us up this whole time." Rueben shrugs miserably.

"She has a tendency to ruin things when I'm happy."

"God." I gasp as I stare down at one of the pages and I read something that hits a nerve.

"Look at this date Roo, she was asking Jenna round to her house the day before my Mum's funeral. Just before she babysat the kids."

"Jesus Christ. I don't know what to say…I'm sorry." Rueben heavily sighs.

"So, what was the plan then? To make me feel threatened. Pushed out? Upset?

During the one time I needed all the strength I could get, your Mum wanted to hurt me even more?" I begin to say calmly but my voice gets louder and louder by the end. So loud in fact I suddenly feel my cheeks burning red with embarrassment as I realise half of the people in the cafe are now staring at the scene I'm creating. To make matters worse my eyes sting as tears fill them.

"I don't know…" Rueben mumbles.

"You never know!" I yell before grabbing my bag and storming across the cafe and out the door.

I'm shaking. I can't cope with the constant stress. Every time I think we are all doing somewhat okay, Joy brings another drama to light. Each one getting worse.

Before I can take a moment to calm down, I find myself frantically finding Joy's number in my phoning and calling it. I hold the phone up to my ear as I pace around the street. I'm seething, I wish I could stop myself from making this knee jerk reaction, but I can't, I don't think I have ever felt this angry before.

"Hello?" Joy answers casually.

"Why do you hate me so fucking much?" I snap into the phone.

"I don't? What's happened, love?"

"Don't call me love. Jenna told us, everything. She told us about all the messages you have been sending her!" I roar. I could keep shouting and ranting and get it all off my chest now, but I stop myself, I want to know what she has to say for herself.

"Mollie, I promise you I haven't been trying to speak to Jenna. It's been the other way around. She's been messaging me." Joy says so confidently down the phone.

What a fantastic liar she is.

"I've seen all the screen shots! I've been sat having a coffee *with* Jenna, she saved every little message you sent her! Are you going to keep lying to me? Or are you going to tell me the truth?" I hiss angrily at her audacity.

Within seconds I realise the phone line has gone dead. Joy hung up on me.

CHAPTER SIXTY-THREE

"Babe?" Rueben gently calls as he approaches me.

"She hung up on me." I snap in shock.

How dare she? We have to listen to her rants over and over again on the phone but the second somebody else wants to get something off their chest she behaves too cowardly to listen.

"Who?"

"Your Mother!"

"Oh Mollie, you didn't. Please tell me you didn't." Rueben sighs as he rubs his hand anxiously over the back of his neck.

"Of course, I did! How could I not say something?"

"I wanted to be the one to speak to her first." Rueben stresses.

"Why? So, she can just shout at you or stress you out? And as always nothing actually gets solved? Yeah, right." I huff impatiently.

"Let's go to the car. We can't just do all this on the street. I'll try and ring Dave and see if he knows what's going on, maybe he can talk to Mum for me." Rueben suggests as he takes me by the hand.

"I really don't care about what your ex-girlfriend and her Mum thinks about me, but I am sorry for storming off without saying good-bye, I probably came across really rude and I didn't mean to react that way." I sigh regretfully, trying to calm myself down.

"No, not at all. They totally understood. They know what my Mum is like. Kathy was really sympathetic after you left." Rueben reassures me but that only makes me feel worse. Rueben wanted us to be a team and I let my emotions take over. I really hate the person I become when Joy has caused an issue. I become so irritable and unable to control my temper.

This really isn't me. I used to wake up in the morning and want to go out and enjoy my day. I wanted to take my children to theme parks, to the zoo, plan future holidays and most of all be happy. I didn't want to be waking up with another argument hanging over my head. Constantly worrying about what my mother-in-law is planning behind my back. I hate being on edge, waiting for Joy to have an issue with something else I have done. Waiting for her to get on the phone and verbally abuse the man I love. This isn't the life I want for myself. I promised myself I wouldn't fall victim again to another toxic person and yet here I am, having coffee with an ex-girlfriend of Rueben's because of somebody's toxic actions. This shouldn't be happening today. This is not normal.

I make my way to the car, both of us in silence. I don't know how I'll get over this with Joy. It's one thing to do something out of anger but a whole other thing to plot behind someone's back for over a year. Especially when there were times during that period when I genuinely believed we were all on better terms and working towards a better relationship. Just like she said she wanted. She even wrote me a letter offering to start again and allowing me to think she accepted me but this whole time she's been trying to destroy my relationship with her son. What Mother betrays her own son in this way?

As soon as we get into the car Rueben gets his phone out and begins calling Dave.

"What?" Dave abruptly answers.

"Dave, I need to talk to you about what Mum has done." Rueben calmly says.

"Oh, whatever your Mum has done is nothing to do with me." Dave snaps impatiently.

"Well it kind of does. She's been sending messages to Jenna and signing your name along with hers at the end of them." Rueben snaps back.

"Why would your Mum do that? It sounds like you are starting on your Mum again, over nothing." Dave responds restlessly and I see Rueben growing more agitated as Dave dismisses it so quickly.

"Is this what you think? That Mum is the victim here?" Rueben asks.

"Well, yes. You and your wife have always got an issue lately." Dave responds and I can feel the anger bubbling up inside of me again. How can he think this? I have always believed Dave was somewhat smart, how can he not see any of this for what it really is.

"Dave…" Rueben huffs whilst he looks for the right words to say next.

"Oh look, I haven't got the time for this." Dave interrupts.

"I'll ring your Mum quickly now and ask if she knows what this nonsense is about and then I'll get back to you."

My heart is pounding whilst I wait for Dave to call back. In this moment I would really appreciate it if he could just at least acknowledge what we are telling him and understand that what Joy has done isn't normal behaviour. It's not right.

"Hello?" Rueben says as he brings the phone up to his ear.

"Right well I've spoken to your Mum." Dave confirms forcefully.

"And she said that she just spoke to Jenna casually as she contacted her on social media. That's all. What was she supposed to do? Be rude and ignore her?"

"No that's not it at all Dave. That's not what has happened here…" Rueben tries to interject.

"It sounds to me like Mollie just can't handle it because she's insecure and that's *not* your Mother's fault. She'll have to grow up." Dave continues speaking over Rueben.

"Dave, enough. Mum was only writing to Jenna because she wanted to use her to cause issues with me and Mollie. We have the proof!" Rueben protests.

"I don't believe that for one second. I don't care what proof you have; I'm not wasting anymore time looking at anything. This is so pathetic and just another attack on your Mum. Goodbye." Dave huffs before hanging up the phone.

"How come things like this happen and people like Dave assume we are at fault? How is it fair that we get blamed? What can I do that's any different? I just wanted to be happy, why can't she help with that? Why does she do stuff like this?" I ask as I feel myself growing panicked. I'm breathing faster and feeling lightheaded, my heart is pounding against my chest and I'm struggling to calm myself.

"Babe...are you ok?" Rueben asks softly as he takes a hold of my trembling hands.

"I think I'm having a panic attack." I say as I gasp for air and frantically unwind the car window.

"Everything is going to be okay. Just look at me. Keep your hand on my chest. Can you feel that? That's the air going into my lungs, just like the air is going into yours. Even if it doesn't feel like it, I promise it is. You're breathing. You're okay." Rueben reassures and I desperately try to listen to his relaxing words and try to slow the racing thoughts buzzing around my mind.

"I'm so stressed out, Roo." I sob in between breaths.

"I know. Believe me I am too. The most relaxed days I had were when we had those few days on our own in Florida. Just us." Rueben sighs gently as he continues to hold my hand against his chest.

"Me too. I loved it." I croak as my breathing slows down a little.

"I've been thinking about this for a while now, a part of me thinks we should just move away. Have a fresh start, just our little family."

"Really? But what about our home?" I ask surprised.

"We'll get another home and we'll make it beautiful." Rueben says so confidently.

"You've been wondering what I have been writing about in my journal for some time now. Here, you can look."

Rueben leans over me and takes out the small black leather journal from the glove box and places it on my lap. I pull my hands away from his chest and open the first few pages and stare down at the notes and memories Rueben has been writing down for so long now.

There's so many. Some I already knew about, some I didn't. I read about how Dave would often grab him by the throat and threaten to punch him when he was just a child. I read about how his only safe place was at his Nan's and that's why he is so close to her now. I read about how Dave would yell at Rueben all the time because Joy would always tell stories on him. So many different incidences. So many times, where Rueben was punched, kicked, verbally abused and threatened. I can't imagine how it must have felt to return back to a house like that. I can't imagine living in a home that doesn't feel safe.

"Why did this happen? It says you were locked in the downstairs bathroom and you had to sleep in the bathtub without any blankets and that you woke up alone in the freezing cold and in the dark? What did you do to deserve that?" I question sympathetically as I carefully read the notes. I feel the lump back in my throat as I picture a mini Rueben, alone, huddled up in the dark, being forced to sleep in a bathtub.

"Yeah. That's pretty much all I can remember. I was about nine or ten years old and I remember they locked me in there in the dark. I was banging on the door and crying to get out, but they wouldn't let me out. Eventually I must have gotten tired and fell asleep in the bath. My next memory, I was waking up and it was dark, it was the middle of the night. The bathroom door was finally open and so I ran upstairs to my bed. It was terrifying." Rueben whispers as if he is worried in case anyone can hear his story.

"What's the note here about the supermarket?" I question as my eyes focus on the scribbled unclear notes on the paper.

"Oh, I was in a supermarket with Dave, maybe around twelve this time and I think I asked for some sweets and he said no, the next thing I know he put his hands around my throat and pinned me up against the wall. A security guard actually came over and told Dave to get off me, but he just sneered at him and told him to mind his own business. I was so embarrassed. I spent the whole night hoping that the security guard might have told the police or something. I hoped someone would help me, but nobody ever did." Rueben explains.

"Did you ever think that maybe the school might have helped?" I ask gently.

"Never. My Mum used to write letters and tell the school all the bruises came from football or falling out of bed. I think I told you this before. For years I went along with that because she told me too. I thought it was too late, I didn't think the school would ever believe me. I was just a kid. Can you imagine if I told the school and they didn't believe me? And I got sent home with Mum and Dave that night anyway? It would have been horrendous." Rueben shudders at the thought.

With each memory I read I find myself growing sicker as I am reminded that these are the people I have repeatedly forgiven and even defended.

"I don't know if I can keep bringing the kids around the people you're describing." I hesitantly say with tears in my eyes as I learn more about my husband's difficult childhood.

"Keeping your child locked overnight in a bathroom is not the act of a loving parent."

"I'm not comfortable with it either. I thought I could be if they were changed people. But all this drama tells me that not a lot has changed. She's still abusive, she's just altered the way in which she does it. I think I had been waiting for something that is never going to happen." Rueben heavily sighs.

"What do you want to do?" I softly ask.

"I need to ring Mum. I need to tell her to back off now. I need space, I need to look after my family. Not spend my weekends unravelling another *Joy*ful surprise." Rueben says as he pulls his phone out of his pocket and searches for her phone number.

"Mum…I need to talk to you." Rueben firmly begins.

"What?" I hear Joy abruptly respond.

"What you have done with Jenna is completely over the line. She showed me everything and even Kathy told me about how you stopped her outside of a supermarket and asked her to send me stupid messages. You have Mollie so upset and stressed out she's having panic attacks."

"Oh, pathetic. It's all poor me with that one! Playing the mental health card, is she?" Joy scoffs as she lets out a loud mocking laugh.

"Don't speak about her like that!" Rueben snaps.

"You have really hurt me too, Mum. You brought back a person into my life who I'd rather forget. You're messing with my relationship and hurting everyone. I need some space, away from you. I want to stop all contact for a little while."

"What about Freddie? He's my grandson. I don't care about Daisy much as she's just Mollie's kid…but Freddie is mine!" Joy scorns.

"How dare you! You said you would never bring Daisy into your arguments again, you horrible evil crazy witch." I scream over Rueben.

"I don't want to talk to you Mollie. You're not family. I would like to talk to my son." Joy screams back arrogantly as I'm a nobody.

"Well I'm telling you Mum, I'm sorry but I am done for a while. You have really hurt me and you're not even sorry." Rueben responds.

"You dare keep me away from my grandson and you'll come unstuck. How about I ring your work and tell them about how you took Freddie out on his first birthday? You weren't sick! You lied. I'll tell them and you'll get fired…" Joy explodes.

"What are you talking about Mum? I didn't call in sick that day? I had booked in a holiday. They knew it was my son's birthday! What's wrong with you!" Rueben groans irritably as Joy continues to scream threats over him.

"I'll ring your Nan then, she'll be so ashamed, she'll disown you! Then I'll ring Mollie's Dad, then I'll ring her work and tell them what kind of woman they have employed. Then I'll ring Daisy's school and I'll tell them she's an unfit Mother. And then I'll…."

"Goodbye, Joy!" Rueben interrupts as he hangs up the phone.

"I'm going to block her phone number. You should do the same."

"Okay." I nod.

"I'm done with listening to her threats. I'm done with her trying to bully me." Rueben declares confidently.

"Enough."

CHAPTER SIXTY-FOUR

"So, let me get this straight. For the majority of your relationship, Joy has been trying to use Jenna to break you both up?" Lana asks with her eyes wide and her mouth open in shock.

"Pretty much." I mumble as I pour myself a glass of wine.

"The thing is though; Jenna and her Mum were pretty decent. The silver lining I have is that they at least didn't entertain Joy."

"I'm not surprised! Who would? She's clearly unhinged." Lana sighs.

"You hear about this kind of stuff in soap operas. Not day to day to life."

"Well hopefully we won't be hearing any more. I've blocked my Mum and Mollie has done the same. I'm hoping this is the end." Rueben adds as he grabs himself a beer from the fridge.

"Really? Is that it for you two?" Lana asks curiously.

"I'd say I'm done with it for now, yes. I need to move on. I want to be happy with my family, not deal with this all the time." Rueben says positively.

"After my Mum died, I honestly felt Rueben needed a relationship with Joy, even if it's just at arm's length. Afterall, you only get one Mum. But now, I don't know anymore. Toxic is toxic, right?" I respond.

"Absolutely. As time has gone on, it's gotten worse. Mollie your panic attacks are back and Rueben you look more and more dejected each time I see you. You guys deserve better than this." Lana says as she stares at us both sympathetically.

"I love the both of you, I want you to be happy."

Rueben looks up and smiles at Lana gratefully as he takes note of her support. We really are lucky to have good friends around us. Lana decides we could do with a chilled night and goes off to order a Chinese takeaway whilst Rueben and I get comfortable in the front room in front of the television. The kids are enjoying a homemade pizza Lana made earlier and it won't be long before it's their bedtime. I'm exhausted myself; I wouldn't be surprised if I'm asleep by seven o'clock too. Another long and emotional day, it really takes it out of you.

I sip my wine and take a deep breath as I stretch out on the sofa and try to relax. The thoughts of the messages from Joy to Jenna keep popping into my head but I try to ignore it. There's no point allowing myself to become so consumed by it. It's over with now, she didn't achieve what she set out to do and everyone's okay.

"I feel a bit sick." Rueben whispers as he turns to look at me nervously.

"Really, why?" I ask, studying Rueben's pale face.

"I'm just not sure whether it'll stop here. I know my Mum. I know she'll have nothing better to do than think of something else to hurt us right now. She'll be so mad that I stuck up for us and told her to back off."

"Roo, there's nothing else she can do." I groan a little impatiently.

"I'm tired of worrying. What else is there left to do? She's gone after an ex-girlfriend of yours and it was unsuccessful. Do you have another ex that you're worried about?"

"What? No, not at all. I told you there was only Jenna. Well I had girlfriends before her, but I mean I would have been like, thirteen. If she manages to find them online, I really will be surprised." Rueben half jokes and I can't help but laugh at the thought of Joy frantically finding all Rueben's childhood sweethearts.

"Then I'm sure it's fine. She's just one person, Roo. Don't let her fool you into thinking she's more powerful than she actually is. She can't hurt you. You're not that child under her roof anymore. You're going to be fine." I assure and I affectionately run my fingers through his hair which makes him relax a little.

By the time the Chinese food arrives I'm feeling much more relaxed as we all get stuck in and chat away about the upcoming summer and some trips we could plan. This evening is definitely a massive improvement from our day.

"OK, guys, well I best shoot off. Mike is waiting at home for me. Don't tell him we had Chinese; I'm supposed to be on some new fitness meal plan with him." Lana winks as she gets herself ready to leave.

"No problem." I laugh.

"Thank you so much for watching the kids today."

"Don't be silly, you know I'll watch them anytime." She smiles before giving me a cuddle.

"Bye Lana, thanks again for today." Rueben adds.

"Bye, Roo. Try and relax. I'm sure everything will be fine." Lana assures before giving him a quick kiss on the cheek goodbye.

As I stand at the door and wave Lana off, I suddenly realise how tired I've become. My eyes are blurry, and I have a huge headache coming on.

"Shall we go to bed?" I ask as I head back into the front room.

"You've read my mind." Rueben yawns as he turns the television off and we head up to the bedroom.

As I pull the duvet up over me and snuggle down, I know it won't take long for me to fall asleep after last night's restless night. When I close my eyes, I think of my Mum. I think about how I wish I could have phoned her tonight and told her everything about what happened and what Jenna showed me. I try to imagine what she would say, the advice she might give. I feel a tear drop onto my pillow as I try to imagine her voice comforting me. I wish she was here right now. Thankfully, before I get any more upset, I feel myself drifting off to sleep with Rueben's arm draped around and holding me close.

When I wake up the morning, I'm feeling a lot more refreshed. I can hear Freddie playing downstairs so Rueben must have got up with him already and taken him downstairs.

"Morning Mummy." I hear Daisy whisper cheerfully.

"Oh, hello beautiful! I didn't know you got into bed with me." I say as I turn over to see her smiling face staring down at me.

"Yep! Daddy said I could. I'm playing games on your phone is that okay?"

"Yeah, sure. It's fine, since you are anyway." I giggle and snuggle into her.

"Oh, Mummy. Grandma sent you a photo earlier." Daisy tells me casually.

"What?" I ask directly as I sit up in a panic.

"What's wrong Mummy?" Daisy asked, confused as she looks up from my phone.

"Nothing sweetheart. I'm just going to need my phone for a minute. Why don't you go downstairs and grab some breakfast."?

"Ow! But I wanted to play games." Daisy whines as she huffs out of the room.

"You can later. I promise." I call after her, feeling bad for having taken the phone away.

I look through my phone anxiously. Joy was blocked. I'm not sure how she would have sent me a message. I frantically search through different apps, but I can't find the photo anywhere. The last app I check is my email and sure enough there's a message in my inbox which has already been opened by Daisy.

I nervously open it.

Hi Mollie,
Here's a photo of my son with a beautiful girl he has been
cheating on you with. Isn't she gorgeous?
Joy.

I stare down at the photo in front of my eyes. I feel sick as I study it and my hands begin trembling. My adrenaline is already pumping through my body and my heart is beating out of my chest.

It's Rueben smiling next to a young woman, she's smiling too. They look, happy. They look like they're together. But I don't recognise her at all, and Rueben has never once told me anything about another girl. Only Jenna. The photo is clearly recent because he is wearing the same polo shirt that he was wearing when I met him.

But when I met him, he told me he had been single for a long time and didn't even have any time to date.

Has he lied to me too? He wouldn't cheat on me, would he? How

302

does Joy know this girl and I don't? And why does she have a photo?

"Daisy just said my Mum has messaged you?" Rueben asks nervously as he bursts into the bedroom. He clearly ran up the stairs because he sounds al out of breath.

"Who is she?" I ask suspiciously as I throw the phone down onto the bed and watch his face fill with anxiety as he stares down at the photo.

"Well?"

CHAPTER SIXTY-FIVE

"I promise you, it's not what you think." Rueben stares at me nervously, waiting for my reaction.

I jump off the bed and grab some clothes from my wardrobe.

"Where are you going?" Rueben asks as he tries to grab my arm.

"Don't touch me!" I scream and I storm off into the bathroom and slam the door behind me.

His face tells me everything I need to know. He is nervous. I can't bear to stay here a minute longer.

I throw on some jeans and a top and shove my hair up into a ponytail. My heart is racing, and I just want to get out of here. I haven't got the strength for another drama.

When I swing open the bathroom door, Rueben is sat on the edge of the bed with his head in his hands before looking up at me with his sad puppy dog eyes, filled with desperation.

"Babe…please!" Rueben pleads as he stands up and quickly moves in front of me to stop me from leaving.

"Did you cheat on me?"

"Hell, no! I swear on those kids lives!"

"So, she's just a friend and your Mum is lying to me as usual?"

"I…she's…" Rueben hesitates nervously as he tries to find the right words, but my patience can't wait any longer.

I push past him and quickly rush down the stairs. I grab my bag and phone and slip my feet into my sandals before heading out the front door.

"Wait!" Rueben calls desperately as he follows me out to my car. Against my better judgement, I spin round and fire another question at him.

"Have you slept with her?"

"No, not at all." Rueben answers sincerely and instantly relieves my pangs of jealousy.

"Where was that photo taken?"

"It was at…" Rueben looks away from me for a second and stares at the floor anxiously before staring back up at me.

"It was at Carmel and Ray's wedding."

"Didn't they get married the first weekend after we met? I'm sure you told me you had a wedding to go to. But you didn't invite me?" I stare, confused as I try to piece together the truth.

"Yes. But I didn't invite her either! I can explain everything if you come inside."

"Explain what?" I snap.

"That you spent the whole week with me and then took a different date to your uncles wedding? And I guess it just slipped your mind to tell me, didn't it?"

I feel my voice becoming strained as I force myself to fight back the tears.

"But thank god Joy was there to tell me!" I scream sarcastically as my voice cracks and the tears flow. I slam the car door behind me and speed out of the driveway as quickly as possible.

I continue driving aimlessly, not sure where I'm going to go. Rueben has called my phone a few times already, but I just let it ring out.

The tears in my eyes make it a tough drive and I decide I need to pull over and calm down for a while.

I head to a quiet little place I know only another five minutes away. It's a huge lake, surrounded by nothing but grassy banks and trees. The perfect
place for some quiet. The perfect place to think.

I carefully walk down the wooden jetty and take a seat right on the edge and let my feet dangle just above the water. It's so quiet here, so calm. I can actually slow my thoughts down here; I can actually take a moment and have a little breather.

It's beautiful.

I stare at the scenery around me and replay the morning in my head. Trying to make up answers for the questions I already have. Trying to persuade myself that everything is going to be okay.

My phone pings loudly and disturbs my peace. It's Rueben.

Please come home. I asked Carmel and Ray to come over. They're here now. I think they can help explain a few things along with me. Please.

Carmel and Ray? What could they know about it? I really wasn't ready to leave yet but the thought of them waiting at home patiently to speak with me makes me anxious. I can't just ignore the message and keep them waiting. I reluctantly get myself on my feet and take a stroll back to the car.

I nervously pull into the driveway as I see Carmel and Ray's car. Sure, enough they are here, and it feels so awkward to have to discuss such a personal thing in front of them. I feel embarrassed as I head back inside. I'm going to have to be polite and act like I'm okay when really, I just want to cry and scream at how frustrated I am.

Another day, another poisonous red apple given to us from the Evil Queen. Only, I'm not sure if this gets the Disney movie style ending, I would hope for.

"Hey." Rueben appears at the front door and greets me nervously.

"Hi." I answer coldly.

"Before we go into the front room, can I explain?" Rueben pleads as he takes a few steps out of the front door so that we are out of ear shot.

"Fine." I shrug whilst I watch him take a deep breath and gather his thoughts.

"OK. One night, a couple of months before I met you, Lily asked me to pick her up from this nightclub near London. I didn't want to go but my Mum was constantly on my case about it, saying how Lily was stranded and it would be my fault if something bad happened to her."

I can't help but roll my eyes.

"Anyway, when I got there, Lily's friend jumped in the car too. Lily asked me if I could take her friend home as she had no money left for a taxi. I dropped Lily off home first. Next thing I knew this girl was totally full on, coming onto me and flirting with me the whole drive to her house." Rueben pauses and catches my stare anxiously.

"When I got to her house, she tried to take things even further, but I just wasn't interested." He shrugs.

"By the next day she told Lily what had happened and Lily kept pushing me to take her out on a date, She kept trying to make me change my mind, I guess she thought it would be cool if her brother was dating her friend. But then Lily let slip that she's married and has kids too. I would never entertain the idea of a married woman anyway. Not in a million years."

"Oh." Is all I manage to add whilst Rueben shakes his head vigorously at the drama that has been caused.

"I didn't want any more involvement at all. I'm not the type of guy to come in the middle of somebody's family. Lily kept pushing it and trying to push me to call her, but as far as I was concerned, it was never going to happen."

"But the wedding?"

"I know the wedding picture looks really bad. I know. But I would never cheat on you, not in a million years. Please, come inside because I know Carmel wants to talk to you about that." Rueben says and he takes a few steps back towards the front door and gestures for me to head inside. Reluctantly I do. I walk in to find Carmel and Ray drinking cups of coffee and sitting on the sofa.

"Hi sweetheart!" Carmel smiles brightly as I appear into the front room.

"Hey." I manage to smile back and take a seat on the opposite sofa.

"It's nice to see you both again."

"So, I hear my sister has been up to no good. As usual." Ray sighs jokingly before changing his tone to a more serious one.

"She'll never learn, Joy. She always wonders why she falls out with so many people and why nobody wants to be around her, and this is why. She can be spiteful, vindictive and it's not very often she'll apologise for it either. Unless she's manipulating you again and wants you to think she's sorry."

Rueben comes in and awkwardly takes a seat next to me.

"I was just checking on the kids, they're playing with the sand in the garden." He mutters quietly.

"You two can't keep letting this witch break you. I mean Rueben you look terrified. What's there to be terrified about?" Carmel interjects loudly as she looks at us both for an answer.

"I just don't want to lose Mollie." Rueben whispers nervously.

"You're not going too!" Carmel says confidently.

"I'll explain what happened. At the wedding reception, Rueben was supposed to be sat at the table with Leah. But, completely out of the blue, Lily arrives, over half an hour late to the reception with a friend in tow. She asked if her friend could stay and I said no because there wasn't anywhere for her to sit. I hadn't paid for another person to have dinner with the caterers. It was too last minute and to be honest, they both looked a bit worse for wear. I don't want to assume it's drugs, but…"

"But the signs were certainly there." Ray casually adds.

"Yes, they were. Anyway, Lily just told her friend to sit next to Rueben. Leah ended up getting annoyed that her seat had been taken and so had her dinner, so she disappeared off at the bar instead. I was so angry, but I didn't want to cause a scene at my wedding. But I asked Lily to come outside with me explain what was going on. She kept saying how her and Joy wanted to set Rueben up with this friend. I told them both that as far as I was aware Rueben had met somebody else, at least that's what Ray told me."

"Yep. Rueben had told me all about you that afternoon, Mollie. In fact, he couldn't stop talking about you." Ray smiles as he recalls the memory.

"I watched them all night, Joy and Lily. Constantly trying to get Rueben to dance with this girl, trying to get him to talk to her. It was all a bit much. Then they were taking photos and I think Rueben got in one photo reluctantly to keep the peace and that was it. I can assure you that Rueben had no interest in this girl whatsoever. I'm furious that Joy would post a picture to you and try to make you believe anything different. I can't imagine how upsetting and confusing that must be." Carmel sighs.

"You can trust me Mollie. I'm not a liar. I haven't got in this relationship just to hurt you." Rueben gently says as he turns to me.

"I do trust you; I always have. But when someone sends you a photo. It…it just looked very bad." I tremble. I feel sick. I'm relieved of course that Rueben hasn't hurt me, but Joy has manipulated me and that makes me feel sick with anxiety.

"I can understand that." Rueben whispers as he takes me by the hand and tries to reassure me.

"Why don't you block her?" Carmel suggests.

"We have, she sent me this in an email." I explain rolling my eyes.

"Maybe delete your email and get a new one if it's not too problematic." Ray calmly suggests.

"Actually, I think she's on my social media still. I'll block her from that too. I don't want her seeing anything we post anymore; I don't want her knowing a thing." Rueben announces as he pulls his phone from his pocket.

"Good for you two. You have a beautiful little family. I know she's your Mum, Roo, but you've tried as much as you can. You deserve better now." Carmel says positively.

"For god's sake…" Rueben huffs loudly at his phone.

"What?" I question cynically. My heart rate is speeding up again and I await what I'm sure will be another low blow.

"She's insane! She's changing her profile picture on everything to that photo of me and that fucking girl!" Rueben growls.

"You're joking?" Carmel snaps in disbelief.

"Why would she do that? She clearly wants a reaction Rueben. Don't give it to her." Ray tries to advise but I already see Rueben searching for her number in his phone.

Rueben stands up and paces the room whilst he holds his phone tight against his ear. His cheeks are flushing red with anger and his eyes look wild and serious.

"Take that picture down of me and *that* girl now!" Rueben yells as Joy answers the phone.

"Why should I?" She smugly responds. I can imagine her smug grin as she feels happy to of gotten under our skin and finally getting the reaction she's clearly been searching for.

"Because I am married. I have a wife! You're being so disrespectful to my family. People will think me and Mollie have broken up only days after our wedding!" Rueben snaps back as the impatience becomes evident in his voice.

"Well, it'll teach Mollie to play games. What about all the pictures she's been posting on her other social media's. The ones that she does purposely to wind me up?" I hear her say so confidently that I'm left sitting in shock, completely bewildered as to what she might mean whilst Carmel and Ray watch me curiously, wondering whether I have entered into some tit for tat petty game with Joy.

"What photos Mum?" Rueben sighs.

"You know the ones! The ones of her Mum and the ones of the kids sending their balloons up to the sky next to her bloody grave. I'm not daft. How do you think that makes me feel? I'm their grandma and Mollie make it all about *her!* She's bloody dead! She should be forgotten about but that bitch of a wife of yours keeps rubbing her in my face!" Her spiteful tongue sends shivers down my spine.

I notice Carmel's jaw has dropped open in shock and Ray looks equally as horrified.

"There's no need for that." Ray mumbles, disgusted.

Rueben pauses as he takes in his Mother's words. He looks so appalled. So embarrassed but also, he looks hurt.

"Mum, I wish Laraine was here every day because she was the best Nana to those kids and I never want them to forget how much she adored them. As for you, I hope they never have to cross paths with you again. Goodbye." Rueben snaps bitterly through gritted teeth and ends the call.

Silence fills the room and I fidget awkwardly whilst everybody looks at me for my reaction. It's like they're waiting for me to burst into tears or run away to my car again and disappear. But to their surprise and my own, I don't.

CHAPTER SIXTY-SIX

I have pretty much been in bed for the rest of the weekend. I feel absolutely exhausted and overwhelmed. It was only a week ago that I was saying my vows and enjoying the best day of my life and now I'm meeting up with Rueben's ex-girlfriends and having pictures sent to me claiming that he is a cheat.

It's so much for my head to deal with. I have already been feeling a little anxious about sending Freddie to nursery next week so that I can go back to work, I really don't need these stresses on top.

"Are you going to be okay whilst I'm at work tomorrow?" Rueben asks softly as he climbs into the bed next to me.

"I'll be fine. I'm going to visit the nursery with Freddie tomorrow and have a little look around. Then I'm going to pop into town and buy some new shoes for work." I respond flatly.

I don't want to tell Rueben that I'm feeling down and depressed. I'm usually the one telling Rueben that everything will be okay and that she can't hurt us and yet here I am, crumbling under the pressure.

Rueben doesn't look convinced as he stares at me with concern.

I can tell by his eyes he is thinking of something to say but he is hesitant.

"OK, well, I love you." He says finally as he leans over and kisses my cheek.

I offer a small smile in return before turning over and pulling the duvet up high over my head. My thoughts and anxieties from the last few days are still racing around my brain and taking over, I desperately try to ignore them long enough so that I can fall asleep.

The next couple of days are bleak and I hate feeling this way. Sometimes I wonder if my mother-in-law is genuinely happy to have caused so much upset. I wonder if she feels like she has won. I really don't think there are any winners here, the kids are without a Grandma now and she's without her grandchildren. So, nobody has won. This whole drama has caused nothing but upset for everybody and as much as Joy might feel mild satisfaction at the time for hurting us, she's only ruining any chance of a relationship with her son and grandchildren. I wonder if she even realises that. Or maybe she doesn't care at the time because she only ever acts out of anger. Maybe she even believes she can manipulate us into forgiving her again by writing a letter or sending an apologetic text, perhaps she doesn't believe Rueben would ever truly walk away.

I try to distract myself from my thoughts and concentrate on getting ready for work again. I iron out a few black trousers and blouses and hang them up in the wardrobe ready. I take my new work shoes out of the box and put them neatly away, I opted for some black plain dolly shoes with a thick sole, hopefully they'll be comfortable. Freddie's little bag with a change of clothes and a few nappies are packed and ready for his first day at nursery.

I hate that I still feel pretty low despite trying to get myself organised and pumped, ready to dive back into work. The only conversation I have managed has been with Daisy on the walk home from school, but other than that I have mostly been very quiet.

I spend the evening tidying up and making packed lunches ready for the next day, only stopping to put the kids to bed. I head off for a long hot shower and by the time I get out and in my pyjamas, I'm already feeling tired again and it's only eight o'clock.

Usually I'd be happily heading back downstairs and cuddling up on the sofa with Rueben whilst we settle down to watch a few episodes of whichever new show we've gotten into. But not this time, tonight I give in to my tiredness and go straight to bed.

By the morning, I wake up almost as tired as I felt when I went to bed, but I make an effort to get up quickly and shake off this feeling.

"Good luck on your first day back." Rueben says cheerfully as tries to sound as positive and upbeat as possible.

"Thanks." I mumble.

"Oh, and thanks for taking Freddie for me this morning."

"No problem, you'll be amazing today, they'll be happy to have you back, I bet." Rueben continues confidently as he attempts to lift my spirits.

"Hopefully. I'll call you on my lunch break." I say and give him a smile before sliding my feet into my new shoes and heading out of the front door.

I turn the music up loudly as I drive to work. Music is one of my favourite things in the world. I can usually rely on a good song to help me when I'm feeling low. The closer I get to work, the more I feel hopeful that stepping back into a routine and putting all my concentration back into my work will really help me. At the very least it'll give me less time to worry about Joy's shenanigans.

I love my job, it's a little intense at times but I love the feeling of being useful. When I come to work, I actually feel as though I'm helping to make some kind of difference. It's the only job I have ever had where the hours go by so quickly and I'm not constantly counting down the minutes until I can get out of there.

"Mollie!" Mel greets me with a surprised but panicked look as I step out of the elevator.

"Hey!" I laugh a little confused.

"Are you okay?"

"Yeah but I've been trying to call you loads."

"Oh, sorry. I had my music up quite loud in the car, I didn't hear it ringing." I explain as I walk towards my desk.

"Wait! I need to speak to you before you go in." She says as she grabs me by the arm and pulls me into the bathroom in a hurry.

I have never known Mel to look so worried. Usually she is the most laid-back person here, she often brightens my day with her sarcasm and quick wit but right now, her sudden change in personality has me feeling on edge."

"Mel?" I stare at her baffled and uneasy as the bathroom door closes behind us.

"I shouldn't be telling you this, but I was in Tricia's office earlier and a call came in about you. The person wanted to remain anonymous, but they told her they're putting in a formal complaint. They told Tricia that they have seen you mistreat your own children out in public and they claimed to be horrified that you have a job here." Mel breathes heavily with a worried but sympathetic look across her face as I take in her words.

I stare down at the ground in shock and confusion before staring back at Mel's nervous face again.

"It's Joy." I mutter as the realisation hits me.

"What, your mother-in-law? Why would she do that?"

"There's so much that has happened that you don't know about." I sigh as I lean over the sink and throw fresh water on my face in the hopes it helps my sudden wave of anxiety.

"I'm so sorry Mollie, I had no idea." Mel whispers as she comforts me by stroking my back whilst I stay hovered over the sink, trying to fight back the rush of anger and anxiety that is pulsating through my body.

I turn the taps off and stand up straight. I take a deep breath before drying off the water from my face with a paper towel.

"Right, so what happens now?" I try to ask casually and act as if I'm strong enough to take any answer she gives me.

"I don't know, Mollie." Mel sighs sadly as she stares down at the floor.

"But you know there's a strict protocol here."

"Wish me luck then, I guess." I groan whilst I straighten up my blouse and head out of the bathroom.

I barely step into the room when I clock Tricia waving me in from her office. Her face is stern and my heart begins to beat faster as I prepare myself for whatever she is about to say. I'm grateful to Mel for giving me the heads up but I'm now so tense and stressed out that I can barely walk as confidently as I'd like too into the office.

"Ah, Mollie. Take a seat please." Tricia asks firmly as soon as I step inside.

"Sure, is everything okay?" I try to ask casually. I can't let Tricia know that Mel has already prepared me for this meeting, so I allow myself to play along.

"Not really, no. I was really disappointed to have a phone call this morning with some allegations about you. A lady called to say she had witnessed you mistreat your children in a supermarket over the weekend." She stares at me stiffly.

"Well they must have gotten that wrong, I was in bed all weekend." I reply calmly.

"Why? Were you sick?"

"Kind of." I sigh awkwardly. It doesn't feel right to go into a lengthy explanation of why I was in bed and what led up to it. This is a serious job and I can't sit here and wallow in a self-pitying rant about my nightmare mother-in-law. The whole thing sounds so far-fetched and crazy that I'm not even sure she'd believe me even if I tried to explain it.

"OK. Well look Mollie, I'm sure you understand that an allegation of this magnitude needs investigating."

"Yes, I understand that."

"I'm afraid when I spoke to my area manager this morning, he didn't feel it was suitable that you stay in work whilst the investigation occurs. I really hate to be the bearer of bad news but I'm afraid for the time being you're suspended." Tricia states with a straight face and I awkwardly look away from her stare. My eyes sting as I feel the tears filling them which only makes me embarrassed. I feel my cheeks burn as they must be turning red and suddenly, I feel as though the air has been sucked out of the room.

"I, erm…should I, should I leave now?" I stutter through the lump in my throat.

"Yes, please Mollie. I'm sorry. I'll be in touch as soon as I know the outcome of the investigation and when you can come back to work."

I nod awkwardly before grabbing my handbag and darting out of the office as quickly as I can. I hold my breath as I stride out of the room so fast that I may as well be running and I desperately try to ignore the few faces staring at me curiously.

As soon as I step inside the elevator, I let out my breath and the sobs flow with it.

I'm suspended from my job that I adore, that I spent years working towards. What will my colleagues think of me? I'm so beyond embarrassed, I'm tempted to go home and pack all my bags and move me and my family a million miles away from here.

315

CHAPTER SIXTY-SEVEN

My hands tremble as I search for my phone through my handbag once I'm back in the car.

I need to speak to Rueben.

I swipe away Mel's missed calls and scroll through my contacts to find Rueben's number. Just before I can hit dial an incoming call pops up on my screen. I don't recognise the number, but I answer it anyway.

"Hello?"

"Hi, am I speaking with Mollie Adams?" A woman's voice asks.

"Yes? Speaking?"

"Hi Mollie, my name is Amber, I work with child protection, is this a good time to talk?"

"Yes. It's fine." I mumble as I throw my head back on the head rest and squeeze my eyes shut in despair.

"Okay that's good. I'm calling today because unfortunately I had two separate phone calls over the weekend, one from your sister-in-law and then one from your mother-in-law. They're both claiming that they have witnessed you mistreat both your children on several occasions and they're quite concerned that you neglect Freddie in particular." She informs me in a gentle manner.

"I know." I huff anxiously.

"I have just been into my work and they had the same phone call.

My mother-in-law really doesn't like me, and I think this is her attempt at hurting me."

"I see, well I made contact with your daughters' school this morning and they confirmed that they were quite happy with Daisy and had no concerns over her wellbeing. Does Freddie go to a nursery yet?"

"Erm, yes. He goes to Little Angels in the high street."

"Okay, well if you don't mind, I'd like to give them a quick call. If they are happy and they don't seem to have any concerns, then I'm happy to close the case and put it down to a malicious phone call."

"That would be great." I sigh relieved.

I'm really not happy with the idea of Freddie's nursery having to be contacted by social services, in fact it's quite embarrassing but hopefully the quick chat will have them realise that this is another spiteful lie from my mother-in-law and nothing more.

"Are you okay?" Amber presses gently and I realise I'm crying to myself and she can probably hear my whimpers.

"Erm, yes." I mumble hesitantly.

"Are you sure?"

"I'm just, I'm just a bit overwhelmed." I manage to say before I burst into tears. I can't believe I'm crying so hard and all the whilst on a phone call to a woman I have never met before, but it's a relief to get it off my chest.

"Please don't worry, I'm sure we can get to the bottom of this very quickly." She responds calmly.

"I did have my suspicions when both Joy and Lily were very vague with their statements. Sometimes families can act out of anger."

"Yeah." I grumble in agreement between sobs.

"Okay, Mollie. Leave all this with me and I'll be in touch by this afternoon." She says kindly.

"Okay, thank you." I say before hanging up the phone. She seemed so kind, but it doesn't take much away from the fact she is still a child protection officer who is having to call me because my own mother-in-law is making false allegations about me.

Immediately I call Rueben, as soon as he picks up the phone I'm sobbing heavily and trying to tell him everything as best as I can. He doesn't seem to catch much of what I'm trying to tell him, instead he tells me to calm down and drive home and he'll meet me there. His voice sounded so concerned and stressed again as he learns about more of his Mother's antics.

I sit in the car for a further five minutes and try to compose myself. I catch my reflection in the mirror and see my mascara has run down my cheeks and my skin looks all blotchy and puffy. I pull out a fresh make up wipe from my bag and rub all the mascara smears away, making myself look a little more presentable again.

When I arrive home, I'm relieved to see Rueben's work van parked in the driveway. As I get out of my car, I see him already waiting by the front door.

I virtually run to him and fling my arms around his neck which takes him by surprise a little, but he soon pulls me in tight and slides his arms around my waist.

"I don't know what to say." Rueben sighs into my shoulder.

"I could ring her and ask her what she's playing at, but I don't think that'll get us anywhere and I really don't want to speak to her."

"No, it's fine. To be honest just hearing that woman's voice right now would make me feel sick. I never want to see her again, Rueben. Not ever."

"You won't have too. I promise." He whispers as he leads me inside the house.

"Do you want a cup of tea?"

I nod gratefully before kicking my shoes off and getting comfortable on the sofa.

"I was talking to a friend at work today and he suggested that I look into some kind of restraining order." Rueben says as he brings in a cup of tea in and sits next to me.

"Really?" I say taken by surprise.

"Well, yeah. Mollie, I'm still needing therapy for my own childhood trauma's and now my own wife is miserable. Do you really think I can just sit back and let this go any further?"

"I guess not. It's just a shame that we have gotten to this point. That's all. I always pictured having a big family, you know. I always wanted to wake up on Christmas Day and have a house full whilst the kids run around excitedly and just feel so loved and everyone get along." I sigh as I take a gulp of my tea.

"I just wanted a happy family."

"And we are going to be a happy family." Rueben stares at me softly.

"But it might just be a little smaller than you imagined and I'm sorry for that, but it'll be better this way than to be around people who keep dragging us down."

"I know." I nod and I take Rueben's hand.

"I think I know now what I want to do with my Mum's inheritance money."

"Oh?"

"I want to move away." I say as Rueben's face lights up.

"Really?"

"Yes, really." I say truthfully and watch Rueben's face break into a big smile.

"Where?" He asks so enthusiastically.

"I don't know, I thought maybe we could spend some time talking about it. I have friends who have moved over to Dublin and love it. But also, I was talking to one of my college friends a few months ago online and she now lives in Australia, she said visas are pretty easy to sort out. Then of course, I have family in Canada. So, there's another option I'm willing to take. We have the money, so why not?"

Before I can even finish my sentence, Rueben hugs me so tight.

"I can't tell you how relieved I am." He says as he smiles again so brightly.

"I have been talking to my therapist about the possibility of moving away for some time now and she agrees it could be a very beneficial thing to have a fresh start and leave my Mum in the past."

"Do you have a preference on where we go then." I smile back excitedly.

"Not really. Although Canada sounds cool." He laughs.

"But honestly, I don't care where we go, as long as we are happy. As soon as we are away from here and my Mum no longer knows where we are, or where we work or how to contact us, I know we will be a lot happier. I know it."

"I think so too." Just then, my phone starts ringing again. I recognise the phone number, it's child protection, the same number from earlier.

"It's child protection again, Roo." I sigh anxiously and I answer it on loudspeaker so Rueben can hear everything they have to say too.

"Hi Mollie, it's Amber again." She says in her polite gentle tone again.

"Oh, Hi." I answer nervously.

"Good news, I'm going to close the case. I spoke with Freddie's key worker today and despite her only seeing Freddie a few times so far, she assured me that Freddie is a very happy little boy and they have absolutely no concerns over his wellbeing and certainly shows no signs of neglect. I will happily make a note on the system that it appears to have been a malicious phone call."

"That's great news." I say as I let out a deep breath and my tense shoulders relax a little.

"Thank you so much for letting me know."

"No problem. Take care Mollie and I truly hope you feel a little better soon and things with your mother-in-law get easier." She sweetly says before hanging up the phone.

"Well there you have it." Rueben smiles as the call ends.

"Another failed attempt. Now your boss will be on the phone by tomorrow and asking for you to come back."

"Hopefully." I nod, although not quite as enthusiastically as I think Rueben would like me to be.

"It's like you said before Mollie, she's not as powerful as she would like us to think. Her feeble attempts are backfiring, soon she'll have nothing else to do. We are going to be okay baby; things will get better from here on out."

CHAPTER SIXTY-EIGHT

"Morning." Rueben says gently as he places down a cup of tea next to my bed.

"Hey." I croak surprised as I rub my eyes and prop myself up a little. "What are you still doing here?"

"I put in a holiday for today, I thought you could probably do with me being at home. I know yesterday was stressful."

"That's so sweet, thank you. To be honest it would be nice to spend some time with you. I feel as though I have kind of closed off a little lately and I don't mean too, I just don't react well with stress." I sigh apologetically.

"I understand completely. I have been so short tempered and snappy at work, which isn't like me at all. Even at home with the kids I haven't been my usual self. I might take them to that new trampoline park at the weekend, to make up for it."

"That'll be nice. We can both do that for them and maybe treat them to ice-cream after." I suggest as I lock eyes with Rueben and we both smile in agreement. It's nice to clear the air a little after the last few days.

"So, back to today? What do you fancy doing?" Rueben asks after a sip of his cup of tea.

"I'd like to go and put fresh flowers down on my Mum's grave, then maybe we should go and visit your Nan? We haven't seen her since the wedding."

"God yeah." Rueben sighs as he realises how long it's been.

"I should bring some photos over for her too."

"I have a better idea, why don't we pick up a photo frame in town and frame a wedding photo of us and the kids?"

"Yeah, she'll love that! Perfect idea baby." Rueben grins.

"I had probably best call ahead first though, make sure Lily or my Mum aren't there."

Rueben stares at me all wide eyed and pulls a silly face mockingly, as if it's obvious we need to avoid her with caution.

"Good idea." I giggle as I roll my eyes.

It's so nice to feel back on the same page as my husband again. Joy may have made our first couple of weeks of married life a very difficult one, but we made it through anyway.

I feel much more refreshed today as I get out of the shower and get dressed. My gloomy mood seems to have passed a little and I'm feeling a little more positive.

We head into town first and pick out a pretty glass frame for our photo. I sit in the car on the way to the cemetery and carefully place the photo inside. The photo is of me and Rueben standing under the arch, just moments after we officially became man and wife. Daisy and Freddie are posing in front of us in the most adorable way. The picture makes me smile every time I see it.

I call in to the little florist just a few minutes away from the cemetery and pick Mum's favourite flower. A small bunch of soft pink tulips. It always makes me feel emotional when I see this flower. They were the same ones that Rueben and I left on her coffin after our final goodbye.

"They're beautiful." Rueben smiles at me affectionately when I return back to the car.

"Yeah, she would have loved them." I whisper as I gaze down at the pretty flowers.

"She'd be so proud of you Mollie. You have made the grave look beautiful and really put a lot of thought and care into it before you laid her to rest."

"I couldn't have done it without you Roo, you're the one who ripped up all the weeds for me and did all the hard work. I mostly supervised." I say with a laugh.

Rueben just smirks and places his hand across my thigh, in the same way he always does when he wants to comfort me.

I'm relieved when I step out of the car and see that the grave still looks as good as it did before we went away for our wedding.

I carefully arrange the flowers neatly into the little vase and I can't help but wonder if she's been watching over me for the last few weeks when I have really needed her.

"Let's go." I whisper.

"Already?" Rueben steps back surprised.

"Yeah. I can't afford to cry anymore tears today. I've used up my allowance over the past few days." I joke, before taking another look back and then heading towards the car.

"Bye Laraine." Rueben whispers sweetly before following behind.

Rueben's Nan only lives a short drive away and so I quickly put away the photo frame in her gift bag and seal it up.

"I rang Nan whilst you were in the florist and she said no one has been to see her, so the coast is clear." Rueben winks.

"Thank god." I laugh. Although it is a relief for Rueben to be able to visit Irene without the added pressure of Joy coming down or Lily attacking him.

"Hi Nan." Rueben says cheerfully as we arrive. Irene's face instantly lights up as she sees Rueben walking over to her.

The pair share a sweet cuddle as Irene wraps her arms tight around Rueben's broad shoulders.

"Are you married now?" She asks excitedly.

"Yep! We're married Nan." Rueben answers happily.

"Oh, congratulations!" Irene beams as she stares at us both proudly.

I lean over and greet Irene with quick hug before sitting down on the sofa next to her.

"We got you a little gift." I say with a smile as I pass over the gift bag and she takes it gratefully.

"For me?" Irene smiles surprised as she opens up the bag and pulls out the glass frame.

At first her face seems genuinely happy as she studies the photo in the frame but after a few seconds her expressions change to concern.

"What's wrong Nan?" Rueben asks gently as he kneels down next to her side.

"I don't think I'll be allowed it up." She sighs anxiously.

"Joy has already come down and removed pictures that she doesn't like up. She only ever lets me have pictures of Lily and Kelsey on display. If she sees this, she'll kick off again and I haven't got the energy for it."

"Nan it's your house, you should be allowed any photo you want up." Rueben points out as he holds her hand comfortingly.

"I know and it's a beautiful photo. So, thank you so much. I'm just worried. All she ever does it come down here shouting and screaming. This will just set her off even more."

"Do you want me to take it home Irene and look after it? That way she won't know about it." I suggest.

"No, no we aren't doing that. I'm sick of Mum throwing her weight around. Nan would you like the picture up?"

"Yes, I do but Joy…"

"Don't worry about her." Rueben interrupts.

"She'll have to get over it. This is a gift from us to you and it has nothing to do with her."

Rueben takes the frame and puts it proudly on one of Irene's side tables.

"I really do love it though." Irene says as she looks at my softly, as if to show me appreciation for it.

I smile in response but inside I'm feeling very sorry for her. It's sad to see a woman of this age be so afraid and so worried about something as trivial as photo's she chooses to have in her home.

I don't understand how Rueben's Mum is like this. I have never known anything like it. If my Nan was still around and I dare did anything to make her remotely unhappy, my family would ostracise me. There is no way anyone would allow me to behave in such a difficult and selfish manner and get away with it. Although I wouldn't dream of it anyway.

"Have you been up to much Nan?" Rueben asks to change the subject away from Joy.

"Not really. Alison was here this morning and she was going to plan a nice party for me for my ninetieth birthday in two weeks, but she

didn't know where to have it, so I don't think anything is happening."
She responds disappointedly.

"Oh? Would you like a party then?"

"Yes, I think so. I never get out of the house do I, it would have
been nice to have done something but never mind." She shrugs a little
sadly.

"That would have been lovely though, wouldn't it."? Rueben mumbles as he notices the sadness in his Nan's face.

"Yeah. As long as Joy isn't there to ruin it and steal all my presents."
She jokes and lets out a loud giggle which makes Rueben laugh along
with her.

Whilst the two of them continue in conversation, my head starts
running away with itself over thoughts of a party for Irene.

I feel so desperately sorry for her, but it needn't be this way. I have
a large garden space; I could definitely create a little garden party. It
could even be a surprise. I'll invite Carmel, Ray, Alison and Irene's
eldest daughter, Olivia. Olivia has children and grandchildren; she
could bring all them too. I'll invite Rueben's other uncles and of course
I'll let Leah know and she can come down with James and her Mum.
It'll be such a surprise for Irene, she'll love it.

I could do a flowery vintage kind of theme. I could put a big spread
on and order a nice cake for her, I'll get vintage paper cups and plates,
I'll even do a music list with all her favourite artists from Elvis Presley
to Dusty Springfield and we can all celebrate her huge milestone.

My brain is buzzing as I start planning everything from invites
to the decor and I only snap out of my thoughts when I see Rueben
waving his hand in front of my face.

"Earth to Mollie?" Rueben laughs as he continues waving his hands
in my face.

"Sorry, I was in deep thought." I laugh back and playfully swat
his hands away.

"I can see that!" He smirks.

"Are you ready to go? I don't want to risk bumping into Norma
Bates, as you call her."

"Shhh!" I respond embarrassed but luckily Irene doesn't hear, and
he teasingly sticks his tongue out at me.

"You're an idiot." I whisper as I jokingly glare at him whilst gathering my bag.

"Bye darling." Irene says as I lean in to hug her goodbye.

"See you soon Nan, I'll call you in the week." Rueben says as he gives his Nan another big cuddle after me.

"I love you." I hear her whisper into his ear.

"I love you too, Nan."

I smile at the two of them sweetly say their goodbyes before I head off to the car.

"What were you in such deep thought about?" Rueben asks as he clicks his seat belt in place.

"We are going to throw your Nan a surprise garden party. At our house." I announce excitedly.

"Really? You would do that for her?"

"Of course! What do you think?"

"I think it's a great idea." Rueben nods enthusiastically.

CHAPTER SIXTY-NINE

"Where would you like these?" Leah asks lightly as she holds up the floral buntings.

"Ooh, I think maybe just draped across the top of the patio doors?" I suggest.

"I'm going to pop out quickly and get the balloons you ordered." Rueben says before he kisses me goodbye.

"Perfect, thanks!"

I head back into the kitchen and neatly arrange some more of the food onto my silver trays.

"Mummy, can I help?" Daisy asks eagerly as she comes running into the kitchen.

"Erm yes please sweetheart, could you empty these pretzels into this bowl for me? That would be so helpful."

"Of course." Daisy smiles sweetly.

Leah and James travelled down on Friday night to stay with us for the weekend to celebrate Nan's birthday and thankfully everybody who I have invited have said they can make it too. Which is fantastic news, but it has made me a little nervous whilst I rush around trying to make everything look perfect for Irene.

It's a beautiful weekend already, blue skies and the sun is shining brightly. It's going to be a fairly hot day.

The garden is coming together so beautifully, I have yellow floral table covers draped over my garden table with matching napkins, plates and cups. I have started to put food out already with the beautiful pink and white cake taking centre stage. In about twenty minutes time Ray and Carmel will arrive with Irene.

Irene thinks that she is going out for lunch with them and has no idea that in actual fact I am throwing her a surprise party and around twenty family members will be here to surprise her. It's been so exciting to plan. Rueben has been a little nervous just in case anyone accidentally tells Joy about the party, but thankfully it's managed to stay a secret.

"Mollie, me and James are going to pop out and pick up Nan some flowers. Do you need anything else?" Leah kindly offers.

"Nope, I'm all set thank you. I'll see you in a bit." I smile cheerfully and carry on prepping the food and drinks.

I set up my speakers and start playing the background music I made for Irene, even Freddie loves it so much he is dancing around the garden excitedly.

I have opted for a bright yellow summery dress today to match with the yellow floral theme and even Freddie is in a little yellow t-shirt with blue denim shorts. He looks adorable. Daisy has gone for her new favourite white summer dress which she can't wait to show off to all the guests.

I finish off making the jugs of lemonade before completing the table with the small personalised brown paper bags filled with Irene's favourite sweets that I made. Rueben soon arrives back with my balloons and my rose gold helium ninety balloons and helps me display them around the table.

Within minutes the doorbell is going off and in comes Olivia with all her children and grandchildren, even two of her great grandchildren which is great as they're both Daisy's age. Two of Rueben's other uncles arrive too along with Alison and her son Matthew and one of Irene's best friends.

Rueben does brilliantly at greeting everyone and getting them sorted out with drinks as they all get comfortable in the garden. Meanwhile I rush around frantically making sure everything that needs to be out is on the table and all the drinks are getting chilled nicely in the fridge.

"Ray has just text me, Nan's here." Rueben says as he quickly gets up ready to open the front door.

Everyone else awaits quietly in the garden, eager to see Irene. Alison and Olivia hold a beautiful bouquet of flowers each that they have got for her and I stand by the garden table with a big smile, excited to her surprised face.

Ray and Rueben help walk Irene out into the garden with Carmel following behind. I notice she's wearing a yellow top and smile to myself at the coincidence.

"Look, Mum. Look what Mollie and Rueben have done for you." Ray beams proudly as he steps into the garden.

Everyone cheers joyfully and greets her as she stares in amazement at all her family sitting together in one place, waiting to celebrate her special day.

"Is all this for me?" Irene gasps with a big smile before she gets a little emotional.

"Aww bless her." Alison says as she comes to give her Mum a hug.

"I can't lie Nan, Mollie did most of this." Rueben says as he nods proudly in my direction and I give Irene a little wave.

"You did all this for me?" Irene stares surprised with a grateful smile.

"I did. Do you like it?"

"I love it. I can't believe all this is for me! Is that my cake?" Irene asks astonished.

"Yes!" I giggle.

"It's all for you."

Her reaction makes all the time, effort and nerves completely worth it. I watch on in awe as Irene sits down next to her cake and is greeted by all of her family who shower her with cards and gifts. She looks so happy.

When I head back into the kitchen to grab some more lemonade, Leah and James appear with another beautiful bouquet of mixed flowers.

"Wow, they're gorgeous." I say.

"Does she know we are here yet?" Leah asks excitedly.

"No, she has no idea. Hang on I'll grab my camera and get some pictures of this." I offer as I rummage through my bag.

As Leah doesn't live in our area, she isn't able to see her Nan as much as she would like, but when she does come to visit, Irene often gets very emotional and overwhelmed with happiness when she sees her. It's the sweetest thing. They have such a beautiful bond.

"Look who I found." I announce brightly as Leah follows behind me with the flowers.

"Oh!" Is all Irene is able to say before she drops her head into her hands and giggles a little at yet another surprise.

When she looks back up at Leah, she has tears in her eyes as she stares at her so adoringly.

"Hello cutie pie." Leah smiles affectionately as she gives her Nan a cuddle.

Irene wraps her arms tightly around Leah and holds her for a few moments without letting go. I can't see her face anymore but it's clear she's still crying with happiness as she embraces her granddaughter.

"Look at you." Irene says as she studies Leah so fondly.

"You look beautiful."

"Oh Nan, you're so sweet." Leah giggles before presenting her with the big bouquet of flowers.

"They're amazing. Thank you so much. I'm so happy." Irene responds as she stares down at her flowers and then back at Leah.

The afternoon continues so positively as everybody seems in good spirits. I make sure to take lots of photos so that I can put them into an album for Irene and she can keep these memories forever.

Everyone helps themselves to the food, especially Irene who seems to be really enjoying it. The kids are running around and playing with Olivia's great grandchildren and the rest of us are sat on the garden chairs in almost a circle. The atmosphere is so easy and relaxed, everybody is chatting and laughing and really enjoying themselves. It's wonderful to see.

"We literally couldn't have done this if my Aunty Joy was here." Leah mutters to me under her breath.

"I know." I nod in agreement.

"She doesn't like Alison or Olivia either does she."

"She doesn't like anyone." Leah jokes.

"It's been lovely though hasn't it, everyone is getting along and celebrating Nan's special day, it's such a lovely vibe."

"Exactly. This is how it should be. She's ninety, she deserves these happy times and everyone looking after her. Not all of the stresses Lily and Joy bring to her house." Leah sighs before taking a sip of her wine.

"That's why I had to get her flowers too, I didn't want to risk buying her something that either of those two could steal."

I roll my eyes at the sad fact.

"She loved those flowers though, but more than anything I think she's just so happy to have everybody here."

"Definitely." Leah smiles.

Before long, we all gather around Irene as Rueben carefully lights the candles on the cake and kneels down beside her with it.

I make sure to take more photos of this moment with my camera.

Everybody is smiling fondly as they sing Happy Birthday.

We all cheer as Irene blows out the candles and she look so incredibly overjoyed.

"I'll have a big piece, please." Irene asks enthusiastically as Carmel begins cutting up the cake for everyone.

"It's your favourite Nan, it's a Victoria sponge cake." Rueben tells her as he passes her a plate.

"It's so nice." She smiles again and takes a big mouthful.

I notice a few times that Irene tries to catch my eye and when she does, she gives me a little smile as if she's saying thank you each time. It makes me feel so warm and happy to know that she is genuinely enjoying her day. Just how she deserves.

As the afternoon turns into early evening, the temperature drops a little and Ray decides it is best to get Irene back home before she gets too cold. With that, everyone else decides they had better head home too.

I remind everyone to take home a paper bag of sweets as they all thank me by the front door for throwing the party.

"You definitely have a good one here." Olivia smiles at me as she kisses Rueben on the cheek goodbye.

"I know, I'm very happy." He smiles back.

We stand a little longer by the front door and wave off Nan as Ray pulls out of the driveway.

"I'll clean up." Rueben offers straight away as he turns to me.

"Why don't you open another bottle of wine with Leah and James. You've done enough today; I can quickly tidy up this."

"If you're sure? I won't say no to a glass of wine." I laugh.

It's a relief that the day was such a success but now that everyone has left, I finally feel like I can relax properly. I throw my feet up on the sofa next to Leah as we crack open a bottle.

"We should play some games." James suggests after a sip of his beer.

"Some drinking games?" Leah laughs, but her suggestion sounded serious all the same.

"Could be fun! I've earned a few drinks." I say.

When Rueben finishes tidying up the kitchen and the kids are settled in bed for the night, we all end up deciding on the new Speak Out game. It's a game where you have to wear a mouth shield and try to read the words from the card and your opponents have to guess what the word is. Although, we changed the rules slightly. We decide if you get the answer wrong you have to take a shot of tequila.

The drinks continue to flow, and I feel the most relaxed I've felt in weeks. The games have made me laugh so much and I'm really enjoying the good company.

"No more tequila for me, I'll be on Dad duties, but you help yourself." Rueben laughs as he turns away from taking another shot and gives it to me instead.

"Go on Mollie! Drink it!" Leah giggles.

I throw the shot back and immediately it burns the back of my throat as it slides down and warms my chest.

"Wow. You never get used to that burn." I laugh through coughs.

A few more games later and a lot more shots, I notice my head is getting a little fuzzy.

I can't quite believe how quickly the evening has gone when I glance up at the clock and see it's almost two o'clock in the morning.

I notice James is falling asleep with his beer still in his hand and Leah and I can't help but burst out laughing which startles him a little.

"Come on Roo, we best head off upstairs and leave these two to get some sleep." I giggle whilst I stumble to my feet. The tequila has definitely gone to my head. I notice Rueben smirk as I sway towards the hallway.

"I'm not drunk!"

"Oh sure." Rueben teases sarcastically as he gets up behind me.

"Do you need anything else guys? Do you want help pulling the sofa bed out?" I call as I climb the stairs.

Rueben laughs at me and mocks my attempts to be a good hostess through my drunken slurs.

"We're fine! See you in the morning." Leah giggles.

CHAPTER SEVENTY

"Babe, wake up." Rueben nudges me anxiously.

"Eurgh, what?" I manage to groan. I have barely opened my eyes and already I can feel how heavy and foggy my head feels.

"The police are knocking at the door." He says with more urgency. "Wake up."

As I sit up and squint at the bright sun coming in through the window, I notice from my bedside clock that it's barely eight o'clock in the morning. My whole body feels trembly and sick. My neck is so stiff, and my head is pounding. I'm worried the tequila is going to make an appearance. I haven't felt this hungover in such a long time.

I slowly stand to my feet whilst Rueben heads straight downstairs to answer the front door. The room is spinning, and I have to steady myself against the wall as I pull on my joggers.

"Is Mollie Adams here? We need to speak with her." I hear one of the officers ask.

"She is but she's not feeling great. Can I ask what this is about?" Rueben asks curiously.

"No. We really need to speak to Mollie first if that's okay."

I quickly splash some water on my face from the bathroom sink and try to pull myself together a bit.

"It's okay. I'm here." I say as I slowly creep down the stairs.

"Hi Mollie. We had a call from your Mother-in-law this morning with some concerns about your children. She particularly seemed concerned that there is some ongoing abuse happening to Freddie, by you. She wanted us to carry out a welfare check."

"They're still asleep." I mumble.

"But you can check on them."

I cannot believe how low she has stooped and done this again. She isn't just hurting me, she's playing games with my children's lives.

One of the police officers' heads straight up the stairs as Rueben directs them to their bedrooms.

Within minutes he reappears again as he casually comes back down.

"They both look fine. Although I think I've woken them up." He announces apologetically.

"Mollie is there some place we can go and talk?" The other officer asks.

"I, Um. I have guests asleep in the living room." I say anxiously.

"No, it's fine sweetheart." Leah says as she pops her head around the living room door.

"We're awake you can come in."

I'm relieved when I step into the front room because it means I can sit down again. My head is spinning.

"Was there a bit of a party yesterday?" The officer asks light-heartedly.

"Yeah, it was for my husband's Nan. She turned ninety so we had a garden party and a few drinks." I say.

"Which is why you have been called." Rueben interjects.

"My Mum wasn't invited, and she's obviously found out about it already and this is how she retaliates. By wasting police time. It's not the first time she's come out with these types of false allegations either."

"I'm assuming the allegations are only about me. And my husband hasn't been brought into it." I ask, but I already know the answer.

"You're right. The allegations were only about you." He responds, confirming my suspicions.

"It's ridiculous guys. It really is. I'm sorry but it needs to be said that my Aunty Joy is absolutely unhinged. She's so nasty and vile. She can't handle the fact that nobody likes her because of the way she bullies everyone around her, and this is how she reacts. She wants to hurt my cousin and his wife." Leah surprises me by speaking up and jumping to our defence.

The officer nods along as he listens to Leah and Rueben weigh in.

"I have had social services carry out some checks too. This is just going on and on." I sigh.

"If that's the case, I really would recommend looking at getting an injunction of some kind." The officer firmly advises.

"I have already been considering it." Rueben says calmly.

"But after this I think it's vital that I sort something out because she's not leaving us alone."

I sit trembling a little as the stress of being woken up with more disturbing allegations make my anxiety skyrocket.

"Are you okay?" The officer asks me gently and everyone in the room stares at me for my answer.

"It's just been a tough year." I manage to say before a few tears fall down my cheeks. I'm so fed up of crying.

"I feel like I have tried so hard, but I never once really got anywhere with Joy. Then my Mum died, and I've been trying to deal with that and on top it feels like my mother-in-law is trying to destroy me."

I don't mean to, but I drop my head down into my hands and break down.

"She won't succeed Mol." I hear Leah say sweetly.

"We completely understand how stressful this must be but all we can do is strongly advise an injunction. We are also happy to give her a call and inform her that you've asked to be left alone?" The officer suggests and I nod gratefully.

"If that doesn't work, I'll be back in touch and reporting harassment." Rueben says forcefully.

"No problem. You can do that. Before we go, you should probably be prepared for another phone call from child protection again. They will probably have to follow up after these new allegations."

"Okay." I mumble before Rueben shows them to the door.

I stare awkwardly at the ground, not knowing what to say. I feel like I want to just go back to bed and hide away.

"I think everyone was uploading pictures to social media last night, Joy must have found out from that." James says carefully.

"Yeah and the fact Lily kept calling a few of my uncles and asking for money. I'm pretty sure they ended up telling her where they were."

Leah rolls her eyes.

"And this is my punishment." I shake my head irritability.

"I guess so. Well enough about that evil witch. Let's go for lunch before me and James have to start heading home. My treat." Leah perks up and smiles at me warmly.

"Could do." I smile gratefully. I really appreciate the support. That's the one thing that takes the sting out of all this upset, the fact that the rest of the family seem to really like me and I'm really fond of them too.

"Why don't we go back to our favourite pub? By the lake?" Rueben suggests as he reappears.

"Leah is right Mollie, we have had the best weekend, we can't let her ruin it. Let's just carry on."

CHAPTER SEVENTY-ONE

Our lunch at the pub definitely helped my mood. Rueben and Leah were trying extra hard to keep the conversation upbeat and take my mind off the morning's events, which I appreciate massively.

After lunch, we take Leah and James to the train station so that they can catch their train back home.

I give Leah a hug and thank her for all her support and she makes me promise to call her if I ever need to talk about anything which makes me feel even more grateful.

I wave goodbye through the window as their train departs from the station. It's another hot and sunny beautiful day, the weather has definitely been on our side all weekend.

"What shall we do for the rest of the day?" Rueben asks.

"Well…" I answer as I smile down at Daisy and Freddie.

"Since the kids have been so good this weekend why don't we buy a little paddling pool for the garden?"

"Yes!" Daisy squeals excitedly and Freddie copies, even though I'm sure he doesn't quite understand what a paddling pool is yet.

When we arrive home, Rueben takes the new paddling pool that we picked up from the shop straight into the garden and starts filling it up with water from the garden hose.

The kids jump around hyperactively as they eagerly wait for the pool to fill up.

"Stand still." I giggle at Freddie as I smother him in sunblock.

"But I'm so excited!" He squeals jumping up and down.

"Five more minutes and you can get in." Rueben calls from the other end of the garden.

"What!? But five minutes is really really long." Freddie sighs in frustration and I can't help but laugh.

"Five minutes is very quick, silly." I respond before my phone distracts me.

My phone is ringing and unfortunately, I recognise the number straight away, it's child protection. I roll my eyes.

Just when I was about to enjoy my afternoon in the garden with the kids, I'm distracted with another pointless phone call led by Joy's deceit and malicious lies.

I head back into the kitchen as I reluctantly answer the phone. Obviously, I wouldn't want Daisy or Freddie to hear anything.

"Hello?"

"Hi, Mollie. It's Amber again calling from child protection." She says in a friendly tone.

"Hi Amber." I sigh.

"I understand my mother-in-law has been on the phone again."

"Yeah. I'm afraid so." She awkwardly confirms.

"She reported to us that she witnessed you slam Freddie's head into a car window."

"I did what?" I ask completely puzzled.

"Yeah, she was very vague again. She couldn't remember when or where it happened and that's all she told me."

"So, was I driving when this supposedly happened? Or did I just randomly push his head into a window? I'm really confused."

"I really have no more information than that." She softly sighs, sounding as confused I do.

"She said that you owe her ten thousand pounds, but I told her she would need to speak to the police about that. As that is not a matter for us to deal with.

Oh and also, she wanted us to enforce Rueben to take Freddie to her house every weekend for visits, but again I told her that wasn't possible."

"Ten thousand pounds?" I blurt before I burst out laughing.

She must be saying it because she knows I have inheritance money from my Mum, Rueben warned me she would try and get her hands on some of it if she could.

"I'm sorry." I say as I compose myself.

"It's just barbaric. Joy is unemployed, I'm not sure how on Earth she could have leant me so much money."

"That's okay. My phone call with Joy was a little vague and incoherent. It became clear what her motive was when she became quite forceful over the idea that we should force Rueben to take Freddie to her. I have made a note of this on the system. Mollie do you think Joy could pose a safeguarding issue?" She asks in a much more serious tone.

"I don't know." I answer surprised.

"If you had asked me this months ago, I would have said no, definitely not. But the things she has been doing and saying as well as the stories my husband has been telling me from his childhood make me not so sure anymore."

"Okay, it's just I have been speaking with my supervisor and I feel concerned that she could pose a risk to the children. What I mean is, her constant barrage of allegations and complaints to the police and your work could really affect you and cause your family a great deal of stress. From this, it could cause a negative effect on the children. They might soon pick up on the tension." She explains carefully.

"That makes sense, I understand that fully. We have been trying our best to keep them separate from all the upset, but obviously there is only so much I can do when the police turn up and wake them up in the morning to check them over." I answer as I start to realise the possible impact on them and how much they could be picking up on.

Maybe I should speak to Daisy about it. She's nearly ten years old after all and she might have questions about why the police were here and why they woke her up. I just assumed they didn't think much about it, but I could be wrong.

"Yes exactly, these are our current concerns. Mollie, would it be okay if I passed your phone number along to our legal team. They might be able to help you with a restraining order."

"Yeah. Okay." I answer a little taken back.

"Thank you."

When I end the call, I stare out to the kids playing in the paddling pool now that it is finally filled. I feel a little sad that throughout this I hadn't prepared myself for the possibility that they could start to pick up on all of this. The last thing I want is for them to end up with anxieties and worry about the police coming over and social services on the phone.

"Everything okay?" Rueben asks nervously as he finds me in the kitchen.

"Yes. Just the usual. Apparently, I hit Freddie's head, I owe your Mum ten thousand pounds - oh and she wants to you take Freddie over at the weekend for tea and biscuits." I mock as I shake my head.

"The usual then." Rueben jokes to try and make me laugh.

"But they did say they were going to see if they could help us with a restraining order. They're worried about the impact that all of this could be having on the kids."

"That's great and I totally agree. The last thing I want for them is to end up in therapy, like me." Rueben says. His face looks relieved at the idea of us getting some help and finally having something put into place.

"I'll let you know as soon as they call back then, let's just please try and have a nice afternoon without all these stresses."

"You got it." Rueben smiles before placing a kiss on my forehead.

"Oh, and maybe a Chinese takeaway later, since you're clearly too hungover to cook."

He laughs teasingly before heading back into the garden. He's not wrong though, my head is pounding. Between the tequila and my mother-in-law, I could definitely do with an easier evening.

CHAPTER SEVENTY-TWO

All things considered, I'm in pretty good spirits this Monday morning as I head to meet Lana for an early lunch.

I'm still anxiously waiting to hear back from work and find out whether the investigation has reached a conclusion yet. What with Freddie at nursery now, my days really are going to be quiet and boring and I definitely don't want to sit at home and stare at four walls all day.

When I reach the restaurant, I spot Lana immediately as she waves me over to a table by the window.

"Thank god you have a day off, I would have gone stir crazy sat at home." I laugh as she greets me with a hug.

"Things that bad?" Lana asks but she knows the answer already.

I take my jacket off and sit down. It's odd, I usually can't wait to get things off my chest but right now, I really can't be bothered. I'm so bored of moaning about the same thing over and over again. I must sound so repetitive to all my friends when I tell them what Joy has been up too and really, I don't want to keep allowing her to invade my life anymore.

"They are but they'll die down soon. I'm sure of it." I say, choosing to take the more diplomatic approach and play it down.

"Are you sure? I can go over there now and beat her up if you want?" Lana jokes and I nearly choke on my water as I giggle.

"Thanks! I'll keep it in mind, but let's not bore ourselves with it all. It's the same old stuff. My mother-in-law is a psycho, but Rueben and I okay, and we are dealing with it."

"For what it's worth, you could never bore me. I mean, I agree, it is the same old stuff repeating but if you need a friend to talk to, I'm here. You have had a tough year what with losing your Mum. And Joy, well Joy has hardly made any of that easier on you. Anyone would break down under the circumstances. I'm here for you." Lana thoughtfully says as she stares at me kindly.

"Now, let's order lunch I'm starving!"

My stomach rumbles as I order a goat's cheese and caramelised onion pizza. This restaurant is one of my favourites for great food. Lana opts for a chicken burger and side salad and we both give in and order a cocktail each.

"I think I foolishly hoped that after losing my Mum, I don't know, that somehow I might become closer to Joy. You know how sometimes tragedies bring people closer? Well that's what I hoped was going to happen for our family. But instead Joy became the worst she's ever been and it's just, it's just so suffocating." I stutter as I nervously open up to my best friend.

"But Mollie, after everything Rueben has told you about his Mum, did you ever really think that someone who is capable of doing such horrible things to their own child, could be so loving towards someone who isn't their own?"

"That's the foolish part." I sigh.

"I don't know, I guess I felt like she could have changed. People change all the time, right? Especially the older we get, we learn, we grow, we become better. Isn't that the way to lead a good life? To be better than the person you were yesterday?"

"Maybe, in a poem." Lana mocks, making me giggle again.

"But seriously, I think you were expecting way too much from Joy. Not everyone becomes better. Some people are more than happy living a miserable life, surrounded by their own negativity, pushing their own hate and drama on to other people. I think she revels in it personally."

"Really? You don't think she's sat at home, regretting anything?"

"God no." Lana scoffs.

"If she genuinely felt bad for any of the mistakes that she has made she wouldn't make them again and again. I hate to sound like a therapist but the more you and Rueben forgave her, the more you both became enablers. You both allowed her to physically attack Rueben, then call the police and blame you for it and then you both ended up forgiving her. You both subconsciously let her know that you have no boundaries. That she can play these toxic games again and again, because in her warped mind, you allowed her to believe that you'll end up forgiving her again anyway."

"Shit." Is all I manage to add. Everything Lana is saying is making perfect sense.

"I knew it was going to get worse after the first time you forgave her, but it wasn't my place to say. I totally believe she's a narcissist. You need to both stay away, permanently now. Otherwise, who knows what she'll think she can do next." Lana says gently but with a subtle warning tone to her voice.

"Wow. I really need to start some therapy, you and Rueben sound so philosophical these days."

"Oh ha-ha! But actually, I'm not in therapy, I've just been watching a lot of Oprah." Lana smirks.

"Who's that?"

I snap out of our conversation and glance down to where Lana is looking down at my phone ringing on the table.

"Oh. It's Mel. From my office, she said she'd call me if she heard anything about my job." I tell her nervously.

"Yay!" Lana squeals excitedly for me.

"You're going to get your job back now! And everything is going to start picking up again."

I giggle at her excitement as she leans forward eagerly waiting for me to answer the phone.

"Hi Mel." I nervously answer.

Please be good news. Please be good news. I think to myself over and over again.

"Hey Mollie, are you okay, how are things?"

"They're okay, I guess. Have you heard anything?" I ask eagerly. My heart is racing with nerves, I need an answer. I need to know if

344

this embarrassing ordeal is coming to an end and if I can just finally get back to work and get on with my life.

"Oh no, sorry I haven't heard anything yet. But that wasn't why I was calling." She says quietly, sounding a little hesitant.

"Oh?"

"There was this weird guy here earlier. Lurking downstairs said he was waiting for you and you told him to meet you here. But he was, I don't know, a little odd. He stunk of whiskey. Is everything okay Mollie?" She asks again with concern rife in her voice.

"I, I haven't asked anyone to meet me anywhere. What did he look like? Did he tell you a name?"

Lana stares curiously at me as I ask Mel questions, she can tell I'm confused and growing anxious.

"He was scruffy. He had a thick accent but I'm not sure where he is from. He said his name was Connor…something."

"Fuck." I mumble in shock under my breath.

"Mol?"

"Yeah, okay. Thanks Mel. Everything is fine though. Erm, if he comes back just tell him I don't work there anymore. Okay? I have got to go, I'm just in the middle of something. Let me know if he comes back." I stutter anxiously and hang up the phone quickly to avoid further questions.

"What? What's happened?" Lana stares uneasily.

"It's Connor. He has been at my work, looking for me. He told Mel that apparently I asked him to meet me there." I panic as I shake my head in disbelief.

"What, really? How does he even know you work there?"

"I have no idea! I got that job a long time after we broke up." I answer panicked. I'm so confused but my mind is racing trying to find an answer.

"I have no idea what he would even want. We haven't spoken in years."

"Mollie…" Lana says quietly.

"Did you tell Joy about Connor?"

"No! Never. She has no clue about him. We never really spoke that much on a personal level anyway, there's no chance that she could know about him."

As the words leave my mouth, I suddenly realise. The thought hits me like a brick to my face. My stomach is in knots.

"Wait." I sigh heavily.

"Lily."

"Lily?" Lana asks confused.

"I confided in her about my deadbeat boyfriend to make her feel better about hers. I never should have said anything." I groan.

"I was just trying to comfort her."

"So, Lily has probably told Joy and given Joy more ammunition to use against you. Typical." Lana sighs as she pieces together the mystery.

"What do I do? They told him where I work! I don't have the strength to deal with him right now, I really don't." I whine as I get a catch in my throat and try hard to fight back my emotions.

"We'll figure something out." Lana assures me as she reaches across the table and puts her hand gently across mine.

"But he knows where I live, my kids are there..." I gasp at the thought. I wouldn't want him anywhere my children. Alcoholics like him are unpredictable. Especially when they're violent too.

"Mollie." Lana says gently.

"Relax. I'm taking the day off work tomorrow to spend with you, I'll stay at your house so you're not on your own and together we will figure something out. Don't worry."

I stare back at Lana as she smiles at me with confidence, I wish I could be as sure as she is that everything is going to be okay.

I begin to wonder to myself how my mother-in-law could be so cruel as to bring someone so dangerous back into my life but then I almost want to kick myself at the thought. Haven't I learned by now that there isn't a level Joy isn't prepared to stoop too. Connor may be dangerous in an obvious way, but Joy is so much worse. She's calculating, vindictive and lacks conscience. She hides it all behind a mirage. She portrays to the world a friendly, warm housewife and Mother who only has good intentions and that is what makes her *really* dangerous. This whole time, I thought I was safe, but actually the real threat was hiding within the family, playing the role of the unassuming, kind, loving Mother-in-law.

CHAPTER SEVENTY-THREE

I can stay with you tomorrow too. In fact, I insist, okay?" Rueben urges.

I roll my eyes playfully as I pull him in close for a cuddle.

"Are you trying to be the Kevin Costner to my Whitney Houston?" I joke, trying to lighten the mood.

"I can't keep you from work and have you acting as my bodyguard. Lana is going to be here all day anyway. We'll be fine together and if there are any problems, I'll call you."

My joke hasn't gone down very well with Rueben who still looks pale and anxious. He has been like this ever since I told him about my conversation with Mel earlier. Even when he came home, he just paced around deep in thought. Barely offering two words over dinner.

"I feel sick. How could she do this to us." Rueben groans as he rubs his face, almost as if he is trying to rub the stresses away.

"How dangerous is this Connor?"

"He's just an alcoholic, Roo. Who loses his temper. He isn't some mob gangster. I can handle it." I attempt to assure him again with humour, but his expression barely changes.

"It's not funny babe. I don't find any of this funny at all." Rueben huffs impatiently.

"Neither do I. But what else do we do? Break down and be miserable yet again? I'm tired of wallowing every time Joy lands another bombshell on us."

"I'm just so sorry I dragged you into all of this. If we had never of met, then none of this would be happening."

"And you'd be still stuck under that roof and having to put up with it all on your own." I snap.

"This isn't the time to blame yourself Rueben. We are in this together."

"It's hard to not feel at fault when it's your own Mother who is doing it." Rueben mumbles awkwardly. I stare at him sympathetically, trying to find the right words to say that might bring him comfort.

"I don't know how to say this without sounding awful…" I begin hesitantly as Rueben's eyes catch my stare. His eyes becoming wide with worry.

"I'll admit, when certain things started happening, I was so stressed out, so fed up and I was in such disbelief at the things your Mum did that sometimes I wanted to run for the hills. There were times I did feel resentful. I shouldn't have, but a part of me felt angry with you because of it. I often wondered whether I was able to cope with it all. But I soon realised that as frustrated as I was, I still wasn't the victim here. You are."

Rueben's stare softens as he takes in everything I'm saying. I watch him patiently as he takes a deep breath in and stands up straight without taking his eyes off me.

"I was the victim." Rueben says before he clears his throat.

"But I'm not anymore. Tomorrow you deal with Connor and I'm going to see a solicitor about my Mum."

"A solicitor?"

"For now, yes. I'll see what I can put into place to end all of this once and for all." He responds with a stern stare.

His stare is sharp and his jaw is clenched as he stares off into space in deep thought.

"Erm, Roo? Are you mad at me?"

"No. I'm not. I'm just tired of being called a victim, I'm tired of replaying the same conversation about my so-called Mum again and again. I'm a man. I'm not that little boy anymore and I know that now. I'm not wasting another second of our lives falling victim to her bullshit or stressing over what she has done anymore. I don't care what it takes, tomorrow I'm going to fix this. You and the kids are my family and I'm going to make sure you're all happy."

I'm almost speechless at the authority in Rueben's voice. The Rueben I'm used to doesn't handle the stress very well and is usually either getting overly worked up or is throwing up on the pavement outside. I usually see the fear in his eyes when the abuse from his own Mum takes him back to those dark days under his childhood roof where he was just a little boy trying to be loved.

But that's far from the Rueben I'm staring at right now. This Rueben is calm and collected, it's new. I'm not sure I have seen him like this before.

He looks the strongest I have ever seen him. When he stands up straight, he could be ten feet tall. It's like he has had an epiphany. He doesn't seem scared anymore, he doesn't seem worried. I'm not sure what has changed in an hour or how, but I don't question it. It's refreshing, it's comforting, I feel the safest I have ever felt with his new attitude. I believe every word he says. He is going to stop this. We are going to be okay.

"Are you going to stare at me all night? Or are you coming to bed?"

"Ye-Yeah, I'm coming to bed." I stutter as he interrupts my thoughts of him.

We have been on such a journey these last few years. It all started with Rueben questioning his childhood and Joy throwing a few tantrums, to getting hit and mistreated and still being kind enough to forgive her. We've argued, cried and had to protest our innocence time and time again, we have been high, and we have been dragged so low but now we are here, in what appears to be the end. Finally.

I lay and watch Rueben as he peacefully sleeps. I feel so proud of him, it hasn't been easy to come out the other side, but he has done it. Just knowing how strong he is feeling makes me feel better. I love him so much. I can almost feel myself getting optimistic about the future, but there's still one thing weighing on my mind. Connor.

If Rueben can be strong then I can too. Without giving it anymore thought, I take my phone and tip toe downstairs quietly so that I don't wake anyone. When I get to the kitchen, I close the door behind me and take a deep breath whilst I search for Connor's number in my phone.

I try to ignore the nausea that washes over me as his phone rings.

"Hello?" The familiar voice answers after only a couple of rings.

"Connor, it's Mollie."

"Well, if it isn't my little southern belle." He tries to tease which makes me screw my face up as I cringe at his nickname for me.

"Look, Connor, I don't know what has been going on, but I can promise you it is not me who has arranged to meet you." I say, trying to sound as confident as possible.

I barely finish my sentence when he laughs and jeers over me.

"Oh Mollie, Mollie, Mollie. You can't just lead me on for months and then try and drop me now, sweetheart. I don't think so." He slurs.

Months?

"What do you think is happening here?"

"What do I think?" He laughs again.

"I'll tell you what I think shall I sweetheart, I think you miss me because you know I was the fucking best. I think you're bored of your little southern pansy and you want me, a real man."

It's taking all of my strength to avoid asking him what real man hits a woman, but I fight the urge. I haven't phoned him for an argument after all and antagonising him would only make this worse.

"Remind me. How did we start speaking?"

"You know how." He drunkenly mumbles.

"You got your work colleague to message me on my social media because you were too scared to contact me yourself in case your little boyfriend saw. Then she gave me your new number."

"What was my work colleague called?" I ask curiously, despite being sure I know the answer.

"Joy. Don't keep playing fucking games." He snaps impatiently.

"Connor, the person you're messaging isn't me and she is not my friend." I try to respond calmly.

"It is. You invited me to your Ma's funeral. Obviously, it's you Mollie. I'm not stupid. Do you think you're being clever or something? You stood me up and you haven't even said sorry and now you're playing some fucking game with me." He says, his voice growing louder and more irritated.

Fuck. Did Joy really invite him to my Mum's funeral? Jesus, it just gets worse.

"Just calm down. Please, I'm trying to explain something."

"Fucking calm down? Who do you think you're talking too?" He roars arrogantly over me.

"Connor, I have been set up by people who don't like me. Please, I'm not trying to wind you up, I'm just trying to be honest." I say as gently as I can.

"Nobody likes you because you're a fat, ugly slag." He snaps spitefully.

I pause as his spiteful words knock the wind out of me. I can't allow myself to get emotional, I can't let him know he has got to me.

"I shouldn't have phoned you this late. I'm sorry. Please just understand that I don't want any more contact, please don't come to my work again."

"I can do what I like now the restraining order is up." He threatens.

"What will you do if I turn up? What will your pathetic little boyfriend do?"

He laughs loudly at himself and I don't have the energy to try to answer over him. I sigh as I pace the kitchen feeling defeated. What was I thinking, did I really think I could reason with a drunk?

"Sweet dreams Mollie." Connor sniggers.

"I'll be seeing you soon."

CHAPTER SEVENTY-FOUR

After my phone call with Connor last night I couldn't relax and spent the rest of the night tossing and turning. The closer it got to my alarm going off for the school run, the more stressed out I became that I hadn't been to sleep.

It was such an effort to drag myself out of bed, there's nothing worse than trying to survive on little sleep, but I have things to do. Lana is coming over shortly and thanks to my mother-in-law, I have Connor to deal with.

Rueben sent me the sweetest message not long after he left for work.

I can't help but smile sweetly as I read the words. I love that Rueben has taken charge, somehow it makes me feel a lot calmer. I know that I won't have to worry for much longer.

> *I'm ringing a solicitor on my lunch break.*
> *I'll let you know how it goes.*
> *Stay positive. Everything is going to get better now.*
> *I love you.*
> *Roo xx*

I can't wait for everything to get better, just like he says. We definitely deserve it after everything we have both been through. I quickly text back a few love heart emoji's and head to the front door as I hear a car pulling into the driveway.

"Hey!" I smile as Lana approaches the front door.

"Hey Mol! Don't worry I'm armed. I have my pepper spray in here." She winks at me and I roll my eyes as I giggle a little.

"Hopefully we won't need it. Although I did phone him last night and try and reason with him which didn't go down very well." I tell her as we both head into the kitchen and I put the kettle on to make us some coffees.

"Really? Was he not his usual polite self?" Lana sarcastically asks, even though she knows him well enough to know exactly what state he would have been in.

"Not quite. He called me a fat slag before promising to pop by for a courtesy call." I joke and Lana shakes her head at his idle threat.

"How worried are you that he'll come by today?"

I pause for a second whilst I think about her question. I know Connor, he is the most aggressive and argumentative person on the planet when he is drunk but when he is sober, it's a completely different story. He is a lot more reserved and almost cowardly; he has never once gone looking for a fight sober, not all the time I had known him anyway.

"I don't think I am really. He probably can't even remember the phone conversation we had last night and even if he can, he won't do much about it whilst he is nursing a hangover." I say, sure of my answer.

"How do you want to sort this out with him? Shall we call the police and see if we can get them to warn him? Maybe that'll be enough for him to stay away." Lana asks seriously.

"Eurgh." I groan heavily.

"I'm tired of the police. I have never had so many dealings with them in all my life since I met Joy. I'm going to try and call him and see if I can make him understand myself first."

"Okay but put it on loudspeaker and I'll record the call from my phone. That way, if he does threaten you, we have proof and I think we should take it to the police." Lana suggests as she pulls her phone from her pocket and gets ready to record.

I nod in agreement, it's probably the best idea. I feel a little nervous as I dial his phone number again but I'm almost certain that I'll be speaking to a different version of Connor now.

"What do you want now?" He snaps impatiently down the phone almost instantly.

"Sorry to ring again. I just wondered if you remembered much of our conversation last night?" I ask carefully, making sure my tone is gentle and I don't aggravate him.

"Yes, most of it Mollie. I'm not an idiot." He huffs. He sounds disappointed, almost as if he is upset.

"So, you understand that it wasn't me speaking to you? It's not fair that you were dragged into this and I am so sorry, but I'm married and not interested in a relationship with you again." I mumble softly. I wanted to sound confident, but I know how unpredictable he is and I'm not sure if what I have just said is going to make him explode. I can't yet work out whether he is sober or not.

"Don't flatter yourself Mollie." He responds casually.

"I'm already on the train back to Liverpool."

"Oh." I respond surprised. This wasn't the reply I expected.

"Well I'm not desperate Mollie. I get it, your mates played some prank. It's pathetic. But I'm not going to wait around and play these games any longer. You're not that special. You never were." His words are defensive but harsh.

Although his intention is to make me feel small, it can't work because I am just so relieved that he has gotten the message and taken this approach, he thinks he has taken the moral high ground and that's fine with me. As long as he is heading back to Liverpool and not anywhere near me.

"You're right. I am very sorry. Well, have a safe journey home." I say awkwardly.

"Whatever." He sighs before the phone line goes dead.

I'm so relieved as I put my phone down, I feel tears sting my eyes. I could cry but I hold it back, if Lana wasn't here though I would definitely allow my emotions to come out. The last twenty-four hours have been a real stress. Even though I played it down with Rueben, inside I had been panicking and replaying all kinds of scenarios in my head where Connor could turn up here and upset my family.

"Well…" Lana sighs with relief.

"That's probably the best outcome we could have hoped for."

"Tell me about it." I say relieved, as I sip at my coffee.

Connor didn't sound very interested at all. He sounded fed up, but genuine. That could have ended up being so much worse.

"Anyway." Lana perks up with a smile as she eagerly announces her news.

"I can tell you all about what me and Mike have been up too now."

I welcome the change of subject and listen intently as I watch Lana proudly tell me all about how her and Mike have been spending their free time helping out at their local soup kitchen.

"It's been amazing but there's this one girl, I really want to help. Which reminds me, have you got any old clothes you don't want? She could really do with some things to wear." She asks hopefully.

"Sure, let's go upstairs and have a look."

"Mike will probably moan at me if he knew I was asking you for clothes, he says we are there to serve food and help out but he doesn't think I should be getting caught up with someone and helping out on such a personal level, but she's only young, I can't help it. Don't you think I'm right?"

"Of course." I giggle.

I love it when Lana gets all passionate about something, she could talk for England about it, but I really don't mind. I'm happy to help her out and surprisingly I find a fair few jumpers and cardigans that she can take.

"Oh, wow Mollie, this is going to help her out so much." She gratefully says as she folds up all the clothes.

"So, tell me about her. What's made you want to become Florence Nightingale for her?"

"I don't know really; she just seems so innocent. But it's clear she's so lost. She's only like twenty-two or something. Her name is Tia and I can't put my finger on it, but I just feel as though she needs support. She definitely doesn't belong on the streets." Lana explains with concern.

"I just don't think she had the best start in life."

"That's sad." I add sympathetically. Seeing Lana care so much for a stranger has me in awe of her. She's so kind and although I have never even met Tia, I feel sad hearing about her struggles.

"Hey! I just had an idea. Why don't you and Rueben come down tomorrow night? You could both meet her and give her the clothes. She's really sweet and friendly. Then you can help me out in the kitchen. We could really do with an extra pair of hands and it'll help distract you both from the past few days too!" Lana says so convincingly.

I had planned to just stay home but now that the Connor thing is sorted, I'm feeling a little spring back in my step and it does sound like a great thing to be a part of.

"Sure." I smile.

"I'll call the babysitter and see if she's available and we'll come along."

"Yay!" Lana squeals.

"I can't wait for you to meet her."

CHAPTER SEVENTY-FIVE

I spend the next couple of hours sorting through more of my clothes and coats, finding more things to donate to this young girl. I barely notice that the day has been flying by until I realise Rueben didn't call me on his lunch break.

I can't help but grow concerned that maybe his meeting with the solicitor didn't go very well and he just doesn't want to break the bad news to me over the phone. I do my best to push the worries to the back of my mind though as I say my goodbyes to Lana and head off for the school run.

I managed to arrange a few hours in with the babysitter, so I promise to meet Lana at the soup kitchen tomorrow night, along with Rueben. She's so excited. I personally have never been to a soup kitchen and I really have no idea what to expect, but my best friend has taken a serious interest in this so I'm more than happy to help out.

Once I collect Daisy and Freddie, we all head home and I put a movie on for them in the front room whilst I distract myself in the kitchen. I decide to crack on with the dinner and make a homemade lasagne, this will keep me busy and take my mind off the fact Rueben hasn't called me.

Worst case scenario, I can call Amber back at child protection, she said someone from their legal team could help me. Perhaps I could chase them up and they can put something in place for us. As I fry off the mince beef, I'm lost in thoughts of restraining orders, social services and my mother-in-law. I want the easier life that we have been dreaming of, we can't give up on that, no matter what the outcome is today with the solicitor.

"Hey." Rueben's voice startles me.

I spin around to find him stood by the kitchen counter with a huge bouquet of red roses. He is smiling and he stares at me fondly. I can tell immediately that he looks like he is about to tell me some good news, but I wait patiently for him to tell me himself. I'm too scared to assume.

"I'm sorry I didn't call you on my break, the meeting with the solicitor ran over. I was even late back to work, so I literally didn't have a moment spare to call." he explains.

"It's fine. I understand." I say softly. My eyes fix on his eagerly as I wait for more information. I can't move from the spot I am stood in; my legs feel like jelly as I wait anxiously to hear the outcome.

"It's good news." Rueben announces as an even bigger smile spreads across his face.

"I told the solicitor everything. I told her all about my childhood and the things that were happening now. I showed her proof of all the hundreds of calls she makes to me and I allowed her to listen to the dozens of threatening and abusive voice messages she has left for me. She completely agreed that we needed a restraining order as soon as possible, especially to protect the kids from any possible upset. She said she'll draw up the order tonight and my Mum should be served it by Monday."

"Oh my god." I gasp as I leave the spot and leap towards Rueben. I fling my arms around him tightly, nearly knocking him off his feet.

"I know that Amber lady said she could help us, But I didn't want to wait another minute longer. I didn't want to give my Mum any more time to do anything else."

"This is the best news. Do you really think this could finally work?" I ask as I pull away and stare at him intently.

"I really do. The solicitor is going to warn her off from making malicious phone calls to authorities and she isn't going to be able to contact us indirectly either. She can't use my Nan or any of our friends, or even our exes to send us messages."

"Oh my god." Is all I manage to say again as I try to get my head around the brilliant news.

"Thank you."

"There is really no need to thank me. I did it for us and our family." Rueben gently says as he brings his hand up to cup my cheek and strokes it affectionately with his thumb.

I pause and bask in the moment before taking the beautiful roses out of his hands and arranging them neatly into a glass vase.

"I have great news too. I spoke to Connor earlier, but it doesn't seem we have much to worry about. He was already on the train back to Liverpool."

"Really, are you sure?" He questions surprised but sounding a little unconvinced.

"I'm almost certain of it, yes. He didn't sound interested enough to stick around and pursue anything." I assure.

"In that case, I'm sure this calls for a bottle of champagne." Rueben smiles triumphantly.

"You hate champagne, remember?"

"Yes, but as I have told you before, if the occasion calls for it, I'll drink it. And the occasion definitely calls for it."

I giggle and roll my eyes jokingly as I enjoy Rueben's good mood. He definitely looks as though a weight has been lifted from his shoulders. I hear the kids giggling too as Rueben goes off to find them and playfully tickles them and chases them around the front room whilst I dish up the dinner. It means everything to have Rueben back like this. His positivity and confidence fill me with the optimism I have been missing.

"I'm pleased you're in such good mood, because tomorrow night I promised Lana we would help out at a soup kitchen she's been volunteering at." I say over dinner.

"A soup kitchen, really?" Rueben asks before taking another bite of lasagne.

"Yeah, there's a girl called Tia who she has particularly grown fond of that she's been trying to help. I sorted out some clothes to donate for her too and Lana wants to introduce us tomorrow."

"Cool. Well count me in." Rueben responds brightly.

My phone pings loudly before I finish my dinner and I phish it out of my bag to see who could be messaging me now.

"It's Mel." I say surprised as Rueben looks at me curiously.

"Is it good news?" He asks, hopeful.

I nod before I throw my head back and let out a huge sigh of relief. The last problem that was niggling away at me has been resolved. I feel like our lives really are getting back on track. I'm so ready to get back to work and get on with my career.

"She said Tricia is going to call me over the weekend about starting back at work. The investigation appears to be over with."

"I told you it was the perfect night for champagne." Rueben beams. "I'm so pleased baby, this has been a great day for good news."

For the first time in months, I feel so relaxed when I climb into bed. I no longer have a million scary thoughts racing around my head that I have to actively try to ignore long enough to fall asleep. Tonight, I have nothing but positive thoughts and excitement for the future.

When I wake up the next morning, I'm up and out of bed with a spring in my step. I'm eager to organise all of my work clothes and get myself ready for my return next week. Today is the best I have felt in such a long time. Even before when I have been in a better mood, I have always felt as though I needed to keep an eye over my shoulder, just in case something else was about to explode in our faces. But now, I feel free. I feel excited for the next chapter of our lives and no longer filled with nerves every time Rueben's phone rings or I get a knock at the door.

I feel sorry for whoever will end up becoming Joy's next victim. After all, people like her rarely stop creating dramas. But at least this doesn't have to be my worry anymore.

I'm feeling quite enthusiastic as the evening comes around and I'm getting ready for the soup kitchen.

It's a little nerve-wracking to go to a place that I have never been before, but I'm excited to help my friends out and do some good for other people.

As soon as the babysitter arrives and the kids are settled, I finish getting ready quickly in front of the hallway mirror. I decide it's best to pull my hair up high out of my face if I'm going to be handling food and I throw my jacket on as Rueben puts his shoes on by the front door.

"Ready?" Rueben smiles as he opens the front door for me.

"Yep." I say before grabbing the remaining bags of clothes I gathered from the cupboard and head out the door.

The soup kitchen is over by where Lana lives which isn't too far away, usually only takes us twenty minutes to drive there if traffic is light.

I'm a little apprehensive when we arrive though, I'm not exactly sure where I was supposed to meet Lana and I don't want to just hang about the entrance looking awkward.

"Let's just go inside, I'm sure I'll spot her once we are in there." I say to Rueben. As soon as I take some steps inside, I peer around eagerly looking for Lana or Mike.

I'm relieved when I spot Lana's face light up as she waves us over.

"Hey! You made it!" She says as she looks at us both excitedly.

"Thank you so much for coming along tonight."

"I promised you we would." I smile. Rueben nods politely but I can tell he is a little nervous. We are both out of our comfort zone and as daunting as that is, we are both still willing to get stuck in and help.

"Mike was just sorting out a huge hamper of food which just got donated by someone a little while ago, if you want to help him with that Roo? And I thought me and Mollie could help out with the serving." Lana suggests cheerfully.

"Sure, I'm happy to help Mike, just point me in the direction he is in and I'll head off to find him."

"OK, I will, but first I want you both to meet Tia! She's just finishing her dinner but I'm sure she won't mind if we head over to her and say hi."

"Great. I brought some more clothes with me for her if she needs them." I respond.

"Oh brilliant! Thank you so much Mol, she'll love them. She's been running out of proper clothing to wear so I know she'll be more than happy with whatever you have."

"So, what drew you to this Tia girl so much, Lana? There's loads of people here." Rueben whispers curiously.

"I don't know." Lana sighs.

"I think it's just because she's quite young and she really shouldn't be on the streets. It's not safe for her. Some people who pass through here can be caught up in some pretty serious stuff. But not her, it's more like she's running away from something."

"Well, if we can help out in other ways, just let us know." I offer as I follow on behind to where Lana is leading us.

"Thanks Mol. I appreciate that. She's right over here, on the end table, I'll introduce you."

I smile politely as I begin to approach the young girl sitting at the table, but I suddenly notice Rueben isn't following on behind me anymore.

When I turn around, I see him through the crowd of people, just stood in the same spot we were just in.

"Roo?" I call as I head back over quickly.

"What are you doing? Lana is about to introduce us."

"I don't need introducing to her." Rueben says so quietly I barely catch what he said but I notice how his stare is still fixed on the girl.

"Her name isn't Tia."

"What? How do you know?"

Rueben's face is serious, but his body language is hesitant. The colour has drained from his face and his eyes look wild with shock.

"Because that's my sister. That's Kelsey."